= =

The crashing of brush became running steps. Tanman Caladrunan lifted two fingers. Two archers laid arrow back to ear and released. Cries of agony rose over the baying. The dogs went into frenzies; while the wounded screamed, Tanman's bull whistled, and the Nando commander shrieked.

Tanman's voice began in his belly, gathering force and timbre as it rose. "Silence!"

Silence reigned. Dogs cringed; wounded Nandos whimpered. Tanman glared round at them.

Against all protocol I looked up. For a heartbeat my eyes locked with his. He read the stories that my ragged clothes and harness showed, studied the dead mare behind me. Last and most intently, he looked in my eyes.

Sweat ran down my back under dirty robes. I hadn't expected this enormous king. As a child my dead brother played with Caladrunan; but I saw an utter stranger. With my face hidden by dirty cloth, no one recognized me. Shadows slipped across his eyes as if things moved, troubled, in his memory.

"Who are you?"

I spoke through the cloth in Tannese. "I am a desert man, Liege Lord of Tan."

The Song of Naga Teot
Book One

TEOT'S WAR

HEATHER GLADNEY

ACE FANTASY BOOKS
NEW YORK

TEOT'S WAR

An Ace Fantasy Book/published by arrangement with
the author

PRINTING HISTORY
Ace Fantasy edition / May 1987

ISBN: 0-441-80083-1

Ace Fantasy Books are published by The Berkley Publishing Group,
200 Madison Avenue, New York, New York 10016.
PRINTED IN THE UNITED STATES OF AMERICA

My thanks to Indra, the Clan, Kirk Hunt, Molly and Beth in NY, and most of all, JCG, who believed even in starving time.

The Great Oath of Tan

I SWEAR BY the Goddess Sitha to wholly serve the Liege Lord of Tan, to use the full extent of my skills and will to further his aims above all others, and to serve in the ways required by him. In the name of the Goddess of Forever, Amen.

Common Bylaws: Also called the Articles of Tyranny.

1. Negligence and disloyalty is punishable by death.
2. Action beyond orders is punishable at Tanman's discretion.
3. Subject will be bound to lesser authority on Tanman's order alone. Unauthorized service of any type is disloyalty.
4. Honorable suicide redeems rejection of Oath candidates by Tanman. Delay is negligence.

Complete Bylaws: Not generally recited.

5. Oath may be offered in lieu of debt repayments, granted agreement of all parties.
6. Term of service may be set to a limited time granted agreement by all parties.
7. Subject will be maintained by Tanman with the appropriate equipment.

CHAPTER

= *1* =

HEAT BEAT DOWN on my shoulders, my face cloth. My armor dragged at the riding sores underneath. Little sparkles danced behind my eyelids, and the strains in my joints were cramping to knots in the muscles. It had been a long ride. A grating call made my shoulders twitch. The carrion crows, who glided after us day after day, were waiting.

At my fifth year, my grandmother named me Beautiful Gold Dance of Knives and spoke of family pride. I remembered that it was very hot, next to the fire when they tattooed and circumcised me; and I cried. I had another hard ceremony ahead of me now. I opened my eyes into the dust and glare, lifting my hands. Now I was a man I had outgrown my name, but I lacked kin to give me another. I no longer was a Dance of Knives. My weapons were larger than knives—scaddas, two long and graceful spans of curved blade. Viper leather grips rasped my palms. The twin blades flashed sunlight in blue arcs as I struck, and the shock of the blow jolted up my shoulder bones. The crows screeched.

The blades hung tight a moment, swung free in a spray of red with a gasping sound. Blood spattered my head. I blinked wet eyelashes and watched the old mare gana fall. The mare's body bounced in a clatter of legs and tangled hooves. No cry, no thrashing . . . just release. I let out a small sigh. The mare's blood pumped vigorously onto dry summer grasses, flowed under the heap of discarded saddle harness; a bubble of red froth bloomed round her muzzle and burst. Gray hairs of age hung motionless around the reddened nostrils.

1

The beast looked like a huge, stringy, horned goat with heavy maned shoulders and dark brown bars on her forelegs. She had five times my weight and once towered above me. But to me, there on the ground, she looked suddenly small and old. Her legs looked like sticks and cord among the grasses. I knelt down beside the dead mare, trailing ragged strings of clothing into the pool of blood. I propped my blades across her barrel, pulled aside the cloth wrapping over my face, and bent over.

I touched my lips to the bloody muzzle, then to the pool of blood. My lips cracked and our two bloods mingled, ran down my chin, dripped. Mine, the hands honored by her final blood. I straightened, let the face cloth fall in place again. The clenched muscles in my chest swelled into a hard, bitter-tasting knot; I dared not cry out this death in the way of my people. Slowly I untied the last, never-released nose straps. She deserved freedom of me, at the end.

My hands remembered as they moved. This gana mare grew from a stilty-legged heap at a desert waterhole—delivered of her burned and crippled dam, the bleating newborn was all I had left of my people. With a charred spot half-healed on my own hip, and great gaping holes of burn sickness gliding about my memory, I had been alone, scared: only a boy. We ate cactus pulp and bleached scrub acorns. She was the one good thing I remembered of that time; after the dam's death I clung to that awkward little beast with all my strength, foraging on the thin fruits of thornbrush desert. It was a lean time; my legs slowly bowed to fit her barrel. When I joined the Nandos, mercenary soldiers, she came with me. And because I was still a Nando, because she gave all I asked, she died. All I could return was mercy. I asked myself, is that all, in the end? A plume of dust spun away in the breeze, stirring hair, drying blood.

I looked up at a noise. The crows screamed, swirling, and vanished into an oak. In the clearing around me, Nandos shuffled past while their mounts coughed through dry grasses and sand. My formal escort into Tan, these: sad by any standard. Misfits of every kind and perversity sheltered within the Nandos. Face cloths hid outlawing scars, and made us all brothers in anonymity. A beast stumbled past, honking on each breath. I looked at their ganas, at flanks raked by goads, at beasts frothing blood bubbles over their nose-rings. Broth-

ers in spirit, no. A dull rage stirred in my chest. There was no
need for it . . . no need. Even an animal as tough as an old
mare gana could be run to death by a fool, in a strange land.

I wiped wet hands on my robes, drew on my riding gloves,
and shrugged tiredly at my leather armor. My harpcase pulled
at my left shoulder, drawing straps and tearing at a harness
sore worn in by a moon's riding. The scaddas drained in a
whirl of blue glints. Then my hands were still. I stared up
into the noon glare. A black shape moved above me.

The commander of my Nando escort was a black silhouette
against the sun's disk. His latest iron-necked and intractable
mount pawed one hoof, ringing stones. He had killed two
others under him on this ride. I slitted my eyes at him.

"Up, Sati," he snapped. He spoke Tannese impatiently, in
the rasping Crag province dialect that made my scalp muscles
twitch in loathing. "We must obey the time in the orders,
make up speed. Your beast was too old. We will give you a
small beast. Your slight weight won't bother one of the tired
ones much."

The Nando had once been nobility of the Crag province of
Tan. Crag was a rebel province at best and tribal at its worst.
The man had chosen a Nando troop made up of his own kind,
gaunt red-haired, secretive men. They argued in their home
dialect, played their own gambling games, and scorned me—
when they dared—as an outsider. The commander remained a
Crag noble to them, outlawed or not, and they took his orders
for it: all the foolish demands, the grudging concessions,
along with merely arrogant routine orders. At least his status
kept some organization in the troop; discipline had been
fraying under stress since they met me at the border.

"Up, Sati," he said again.

I narrowed my eyes to deeper slits. This man's orders had
killed my mare. We both recalled days wasted on the commander's discretion, running from one brothel town to another, hiding from Tannese border patrols. He wanted not to
enter Tan at all. It took death threats to force him into Tan, to
do his duty by me. He promptly ordered jagged runs and
stops to make up lost time, piously abiding by his duty
without thought for beasts. These ex-Cragmen took pride in
riding until mounts dropped under them, and sneered at my
aged mare. The troop had lost six ganas, stolen new ones and
killed them in turn. The commander purchased his remounts

from a smuggler, costly folly. We ran ragged and pinch-bag for it now. I thought of lifting the bloody scaddas and cutting his arrogance in half.

"Sati," he repeated, while his beast shrilled and jerked at the lines.

Sati was my rank among the Nandos. Sati of scaddas was a skill grade, not a common one in any army. I had an ancient pride to avenge, in the deaths of my people, and no qualms about my revenges. Even for other causes, the hate was still there . . . hot and steady fuel. Satis hate more than other men.

One of my scaddas made a lazy arc in the air. "Go away," I said quietly.

The commander muttered something about witchcraft and unnaturally old ganas. My left scadda flickered; an ornament came neatly off his robe. The man yelled, wheeled his beast into an ungainly trot, dug in his goad. I went after him.

The ride had punished my body severely. I tottered three angry steps after the Nando and pulled myself up with a jerk: I must not kill him. Then my boot nudged a gana hock. I gazed down at the corpse of my gana, told myself over the reasons not to kill the fool Cragman, and slowly wiped my scaddas on the tail of my leathers.

In training I had learned patience. I might never gain the dispassionate serenity of a Master of Scaddas, but I knew how to wait. Such a slim chance; I had an Oath to uphold, and he was the only guide I had. Manoloki paid the fool to escort me to Tan, to pay bribes, to get me past guards and courtiers. I wore envoy seal, yet I needed the idiot. But fury trembled close, so close. Startled men made witch-signs as if I might blight them with a glare—the rage surprised them. I was desert Nando and it was said such men felt nothing for man or beast.

Or so the stories ran. True ridge-runners had a greatly feared and ghoulish sense of humor, but they left no bones as trailsign of their angers. I will someday crack that man's bones, I thought coldly. Prickles of light dazed my eyes between narrowed lashes.

A noise . . . I turned with a lurch, quartering the towering oakwoods round the clearing with my ears. The air hung too quiet, sharpening the one faint bell-like cry. A clear, faraway sound came ringing through the oakwood stillness,

fading and repeating—the baying of a dog. Then many dogs.
No insect whine, no birds had set off alarm; only the crows,
cawing like laughter. Hair lifted on the back of my neck.
Straining for the source of that echo, I took a few stiff-legged
steps.

Others heard the sudden loud belling of dogs on renewed
scent. Hooves thrummed; shouts of riders echoed in the trees
as if they feared no one. Ganas appeared on a hillside. Patrol
blue flickered past dun rocks and over fallen logs: a Tannese
hunting party in full cry. The Nandos boiled into uproar,
throwing gear, swearing. I did not move. I heard something
rushing toward us, flying over leaf litter and twigs at a merest
whisper.

A redbuck soared out of the trees in a single great bound,
horns high. It swerved across the clearing in long evasive
leaps, supremely graceful, brushed the robe of one startled
Nando and darted aside with a white-eyed glare of fear. Froth
hung on the buck's jaws. It plunged into a gap among the
brambles and vanished. I looked up the hill. Huntsmen rode
across a bald ridge. I counted thirty-three riders. That meant a
Tannese military party.

The Nandos were as frantic as smugglers. They screamed
at one another. The commander's voice broke shrill in volleys
of orders. Men ran after wild-eyed ganas, threw straps on
beasts that kicked. Windbroken mounts puffed, head down,
useless, but packsaddles were thrown on them anyway. Two
staggered and fell. I judged our chances. We were dismounted,
surprised on poor ground; we'd scared the local animals that
gave alarms, and the commander had set no pickets—a gamble he'd lost. We were outnumbered. If we fled, the Tannese
could follow scent trail with their dogs: no escape there.

I drew out the envoy seal on my neck thong; diplomacy
must make the best of it, since the Nandos had no hope of
getting away, and I still needed the commander. Earth hummed
under my boots while I strapped my harpcase tightly under
my left arm for a fighting shield. I heard shouts and the crash
of brush under hooves: many hooves thrashing forest litter,
thumping saplings and fallen logs.

My head jerked up. Brassy bull-rage roared through the
woods, a trumpet of battle fury. Men cried out in fear. Were
Tannese insane? A bull—no rider could stop a raging bull, we all
knew that. My Nando escort fell apart; men bolted into the

trees, others stumbled over their gear. Beasts wailed in fear.
By training and reflex I covered for the weak. I saw the bull
first.

The matting of vines and thornbrush split apart between
two oaks, streaming away in torn strands over wide horns and
a black muzzle. That head kept coming out and out and out
. . . even for a Tannese gana it was a monster. Lips writhed
back, tusks parted. I glimpsed one gleaming red eye, a glint
of armored legs; shoulder muscles rolled in streamers of vine.
It lunged out of the woods in a cloud of dirt. Grass, litter and
earth sprayed under hooves.

I was pivoting even as the monster hurtled across the
clearing. The thick neck stretched out; I arched hard aside. I
saw stripes as the horns swept up. The right horn-tip knifed
gracefully past my face, fanning air in my eyes. My outflung
hand brushed a saddle fitting. I saw the rider, a blaze of gold
and blue, vine leaves and a vague shout, wrestling with the
bull's reins. The bull roared as it missed me. Then the long
body was past me—and a hind leg lashed out and hit me.

There was no pain; it happened too fast. Dry grass blurred
away. I flew, balled up in an airless gasp. Sapling whips
thumped my back. Then I rolled over and over in the dirt,
thudded up against something, and sprawled. I stared up with
glazed eyes, ribs heaving. My head lay against the belly of
my dead gana. At a shadow I wheezed and rolled aside.

Black horns stabbed the earth. Slam, rip, slam—the horns
plowed the ground as I ducked around my dead mare. The
bull charged, I rolled aside. The bull skidded past me on its
hind legs, whirled in a spray of dirt, and came back chop-
ping at me with forehooves.

Any other bull would have plunged past, berserk, and
slammed into a tree. Not my luck: I ducked, heard teeth snap,
felt a thudding wrench at my left shoulder that threw me
down. A hoof raked my right thigh. My robe collar jerked up
and strangled me. I kicked in midair, grabbed my collar to
support my weight, clenched my neck muscles. Sky and
forest whirled about my head while the bull spun me round
by the neck. With the razor spurs on my left boot I gouged at
the beast's iron-armored head; my right leg flopped at it and
failed, oddly weak. I scrabbled and poked and kicked. I gave
up my grip on the cloth, got my scaddas out, strangling, and

slashed at his ears. The bull flung me up hard at that, and the rotten old cloth tore at my neck. Air!

I fell hard in the dirt. The air went out in a honk. My left scadda clattered out of my hand, my harpcase spun out of reach. I threw myself hard to one side, sprawling over on my face. My right leg collapsed under me. I rolled.

The bull slashed after me with dirty vine-streaked horns. The tips vanished in dust billows, reappeared. I whipped over and over erratically, flipping end-for-end and sideways like a snake flopping in the dirt. Hooves slammed closer with every escape. The right forehoof smacked on a shoulder strap and pinned me to the ground.

An armored bull gana in a rage is a killing machine. A wise man hides; a fool climbs a tree and hopes the trunk withstands the rammings, nobody fights—not pinned to the ground. I rolled up on my shoulders, threw my good leg in the air, and jabbed at the beast's underside. My spur sank into thick belly fur. My left hand scrabbled to release the strap. I swung my right scadda, clanged off iron armor. I put a good dent into one shin-guard. The bull growled. Black gana hide swelled over me.

Yellow teeth yawned slowly in my face, hot and hay-scented and horrible. I held my scadda poised to bar tusks away, knowing the slender blade would crunch in one bite, while I dug my spur at the bull's furry belly.

I gasped then. The blue and gold rider hauled nose-lines up by brute force in a trembling match of strength against strength. The bull yawed, gagged and foamed at the nose-ring, couldn't reach to shear my head off. Instead the free left forehoof lowered toward my face. For a blurred moment I saw the rider—he seemed to be shouting—but I didn't hear words. I was too busy jabbing and trying to jerk that strap.

The rider dragged with amazing stamina, pulling up the ugly black head. Tusks swung toward the sky. The looming hoof planted down gently beside my head in a little puff of dust. Head drawn tight back, the bull whistled and shrieked battle rage, horns whipping in arcs. Black shoulders clenched. The monster reared. The deadly hooves flung up, kicking dirt in the air.

I rolled aside. For an instant the beast hung above me, shrilling, rearing higher and higher. Armored legs and neck thrashed, hindquarters bunched. Caparison and robes flew back in a blaze of color. Shadow passed over my face; the long body leaped soundlessly over me, hooves flung dirt over me, and then the bull charged trees full of frenzied Nandos. I gasped, clutching my battered thigh. My left hand automatically groped out and picked up my lost scadda. I twisted around, peering over the belly of my dead gana, as I wheezed.

The bull raged against its rider. Nando mercenaries screamed and scattered; the monster slammed three Nandos into the brush, slinging each body off the flat of its horns in great sweeps. The vicious hind leg kicked other men. Bull-rage rang through the woods: the rider fought the beast away from one victim, then another. The mount plunged to a stop in the clearing and screamed. The little red eye glared. It swung its horns in short vicious arcs, panting. Ears flattened back, the bull shrilled a challenge.

Horned heads waved against the sky glare. Ganas cowered silently at clearing edges. Only the Tannese beasts trumpeted answer, like a united wild herd: all bore the whorled horn-bases of battle mounts. Bows arched black against the pale sky—and long hunting arrows nocked gana-hair cords. On those recurved Tannese bows, the heavy game arrows would not slow in passing through a man. I'd seen such archers transfix a redbuck in flight, cripple yedda lions, crash a wild boar in midcharge. The second rank of Tannese held back snarling war dogs on leashes—not the hound pack that earlier bayed on scent. Hunting was an excuse; this was a troop, well armed, disciplined. I blinked. The bull rider wrestled fiercely; that he could control the monster at all was astonishing.

Within the orderly Tannese arc, the Nandos were in chaos. The Tannese bowmen could pick off running figures as they chose. Beasts crashed among the brambles, dragging riders. Nandos stumbled over gear and screaming wounded; the able kicked off the grasping hands of the injured. Five Nandos waved swords, wrestling terrified mounts. Others scuttled back and forth in the Tannese trap, the fear working in them—while their commander sat his mount in a thick tangle of brush and shouted at them.

I crouched next to my dead gana, at risk from both Tannese archers and crazy Nandos; the bull rider was nearest. I turned my head; three Tannese archers sighted on me, and they didn't move or blink. They'd shoot only to orders. With great

care I sheathed my scaddas. I got slowly to my feet, holding
out empty hands; I had to stand on my left leg. I turned
carefully toward the bull rider, holding out the envoy seal at
my neck.

The bull let out a blast of air, hissing like a kettle, but the
rider held the lines taut. I blinked. The man was huge even on
his bull; he tossed back the tail of his outrobe, flinging away
bits of torn brush. Silver embroidery glittered in the sun. He
looked down at me, beard curling and shifting over his chest.
His hair was the color of pale summer hay, red hair curled out
of deeper layers; his eyes glinted yellow under thick brows.
He would have had majesty in any size, it was innate—and it
was a long time since I'd seen any grandeur or dignity. In
answer to my envoy seal, he drew his sword out of its black
saddle scabbard.

A creeping chill went down my back. My eyes flew up to
his face, and down to the revealed sword: a massive weapon
with a two-handed grip, forged of silvery metal. The sword
glittered with script on pommel and blade, glinting white
along its length. It bore its legends with regal grace, every bit
a ruler's sword.

All Harpers knew the sword of Tanman, called Devour. No
man made metal these days that glimmered so pale; it was
said never to corrode. I shuddered. Wise men avoided drawing
the blade. Devour might be a fair and just blade, symbol of
clear wisdom, but it was also old and very terrible. Devour
had a chill presence as tangible as a living man, strong as the
ruler's own—and I felt that live, fey aura quickening at the
hint of a kill, glittering silver in the sun. Desert witches
howled from too many of the Goddess's other worlds in them;
but that whisper of impulse saved my life. I gave full Tannese
salute: bending, as I must I stood one-legged, and touched my
palms to the ground until I felt the pressure of awe easing on
my neck. I straightened slowly.

No one else saluted the revealed Tanman; the Nandos stood
among the brambles gaping like silly birds, their real loyalties
exposed. The bull rider flicked a disgusted regal glance at them,
dismissed them from his gaze. His eyes went to me. He
twitched the lines. The black gana stepped toward me in
single paces, snorting at my scent.

Slender white dogs trotted out of the woods to Tannese
handlers, avoiding the menacing war dogs. Two Nandos rus-

tled in the woods—the pack of war dogs barked and lunged at their leashes, baring teeth at the noise. In his thicket the Nando commander yelled, to no effect; the crashing of brush became running steps. Tanman Caladrunan lifted two fingers. Two archers laid arrow back to ear and released. Cries of agony rose over the baying. The dogs went into frenzies; while the wounded screamed, Tanman's bull whistled, and the Nando commander shrieked.

Tanman's voice began in his belly, gathering force and timbre as it rose. It erupted from his mouth basso, a booming shout that shattered through the clearing. "Silence!"

Silence reigned. Dogs cringed, the commander slunk deeper in his thicket; wounded Nandos whimpered softly. Tanman glared round at them. "Back, you bandits. You've lost me a perfectly good hunt." Devour's tip angled toward me. "You stay."

Against all protocol I looked up. For a heartbeat my eyes locked with his. Palest hazel eyes, yellow with the blaze of temper; deep lines cut hard between his brows. A puff of wind rippled his hair and robes. He looked monolithic—a grim work of stone risen native from the yellow Tannese earth. Rulership showed briefly in his face, strata of flint roughly blasted and hacked to sight out of softer chalk; Tanman's cold pale eyes went to my gear then, and the slatey veins were hidden. He read the stories that my ragged clothes and harness showed, studied the dead mare behind me. Last and most intently, he looked in my eyes.

Sweat ran down my back under dirty robes. I hadn't expected this enormous king. As a child my dead brother played with Caladrunan; but I saw an utter stranger, and my insides twisted in my chest. Who could expect help here? I took a limping step back. With my face hidden by dirty cloth, no one recognized me; and my brother had died years ago. But I couldn't look away—shadows slipped across his eyes as if things moved, troubled, in his memory. His gaze grew less cold. The flick of temper faded into something else: curiosity. "Who are you?"

I spoke through cloth in Tannese. My voice came hoarse, from a bruised throat. "I am a desert man, Liege Lord of Tan."

Tanman said, "Oh? A desert Nando carrying Manoloki's

envoy seal?'' He pointed Devour at my fallen mare. "And that?''

I said, "Windbroken, Liege."

He said, "In the old days desert Nandos didn't serve Manoloki at any pace. Very odd. Do you have his debt payment?''

I blinked. Payment—what had the old traitor done this time? I said, "I know nothing of payment. I fill a position you hired for, Liege, among Manoloki's Nandos."

The amber eyes flashed light. The lines of his face turned icy as hill granite. "I hired for nothing with them after their games! Make payment, envoy of Manoloki."

I stared, puzzled.

The Nando commander pushed aside branches, grating, "*I* answer, not this one who knows nothing!"

Tanman looked fiercely at the man—a look of little patience and no tolerance. "Explain yourself."

The Cragman wrenched his nervous mount about in the thicket. "Manoloki pays debt now, Lord of Tan—we have it with us—"

Tanman cast a skeptical glance at the Nandos. The commander said hastily, "To pay the debt, we offer a man's services—servant for your tomb—guard for your everlasting. Great rarity, a Harper and a Sati of scaddas, two skills so advanced—the Master of Scaddas Reti was his trainer—a Great Oath candidate for your tomb, Lord—"

Blood rushed up in my ears, rang like hooves drumming clay.

Tanman snapped, "What are we, savages? Why should I accept one of your lot? Useless dead flesh for my tomb, at that!"

Manoloki and his Nandos offered me up to die, my soul in bondage forever. I swung around, started three stiff steps at the betrayer, who had known all along.

"Stay!"

I stopped.

Tanman's word was law, yes. Devour glittered icy lights. But his voice had that crackle that made me—me, a Sati of scaddas!—jump. He murmured, "There is time, desert man."

I tried to think past rage. So: the Nandos gave me this post to get rid of me; on their terms I must go to an obedient death for the sake of my Oathsworn soul. Manoloki wouldn't get

Tanman to accept it; Tannese no longer practiced such barbarities. But because of my rank, Manoloki could say he offered a valid debt payment—too bad Tanman would turn it down. I was only a stray, not trusted, easily spent. But if Tanman refused to accept me on their terms, he refused my Oath, which was death: If I could not fulfill the Great Oath, I must suicide.

Tanman snorted. "I didn't watch this Oath being sworn, I didn't accept any terms of it. I never contracted with Manoloki for a man. No agreement. On that basis, it is invalid."

The Nando protested among the saplings, "But a Devotee of Sitha performed the rites—"

Tanman's brows came together. "So? I did not agree. Did the Sati himself agree to this use of his Oath? I think not."

I met Tanman's eyes bitterly.

Oak thicket sputtered, "Manoloki rules! And the Sati swore—"

I said, "Manoloki does not rule all Nandos, fool. As one of Reti's pupils would know best." I watched the Cragman go rigid; this was not something Manoloki's man wanted argued before Tanman. I smiled, baring teeth inside my veil. I'd do him as much damage as I could before I went down—him and Manoloki both.

Tanman gazed at me. "Now that *is* interesting."

I felt my pulse pushing in my bruised throat. My marathon ride was over but the things I had struggled so long to achieve lay in danger of dying unrevealed. I could see no honorable way out of the mess. My right hand went to the envoy seal at my neck; I jerked it free and dropped it in the dirt. I twisted my weak right foot into it; the seal cracked. The Nando shouted.

I stared at him as I destroyed the seal. I had a memory sharpened by the harp. For my dead mare, I'd not forget him, in any future I might have. I shuffled my boot. The seal lay in pieces. The Cragman shouted dire promises; and subsided into mutters. Seal gone, his men were no longer a legitimate envoy's escort, just trespassing Nandos. Tanman's black bull let out a horrid low hiss like steam escaping from a pot. Tanman wore an odd expression, almost a smile. My Oath lay in his hands now.

I waited. Speckles of yellow mud lay caked on the wings of his blue outrobe; the pattern of it splashed indelibly across my memory. He sat very straight, parade-correct, in his saddle. I lifted my eyes to his face. A muscle jumped in his jaw. He said, "Reti's man, desert or not, after Pass of Bones, what use have I for any Nando?"

I said, hoarse and low, "Liege, please tell me what happened at Pass of Bones." Devour sparkled against the dark trees.

His jaw muscle leaped again; by that, I knew it was bad. But his voice ground it out. "Manoloki contracted last spring with one of my nobles to send Nandos to Pass of Bones. The bunch continually made trouble. At battle they fled the field—on Nando orders. They had no casualties. We fought on anyway. We lost the Pass that day, and most of the Pass-controlled territory. Manoloki owes me six hundred jade bars as war debt to clans who lost men after the Nando desertion. One man's services—however superb—do not compensate for whole companies of dead, especially if he is slaughtered for nothing!"

The Cragman stuttered, "A Sati of second degree rank earns more pay in five years, and we've offered him for a tomb servant forever—"

My voice cut through the yelling. I said, "Liege, Pass of Bones happened the same in other places. You will wish to know more. *That* is what service a Nando of Reti may give you."

Tanman shot a look at me. "Reti and Manoloki were always enemies. How does Manoloki offer me one of Reti's pupils?"

The escort commander shouted, "Many came over to us when Reti died. Many—even witch-ones like this!"

I glared at him, then at my dead mare, the price of my work: Reti had told us, fight within. "Liege, they accept such as me. Manoloki sends us out into Wasteland exile to hard labor. It was in one of those pest-holes that I heard of a post, working in your name, with your troops; it required Great Oath. I competed for it—" I paused, remembering the fighting among a hundred ranking officers from all over Manoloki's commands. "—and I won. At riding time, the envoy seal was one of Manoloki's personal seals. There was a power shift; he is dictator over most Nandos now. We were taken by surprise."

Tanman frowned as if this was fresh bad news. "Yet you came here anyway, under his seal. Why?"

"I came for the dead, Liege. I came because of holds lost

as you say Pass of Bones was lost . . . as Redspring Hold was lost.''

For a moment all was still. Then Tanman leaned forward to stare harder at me, and the Nando in the saplings pounded violently on his saddle, alarming his beast, shouting, ''You swore to serve—''

Slowly and carefully I made a witch-sign at him. *Death to you*, my hand said. Men rustled uneasily and muttered among themselves. I saw Tanman's eyes dart between me and the coward in the thicket. I said, ''Liege Lord of Tan, Tanman Caladrunan: my trainer Reti charged me with messages and duties to you before he died.''

The Nando shrilled, ''You'll guard Manoloki's everlasting—''

''Nando, you are a brother-slayer. There are punishments to fit that crime.'' I turned my side to Tanman and lifted my arm to exhibition throwing stance—well away from scadda hilts, ready to slap and throw. ''I won Manoloki's false post over a competition ladder of a hundred. Liege Lord of Tan, I wish to test my speed on this Nando. It would please me.''

Silence. Among the branches my enemy's eyes went wide and chilled and afraid. Behind me, soft creaks of bowstrings; the Tannese feared I might slap and throw at Tanman. But the Lord of Tan shifted in his saddle and spoke to me in an easy, calm tone. ''Sati, did you give your Oath to pay Manoloki's debts?''

My stance didn't change; my arched hand could slap to my scadda and whirl it as I spoke. ''No. I was never asked.''

Devour swung high, ghostly silver. ''Yet you did swear Great Oath?''

I inclined my head to him, to his sword. ''I did, Liege.''

He said, in a dry tone, ''I did notice that you saluted properly, while these others act as if I did not rule them too! So. The Sati is mine to keep or reject as I choose.''

The Nando commander gave a bleat of protest.

In the same instant Tanman said, ''Sati—stay.''

''I obey.'' My hand poised. ''Speak the word, he drops.''

The Nando howled, ''He swore to serve—''

Tanman turned back, lifting one thick yellow eyebrow. No one had to tell *me* it was a sign of dangerous temper. Softly he said, ''This is the law, faceless one: to pay a debt under Great Oath, all parties agree. There has been no agreement. Second: when the Sati completed his Oath, he was no longer

a Nando brother. None of your laws overrule Great Oath in
Tan. What he swore applies as strictly and openly as anything
my liegemen swear. He owes nothing to you, nor you to
him—as Manoloki clearly knew in throwing him away to be
killed. Finally: I accept no trickery on Great Oath. I take it
ill. You tell Manoloki that, within the next ten days. After
that my hunting parties will mark you out on sight.'' He
leaned forward on his saddle. "Tell your master that his
debt is overdue, and he will rue it.''

Tanman was the supreme judge of his land, his court gave
no appeals—save to diety. And Tanman Caladrunan lifted
one finger. The Tannese arc opened an exit while archers
sighted eyes along their shafts. Three sighted on me; hand
still cocked, I stood quite still. Tanman said, "Get you gone,
faceless ones.''

Three war dogs burst baying from the pack, leashes trailing. The Nando officer cursed, jerked lines, thrashed with his
goad—his gana crashed with a snort through saplings. Nando
mounts backed into the brambles, danced terrified among
snapping dogs, screamed and rolled their eyes. Hooves trampled wounded; men on foot, tangled in gear, lunged for
escape. Men fought one another to pass first, the whole
awkward crowd scrambling at once for the hole allowed
them. The commander shouted for order, swung his goad at
men, cursed the ones he missed, and wrestled his panicky
half-trained mount. A war dog nipped its hocks. Man and
beast crashed away through briars; the gana gave an odd
whistling shriek that faded with distance. War dogs raced
after, nipping hocks. The Tannese watched the disgraceful
flight in silence.

And I—I stood there with a wild swell of relief rising in
my chest like a bubble through streamside forth. My body felt
thin and weak, as if I might drift off, thistle-blown, behind
my ballooning head. I blinked. *"Yek-shin,"* I said. Hill-
robbers, cowards, Manoloki's outlaws were that—I should've
killed them. I dropped my throwing hand and ground the
chips of envoy seal under my boot.

Tanman's bull snorted quick hard breaths, as if he drove
off the foreign ganas, and dared any to come back. High
breeding showed in every powerful movement. The bull pawed
the grass, hooked the air with proud briar-decked horns,
screamed out a challenge after the crashes and cries. Beneath

costly armor the black coat rippled with muscles. Tanman said, "I think we need to work with this bull, Pitar. That temper tantrum nearly wrenched my shoulder apart."

A Tannese officer inclined his head. The bull trumpeted again.

From that towering magnificence my eyes dropped to my dead beast. She lay flattening on the earth, a common dun mare sprawled on dry grasses, skinny forelegs splashed with blood. A wasp buzzed close around her eyes. I knelt, smoothed her neck, and closed the staring eyes gently. At a sound, I glanced up.

Sunlight winked off Devour's hilt above me. It was perhaps a bell pass after midday and the sword caught the hot light. The Tanman named Caladrunan, Heart of Iron, lowered his sword. He said, "Take off that face cloth, little man."

CHAPTER

= *2* =

I TOOK OFF my riding gloves. My hands went to my face
cloth, my hood. Loops of cloth fell to my neck. The archers
stirred, murmuring—oh yes, they were surprised at my dark
Upai face, startled that I bore no damning outlaw cheek-
brand. I crossed wrists in salute to Tanman, inclining my
head low. "*Kinai denar shi,* Liege Lord of Tan." I added
softly, "*Kigadi.*"

When I lifted my eyes, his face had changed. His skin had
pulled back taut, the eyes opened. *Kigadi* was a reckless
word, a complex web of meanings and obligations: the friend
who spared nothing asked of him, to his own life, who gave
his friend merciful death when dignity and hope were lost,
who slayed his friend's enemies with ferocity. *Kigadi,* hunter
for a dead friend's wife, uncle to the children—a man's best
brother.

An outrageous word to utter to Tanman Caladrunan. I'd a
right. The spirit invoked, demanded a courage perhaps foolish. I knew Caladrunan and my brother had shouted it together, fine and wild as redbuck on the peaks; the word
braided me to my brother's rights. Kigadi—I gave the honor
to no other, I never asked after another man's soul. I could
only hope the spirit was in him yet, to remember. He looked
pale.

Tanman said, in a flat, quiet voice, "Get up, Naga." I
tapped my brow with my thumb and stood up. Devour's tip
sketched a gesture in the air; Tanman nicked the back of his
hand, wiped away blood and sheathed that awful weapon, its

17

fires dimming as he slid it into leather. "What happened to Redspring Hold ten years ago?"

I said, "Five days after you left Redspring, Manoloki's Nandos gave passwords through the perimeter, forced open gates for raiders with large weapons. They destroyed the hold down to the cellars and my people's camp. They executed everyone. I found no one else alive."

His brows drew hard together. He rested one clenched fist on his thigh, looking into my upturned face. His bull inhaled deeply of my scent, whuffed a blast of air at me. "No messages got in or out—rebels, we thought. After, nothing left. Total silence from your clan . . . So you joined Reti, became a Sati and a Harper."

I inclined my head to him.

In a soft, soft voice, he said, "Who were these raiders with large weapons? Even if they got the main gates, Redspring Hold was strong: barbicans that could hold, walls, watch towers . . ."

Answer writhed off my tongue in five distinct Upai tones, fouling the summer air: "*Osa'aa'ei.*" Enemy, atrocity, hatred, death by fire—all bred together in one monstrous name. The Osa! Murderers of women and children and helpless wrinkled old men. Tanman blinked at me. In Upai, in my gentlest voice, I said, "The Osa aimed at you, Liege—five days sooner, they would have got you." Long I'd cursed his name for that, and my brother's, even as I hoped for his aid now. If Caladrunan had not been at Redspring, my clan might yet live. Perhaps.

Tanman looked at me expressionlessly for a heartbeat. His eyes moved down to the scaddas sheathed at my waist. Then he turned his head. "Pitar, arrange a beast for the Sati to ride."

The archers cased their bows, formed a column; huntsmen whistled for stray dogs. Men rearranged a redbuck carcass slung on a pack beast; I swung up to sit across the packstraps like a farmer. My right thigh gave way awkwardly as I mounted, red sprites spun past my eyesockets. They'll be watching, I thought, and fought it. Bony angles of redbuck nudged my thighs.

When I opened my eyes, Tanman had ridden off, his bull moving with stately dignity. A trio of burly archers rode up behind me, bows held ready across saddles. A placid

packmaster's gana towed a dozen leashed war dogs all straining and growling at me. Indifferent to clamor, my new mount
followed them in the column. The soldiers were veterans all,
by the scars; they rode well, looked fit; their harnesses showed
wear; but they seemed plump by my standards. I looked back
slowly, reluctantly.

On the churned ground, my old mare lay abandoned in the
ruck of her gear, and no one mourned. My last glimpse of her
was of a dun-colored patch among the oaks. My only words
to salute her translated from a History: "How your eyes have
darkened, my brave one. Your heart was as the rock lion.
This your saddle shall never be ridden again. Hunt the oakwoods
of your everlasting under a greater Lord than I."

Dull green oaks arched over the dusty trails, lifting ragged
heads ninety feet tall. Limbs bent down, corky and black.
The woods ended on a long slope, rolling terrain covered with
yellow grain that brushed my boots. I stirred uneasily, riding
thus on a following wind. My eyes flowed around the strange
circular horizon, so unlike the jagged gorges of the desert. I
could see everything and everything could see me. The dark
oakwoods made no barrier at all to that vastness. I scowled.
Long days riding under the wide pale Tannese sky still did
not make me used to it.

A clump of reddish towers rose small and sharp against the
sky-haze ahead of us, rose and fell slowly against clouds as
we rode gentle land folds. The column found shrubby trees,
fanning out among them—an apple orchard. The trees hid the
sky in a thick mesh of branches, leaves gone dull in the long
sleepy decline to fall. Moss grew on trunks. The air smelled
of sweet rotten windfalls. I snared apples, fresh apples—I
hardly tasted any, hunger cramped my gut so bad I wolfed
smaller ones whole. Just as promptly I clutched my belt,
leaned over and heaved. My lips tasted of sour acid and fruit.
My trio of guards tensed.

"Problem?" Tanman's bass voice rumbled. He rode up,
glancing over the column's gear. I shook my head; he tossed
me a leather bag and rode on; the column moved after. His
bag poured grain into my hand. Judge a noble by his men's
gear, I thought, chewing parched kernels, and relaxed into
motion. The man did not waste things; he'd use me, which was
all I asked. My head nodded down, and without knowing when,
I slept. The body has its own wisdom.

The pack beast thudded onto a cobbled road. My eyes jerked open; I put up my hood, wrapped my face—Nando habit. We rode quiet town streets past whitewashed houses with yellowish tile roofs; distantly I heard the bawl of market, animal pens, mills, clanging ironsmithies. Houses grew larger, ornate slate-roofed compounds lapped at the base of a massive yellow wall. We had arrived at Tan's seat of government, the Fortress of Tan.

I knew the siege walls of Tan's Histories. This wall looked as thick and tall as Histories said—but there were no surrounding river channels, no stake-pits or trenches, no engines of war, no sentries visible. Only houses! After losing so many outer holds, I'd expected a fortress strident with the trades of war. Nothing warlike here—only the broad brownish scar on a hill across town that marked a beggartown. They'd herded unpleasantness out of sight, slammed the gates of the beggartown on warnings. Faintly, as the wind veered, I heard the keening of refugees. I gazed somberly at Tanman's back while my insides plunged into icy knots. I thought: he knows. Enemies hamper him. Manoloki has allies here.

Tanman's head lifted. Spiring above us on the far side of the siege wall were pink sandstone towers capped with pale slate. Ornate statues in niches climbed up the towers. Weathered green copper pierced the air at each roofpeak: lightning wards molded into wands, wires, flame shapes. The towers were round, angular, close-ranked in a jumble of heights—a jagged skyline packed with intricacy, not a place of defense. Fire lodged well in such assassin's crannies. I scowled at an ox-gana yard beside the wall ahead.

A slow merchant caravan turned aside, throwing dust over the cobbles; drover faces stared at us, floured with their own dust, as we passed the yard. Caravan leaders and merchants stood talking at a low, common-house door, passing a wineskin; drovers smacked goads and jostled teams to water troughs. Tanman lifted his hand to greet them. Men shouted back, grinning, waving.

By the great wall a group of women in gauze veils sang to a tambour beat. Their girdles shook. I turned my eyes from arms shining bare and pale in the blue shadows below the Fortress wall: I knew natives better look aside, or risk hard lessons in manners. But white waving hands stayed vividly in my mind.

We turned into a broad postern gate in the wall; over the years caravans had gilded the subtle-grained stone with yellow dust. Fine houses outside might be whitewashed, but the siege walls were not, and showed their age. Hooves clattered on old cobbles; everyone else I saw—all in military blue—dismounted at the gate, led their beasts well aside, while our troop rode on. Tanman's bull whistled shrill warning: give way! The noise of shod, split hooves echoed and shattered between tower walls. I kept craning my neck up, shifting in discomfort: this was the old section. It felt like a desert gorge set for ambush. Limestone catwalks leaped the streets, stone and brass balconies filigreed the lower levels of the towers. Slit-windows and arrow-loops angled everywhere. Marble statues crowded the barrage of culture: men, beasts, fantasy creatures, copper engravings bolted to monoliths in the street. The country had been too open; this narrow place was a sniper's dream. A man crossed a catwalk and disappeared above like a bug in a hole.

I understood suddenly the planning in these towers. Past Tanmen never expected this section to repel heavy engines of war; this was desperate, core-area defense once the outer curtain walls were lost. The narrow ways would fracture a large invading army, provide cover for defenders; catwalks with high copper-sheathed doors could sling stones and hot tar on invaders, slits housed archers. For such old work, such intricacy, I saw no visible wood; seen close, the tower walls at street level looked fire resistant.

But these days Tannese weren't planning for war; they were building houses outside the walls. I looked at the soldiers around me, so sturdy, so heavy—and so clean—and I felt tired. Likely such men walked the beggartown perimeter and herded the war-weary out of sight of Tan's nobles. I must explain the urgency to men like these? Stupid of me, not to have foreseen Tannese inertia—more struggle than I expected when I poured out my strength recklessly to get here. I shifted position across packstraps and felt damp trickles along the cloth bound about my loins and padding my leather-armored seat. I touched my corad, lifted bloody fingers. The pain felt no worse than before. I closed my hand over the stain on my harp calluses.

We rode across a wide unpaved parade ground churned by formation drills; the column stopped at a low limestone sta-

ble. The stable was cracked, battered, hoary with age, but its
outside pens were flanked by crisp new pink sandstone barns;
the squeals and challenges of ganas split the air. The acrid
fumes of an impressive dung pile cut through my face cloth.
My pack gana meandered to a stop. I swung off the straps,
gingerly slid weight onto my good leg; the ground heaved
about at gana pace. I stumbled through the mill of soldiers,
flanked by my trio of bowmen. I saw officers wrinkle their
noses as I wandered past—I knew I stank, and I didn't care.
Hunger made me ill-smelling, let alone the long embrace of
ganas, dirt, and saddle leather. Food and sandbaths should
tame the cheese-mold aroma, if I lived that long.

Tanman was giving orders to a soldier. I halted a courteous
twenty-five paces away, before anyone yelled; I saluted him
with crossed wrists and waited. I was good at that. Tanman
looked at me. He gave an odd, frustrated gesture of a hand;
he dared not come within kill range. I looked back. The trio
of guards watched me, arrows nocked. He said, "What is
your message from Reti? You can talk here."

I gathered my strength and spoke in a low, controlled
voice. "This is for you alone, Liege, not for gaping formation soldiers preening their ornaments and tin rank bangles."

Cords creaked softly. A voice, clipped and crisp, said,
"It'll be your back, little man, if you go on with insults."

I said evenly, "I know. I heard them pull cord."

"Easy." Tanman's eyes narrowed and paled. Staccato
Tannese mutters hushed. "Better," he murmured coolly, and
the amber eyes came back to me. They were very cold. "The
message?"

I spoke, in my native language, five opening lines of Tan's
Fourth History. In Upai the message was compact. *"Bilouros
ara aedoo Sitta paroerissar sai xojia soforu . . ."* Pleading
those lines in Upai, an envoy named Kirot uttered his message of warning and grief: mine was for the same grief, the
same danger. When I saw the glitter of light in Tanman's
eyes, the knowledge, I continued in the antique Tannese of
other men in the History. "I have carried bitter news and I
call you to hear of great misery."

He lifted a bushy brow. "Indeed—quoting Histories at
me." Men muttered behind me; seven of them lingered back
there now. Tanman frowned. "You claimed you were from
Manoloki's Nandos."

I glared. "I crushed his seal for the traitor he is!"

"Oh? Just for selling you off as a tomb servant?"

I shook my head once. "For other, larger crimes. You told me of Pass of Bones. There were others. Will be more."

"You swore Great Oath to serve me. You were a Nando. First you come from Manoloki, then you don't. Now you claim to be envoy from the Upai. How can you—" He glanced at the men muttering, so they shut up. "—how can you be both Upai and my Oathswearer?"

"The two are one. Desert Nandos were never rebels against you, Liege, nor Upai. Both could be of incalculable value to you."

One of the mutters behind me ended in a harsh laugh. "Sounds like that talented Marsh noble who turned traitor on us last year."

Tanman glared fiercely. The noise stopped. Tanman said, "Upai, tell that to our mutilated dead on the desert border."

I said, "Those were not dead by Upai hands. Upai do not touch the dead." I lifted one hand carefully to the muttering. They quieted. I said, "We mutilate living only." *That* caused an uproar. Tanman made a sharp gesture, cutting it off. Then he looked hard at me.

I lifted my thumb slowly, pointed northwest. "Manoloki and his Nandos, who are your enemies." I pointed eastward. "Marshmen in revolt against their nobles." I pointed west and southward. "Cragmen in revolt against Tan, pirates fighting for anyone with jade. Those are your border rebels, Liege. I know the Wastes—the Upai alive yet are loyal to you. Others lay false trails. I know who rules those lies; I've tried to learn it for two years, as Reti ordered me to do. I offer what I know for the safety of your land, Lord of Tan. And I beg you to help the Upai who flee here. They flee what is taking your holds."

The crisp voice behind me said, "Scaring Manoloki's curs, giving information—open war between Nando and Nando, Liege?"

Tanman shook his head. "This is an old feud come to light. Reti and Manoloki were enemies. Reti had fewer men, he was loyal to Tan. One of his pupils is a rare prize. Manoloki was a fool to throw you away, Sati." He smiled a strange wry smile. "But you didn't like what he offered, did you? I never saw a man tangle with my bull and get up to talk

about it later.'' He folded his arms, looking me up and down.
''You don't argue quite as your brother did. Are you done
popping up with surprise affiliations? Good. You say you are
an envoy from the Upai. You know the obligations of an
envoy? You can start by acting like one. I will be up to talk
with you after you have disarmed. Pitar, take him up to the
tower.'' Tanman walked across the parade ground to a long
block of a building, up broad steps to a door arch; ten soldiers
flanked him. A last swirl of gold and blue and silver and he
was gone.

Pitar's crisp voice said, ''Come, Sati.'' Air lay dead and
thick inside the building we entered. The only light came from
torches soldiers lit by the entry, and from a few closely grilled
windows. Scuffle marks showed along the dusty limestone
floor. At a stair landing Pitar led the way up. He went
swiftly; after five stair landings, I was limping and reeling
shamefully off the walls. Pitar unbarred a wooden door
banded in brass and waved me in.

I stumbled into a pattern of colored light on the floor.
Streams of yellow and red and green, alive with dust motes,
came from a window of colored glass. Air whistled through
tiny holes where panes had fallen out and shattered on a
semicircular floor of stone. The chamber held two wooden
chairs, a straw mat, a chipped porcelain slushpot of another
era at an iron waste grill; nearby, a dusty copper pitcher. One
man grabbed the pitcher and departed; that left six. Pitar
rubbed glove knuckles, gazing at me.

A prison cell, I thought. Built for someone of noble blood,
with that glass window. Tragedy shimmered over the mute
relics. The colored glass rippled my view; but out of an open
hole, I saw a dark edge of oakwoods on the land far away.
Sun passed toward night in a golden summer haze on grainfields and woods. The air fanning my face smelled wet and
salty, as men said of the sea. The cliff wind, Histories named
it, caught only in the highest Fortress towers. I had never
smelled the sea before.

CHAPTER

= 3 =

THE SOLDIERS TENSED, lit by window glow, partly obscured in their own shadows: farm-born young wrestlers, rawboned bargemen with red knuckles and long sad faces. I reached the shoulder of the shortest one. Pitar said, "How shall it be, Sati?"

I slid a look at him and held my hands out lightly before me. Pitar gestured. The heaviest of the men freed my scabbards and harpcase, jerked away my face cloth, uncoiled braids; he opened my outer robe, unhooked my leathers, poked inner robes. By most standards he was thorough. He even prodded my corad, the most private garment of all, with some force. He wiped his hands on rags, for his hands came away smeared with fluid-seep and blood. With brisk disgust he said, "That's the lot, Commander. Garrote cords, prayer stick, wrist and chest knife, and spurs."

Pitar stared disapprovingly at the spurs taken off my boots. The razors, set in prongs, caught light and glittered—for battle, not for kicking ganas. Few learned spurs in Tan; it made me look better than I was. They were ugly, used—I'd been lucky not to cut myself in the tussle with the bull. While I closed my robes men carried out my stripped gear, other soldiers filed in. The door boomed hollowly.

Tanman strode in holding my prayer stick. He scowled at it. Nando sticks weren't prayed over; they made good weapons. On mine Reti's dune-line insignia was subtly carved within prayer glyphs. Tanman looked from it to me, as if he expected me to speak.

25

So I did. "Liege, as a Nando I carry information from Reti to you. As Upai, my clan named as Naga Asaba Imuto Teot sa Inigrev sa Orena sa Efresa Scaso sa Kirot, Kirot of the Fourth History. My own name means Beautiful Gold Dance of Knives. I ask formal recognition, on this name, as an envoy from the Upai."

Silence, louder than words; I'd offended Tannese protocol in speaking first. Tanman considered, and set my prayer stick on a chair within reach of anyone in the room—including me. I met his eyes. He gestured; Pitar stowed the stick away. Tanman said, "According to the law, your name does make you envoy. Now, the entire message. What did you bring?"

Joy lifted in my middle. "Give me a slate." Slate and chalk were brought. I gentled my cut leg to bend as I sat down on a battered chair, and I drew. My duty burned through my fingers in rapid stabs of chalk. I drew a scale diagram of a flamethrower, Osa trailsign, travel and battle movements in lines and arrows. On the slate's reverse I marked glyphs of holds lost, a long list. That didn't betray literacy; most officers learned hold symbols. These days no Upai admitted he could read; we had died of it. I put the slate down and limped to the glass. My head dropped to the open hole; the seawind felt so pure, so clean. Alertness renewed, I gazed at my new ruler.

Tanman scanned my work with puckered brows. In low tones he called for food, clothing, water; he stood half a head taller than Pitar. Goddess! I thought, surprised how far my head tilted to see his face—he'd looked big on his bull, but anyone would on that monster. My brother once called this man *Kigadi*—and so had I, today. Against a creeping awe, I wondered how he knew where to set his feet down, he was so far from them. It helped to think about that, rather than the pain in my leg and the weariness gaping before me like a void. Sleep, muscles whispered. Please. Sleep. My lids drooped; I jerked them open.

Tanman paced, frowning; waved his hand at Pitar. "No, let him slouch. I want to ask him a few questions." I leaned on the wall, with such permission, and tipped my head onto stone. "How did Manoloki trick you, Naga? How did he get you to swear Great Oath at all, ignorant of debt payments?"

My spine felt like a rod of chill; I stood up straight. I glanced at soldiers, judging their steadiness: they weren't going to like this. "I was to send plans of Fortress. Manoloki offered me a hold to rule, Liege, if I killed you at signal."

Tanman jerked up, staring. For a heartbeat he looked like a great red stag at bay. Then his shoulders and the line of his neck relaxed, and he folded his arms. I thought, if that shocked him he hadn't much military experience. He took a pace around the room; asked calmly, "You could do that, Naga?"

"Kill you?" I yawned, rubbing my face. "Now? Yes. If I didn't care what happened to me after." I met the unblinking amber gaze.

"You knew Manoloki would trick you—"

I smiled grimly. "Kill Tanman, for a hold! It made me laugh. I knew they'd kill me after; I believed them *that* far. I meant to snarl the plans. His debt tricks were the real plot, but I didn't know about all that. I was at Bitterspring. Wrong end of the desert."

His eyes narrowed. "So the Nandos have poor communications. Bitterspring is a sixty-day caravan, no wonder you look this way."

I said softly, "Thirty days on a good mount, if you care for it. They owe me for my mare's death." I tilted my head back. "I have information about my end of the border. . . ."

"Tell me. These are all trusted men. Pitar, record it."

I pressed cupped palms to my eyes, pushed away fatigue. Data rolled out of me in Harper recall; I was far too tired to think clearly. Propped against the wall, I pressed my fingers hard into my forehead. I detailed routes for smuggled drugs, weapons, and food; the financiers; Nando garrison strengths, strategic supplies, weak points, common difficulties; and the routes Manoloki used to channel masses of men from Marsh swamps to camps on the Tannese border. "Such precision!" Tanman murmured. Then I turned to Osa.

I told where Osa flamethrowers were, and in what state of repair; where stolen or improvised parts lay hidden among allies for future use on the Osa themselves. The Cragmen and Manoloki's Nandos grew restive under foreign yoke. Squinting between my fingers, I said, "Manoloki deals in drug trade to support two armies eating jade. His Nandos fail contracts as the Osa require, such as at your Pass of Bones. He also runs masses of raw Marshmen as Osa foot troops, solely on plunder. The Osa promised incredible pay, but no jades have passed hands. Drug trade has to support his Nandos and his expansion as an Osa ally.''

Tanman's face grew hard. He paced while Pitar scribbled on slates. I gave tactical details: Osa flamethrower range, their great speed, the Crag-mined coal moving fuel; how flame-fuels were made of bitter earths and oil. I described the rarer engines modified to hurl explosives. I diagrammed exploding an Osa flamethrower or the cobbled-up imitations built in secret by their traitorous allies. I told of Manoloki's plans to take Tan and obliterate the Osa, after they served his purpose. The irony was, the Osa likewise meant to rid the world of Manoloki after all use was squeezed out.

''You say the Nandos are not solvent, that some drug raids would scramble Manoloki's financing for his expansion. That the alliance is unstable. You call us blind! I never heard of—''

I shook my head. ''Few victims escape if they're close enough to see flamethrowers. At Redspring I was lucky. I was in . . . I was in rocky country.'' I lifted my head, flames filled my sight; I almost brought up my arms against stench and smoke. . . . I blinked, and there was only sun winking off colored glass. I whispered, ''Yours is the last strong country before the sea, Liege. The Osa murdered sixty Upai clans back in Fourth History; they pursue my people yet. They meant to kill you too, years ago. Reti hated them—as both Upai and Reti's pupil, I offer service to you under Great Oath. I plead with you—fight these weapons. I don't want to see my people—yours—massacred.'' Amazing eloquence a man can deliver when he's desperate.

Tanman paced. Dirt rasped. ''You've fought the Osa?''

I angled the rough strike-edge of my left palm to light. Six scars ran among the callouses. ''I exploded so many throwers.''

He lifted thatchy brows. ''You're a significant irritant. How many Osa soldiers did you kill?''

''With my hands?'' My hands flexed. Tanman's face changed while he looked in my eyes. No one moved. ''Reti had standing orders: capture and question. I've questioned eight true Osa.'' Nobody spoke, but they shifted; desert methods were not gentle. Tanman turned away, paced. I spoke in a slurry Marshman account perfected in two years under

Manoloki. "The Nandos never knew. No one cares about a flawed Sati sent off by Reti for gambling."

Tanman gave me a straight, understanding look and gazed off at the window. "I hear interesting rumors on someone called Tokori Efresa. Shadow, I think the name means. You know of him?"

Though I was exhausted, I straightened against my wall. I said, "I do."

Tanman glanced at me. "Allegedly Tokori Efresa unites a dire outside force, like your Osa, with two thousand rebel Upai."

I opened my mouth and laughed. The noise rang harshly in the cell. I wiped my eyes, laughing, and shook my head. "No, Liege. Upai and Osa!—not while sand shifts in the wind. Tokori Efresa means Shadow-of-Thorn, also Warleader, the Swift Death. He preys on Osa and Nandos. Tannese need not fear Tokori Efresa of the Upai."

Tanman strode up to plant his tassled boots two paces from me. If I wanted to kill the Lord of Tan, this chance was it; the chamber was full of nervous eyes. He stared into my face as if daring me to do my worst; I stared back. Naive of him, I thought. Then I took a sudden fierce pride in him, for choosing him my liege: he had courage under his early caution.

He said, "So you know Tokori Efresa's Upai and Reti's men. How many are loyal? How many would fight for me?"

"Reti had seventy-two high level officers hidden as I was." I heard someone whistle in surprise. "There are not two thousand Upai; there never were. You mistake Manoloki's dark Marshmen for Upai—as Manoloki wanted. I count three hundred Upai warriors in the Wastes, the desert; a hundred on the border. Maybe more among your refugee camps, but I haven't talked to any yet." My scarred hand turned edge up. "They will all fight for you, Liege."

He looked at Pitar. Then at me. Quietly, "And you, Naga? You will fight for me?"

"I named you Kigadi; to me, I swore Oath—I always fought on your side—" I stepped forward to salute. Pain flared from knee to hip socket, agony in the tear left by the bull, knots seized in both legs. I hadn't dared stretch to keep muscles usable. It conjured violent cramps now—the cost of such a ride. One leg buckled ridiculously under me, then the other; I grabbed stone to break my fall, but I went inevitably

to my knees. I could not stand up, I could not even straighten—
obscure little muscles spasmed while the big ones clenched in
seizures. Slowly, gracefully as the fall of a feather, the knife
hidden in a scar-hollow at my jerking right shoulder slid
lazily out.

The knife dropped with a soft thump. I stared at it. I didn't
pick it up; I was not stupid. Hands snatched my hair, my
arms. They twisted my elbows back, flopped me on my belly,
yanked my legs out straight. Knots clenched. "And I asked
about Tokori Efresa," Tanman said bitterly. They ground my
jawbone into limestone paving, cracking scabs. I supposed
their mistrust was now justified. My leathers exploded under
so many hands. They shredded robes, ripped and searched
seams. Then they started on my body. This time, they were
thorough. It hurt. They turned me over a few times, like a
child playing by the cookfire with a greasy grilled rib. They
found it at last, no longer than a fingernail: the suicide knife
wrapped in my braid bindings. Tanman examined it grim-
faced. "You yourself are one of Tokori Efresa's men."

"Yes, Liege." They took my flat tone for defeat. I lay on
my back staring up at hard competent faces, three big wrestlers to each limb—they could easily tear me apart. My
private parts ached, blood brassed my mouth; my torn thigh
shot jagged stabs and convulsed into shivering. Tanman's eyes
moved to my leg; I bled all over, now I was naked. None of
that bothered me so much.

What bothered me was Pitar. The guard commander held a
sword tip on my belly. Each convulsive jerk of my legs
pricked skin below my ribs. I learned anatomy to kill; Pitar
had too—his tip was angled to slide through my diaphragm.
He stared into my face, head cocked, waiting for Tanman's
word. Pitar's eyes were pale gray, his chin beard was scrag-
gly; I saw a slash-scar on his temple. His sword looked ten
times normal size. Not for me Devour; no, a common blade
nicked from use would finish the last-born of Clan Teot,
rulers once, noblest clan in a land larger than Tan.

I did what I came for, I thought. I tried to relax my
cramping body, to go limp. From the faces, I'd not long to
compose my life. My long task was done—Sitha Goddess of
Mercy, I prayed, make it fast, let it be swift and kind, like
sleeping. I am not very brave. When I heard Tanman's robes

rustle I shut my eyes, waiting for pain. I knew there would be pain.

Pitar said, "Forgive us for missing that knife, Liege."

"You knew he was a Sati, Pitar. Let's not miss things." I opened my eyes a slit. The sword dug into my skin and cut a narrow little burn. I closed my eyes swiftly again. "Thirty-five lashes owed for concealed weapons in my presence—I doubt it'd impress him in this state, and it'd probably kill him. Loose him. He'll talk about Tokori Efresa eventually."

I opened my eyes. Tanman's figure wavered in front of me with absurd flickering lights, red dots and colors. A strange slurred voice said loudly, "I may tell you those things, Liege Lord of Tan—but I will not talk under sword edge!"

Me. I said it. A stranger inside my fool head yelled it out. Pitar's blade massaged the crease between my stomach muscles. I'd seen eyes that cold before: Manoloki's eyes were that cold. The fool in my mouth whispered, "Everything you do, natives like me taught you— Sek-bloods gave you all you know. Your people crawled up on the beach, worthless ship-wrecked outlaws, and the Sek took you in. Now you have pretensions of—" Pitar growled and someone wrenched my head back so I couldn't breath. The dots were black now.

I heard Tanman's voice rumble through the roaring in my head; the grip relaxed, I breathed again. I gasped. He said, "You're probably right—no need to insult us. Is the water ready, Pitar?"

Pitar murmured, in a civilized voice, "Yes, and food waits. This offense to your person, Liege—"

"Enough," Tanman said. "We touched his honor. Desert men do such things; and they have different punishments. Bring in the water, and respect his temper—we're lucky he's so weak. Manoloki may have forgotten what Reti's Satis are like, but I haven't."

There was really no excuse for what I did then. I yelled, "Manoloki's pigs can't lap blood if you hold the pan for them! Reti's men slop guts on every floor of their competitions—bunch of waterhole leeches infecting snake intestines with pickled—"

Tanman said mildly, "Did Reti teach you to swear like that?"

I shut up. Hands lifted me, forced back my elbows; my feet were set on the waste grate. I demanded fiercely, "What the pig are you farmers doing—,'' when I heard the door. A man carried in the pitcher; steam wisped off the spout. I stared incredulously as he tipped it over my head—my reflexes seized, but the hands held firm. Steaming water poured down my face. I shrieked in heartshaken, utter outrage.

The water was hot, yes—but now it was dirtied, ruined. That was greater outrage! More pitcherfuls doused my head. Slippery wet, I jerked free, skidded in the water splattered on the floor, fell on my knees. Water splashed on my back, ran down my thighs and puddled the floor about the grate, muddied brown and yellow and streaked with blood. Clean drinking water poured over a body as filthy as mine—no greater sin existed. I scrabbled at the grating but they jerked me in the air, upended me. Two of them scrubbed me with a clothbag of soap as if I were a slave fighting before the block in Manoloki's camps. I heard laughter when I strained against too many hands and yelled. For a Sati, I gave poor fight for myself: whenever I broke free, muscle spasms felled me. They found that hilarious. I was appalled at their casual attitude—a dozen rations of water ran down the waste drain. They didn't care about tainted water. I was ruining the water, it'd be me the Goddess pursued in rage. What did She care about how it happened?

The extra soldiers laughed when I swore and shouted; only the wet restrainers shouted back. Even Tanman stood out of range and smiled. Sitha, how they poured on the water—and the bellowed jokes flying about! When I lost my temper and screamed at Tanman, he only threw back his head and guffawed. They doused my face with a pot of water. I hung upside down, coughing.

''Enough,'' Tanman said. I blinked water from my eyes, snapped two pungent words. The chamber roared with fresh laughter. Pitar clapped my shoulder where I hung in midair, spoke; his men tumbled me onto a thick cloth on the floor. I rolled over, sat up, and bared my teeth. Men scrambled out of reach, pelted me with rags. Pitar dropped a blue robe nearby, gestured; the pelting stopped.

I pushed aside their rags. My hair was a sorry draggled mess and my skin was lighter than before, while saddle sores bled and stung from the soaping. My hoof-cut thigh welled blood in sullen trails. Pitar told me, ''Use the rags to dry off.'' I glared at him and swore instead. I felt skinny and

stripped of dignity sitting there on the floor, unable even to
stand up. I knew, oh yes, I was amusing to them: a desert
Sati too weak to fight while they defiled good water on me
and joked—punishment! Tanman was right about that.

Pitar dropped a pile of white strips near me: bandages. I
cursed him and he laughed. I held my face wooden against
pain as I wrapped my cut thigh and worst harness sores.

I saw Tanman's eye watching me; his face looked grave
and not at all amused now. He said softly to Pitar, "Believe
me, old friend, he only wanted out of it. Killing would be
easier for Satis than trying to wrestle free." Pitar muttered,
glancing aside. Men carried in a table, set out trays of food.
Three of the soldiers stalked toward me, big hands out-
stretched. They grinned.

I stretched a loop of cloth bandage between my hands.
They eyed it, and each other, and looked uneasy. Tanman
said, "Put that down, Naga, it's time to eat. They'll help you
over here."

"As they helped before?" I snarled.

He smiled. He walked over and extended his hand for the
bandage. I growled a word and threw the thing aside. He
pointed at the rags and my wet chest. "Dry yourself." I used
a rag, flinched at such waste. The bigger drops I licked off,
conserving as much as I could. Tanman bent and handed me
the fallen blue robe, chuckling at the expressions of his men. I
put it on, because he told me to; then Tanman gripped my
upper arms, hauling me up off my feet with a grunt. "Heavier than you look." He handed me gently to the three soldiers. They carried me, plopped me in a chair like a limp cloth
toy.

I sputtered, "Why did you do this—this—waste all that
water—"

Tanman smiled as he sat down. "Because, Sati, you stank."

I pointed my thumb at him and told him what his sacrilegious
use of water deserved. It made me sick with shame that I
failed to prevent it. I told him so. Profanely, because I was
very angry. Soldiers nudged one another, grinning. Tanman
began to grin, then to laugh, shaking with deep belly roars.
He leveled a finger back at me. "The Goddess is more
generous here than in your desert. You need fear no sin over
that. Now shut up! I'll hurt if you amuse me any harder!"

I shut up. I sat there, lips clamped shut like a turtle;

blinking, confused, humiliated, and angry. I looked at Tanman, who was wiping his eyes of laughter-tears. He looked as if it felt good, as if he had long needed it. My rage faded fast; I wasn't angry then, I was just tired. I yawned, surprising everyone, rested my head on the table, and closed my eyes.

Tanman called hastily, "Ben, that food—" I jerked up, startled. A man set dishes before me. I drew breath to smell. Pale green dishes on a long tray, perilous temptation! There were arcane eating tools, steaming bowls, low dishes of cold food: a Tannese midday meal of noble dimensions. My left hand scooped hot grain, and all thought trickled out of my mind. I tasted. I promptly choked, eyes bulging. It went down in a painful lump. Salt! Enough for ten bowls of any Nando food. Salt wasted like precious water— I'd never get used to this crazy land. I glared, while they laughed at the sight I made.

But my gut didn't care about funny tastes. My stomach let out a horrid growl with a surge of hunger that blurred sight. I grabbed a dish of venison in a bland sweet sauce, gulped it down. The guards whispered, made faces and gestures. Perhaps it revolted them. I ate as I always did: snapping large hasty bites, guarding my food with spread hands, snarling at anyone who came near. I gorged down a dish of nuts. Another of vegetables. Only then I realized it was too rich for a stomach shrunken by the long ride; whatever I ate would come back up. I was disgusted. I picked up an empty bowl, bent over, and gagged. After I quit heaving, I wiped my mouth on my hand. Shout about blasphemous waste; this was disgraceful. When I dared, I slid my eyes up to Tanman's face, trying to think of some contrite word.

He hadn't moved. He looked straight in my eyes with all the directness of a born Upai. He remembered *that* part. "Liege," I muttered. I folded the robe closer, pushed wet trickles from my hair out of my eyes. I felt cold. From a silver flask Tanman poured wine into a goblet, waved for me to drink it. I swirled the fluid, sniffed it, dipped my tongue tip: it was red wine laced with herbs and honey to an invalid's syrup. I glanced up once at Tanman—the smoky taste of a drug lay in it too. He waited, gaze cool. I drank it slowly, fighting renewed hunger; my stomach heaved once, and settled. The stuff stayed down, warming my belly, numbing my aches.

I blinked stupidly at Tanman's face in the window glow. When he rose, I stared up through wine haze; I felt numb. By his expression he expected me to get up too. I did. I took one step, found myself on my knees. It hurt, and I was too drowsy to care. My goblet fell on my leg, rolled across the floor; red wine trails glittered on pale limestone. Then my shoulders and my ribs grated on the floor: all sprawled out. Odd how hard the wine hit me. Hands lifted me up . . . I let them. They put me on a cloth pallet, their faces all lit by the colors swirling from the glass.

I slurred, "Liege—please. Have my gana buried. I beg you."

Tanman stood over me with a grave expression. He muttered, "It was wrong to laugh at him, Pitar."

"What?" Pitar spread a white cloth over my body.

Tanman shook his head. "Nothing. The man's half-dead—Use thick furs, see he's kept drugged and fed until he's better. Call me if he asks for me, if there's any sickness, or if someone makes an attempt on his life. If they do . . . catch the bastards."

Someone threw a fur over the cloth on my legs. The silver hem of Tanman's robe brushed my outflung hand. I whispered. "Always . . . fought . . ." He knelt down beside me. His boots smelled of straw and oakwood loam and gana sweat. ". . . mare . . ."

Tanman Caladrunan's voice murmured, "Your mare will be buried. Sleep, Naga, Dance of Knives. You can sleep now." I fell over willingly into that waiting canyon, with the feel of someone's tasselled hunting boot touching my cheek. The scent of hay and gana and dusty leather came winding down in my darkness, and faded with me.

CHAPTER

= 4 =

I DREAMED OF heat. I stirred. But nothing disturbed the shimmer of blinding midday heat. During the Moon of Yellow Grass, fire alert ruled our camp. I was twelve years old; remembering the stern warnings of my father and uncles, I had been careful when I sparked leaves to roast my dawn-caught fish.

Dryland fire meant nothing to the Osa. It was just after midday they came rolling out of the hazy red distance in their flamethrowers, gray metal monsters that lumbered through the dust at a terrifying and unnatural pace. The Osa never concerned themselves with escaped flames, fire was their weapon. They used the great jets of flame in the same way a man kills locusts with a torch. It'd happened before, in Tan's Fourth History, but I had not learned about Osa yet. I only knew what I saw.

At midday I was fishing, too hungry and too stubborn to gauge fish better; I was always hungry. I was below my clan's camp, in a boulder field on the rusty stream called Redspring. I had just set bait on a fishhook when I heard someone screaming. It was faint—a faraway sound, quavering away until I was not sure I had really heard it. Then another voice screamed. The ground began softly rumbling, and the pools of water around me trembled. The hair rose on the back of my neck. Very clearly in the still air I heard a deep cough—a roar—and an abrupt cessation of the roar. The cough was louder than any animal cry. It came again and again, reflected by trembling water.

36

I dropped my fishing line and my fish basket and I ran. Smoke billowed in thick columns above Redspring Hold. When I finally reached the main track above the hold, the walls had already fallen in all directions—they had built the hold of stone braced by timbers. Now, the walls were braced only by ash. Men lay everywhere, dead and scattered, dying of burns amid charred timbers and fallen granite. Fires smoldered in the drifts of ash. The roaring noises came from the camp of my people. I ran onward, coughing, stumbling at times.

The rest of that day sank down featureless in my mind, a blind searing pit of horror. No distinct memory remained—only bad dreams. I had the same nightmares over and over, but they never grew less frightening for my knowing them as they came. The worst one was when I saw my mother.

She ran slowly among flaming camp tents, waving her arms and screaming. A curtain of fire licked up her long hair all across her back. Sparks showered from her sleeves, she set dry brush on fire with each step. I twisted about at a cough and roar from behind me—to look straight up the blackened nozzle of a flamethrower. I screamed into the choking oily stench. My mother waved her arms at the flamethrower, and slowly, slowly, its firetube swung grinding round from me. I scrambled onward among the tents, it seemed very clear but so failingly slow. I fell among charred rocks. With a shriek I was up running again, clutching burned hands over one smoking hip. In some dreams I fell on the blackened body of my father. He lay over the bodies of my brothers and sisters, his limbs strained as if trying to protect them in their little rock hollow. What horrified me was that none of their faces were identifiable—only the remains of their jewelry. They could have been any of the bodies I'd seen. The flamethrower roared briefly behind me. I looked back where my mother had been. At that point, I saw . . . something. And I screamed. I always did.

"Ahh," I gasped, and fell back limply. A scent hung close around me, vaguely familiar in the dark. Herbal, clean—civilized. I had not smelled sweet herbs since Redspring Hold fell.

Caladrunan said softly, "I'm here. You called for me."

"Uh," I grunted. I felt his hand pat my shoulder. The big

Tannese palm smelled of lavendar dust and writing chalk. A sore twinged on my collarbone.

"Drink this," he said, and a bowl touched my lips. I lifted my head and gulped down sweetened wine. My breathing sounded loud in the still air. He said, "Just a dream, that's all."

I wiped my lips with shaking hand, lay back; I seemed to be wrapped in thick furs. "Dream." My hand dropped down to the lumpy patch on my hip, the burn-scar left of that day I could no longer remember, only scream about. Perhaps someone died saving my life, just as in that nightmare image, but only the dreams knew. The Osa raid haunted my waking life like shadows: faceless, blank of detail, formless. Terrors all too vivid by night, by day it was a death-place where my mind would not go at all. It was from that tortured place that my hatred grew, and from that place I became a Sati; and out of that place squirmed a coward's dread of fire. Even at an age of twenty-two summers I could not overcome it wholly; swords could not frighten me at all, compared to a simple open flame.

A tiny lamp bloomed in the dark, lighting Caladrunan's face. He set the lamp on something nearby—and he pushed it farther away when he saw me flinch from it. He glanced at the lamp, then at me. "Better?" he asked softly.

I dragged myself up. He was really there. "You came," I said, amazed, and then the drug in the wine came down over my brain like a black cloth. Vaguely I felt my head hit the furs, then nothing.

At the crackle of a torch I opened my eyes. Standing over me, in the darkness and the torchlight, was a lean old warrior with iron-gray hair—a stranger to me. I felt only a mild drugged curiosity. He knelt down and with his thin hand turned my chin toward him. The old man smiled, nodded once to me. He lifted his other hand, dropped a robe similar to his own over my fur bedding, and walked away. I turned my head to follow him: he spoke softly with three soldiers in Tannese blue standing in a pool of torchlight. One of the men was Pitar; the guard commander murmured something, glancing at me, and departed in a grating of door bolts. They knew I was awake.

I rubbed at my eyes and shifted my legs in the fur bedding,

feeling my bandages with my hands. The windings had been
changed while I slept. My body was warm and clean, there
were no muscle cramps. My head felt tight and hot; I'd been
drugged for a long time. I thought, yes! cupflower sedative in
the wine that Tanman gave me. They must have fed me
sometime in my haze, because I had need of a slushpot.
Perhaps I should get up and start acting like an envoy from
the Upai to Tanman, I told myself, or they may do more
outrageous things to me. Such as addicting me to cupflower.

I sat up in the ruck of my bedding, grimacing at the drug
taste fading in my mouth. I stretched out my arms, flexing
them until the weakness left. I put on the blue robe though it
was far too big. I leaned against the wall and got to my
knees, then to my feet, testing my bandaged right leg. Easing
slowly onto the hoof-dented leg, I turned to a slushpot on the
floor near my furs.

The sight of me over that pot, naked under that great
flapping blue robe, must have been hilarious. The soldiers in
the torchlight grinned at me like dogs. They looked stupid
and young; I doubted they really were—no one puts idiots to
guard a Sati. The old man watched me too, but he didn't
laugh. Neither did I. It wasn't just my legs that suffered
during that ride. I felt an impulse to make a rude gesture with
my penis, but they wouldn't understand a desert insult. It
angered me that I even felt anything for their laughter.

Instead of the rude gesture, I folded the big robe, tying its
loops to keep from tripping over it. I was still not wholly
steady on my feet; I moved carefully toward a table near the
soldiers. One of them pulled out a chair and gestured for me
to sit there. I looked at the helpful guard, surprised, and sat
down. He startled me again: he shoved a food tray in front of
me, thoroughly tasted it before my eyes, and withdrew out of
reach. For a moment I stared after him: giving food away to
me? I sniffed the food steaming in the cold air. My tongue
moved dryly in my mouth. There was a pewter water pitcher.

Slowly—watching the guards from my eye-corners, I tipped
up the water pitcher. I tasted minerals: lime and iron-bearing
rock. The water must have come of the spring of the inner-
most Fortress citadel, famous in many harp songs: for a
moment, shocked at such honor, I blinked without swallowing it. Life sprang tingling into my mouth tissues. The foul

taste of the drug faded away. I took a few deep swallows of water, and hastily put down the pitcher.

In the desert, an envoy did not steal more water than his share. But the pitcher was not marked for shares; and in Tan, the Tejed River ran wide across lush grainlands. After a moment's contemplation, I drank deeper. The unwilling bath had cured me decisively of one desert taboo: I was certain the Tannese wouldn't waste water on me unless they had more water than they could ever use, river or springwater alike. I couldn't remember anything so fine as that cold iron-flavored water. I half closed my eyes, drinking it, and nearly forgot to watch no one stole my food. Then a wisp of aroma tickled my nose and I opened my eyes to the food.

The tray carried the pitcher of water, a bowl of steaming kinash grain, and a celadon-green bowl that held chopped spiced meat. I dipped my fingers in the bowl of meat; I took three quick bites, not believing. I tasted the kinash grain, and it was the same. The spices were joltingly familiar—the sage aroma, the small portion of salt, the hot red spices from summer harvest: a Upai hand had spiced this food. Tanman must have ordered this. He had to, nobody else knew. Tears, tears of outrage and longing, gathered in my throat. I thought of my dead clan, of my dead mare gana who loved to eat red spice raw from my hand, and I swallowed the bite in a hard gulp. The old man in silvered robes smiled, took the other chair, and sat down opposite me. He looked pleased with himself.

"Who made this food?" My voice grated harsh, unused. My hand gripped the tray tightly.

The old man spoke in a soft, whispery, dry-grass voice. "One of the servant women, of your blood. Tanman felt that you would like some of your own food when you woke. You've been asleep nearly two days, they tell me."

I blinked. Another Upai, a servant alive in this Fortress— and risen to the notice of Tanman, too. I scooped up another bite in my fingers, eyeing the man, but he didn't move; I popped it in my mouth. Then another. Then I was wolfing it down. There was not a great deal of food, and I was left a little hungry. For a moment I wondered if I would vomit again, but nothing moved inside me. I drank more water, gratefully. I made the Goddess-thanking gestures and mur- mured the prayer words. I meant every thankful word: so far my luck had been good. Then I thought suddenly, two days' sleep. So much could happen in two days—two days!

The old man murmured, "You are a Harper?"

I nodded. His eyes were bright green—intense, shrewd eyes. His skin had drawn back leathery brown against the bones as he aged, so that his face gave the impression of thin flesh and a strange toughness. I said, "Who are you?"

He smiled dryly. "I must look familiar. My eldest brother commanded Redspring Hold while you were there. So do you know what happened to my brother, when Redspring Hold fell?"

Dream images sliced across my mind, unsought, unwanted. I slammed that barrier tight and the bitterness faded before it touched my tongue. I looked up at the old leathery soldier, and down again. I said, "He died."

"Did he die well?"

"No one died well at Redspring Hold. There was no honor in it. He died." The soldier looked silently at me. I looked aside and forced back the images.

He extended his hand to me. "I am Strengam Dar, Tanman's Head of Army. I needed this information for my clan. We have waited a long time."

I looked at his extended hand. What did he expect me to do, spit on it in the desert way? I was not yet his friend. But I touched his hand in the Tannese manner of greeting, and satisfied him. He withdrew his hand and folded his fingers together. I said, "This is the reason for your visit?"

He smiled. "No, but I see that you would not discuss military news unless Tanman so ordered. Another man perhaps . . ." He shrugged.

I stared at him. "There are some of Tanman's own men he dares not trust to keep quiet? And you suspected me—"

Strengam Dar met my eyes. He tapped the table lightly, studying me. "You are truly far back desert, aren't you? Don't be insulted. We will try to get you used to Tannese ways quickly. You had better give a large public harp performance soon, to establish your right to enter the Great Hall freely. Your people have no citizens' protections within Tan, and your recent Nando past puts you under suspicion— We have had trouble with refugees stealing and picking fights; you could be mistaken for one. You must be widely known, or hostile groups will find it easy thus to harrass you until you cannot perform your duties. That is—duties given if Tanman decides to accept your Oath and your service.''

I looked hard at the Head of Army. It was true that Tanman hadn't formally given his acceptance of my Oath.

After a moment, Strengam Dar added, ''He has set a time for publicly testing your Oath. Then no one can say you were not fairly tested and judged.''

Including me, I thought.

He beckoned. One of the soldiers went out of the tower room and returned with a leather case: my harpcase. He set it on the table. Strengam said, ''If you would play a bit for me, Harper.''

I frowned. ''Why did he send such an important man as you, Head of Army, for this?''

Strengam Dar smiled a small dry smile. ''Your messages from the desert concern me quite as much as Tanman.''

I glanced over at my harpcase. ''When is the first chance for a public harping?''

The green eyes inspected my face closely. ''Tonight. But it would be rude to put you, ignorant of protocol, up there tonight with the finest musicians in the Three Countries.''

I smiled at him. ''Don't you grow bored of hearing the same voices, the same styles, over? I thought the eternal Tannese quest was for the new, the unusual. Wouldn't a Upai who sings Tannese be freak enough to amuse you all for a few moments?''

Strengam Dar said, ''Tanman did not tell me you had such a saw-tongue.''

I said, ''I try to follow the manners I observe.''

His face suddenly wreathed up into tiny smile wrinkles. ''Spoken like Reti himself. You'll certainly catch attention.'' His face turned sober. ''Be careful whose it is, desert man.'' Then he left the tower room.

They gave me blue robes; there was a soft black silk underrobe and soft black doeskin boots with them. Not clothes to run away in, these, though everything fit me. My Harper jade-bag was folded in the robes, its knot intact, so I hung it around my neck as always. They gave me my weaponbelt then, they carried in all my weapons, piece by piece, even the hidden ones. I winced with every abraded sore as I put them in place. I might have saved myself the trouble of arming my belt; five flights downstairs I had to give them all up again.

My guards and I joined a line of soldiers going into a door where tapestries fluttered and torches flared in drafts. After a few sharp glances the soldiers gossiped around me as if I wasn't there.

"Rafai, I thought you on duty out at the beggar camps."

"You're joking."

"Didn't like it—does anybody?"

"I heard the shifts were all rearranged—"

They gave their weapons good-naturedly to a huge fat man at a table before a rack of weapons. The rack looked like a hold armory. Everyone seemed to have his own harness peg.

The fat man had the quick pointed fingers of an expert fourpeg player or a thief. He bellowed at me, "You're a new one. Who are you, soldier?" The deft hands opened the harpcase and searched it.

"Naga Teot," I said, unlatching my weaponbelt. "I am a Harper."

The fat man roared at me, "Coming in through the soldier's door? Rafai, what's damaged your brain?"

One of the two guards flanking me said, "He's a soldier, too. Sati level with those scaddas, Lumi."

Heads turned. The fat man guffawed. "Sati? You hoax me every tenday, Rafai. A Sati with a harp! By Sitha, you ever see a Sati's hands?"

I set my belt on the table, and the scaddas slid lightly out of their sheaths. Briefly, I showed my hands to Lumi. One piece at a time, I stripped off my open weapons from the belt and my robes; I unbuckled and set down my spurs. The silence spread as the tabletop began to fill. The guard called Rafai said gently, "Sati level, Lumi."

The fat man fingered my weaponbelt, hung it up. "Got a lot of wear on that, soldier, better get a new buckle. Sure you didn't steal the miserable thing?" He rummaged in my harpcase.

Out of the corner of my vision I noticed the soldiers looking at me, waiting for my answer. Without speaking a word, I flicked the knot and reached into the Harper's jade bag at my neck. I flipped out a white jade. It startled me quite as much as anyone else there—it got in there while I slept, for I'd never had a white jade in my life. Lumi's little stony eyes narrowed. I tossed the jade up in the air, Lumi's pointed fingers darted after it—but he was not as fast or deft as he obviously thought he was. I whipped back the jade and gave

him a good rap on the knuckles for his greed. He let out a
yelp, clutching his hand with a pained look. I tossed him a
jade chip to keep, though he'd lost. With more respect he
thrust the searched harpcase back in my hands. He pointed
at the door. "In! And no dirty-neck camp-thief trouble,
understand?"

I gave him a brief look. Then I glanced around at the
others, looking for anyone who might challenge me for the
white jade. Their eyes followed me, but no one moved. I
passed through the door between the tapestries.

Just inside I took a quick step to one side, squinting in the
dim light. I stood at one end of a long rectangular room. The
place went up two levels overhead, up into dark smoked
beams. A stone draft-oven dominated the center of the room
with multiple mouths. The largest of the many fireholes held
a whole deer carcass on a spit, elaborately dressed. A servant
swung the spit out of the fire and began carving the carcass.
Intermittent blasts of roasting venison aroma, burning lamp
oil, and oakwood smoke swirled around me. The smell made
me ravenous all over again. I edged to one side of the oven,
snatched a gobbet of meat from a passing platter, and I ate it.
It was glorious. As I tore at sinews, I looked around.

Beyond the draft-oven, people sat along broad dark trestle
tables; all of them wore beautifully colored and embroidery-
silvered robes, talking, while servants in blue robes served
brass platters of food. The Great Hall fed Tan's nobles at
court: their faces appeared and vanished in the orange light as
guttering drafts of air made flames flutter. Brass oil lamps
hung low, little fat pots bellying in racks on long chains to the
beams far overhead. By their light, jewels and silver threads
glimmered; gold thread in the wall tapestries caught splinters
of light when the lamps flared high.

Away at the opposite end of the Hall from me, a circular
white marble dais rose above the common stone floor. Lamp
flames reflected yellow streaks on the black polished wood of
two chairs and a black trestle table on the dais. The ruling
chair of the pair was fan-backed, inlaid with white swords
filigreed in silver. The white inlay swords turned orange and
brown and red as the lamplight caught and left them. Below
the dais lurked a clutter of low stools.

At my side, the escort guard Rafai murmured, "We made
it just in time. You go there. *If* you're through eating." He

pointed a pale finger past me to the stools grouped by the
dais. I glanced at him: but he had no expression. I walked
through the benches, sniffing. I smelled venison and women's
perfumes and wine, and sweat from passing servants. No one
noticed me—quite. Their eyes slid about covertly when they
thought I wouldn't see them.

I sat down on one of the stools at the foot of the dais,
holding my harpcase and thinking about songs to play. My
guards deployed behind me. I turned when I heard a man's
step. A man in wine-red robes strode out of a shadowed
doorway near the dais. He carried a harp. He said in a light,
crisp, trained voice, "You're lucky it's only me tonight,
newcomer. The old swine doesn't like competition these days."

"The old swine?" I asked politely.

In stronger light, the noble in red became a young man
with dark blond hair, holding a fawn-colored harp. For a
moment he just stared at me, smiling. "Say that again," he
commanded.

I asked, "Who is the old swine?"

The young man burst into a broad chuckle. "You have the
thickest, slowest border accent I've heard in years! Oh yes—the
old man: Tatéfannin. You've surely heard his stuff until you
puked. As I said, you're lucky the fuddlebrain isn't out here—
oldest bigot in Fortress. Say something; you're delightful."

I swallowed. Tatéfannin the Harper was known throughout
the Three Countries, mostly for his wealth. Some said he
only harped at sacred ceremonies for pay, which was against
Harper oaths. I said, "Who are you?"

He laughed. "Lado Kiselli, from Birchwoods Hold. I might
ask you the same question, Black Man."

I glanced down, astonished. "I'm not black."

Lado said, in a languid drawl, "Are you any good? You're
black as a riding whip in this light, Harper, so you'd best get
used to being called it. Taté, the old frog, will never let it rest.
Where are you from, what's your working name?"

I lifted my chin higher. Strange how deeply the Nando
name-taboo ingrained itself into my habits. False names sprang
to my lips. Instead, slowly, I said, "Naga Teot, from the Po
desert."

"That is not a common desert name," he said lightly.

"You ask a lot of questions." I had never met a man like
this before, so mild, so unwise. He wasn't in the least afraid

of me—demanding names! I didn't even know how to turn
his interest in me.

He laughed. "I apologize. My curiosity bolted with me.
You've got an incredible accent— I can understand you, but I
felt like the first Tannese to step ashore, with a Sek-blood
rearing up out of the grass yelling at him. I almost didn't see
you here. Startled me, you know. If you sing off-key, I'll die
a thousand times."

I blinked, startled . . . and amused. Harpers I understood. I
pointed at his harp. "That's haddoka wood, yes? I've never
seen haddoka that pale."

He nodded and sat down. "Spent a fortune getting the
materials. Now I just have to do it justice. Take your harp
out, let me see it, could you? What do you find in the desert
to make harps of? Tanman is taking his time. Have you eaten
yet?"

I nodded, eyeing him warily. But I handed him my harp.
He obligingly handed his to me. I touched the creamy satin
wood with my rough fingertips, gingerly. I said, "What kind
of people do you get in here at night?"

In a dry voice he replied, "How many taverns did you
work on your way here?"

Surprised, I said, "None. I killed my voice on well-digging
cadences for two years. So I let it rest, mostly, on the trip.
Wore out the rest of me, but I saved the voice."

He made a smothered groaning noise. "Perhaps we ought
to do this as a joint performance this first night—"

I dared to stroke the strings of his harp. Ethereal notes . . .
I shook my head. "You don't have to cover for my im-
perfections."

He shrugged. "I'll go first, then. We all suffer if someone
messes up and puts Tanman in a rage. He's got a good ear.
This is thornwood, isn't it? Unique material. And very nice
gut strings. You haven't tried metal ones— Do you know
how much easier it is to keep brass strings tuned? I look
forward to hearing it. Believe me, when old Tatéfannin forgot
a line in one of the holy songs out of the Histories—senile old
frog—Tanman knew which line it was. We were all in dis-
grace for thirty days, cleansing ceremonies, the lot. So you be
careful." Lado Kiselli turned my harp about gently with long,
heavy-tendoned fingers.

He continued, "Tanman knows Histories pretty well. He

can translate from the old dialect into modern and back line by line as he hears them. He uses them for strategy. Battles is all he wants. What is this on the wolf here—the bone inlay?''

I glanced over. ''Blood. Three Harpers before me died over that harp. I respected them too much to clean it off.''

Lado looked up sharply at me, speechless. He smoothed his fingers over the stained bone inlay and handed my harp back to me. Then he turned his head. I heard it, too: the unbarring of a door, a creak, and the rustle of heavy robes. Lado gestured for us both to stand, took his harp back, and hissed, ''Here he comes.''

CHAPTER

= 5 =

TANMAN HELD THE hem of a dark fur outer robe aside as he mounted the dais, and a flash of silver embroidery caught the light on his inner robe. At his left side walked a veiled woman in a gemmed headdress; tiny silver mirrors hung embroidered with silver thread in her robes so that she flashed bits of firelight as she moved. She mounted the dais beside Tanman. The man on Tanman's other side did not go up the dais—he came slowly around it to our stools.

The man was stooped forward, almost totally bald; I rather stared: in the desert such an ancient was a rare sight. He carried a harpcase, and he regarded Lado and me with a filmed and hostile eye. Lado only smiled, and saluted Tanman. The people in the Hall saluted their Lord in the same way, rising and bowing; I heard jade chimes ringing, and the rustle of rich cloth. Past the strange old Harper's head I caught Tanman's stern pale eye upon me. I inclined my head and crossed my wrists to him.

Lado murmured fiercely at the other musician, "I thought you weren't coming."

The stooped man bowed stiffly to his Liege Lord and hissed back, "Tatéfannin I still be—I refuse to yield a Harper's place to savages! Overrunning our holds, insulting our people—this is too much." He gave me another rheumy glare, shaking out the folds of his fur-edged robe.

I said clearly, "That is Tanman's decision to make, not yours. Which is a good thing, if you believe it was savages who threw down Tannese holds, Harper."

Lado smothered an odd burst of giggles.

Tanman, above all this Harper in-fighting, sat down on his black fan-backed chair. Everyone sat down. Poor Tatéfannin let out a terrific grunt as he lowered himself to his stool. Lado smothered another unkind giggle.

I looked at the old Harper. He drew out an instrument of haddoka wood thickly inlaid with black and silver wires and pearl-colored shells and a sprinkling of faceted gems; it hardly looked like a harp at all. And his eyes, over his harp, glared at me so angrily I didn't think he actually saw me at all. I stroked the arch of my thornwood harp, and smiled back at him. Satis do smile . . . sometimes.

Tatéfannin looked away from my eyes. He cleared his throat and told Lado, "You wouldn't laugh if you heard how they caught this half-blood thief. They caught him with a dead stolen gana— "

Lado glanced at me with a gleam in his eye. "Tanman must have had his reasons."

I saw Tanman's hand flick above us in a gesture. One of the guards stepped forward and whispered in Tatéfannin's ear. The old man gave a loud sniff and glared at me. "Stolen ganas," he muttered, and subsided.

I whispered, "It wasn't quite that way." A lance of pain went through my chest.

Lado gave me a sharp glance. He muttered, "You better do very well tonight, Black Man, or we're all in trouble."

I had no time to reply—there was a noise among the main Hall tables. My pulse picked up pace. I knew the sluffing-scuffling of loose Marshmen boots better than anyone.

A little knot of men in striped brown outrobes pushed among the tables at the far doors. They wore wrapped white face cloths, which only Nandos wore. "Get out of the way, then, worms!" one of the Nandos snarled. No one challenged them. I didn't know them or their group insignia; and they walked like men just come in from a long ride. I felt my neck hair rise. I said between my teeth, "Lado Kiselli, who hired those Nandos?"

He glanced around, surprised. It took him a moment to notice them—then his face changed. "You have sharp eyes. Those are some of Manoloki's local lazy dogs. They work for a Cragman lord at Tanman's autumn court. He buys or sells or something to our charming Devotees of Sitha."

I read the knowledge in Lado's eyes; somehow, Lado knew, just as I did: they were enemies. I said, "How did they get the right to come here? Why did that doorman, Lumi, let them in?"

Lado snorted softly. "If their employer is fool enough to insist on bringing Nandos in as his personal guards, who's going to argue?" He gave me a sharper look, and gripped my arm. "No, don't move. You have an accounting with them?"

I settled back onto my stool. I said, "A small one."

Lado said, "Keep it for later—with about eight or nine of my friends to help us *both* settle it. Preferably in a dark alley with a few *slightly* illegal tools."

I lifted an eyebrow at the force in his soft tone. I thought, I could get to liking this Lado Kiselli. We both looked around at a movement from Tanman. The old Harper, Tatéfannin, harrumphed, grunted, and stood up, holding his harp wedged against his belly.

Lado muttered, "He's stupid to insist on going first, but let him, I say."

We sat through a proper but dull recital of holy songs. I learned interesting effects from the way Tatéfannin's voice wavered in his notes—I had never heard such an old man sing before. In the desert, they generally died of one thing or another before they reached half of Tatéfannin's years. He'd probably call me a young brute. I stroked the wolfhead carved into the arch of my harp. Lado muttered, "At least he got the last triplet correct this time."

Lado winced at the next. I glanced out among the tables, watching the Nandos. Men drifted by, speaking to them as if they were merely talking among themselves while passing—chatting. I was amazed how blatant they were at it. When I glanced up, I noticed Tanman was watching too. Lado Kiselli seemed not to be noticing it.

When Tatéfannin finished, everyone rose. Tanman smiled at the old Harper; if I read boredom in Tanman's face, perhaps I was the only one to interpret his look thus. The woman at Tanman's side thanked the Harper in a polite, high-bred voice. I thought uneasy notes of falsehood disturbed her voice; and it was Tanman, impatient, who at last dismissed the old man. Tatéfannin muttered off into the darkness, going away to eat. Tanman turned his gaze slowly to us. I lifted my eyes. Tanman was staring at me. His name in

the old dialect of Tannese, I recalled—my eyes felt pinned in
the strength of his gaze—meant Heart of Iron. He will need
that iron, I thought somberly.

We shared the locked stare of our first meeting. He looked
more regal than ever; with Devour standing in a gilded sheath
beside his hip, he was the only openly armed man in the Hall.
The dark blue outrobe he wore made his hair a halo of light,
the tips turned to a curly white ring in the back light; his eyes
glowed like golden cat-stones on jeweler's cloth. I thought,
not once in ten thousand years does any country have a true
ruler. And the feel of it breathed over my skin, crisp and
distinct as cold air. Like the joros—statues found in the deep
desert, seven feet tall and endowed with a prickly aura of
awareness—this man, Heart of Iron, looked down at me
silently from his great height. There was a mildly amused,
serene cast to his face . . . and the eyes, like the joro statues,
watchful.

Lado hissed at me, "Don't you have any manners?"

Tanman smiled, became human. He waved his hand at
Lado. We both inclined our heads. Lado whispered, "Well, I
get to go first. Wish me luck." He took a step into better
light, shifted his harp on his hip, looped the harp strap to his
belt, and began.

Lado's was a wildly different sort of performance than
Tatéfannin's. Lado's songs were all romantic poetry, very
modern and very unlike the historical repertoire; lots of trill-
ing and impossibly technical runs on the high strings. He
didn't use the old rhyming phrases polished to fit the proper
situation, he had made his own. He changed keys casually
within the same verse and adjusted his timing to match his
subject, a shocking breach of tradition. But he was no shouting verse-grater like the moderns I'd seen before. Despite all
the wizardry he achieved a soft, pastel effect, soothing as
mulled wine.

I sat transfixed. This, I thought, was worth my ride. Such
technical accomplishments used in a truly heroic song would
make courage bellow out, plain to all. Even for this light
entertainment, people grew quieter; many of them listened
attentively and actively to Lado's work. When Lado finished
his songs, there was a respectful hush. Lado flourished a
salute to Tanman, turned to me, and took in my expression.
He grinned, wiping sweat off his face as he sat down. Then

he cocked his head warningly toward Tanman, and I glanced around.

The woman was speaking to him, but Tanman sat tapping his fingers on the table, looking vaguely bored. His eyes went roving over the Hall and kept coming back to me. It was difficult to resist staring back; his eye was commanding. I wondered if I'd alarmed him or offended his sight. He looked again, and abruptly waved his hand.

When I stood up, Tanman's head came up with a tiny jerk—and his eyes were not bored at all now. I stepped into the better light, adjusting my harp on my harness. The run of mutters in the crowd fell slowly into hush. With a glance at Tanman, another glance at the Nandos I did not know, I began to play.

I knew to avoid the soft songs; I had not the range of high voice, I could never compete with Lado Kiselli on those. No, mine were the rough-edged songs, the ones of hard life. I began the Ballad of Iahri with one hand, looking out into the fireglare and the faces. My fingers dropped into the familiar patterns as into an old harness.

The Ballad of Iahri was the hardest traditional song in the repertoire of most Harpers. Reti had insisted, over my harp trainer's protests, that it be my final testing song. It had not been easily mastered. Even now, it was like riding an unruly mount—but it had made a Harper of me. After singing work songs all day at Bitterspring among Manoloki's Nandos, I went out into the desert above camp, and I performed this Ballad to remind me I was a Harper, not just a shrieker of bawdy digging songs with my hands full of mud and splinters. Out there alone with the hard night stars, I taught myself new twists of chord that enhanced the melody and the rhythm, making the structure of it stand out in satisfying perfection. Now, after those long nights of work, I felt the Ballad rising under my hands, carrying me as it sometimes did—yielding to it gave my best performances.

The Ballad was a warrior's song; it must sound like a man singing across a broad empty plain, a man singing across a quiet battlefield in the night before his last, and most glorious, fight. A song of knowledge, the Ballad of Iahri.

I had never had such a quiet audience before, such a beautiful staring silence in which to stretch and flex my art. Lado's performance had proven to me the quality of this Hall;

I could raise my voice without jarring reverberations, without drunks shouting me down. The slightest whisper carried. I added vocal flourishes and more complex harmonies that I could not use in a less perfect hall. One hand held the main harp chords while the other flowed in and out and punctuated the main line. And I knew I had them all, nobles and soldiers, gripped tight in the song. I felt chills rise on my skin; after Lado's mellow tones, my voice sounded like a carrion crow given human tongue. It fit the Ballad.

Until I chorded off the last note, I could not guess how they would react to my work. The mood of the Hall now was cold sober, only the faces embroidered in the fine wall tapestries smiled. No one moved or spoke. I unhooked my harp in silence. It was the veiled woman beside Tanman who broke the hush. She said, "Amazing what rides out of the Wastes now and then." In a lower voice, to Tanman, she murmured, "That voice—he makes my flesh crawl."

Tanman only grunted in reply. She murmured more softly yet, and laughed. He said nothing. He toyed with a plum in a lapis–blue bowl, and looked under his brows at me. His fingers shredded the purple skin from the plum. Now and again a muscle high in his jaw leaped, as if in anger.

I heard nobles among the tables whispering among themselves. I turned and sat down on my stool, head bent. I wiped the sides of my sweaty neck. I clenched my hands on my harp. It was a bad moment.

Lado Kiselli murmured dryly, "Enjoy the rest, Black Man."

When I looked up, he was gazing at me expressionlessly. He said, "I could have saved myself the trouble of protecting you, I think. I told you—rest while you can. They'll call you out for more."

I felt a rush of profound gratitude. No one else had given me a sign of accomplishment, only that unnerving total silence. I thanked Lado softly for giving me that attentive and quiet audience; I knew he could have made them impossible. He only sighed, hugging his harp a little higher on his lap. At last he said, "I always wanted to be a monumental Harper. Dreamed of it. Never will be, haven't the voice. Oh, I know what to look for in others! You walk on right out of the desert, get up here all ragged at the edges—and you're the next great one. Look at them! You had them hanging on every breath, not a whisper out of them. While I run about

with poetry exercises.'' His hand made a fluttering and fell
still on his harp.

I stared at him, bewildered. I wouldn't call the dead hush
after my singing praise, exactly. I said, "Lado, we have a lot
to teach each other. You are much—"

"I haven't the voice," he said, so bitterly factual that I
looked down at my harp in silence. His tones spoke of such
expert knowledge that I could only wedge it down my throat
and accept that it was as he said. But I didn't have Lado's
high vocal range either, his string technique, his light and
humorous touch. Nor did I have his painful and unexpected
honesty, to give himself away to a raw rival like me.

Tanman's voice made us both jump. He growled. "Give us
Fourth History."

Lado silently gestured me to stand and take the task. I
glanced from Lado's closed face to Tanman. I drew in a
breath to ask which part he desired.

"The Pass of Bones battle," he rumbled, before I spoke.
Caladrunan lifted up his wine goblet, as if the request meant
nothing to him. But I knew better: a thrill of fear and exulta-
tion shocked through all my bones. I feared that Tanman's
enemies might guess by this recital exactly what message I
carried—for the Battle of Pass of Bones told of a failed
invasion by the Osa many years past. But in the same confused thrill, I felt a deep happiness that I had earned the right
to a second song in this Hall, and that Tanman knew Histories. He knew of the Osa threat. Caladrunan read History
scrolls when he was a boy in Redspring Hold; it lightened the
wounds in my soul that he still read them, and remembered.

I began Fourth History in the archaic dialect it was first
written in. It was not modern Tannese at all, and during holy
day recitals of it people grew bored. My accent being vastly
different from Devotee voices, I dared to regroup it into
common words instead of artificial drone chants. It was plain,
from the faces looking at me, that it was simply music to
them. I hoped that the sole person I desired would be the only
one to understand my actual words—Tanman, not his enemies. I wondered, too, why he wanted it recited now; who
did he want it to affect? Me?

Fourth History, Pass of Bones Battle, was essentially a
tactics lesson. It explained how that old and bloody place,
Pass of Bones, defended the fertile Tannese valleys from

desert-crossing invaders: the Osa. Warned by one of my own
Upai ancestors, the Tanman Kasin had arrayed a great army
in that waterless slot in the ground. The exciting parts of the
History told how the Tannese soldier-hero, Ganek Tanedi,
scouted the Osa flamethrower positions in the night by the
acrid oily stink of their weapons. Most Harpers treated Fourth
History as a hero fantasy, in which Ganek Tanedi crept upon
the enemy with great skill, and battled monsters; in truth,
even the hero's help did not save much of the Tannese army.
The Devotees regarded the whole thing as one of the overac-
tive texts, a fantasy for less than scholarly minds. In cold
truth, the History was an accurate account showing what the
Osa once did to Tan—a warning to the future. If I could have
gathered proof sooner, come years back as a boy with my
information, come with warnings as this History did, all of
Tan might be armed, not slumbering in the Osa advance.

Standing in Caladrunan's Great Hall, singing that ancient
History, I stood again on a hillside watching the valley of the
Redspring turn to a fiery caldera. Trees exploded into torches.
Fire hosed out and bathed the hillsides and fallen walls and
running people. I heard the screaming again.

Many Tannese soldiers would insist that fire did not drip,
flow, and jump to attack under intelligent control, that no fire
burned on after dirt and water are thrown on it. But I knew. I
had smelled the oily stink that Ganek Tanedi tracked the Osa
weapons by. It never came out of cloth or leather it touched.
Faintly, I could smell it now, eddying from somewhere near
the far doors among the Nandos in the white face cloths.
Perhaps their Devotee friends used it! Such arrogance they
had, wearing such stains here! Even so many years later, the
slightest trace of that smell put me into a sick, berserk chill.

The relivings came on me less often now. As in the dreams,
the whole blind terror of it crawled over me, making me see
over and over images of horror burned in beyond memory. I
once saw the remains of a whole people charred to death—
and it drove me mad. The deep ceaseless roar of heat beat and
echoed in a cave inside me, flickering the images rapidly in
my mind. I could not hold it, could not contain it. I started to
sweat. In midsong, I heard my voice change, deepening in
the air like a rope straining under tension. In a moment, I
would break under it, and I would run for the doors. I would
flee blindly for some place to hide—fierce as a stricken child,

rocking and talking to myself, huddled up in the dark. It had happened to me before.

Once a man tried to stop me in the grip of a reliving. I was already a Sati, I struck one blow. It almost killed him, he was never the same again; I damaged his brain. He never sang again, not once, to the day he died in my arms over his harp. It was his harp I played; and his blood darkened its inlay. I plucked singly the last notes of Fourth History's battle, lowered my thornwood harp. I breathed in deep gasps, silent, but ragged; my legs kept twitching and cramping. I lifted my hand and felt a single bitter tear run across my cheek. I turned quickly out of the light to my stool, bending all my will and long training into choking off the shrieking wilderness inside me. I shoved frantically to shut the door on that echoing nightmare in my head, full of the screams of the dying. My harp felt the grip of my hands many times before; it bore up under it now as it always did.

Lado murmured, "Look behind you, Naga."

Tanman was standing up. A sword embroidery on his shoulder glinted rapidly with his breathing. Then they were all standing up in a rustle of gemmed robes and furred sleeves, their robes made the only sound. No one broke the hush. Tanman looked directly at me with terrible eyes. No one should have eyes that wise, that sad, and that angry.

I set down my harp and stood up, driving my nails into my palms to keep away the inner demons. Now, I thought, now Caladrunan knows what happened to Redspring Hold.

Tanman Caladrunan held up his wine goblet slowly, saying, "I am privileged to hear the courage of Ganek Tanedi given such justice as it deserves." He set the silver goblet upside down with a hard clink and a splatter of wine. Then he looked at the woman beside him with blazing eyes. She put down her goblet in the same way. All those people in the mass of tables did the same under his glare, spilling wine over half-eaten food.

Tanman turned and swept across the back of the dais toward a door. I saw a sheen on his cheek as of light on polished, shining stone, or firelight on water. The woman and his guards followed after, and the door shut them away in silence.

I turned to Lado, tense, angry, still smelling that Osa stink. I never meant my harping to make innocent people spoil good food. I glared around fiercely. Nobles were milling about. Many of the Tannese murmured rapidly together, throwing glances at me; too many of them. The Nandos had vanished somewhere into the crowd. Tanman's soldiers formed up a cordon around Lado and me. Lado demanded hotly, "Rafai, is he a prisoner after that? Liege didn't have many guards with him just now, he may need these louts."

"Orders, keep everyone from harm. Lord, if you want to come with the Sati, a quiet goblet, very good—but not here." Rafai cast a dark glance toward one agitated corner of the Hall. "Cragmen are getting ugly over there. Might be trouble. Hope they don't take a fight into the back corridor after Liege."

"You know they will. Sitha's first law of mistakes." Lado sighed, bent down, picked up both his harpcase and mine. "Come, Black Man—allow me to carry it for you. You look like you've fought the final round."

I tried to speak to him politely, but I was watching men pushing hard and quickly toward us—pushing toward the door Tanman had left by. Something flashed. A guard fell. Someone pushed Lado, knocking him down, and then the wedge of attackers was past most of the guards, closing toward Tanman's door. Only my two escort guards and I stood in their path. The white veils were gone, but they were the Nandos. The odor of foul oils followed them.

I felt something inside me rush up from tailbone to fingertips and explode in a fierce, joyful tide: that berserk rage that had nowhere to go until now. Events seemed to unfold in that odd slow way that battle rush always brought on me. I lunged and caught an uplifted hand before it drove a knife in a guard's back. My free hand crunched across the elbow. Then I grabbed another man plunging past me, spun him around, and felt armor beneath the brown-striped robes. I punched him hard in the ear. He fell with a cry. A man fell near me; about to roll up again, he whipped out a knife. I stepped on his face. Hard.

Rafai crouched near me, grinning ferociously with a long dagger in his hand. One assassin already lay clutching his guts at Rafai's feet. Tannese soldiers swarmed out of everywhere in the Hall, running with irritating slowness among the oil lamps and tables, pushing aside confused nobles—like ripples of wind in a field of brightly colored wildflowers.

Lado struggled slowly up to his feet. I knocked an assassin away from him with a side-kick of my bad leg. It hurt. But I had to protect him; he had my harp, after all.

The guards massed to defend the door behind us. A lone Nando spun, fleeing that force, and lunged back toward us. I blocked the man, but he dodged my first punch. He tried to force me back on my weaker, gana-slashed leg, slashing at my ankles with fighting spurs, small spurs that a man could hide and put on later. He was a heavy man, not as light on his feet as he ought to be to wear them. I raked his face with my long fingernails while we both skipped about among the hall pillars. I punched him, delayed him, tried to land blows to cripple him. Lado Kiselli abruptly clapped a wooden serving bowl down hard on the man's head. The Nando went down in an ungraceful splatter and sprawl of limbs, and I finished his day's fighting by kicking his head on a pillar. Then I hurled Lado aside out of the path of a flung knife, ducked, grabbed the hilt as a second blade hit a table, and returned it with greater accuracy. The knife-thrower choked, clutched his face, and fell over. Then Lado and I both gazed around blinking; there was no one near. Our part was done.

The last three Nandos were running toward Lumi's door at the far end of the Hall, abandoning their dying and crippled fellows. A huge guard snatched the robe of the first one. The robe gagged its wearer; the big guard promptly spun about and slammed the assassin into a tapestry with a wall behind it. The Nando goggled a moment and went limp. Lado cheered.

A Tannese noble threw a heavy lacquer tray at the second Nando; the tray arched leisurely through the air, spinning end for end, and hit its moving target with a thud. Half-stunned, the assassin stumbled and went down in a heaving tangle, covered in guards.

The third Nando vaulted into the confused crowd. That undid him. A simply enormous woman in a red veil and plush fur outrobe took him up, redirected his motion as he passed, added some push and a loud yell to help him—she flung him in the open mouth of the main fireplace hole. He screamed louder than she did when he landed among the red coals. Lado shouted at the woman, cupping his hands, "Good toss, Nella! I'll have some roast Cragman to go with him!"

It caused a general roar. Riot, I thought. Guards converged around us in a solid mass. We were hustled out of the Hall as fast as we could go, leaving the wreckage behind. Someone promised to fetch my weapons from Lumi at the door—Lado made them promise. Why bother, I thought: Lumi let those Nandos into the Hall with concealed weapons. He'd soon be in a cell for questioning, if anyone had any sense.

Lado said sternly to me, "Look at this! one of them almost marked my harp. And that shove made me drop yours! I barely caught it."

I gazed at him; he was laden with two harpcases on his belt straps. I said humbly, "My apologies, Lado. I was not at my best. I will be more aware, sooner, next time."

He stared at me and began to laugh. "Apologies," Lado wheezed, doubling over the cases and laughing until he was gasping and weak. I studied him doubtfully; he hadn't seemed like the hysteric sort. He said to Rafai, "Bandaged and weaving on his feet, and he apologizes for smacking down Nando assassins like flies. Can you believe it?" He gestured weakly at me. "Cragman Nandos, too—you saw that red hair?"

I said, "They weren't very good."

Lado's head came up. He stared into my face. I said, "I should have seen them coming earlier. Cragmen are not the best assassins, Nandos or not."

Lado said, smiling, "You could actually do that again—better?"

"Yes." I remembered my hot rush of rage, and Lado's refined face gone contorted as he smashed the bowl down on a Nando's head. Lado held out my harpcase, and I slid out the harp to check it.

Lado said, with no laughter in his voice, "I believe you. Swat them down like flies—is that what it means to be a Sati?"

I glanced away at my harp, taking it and smoothing the bloodstains on the white inlay. "Yes."

CHAPTER

= *6* =

I SAT WRAPPED in my bedfur. I looked out of the open windowslit of the room given me; I saw a single star glittering in that black stretch of sky. The breeze came in puffs to me. Across the room, near a small brazier, Lado strummed his harp. He wrote words on a slate now and then, humming to himself. Songmaking, I thought. He got up restlessly and stirred the oak knot coals in the brazier. This chamber belonged to Rafai's family; it seemed they were all friends of Lado Kiselli, who apparently chose his friends wherever he liked. I still didn't have any weapons; Lado said it wasn't polite to go armed as a guest. Somebody had my weapons, he said soothingly, someone would see why Lumi at the Hall door had failed to catch the hidden weapons the Nandos used. Someone, I told him nastily, had better check on Lumi.

I lifted my wine goblet and drank. Lado's magic had given me a wine too strong for my coarse palate. I was thoroughly, disgustingly drunk. Thirty days of riding, my message given, a reliving in public barely averted, my first harping and my first Tannese fight a success—Lado poured more wine into my goblet, and I let him. I didn't care about inept assassins bothering me again, I'd kill anyone who tried me. That was how drunk I was. I was full of wine peace, the Goddess's peace, and I was content.

Lado sat at the table a moment, fingering his harp while he stared at me. A lock of hair fell over his forehead. He said apologetically, "Tanman called me in to check if you were really a Harper, the day after you arrived."

"How did you do that?" I asked.

"Callous patterns on your fingers."

I nodded.

Lado picked out random notes on his harp. "You were unconscious. Drugged. They looked you over pretty thoroughly. By Sitha, I think they even dipped you for vermin and wormed you. Do you mind?"

I laughed. "You saw my legs?" I saw from his eyes that he had seen it; he had seen my lolling there like a puppeteer's half-dressed ruined toy. I said easily, "I don't mind the drugging. Saved me some pain, let me sleep. Nobody minds losing their fleas! Now, getting my throat cut—*that* I would mind."

Lado said dryly, "Little chance of that. Not many of us want a screeching ghost like yours would be."

I laughed. Then I said, "How did you get this wine? You just waved your hands—"

He sat up straight. "This comes from my hold's vintages. I'm part of the Council, not just a Harper. I'm one of the few loyal men Tanman has, these days."

There was a silence. So there's more than frivolity to this one, I thought drunkenly. He saw the blank look on my face and went on, "I'm from Clan Birch. Father's too old to be a Council member. Besides, he drinks like a sailor. The rest of the Council says I'm either a radical or a hidebound traditionalist, they never agree which. Tanman is the only one who seems to understand what I want to do. The harping was what I trained for. It was my brother who was to be Council delegate. . . ." His face darkened to an angry, chill look.

I said, "There was a raid?"

He looked at me, his face hawklike and no longer young. "Ah, you're quick, Black Man. I heard the raiders talking. They were dressed to be Upai. But they were talking Marsh dialect in the middle of Tan—in midwinter, prime Marsh fur-trapping season when any honest Marshman is busy. That makes them Manoloki's Nandos. I have no proof, of course, it happened out at an isolated hunting lodge. Loyal nobles have been avoiding isolated places lately. My father's men came in time for me. Not for my brother." After a moment, he added, "By the way—I owe you for those assassins you swatted down in the Hall; you saved my skin. Maybe Tanman's, too."

I waved one hand, dismissing the general brawl, and stretched a little. Lado looked at my hands; I kept my fingernails long for harp techniques and for fighting with. Thumb and forefinger nails were shorter for my scadda grips. I looked at my complicated fingers and scratched my cheek.

Lado said, with sudden force, "Would that I had your skills, Sati! I'd go down in a blaze—"

I gave him a slow, placid smile. "Lado, one man can do nothing. An army changes the whole country. Save your rage for those Council battles. And monumental harp works."

Lado's face darkened again. "I haven't the voice."

I said a pungent and very rude word. He looked at me. I told him, "You give me hope we can prod this country into getting ready for war, Lado. Hope, that is something. You know . . . you've got me drunk."

Lado looked uncomfortable. "It'll numb those sores."

I laughed. "Then pour more. I accept." I didn't care whether Lado had orders to pump me full of wine or not; I just liked him to be there, friendly and dogged and slightly silly. I felt for him in his anger, frustrated by his upbringing and his culture. His only weapon was a jeweled dagger in a waist sheath—the kind of knife that often snapped when it was actually used. He certainly hadn't used it in the Hall. I said, "Lado Kiselli, do you often make friends with strange Harpers?"

He snapped, "Never. If you weren't a Sati besides, I wouldn't now. The last foreign Harper I spoke to was years ago—turned out to be Tatéfannin's sort, and worse than the old man."

I laughed. I lifted my goblet to him, saying, "Then let us watch each other's backs forever." An old Nando pledge. I was very drunk.

Lado said tartly, "Past your hangover in the morning will do fine."

I giggled at that. Lado remarked that I sounded like a badger gargling in a hollow log. I had to ask what gargling was, which made him laugh. I must have fallen asleep, for next thing Lado was standing over me, tugging at me. "Come, get up. Tanman's here."

The words made me glare. He took the goblet away from me; wine had spilled on the floor. "What does *he* want?"

Lado heaved me up on my feet.

I was all right once I was up. I was steady—if Lado caught me now and then. Soldier's faces moved around me with the disturbing tendency to drift up and down and to laugh out loud when I spoke. A voice bellowed from the other half of the room, behind a hide curtain, and then a vast blue figure loomed over me, dancing blurrily up and down in front of me. "You're drunk," Tanman said.

I said something rude. Soldiers gasped, and someone behind me swallowed a laugh. I straightened up, feeling that I should be careful of my bearing with Tanman. I smoothed my robe with one hand and happened to stagger sidewise just a bit. Lado's hand propped me up.

"Why?" Tanman demanded. "Why are you drunk?"

Lado began speaking to him in low tones. I didn't feel like being excused or swept innocuously out of sight. I cut it all short. "Excuse me, Liege. I'm very drunk. Lado Kiselli . . . these people are your friends . . . whoever they are. You better find me a place to sleep . . . one of these people must have a bed. I'm very drunk." I gestured too wildly round at all the faces, and Lado had to prop me up again.

Some of the faces were children hanging upside down from sleeping-loft rafters. It made me dizzy to look at them. I turned and looked up at Tanman instead; he was nearly as blurred as the children. Irritated, I barked, "Liege, how come you're so far up there, anyway! Am I supposed to shout at you?"

Silence. Lots of staring eyes. Then two large hands closed gently on my arms and lifted me into the air. My face came level with Tanman's. "Is that better?'

I blinked into the amusement in the amber eyes. "Yes, Liege. Thank you."

"Why are you drunk?"

"I don't know. Sorry, Liege."

"You'd better be sorry. In fact, by the look of you, you will be sorry tomorrow morning."

"Yes, I expect . . . I will be." It took effort to get the words straight.

"You belong in bed. Am I hurting your sores?"

I smiled. "Can't feel it if you are," I said hazily. "I'm very drunk, Liege."

"Do you like hanging in midair?" His face was reddening with effort.

I glanced slowly down. Things waved about. "It's fine. Better than trying to stand up." I didn't know why they all laughed.

Tanman said, "Have you ever been this drunk before?"

I blinked. "No. Never had enough wine." I heard laughter again.

"Do you want to go to bed?"

I smiled agreeably and he put me down. I promptly got tangled up with my sore right leg and fell over on the floor. I blinked up at the spinning faces. Somebody picked me up and slung me over his shoulder and carried me along. It was a long way up from the floor, and his shoulder jolted into my belly. I half closed my eyes. My arms were banging against a broad sword belt. The hilt of Devour winked silver lights up at me. "Good evening," I told the sword politely.

Tanman turned his head and said, "Shut up and go to sleep, Naga." He rolled me over and dropped me onto a bed.

To the blare of voices and torchlight, I said firmly, "I'm asleep. Go away." Murmuring and shuffling of feet. And then they were gone. I huddled up into the thick furs and sighed.

Naga Asaba Imuto Teot, Upai envoy, Tanman's Oathswearer, Sati of scaddas, woke in the grip of an undignified, skull-cracking headache. A little hand was patting my face, by the light of a tiny oil lamp. I squinted, reflexes briefly stilled: I lay face-to-face with a plump, pink, girl child. The baby examined the tip of my left braid and studied me with large thoughtful blue eyes. She gurgled and pushed at my chin with a fist. I closed my eyes. After several eons there were footsteps, and torches, and other children, all of them yelling. Someone took the child away and they all trooped out, proclaimed by the two-year-old's shrieks of outrage. Lado said irritably to me, "Can't I turn about without you getting in trouble?"

"Visit Tan and learn court manners," I said. I heard the child's howls grow fainter with distance, and Lado's footsteps following after. But the headache did not follow them, and leave me alone.

After several unpleasant bell passes of time, I opened my eyes a squint wider. There was a window: a slit about four fingers wide, showing the gray that was neither night nor dawn, that vague time before true light. Doves cooed outside.

I thought uncharitably of uses for bird flesh, but thinking made me ill. At a noise, I turned my head carefully, slightly.

Beyond the broad hide curtain across the chamber, somebody was enjoying themselves. The noises grew into a huge racket—bed straps squeaked and creaked near breakpoint in a pandemonium of satisfaction. Passion ruled, straps suffered. I gingerly lifted a roll of fur over my ears, but it didn't muffle the wild shrieks and groans. The very sound made me queasy. I had urgently to urinate, but I didn't for any purpose want to move.

Need finally drove me out of bed. I sat up, carefully holding my head together. The limestone floor felt cold to my bare feet. I thought numbly, have I lost my new boots? Slowly I bent over, put my knees on the stone floor, and rested my right cheek on that cooling stone. The chill held my head together better. For a time I knelt with my face resting on the floor. It seemed to help. "Visit Tan and learn dignity," I told the stone.

Kneeling with my tailbone in the air made my unbelted robes flap open—at least I still had those. Looking upside down at myself, I poked at my sores and bandages. I still didn't want to move all the way over to the slushpot: it seemed so far. I turned slowly about with my cheek on the floor, and looked at the slushpot. My boots were next to my harpcase, stuffed underneath the bed. No weapons anywhere. I blinked. In most Nando camps, drunk as I had been, I wouldn't have awakened at all, let alone clothed and still in possession of the boots, harpcase and the jade bag at my neck. I really had been a fool, I told myself. I reached for my harpcase.

Well, I moved too far. I fell over on my side, cracked a dozen riding sores, and scrambled for the slushpot in a great hurry— where I did everything at once, including losing my stomach. Somehow, after it was over, I was sitting against the wall with my face pressed to the stone window casing; boots in one hand, my harpcase in the other.

I told myself, that's the last time I get drunk. That is the *last* time. Memories of how I had treated Tanman's magisterial person, tripping over myself and saying rude words and acting like a crazy dung beetle, all came sluggishly to the light in my head. I leaned on the window casing and pressed my face to the cool air and groaned. The abused bedstraps beyond the hide chamber-curtain again reached a thumping crescendo.

When I finally dared move to put on my boots, to latch my weaponbelt and hook the harpcase on my bandolier to hang under my left arm, I heard a baby in the other room start to cry. A door banged and children ran in yelling for their mother, arguing. The sounds made my head threaten to fly apart.

One yelled shrilly, "I get to see him!"

"No, you promised me—first this morning, you got to see him last night first—that's not fair—"

An older voice hissed, "Shut up, all of you. Plenty of room for everybody. And keep it quiet, you pudding-heads!"

I got slowly to my feet and went a second time to the slushpot. Instantly all the noise hushed. My urinating sounded terribly loud in the quiet. When I looked at the hide curtain, blond heads drew hastily back from holes and rents, and the curtain waved in the air. I fastened my robes. By the time I finished tying my boots, round bright eyes watched me from every slit in the hide. Bare feet of all sizes showed at the bottom. I even saw short pink legs.

The two-year-old girl toddled backwards underneath the hide and stumbled toward me, thoroughly confused. Her belly was round and fat. She peered up at me inquiringly, one finger stuck in her mouth. She came fearlessly to me, patted at my leg, and toddled back to the curtain. A large fat arm shot out, snatched her up, and vanished in outraged wails. The noise! I clutched my head, stood utterly still, and prayed— until the screams faded into gurgles and slobbering noises.

When I could, I dragged myself about the room, searching. I suppose it took entire years—it felt like it. I saw no weapons anywhere. I pressed my face against the chill stone of the window; nothing in the unpromising gray fog outside had changed. I took a deep breath and went at the hide curtain.

Children's feet pattered in all directions. I pushed through, and stopped. My half of the chamber was spotless by comparison to this. Bedding and children and strewn robes lay everywhere in tenebrous gloom, rags and leather and stray toys and wooden animals scattered about. Worn-out knee guards, giant mismatched boots without soles gnawed over enthusiastically by a litter of puppies—this family lived in awesome clutter. Round critical eyes gazed at me from all angles. I supposed that the bedstrap uproar explained the incredible number of pink young faces everywhere around me.

I glanced around at a soft laugh. The Head Armorer sat on the edge of his bed. I had no idea why I knew who he was; Lado must have told me that. In his lank gray braids, he was about as noticeable as the lard scraps left by the dogs, the scrawled walls, and broken furniture. I thought to myself, he might well look so smug after his wife's attentions; I heartily pitied those sagging bedstraps. I picked my way carefully across the chamber.

Near the doorway, the confusion was dominated by the Armorer's wife: a monumentally motherly figure who shook two fingers at a grown son twice her height, while she nursed the two-year-old at one large pink nipple. I could not imagine husbanding such a huge woman, but I gestured respect to her hastily: it does not do to offend the tent-mother. I thanked her carefully for giving me a bed and safe haven for the night.

The giant son turned in apparent surprise and looked at me. It was Rafai. He still wore military blue. Staring at me, he no longer looked quite so adolescent and sheepish as when his mother was chewing him over.

Behind me, a child's voice hissed, "But he's too little to be—," and someone else made hushing noises.

Rafai said to me, "Good morning, noble-born." He saluted me. I gazed at him in some astonishment. How did this Tannese soldier know I was nobility among my own people? Later I learned from Lado Kiselli that such information just floated around like swamp gas. I was careful not to ask him what swamp gas was; he would have laughed at me. I ran my head over my hot forehead, acknowledged the salute, and went on toward the door.

The door was guarded by a trio of young boys and a plump young hunting pup. The pup yapped at me and yawned and wandered off to a corner, belly bulging. There it did what dogs do, and a child yelled at it. My hands clenched at the noise. Two of the boys ran away and hid behind their mother. The third boy at the door did not run. Perhaps six, his belly hung out of his untidy corad exactly like the puppy's, with a belly button like a great round bead. He straddled a puddle of dog urine and pointed a toy arrow on a boy's bow. At me. And he yelled.

Sitha, how he yelled. This child insulted me in the best
warrior's manner, shrilling with excitement—and he drew
back the arrow with every sign of shooting me. I started,
puzzled somewhat; no desert child would have done such a
stupid thing. When his finger shifted on the bowcord, my
hand went up.

My right hand swung up and down in reflex and smashed
the weapon out of his grip. The fine little bow hit the wall
and broke into three pieces. I blinked at the child. He backed
up, gave a horrified look at the pieces dangling in my fist,
and shrieked for his mother.

Rafai strode toward me, hands out, and the Armorer no
longer looked complacent in his mess. I said, gritting my
teeth against the pain in my head, "Such a warrior should
fight men his own size. Perhaps a new bow from your father,
fierce one, while you learn better wisdom?" I held out a jade
chip from my Harper's bag. The howling softened to whim-
pers. Eyes round, the boy held out a grubby palm. The instant
I let go of the chip, boy and bribe were gone. I opened the
door and went out. My head may crack, I thought in amazed
pain.

Now I was out the door, quick as a snake Mother's arm
shot out and snatched up the little boy and gave him a sound
boxing on the buttocks. Fresh howls broke out. Shrieks of
motherly imprecation lashed the air. Her two-year-old, secure
in the other fat arm, suckled on undisturbed . . . while I
winced. Rafai came out behind me and closed the door on the
uproar.

I made the effort: I didn't actually clutch my head. Opening my lips gingerly, I said, "I hope I've broken that habit of
the child's."

Rafai looked at me, startled, and suddenly grinned. "I
think you did, noble-born."

"Don't come at me fast like that again, soldier. Next time I
might mistakenly think you were attacking me."

The square face sobered. "Pardon, noble-born."

I walked on aimlessly, restless. "I understand your family
concern. Stay with me, unless Tanman orders otherwise. It's
been a long time since I saw a soldier ready to lay hands on a
Sati to defend his family."

Rafai gazed at me. "Anybody would—"

I laughed grimly. "Soldier—no. They run. I never had

many women or children abandoned to my tender mercies; there weren't many left in the places I've been. But on the border, they run.''

Rafai's eyes went round and sober, but he digested it silently. At last he ventured to say, ''Where are you going, noble-born, with the harp? The ceremony is supposed to be—''

''Ceremony?'' I looked blankly at him.

The man's face became appalled. ''No one told you? Your Oathswearing is today. You're to do it over new, all Fortress will be there, it's going to be part of the holy day ceremonies. We—I thought you knew that, noble-born. That's why they took your weapons.''

I said, ''Any Oathswearing should be at dawn.''

''It is,'' Rafai looked even more horrified. ''Lado—he's always getting me in trouble. Someone should have come down to fetch you a long time ago. If you turn that way—''

I said firmly, ''Tell me which way we turn to go outside, toward the stables.''

He gave me a look. Then he pointed, suddenly subdued. Like his land, Rafai was lush and lazy in apparent peacetime. He smelled of babies, wine, and a rich diet—and the scent of woman. He probably had his father's randy propensities, too, a continuation of generations that was oddly comforting. I dismissed the thought of that and walked on. Together, we stepped out of a wooden door onto the big dirt parade ground.

We passed a group of young Tannese nobles. Their voices trailed about us in incomprehensible court dialect like languid sunlit streamers, bored. The crisp, light, staccato note in their drawling voices I had never heard anywhere else; Tan's common voices were choppy and guttural. The courtiers smelled of deer musk perfumes, flower garlands, wine, and fish in the cool wet breeze. They didn't, any of them, look at me until they thought I would not catch them at it. ''. . . beggars . . . don't know why they let . . .''

There was mist among the buildings, haze at all distances. I could clearly smell the sea; the air felt cold and still and heavily damp. I recalled a line from one History that I had never understood before—it was that smell: *water and blood and wet fisherfolk clothes.* I turned toward a gana stable marked with a flame-shaped lightning ward at the peak, where boys moved about.

Boys leading ganas walked past me nervously, ducking

their heads. As I went into the stable, I heard bare feet patter out the back. I stopped inside, staring; while I gaped, Rafai and another new soldier came up on either side of me like an honor escort. I gazed silently.

Torches were hung on chains from the stable's main beams. Torches in a stable! The floor was clean-swept sandstone, and the pens were built of quarried blocks, no scrimp-work economy here. All the gana boys seemed to have vanished into the deeper gloom. I called out, "So you leave your beasts to my mercy and my ignorance?"

"Noble-born," small voices murmured from the shadows of the deeper pens. So, I thought. The gossip-line in this Fortress impressed me.

I said, "I don't eat beast boys. Show me the animals." Behind me, Rafai shifted his big boots anxiously about on the stone floor. I said aside to him, "Those jade dangles and mirrors have no place on a soldier's robes. I can hear you breathe."

He mumbled something. I glanced around as a boy came scuffling barefooted out of the stable's back stretches. This one seemed older than the boys walking beasts in the square, his cheek was scarred with knife-work; his eyes wary and sullen. He wore a black Devotee robe too small for him. He went about the stable naming the ganas, giving their histories carefully and precisely in low tones. He ended with more confidence than he had begun when he showed me a light, large-boned bull at the far end. This beast was truly handsome. I leaned my arms on the pen and the bull glanced round at me and continued to crunch grain. Most bulls were bony to ride, impossible to confine in a small pen, and even worse to tame. Not this one. "Yaaah," I murmured, and one ear flicked.

The beast boy smiled a little, and admitted to me that the bull was the one he fed and groomed and mucked out. The boy also admitted that his own name was Esgarin. I told him I liked his work. He ducked away back into the shadows as soon as I let him go; I thought that nobles had never been kind to him. For some time I studied the bull, thinking out the Tannese breeding lines the boy had listed for me, learning what they were trying to accomplish. I was also trying to make my hangover go away.

"So," a familiar deep voice pierced the barn's silence, "you're admiring Tor, are you?"

I glanced around. I threw back my outrobe hood and respectfully inclined my head to that voice. "How much do they want for him, Liege?"

Caladrunan waved Rafai away to his escort, six soldiers who stood at guard around him. Caladrunan fingered his beard. "All of these belong to the Devotees, who never sell. They keep Tor at stud, getting fat."

I wrinkled my face into the required envious look. "Yaya, such a life. He's a fine one."

Caladrunan said coldly, "Why did you come out here right before the Oath ceremony?" A ceremony which would, by his look, condemn my faulty character should I fail—the full and most binding Oath, whose cost could be my death.

I did not even glance at Rafai; it was futile to mention my ignorance of any ceremony until moments past. I said, instead, "I'm going to need a beast, Liege. Soothing, I guess, haggling over animals." Out of the corner of my eye, I noticed that Rafai's body relaxed. He wasn't going to be reported by me for negligence. Then he tensed up again, warning me.

Caladrunan said, "Do you need a pleasure woman, too, before you feel ready?"

My eyes flickered up involuntarily into the chips of ice that were Tanman's eyes. I was startled at the bite in his voice. I inclined my head to him, saying, "No, Liege. I meant no disrespect."

Caladrunan swung around angrily, abruptly, interrupted by a sound. A tall, thin reddish man stalked the length of the barn, squinting in the torchlight; he held an ornate ceremonial sword bare in his hand. He led a quartet of green-robed soldiers toward us. All of them walked out of step like Cragmen. The officer's face was classic Cragman: dark reddish freckles, red hair, a narrow face with a plow-blade nose. His inner robe was even the classic Crag green, though his outrobe was Tanman's blue.

The officer carried his head high, as if he were a noble raised from birth with superior status. But noble or not, his blade moved in a businesslike manner. When he saw me tense toward a ready stance, his eyes looked me over in professional assessment; the instant he was sure I was unarmed, his eyes shifted arrogantly, dismissing me as trivial. His voice had the loud crisp snap of a field commander; he spoke to Tanman as if I did not understand him at all. "They tell me everything is ready, Liege. A Sati, Liege—this may be dangerous." His voice emphasized the word.

Strange, I thought, when words and action did not agree.

Caladrunan raked my face with a swift cold look. He said, "Any other good advice, Keth?"

Keth Adcrag, I thought. One of the names I had memorized, a prominent one. I thought, you are in danger, Liege Lord of Tan, with this one.

Keth's lips thinned. He said, "Do recall that he could do to you what he did to Manoloki's service—betray your trust with foresworn promises. Remember that Marshman traitor who marked you, five years ago."

Caladrunan's irises snapped light-sparks briefly, just a glint of cold, then control. He did not like that memory, nor the reminder. He turned to me and said curtly, "Give us the harp."

I put it down on the stone stable floor. Keth reached for it. I said sharply in Tannese, "Treat it with the respect due it."

Both of them looked at me. Keth Adcrag jerked open the harpcase, reached inside and rummaged roughly among the spare strings. He held out his hand then. On his palm was the small scar-hid knife that fell out of my robes during Tanman's questioning—and I knew it hadn't been in my harpcase. Keth had palmed the knife. I could not read Tanman's blank face to see if he knew it, too. But Keth knew about the desert trick built in that knife. Its odd balance told the secret.

Keth grasped the knife and unscrewed the pommel. A small gray lump fell out of the hollow grip and hit the stone floor with a clang that made everyone there jump. *Liar!* my nerves screamed. The lump was wrapped in cloth when I carried it. Keth prodded the lump with his boot, staring at me. His gaze said, Assassin.

Tanman said in a flat tone, "It appears to be one of those slag pieces you see at forges."

Keth turned his ornate sword and smashed the flat on the lump. Sparks flashed, the blade jumped, hit the floor, and screeched. The sword scored a deep mark in the floor stone, but left nothing on the lump. He tried unsuccessfully three times to mark the lump, using edge and flat both. "Perhaps you could, Liege—"

Tanman waved him aside and closed his hand on his sword hilt. A silvery rasp whispered on the still air of the barn, Devour rose up out of its scabbard under his scratched, sun-browned hand. My eyes went down the massive hilt and the long, perfect, script-laden blade. Tanman lowered Devour's tip toward the lump slowly, as if thinking exactly how to test the lump with Devour's arcane metal.

Or perhaps he meant to test my nerves. I could not take it. To crack Tan's most sacred sword on that lump would shatter my superstitious faith in Tan, and some tests were better avoided.

"No," I said, and knelt, putting out my hand in Devour's way. "Liege, please. Do not desecrate the holy blade with that." I forced my eyes upward to Tanman's eyes. I tried to keep my expression calm and my hand steady, as if I felt nothing. But Devour's tip hung at my left side, where my arm was lifted and my ribs exposed and my heart pounded. I whispered, in Upai, "A dishonorable relic of the Osa if it has not been exchanged for another."

Tanman looked steadily at me. I could not tell whether he understood. He said in Tannese, "Where did you get it?"

"Redspring," I whispered. I lowered my hand to the stone blocks. Yes, a relic; one I hated. The death of my clan lay in the secrets of that ugly lump of metal.

He must have read something in my face. He said softly, "From one of their weapons?"

I nodded.

Tanman said, "Let us turn it over to my metalsmiths, Sati."

I glanced up at Keth Adcrag. The Cragman's face looked rigid, expressionless. I thought, Keth does not want this, he tried to frame me traitorous. I said, "Desert smiths cannot work it, Liege, it is too hard."

Tanman smiled grimly. "This is not the first such sample my smiths have got these days. Get up. You owe me an Oath at dawn."

I looked up at him, startled. Not the first such sample? Then—but he was not answering questions. He gestured to one of his own escort soldiers to take the lump, waving away Keth's Cragmen. Another of Tanman's men took up my harpcase, and took the Tokori knife firmly from Keth. In a casual gesture Tanman nicked Devour's tip on the back of his own hand, amid a welter of other similar scratches, and wiped the blood away with a rag. But he looked at Keth as he did it, and the look was not casual. Keth stared back.

The Cragman said, "Or he owes the Altar a death."

Caladrunan said calmly, "We shall go now. It'll be dawn soon, and you have a ceremony to go through, Sati."

CHAPTER

= 7 =

ONCE IN THE looming massif of Fortress, night and dust and the stink of ganas gave way to the odors of the soldiers' torches, salted fish, baking grain, and the sweat of men. Deeper in the place, a miasma in the thick corridor air, came the cesspit smell of the drains and lower-level garbage pits. It made my hangover ache sharply. We paused before a set of wooden doors carven with old flame motifs. A Devotee priest in black robes came up, jangled a key in the iron lock. The stiff door hinges squealed. A wave of air from the cold rock gut of Fortress flowed over us and past; our breath puffed torchlit steam in the chill. I followed Tanman through a flickering darkness along tunnelways. Constantly I looked back, for Keth jostled at my back, muttering in Cragman under his breath.

Forms moved against a misty rectangle of light; Tanman stepped into brilliance dazzling after the darkness, and beckoned. I followed him onto an expanse of red-speckled sandstone floor—and I walked into a great shaft of rose sunlight, first light, before the largest single mass of humanity I had ever seen in one place. The light bounded from the pale stone and diffused everywhere.

I lifted my eyes, sight blurring over the ranks and ranks of people: nobles, military, clan leaders, commoners and tradesmen of every sort. The noise of the assembled multitude rising to its feet made a rumble and rush like falling rocks. The air tasted of salt and fog.

As proof of Tan's wealth and variety, they could have

covered a hillside—blond and brown and reddish, misted in rosy light and endlessly repeated, blurring into a color like Tan's grain fields. It was all enclosed in sandstone walls, an ancient siege-wall keep. This was the Great Altar of Tan during a holy day ceremony.

I swept an awed gaze over the vast expanse, over the faces. The shaft of dawn light touched my face with the dimmest warmth. That misty brilliant light was the only source in the place. The length of light measured the height of the first, original Fortress, from the stone floor under my boots, to the huge vents streaming mist so far overhead. This had been the first fortification of Tan, sanctified in every History, seat of Tan's dominion. Pointed stone arches fretted the walls and ceiling, a rising chasm of rock twisting and calling to the sky many floors above me. At each floor hung balconies, each balcony packed with faces. The sandstone Altar floor stretched out so far that it dwarfed even Tanman into a tiny figure.

I turned to look at them all, with a scrape of boot on rock. It was amazing that so many people could stand so quietly; I heard someone three floors up cough and beg pardon of his neighbors. "My Liege," I whispered out against the hush. In the still moment before anything started, I realized what I would suffer: my test, and my Oathswearing would be a public celebration on this holy day. And my death, too, if I failed that test.

At my back, the soft blossoming roar of a fire started. A large fire. My nerves jerked in my skin, I spun about—hands out, body low. I stared at the back wall of the Great Altar.

That wall was the seat of holiness in Tan. In the new light a seal of the Goddess leaped out in a relief carven into the wall behind the main Altar slab. All the place was visible, all the faces. The hair on my neck went up rough in fear, my lips pulled back from my teeth. The Bowl on the slab contained the living reality of the Goddess: a cauldron of gold-washed iron, big enough to hold a whole man in it. Rivulets of rust marred its shining sides; it was very old. Within it stood the very flesh of the Goddess, which is fire.

Then I dragged in a deep shuddering breath, and my mind began to work again. I was a coward, terrified of fire more than of anything else. If I gave way to that past . . . Inside the Bowl, the Flames of the Goddess shot up six feet high—long, pale, white-and-blue shafts. I covered my eyes with one hand. Blinding bands of red danced over my sight. These Flames were Sitha's real face. Never had I seen a holy thing like those six-foot pillars of fire. If I could, I would have crawled right down into the red speckled stone under me.

"We see you," Caladrunan's strong hoarse voice said through the fire, and the Devotee choir softened to a hum. Later I learned how these things were done—but for a desert Nando, it was devastating. I lay on my face before my deity, and felt exceedingly tiny and very unimportant. Tanman alone stood upright before those flames; the rest of us hid our faces under our hands.

Tanman's boots grated on granite. Close above me, he said, "Naga Teot, your spirit stands under my gaze on this holy day. You may flee these Flames of Judgment now—if you fear Us."

I lifted my head with a startled jerk, which made my hangover ache harder. At one side, a Devotee held open a wooden door just wide enough for me to run through; the back of the door was marked with an odd abstract pattern of lines I had never seen before. That door—I shuddered. That way, I was sure, led to a bloody flight through the streets that I did not know. I could never outrun a killing mob if I fled this test. Already some of the Tannese were craning their heads. "Will he run? Can't see—"

I clenched my jaws tighter. No. That was not why I'd come to Tan. I lowered my head to my arms. Lifting my hands from the floor, I crossed my wrists and turned my palms up toward Caladrunan. I had no words in me for answer.

Caladrunan held the sword Devour bare in his right hand; the script on it glittered. The strong dawn light and the Flame glow poured over him with a dazzling radiance on his light hair, shining on the silver in his robes. I looked up edgewise at him, meeting his stare.

Caladrunan's lips quirked at my unorthodox reply, and he said, "Very well, Sati, Harper. Obedience is my order to you." He gestured; the Devotee closed the escape door. There would be no fleeing Tanman's demands now.

Caladrunan made a grand sword gesture at the watching Tannese masses. They settled with shuffling and sighing noises into the ranks of wooden benches. I heard some of them talking, babies started to cry. A droplet of sweat ran into my right eye as I knelt there on the floor, wrists crossed. Stone grains grated under my knuckles. I blinked. The same pattern of lines I saw on the Devotee door was also scratched into the underside of the great golden Bowl, where no one normally could see it. I wondered if I should figure out its meaning while I thought out chants, preparing myself for physical demands—for torture, a common Nando test. I saw Tanman's boots, with a red tassle on each toe, walk around behind me.

My skin crawled. A cold breath of chill touched the fine body hairs on the bare nape of my neck above my robe. Tanman, silent as an owl, touched Devour's tip to the hollow at the back of my skull. I gazed up, moving only my eyes; Keth Adcrag nearby looked at me with an odd smile I did not like at all. Last, I looked round at Devour's hilt. The scripted noble blade, long enough for me to see at one side, glowed silver. I held myself still while the tip glided lightly across my outrobe, down my spine. I had heard of such coward's tests—a waver, a shudder, any sign of fear, and it was over. Forever.

Tanman rested the flat of that sword on my shoulder and pressed, saying, "Down." I leaned farther, until my arms stretched forward full-length upon the stone. My nose touched the rock between my knees. I watched Tanman from the corner of my eyes, straining to see, but I saw only boot toes, speckled stone grains, and the underswell of the Bowl, mysteriously mapped with lines.

Devour's tip caught suddenly in a fold of my outrobe and skipped on, with a loud ripping noise. At each shoulder in turn, the dressing loops drew taut and snapped with sharp popping noises. My neck hair stood on end. Cold air shot through the slit robes, twinging on my harness and riding sores. Outrobe and inner robe flapped open, loose folds lolling aside of the cold touch on my skin. The neck of my robes slithered open and the clothing fell apart over my arms, the fittings hit the floor with a flat slap. The sword edge touched my bare back. I felt Devour trace pointwise whorls across my shoulder blades, chill as a lizard's foot, sometimes scratching me. Then Tanman laid the cold flat of the blade on my back. He said, "Do you know the legend of Devour, Harper?"

With some difficulty in my bent posture, I said, "Devour was forged by sixteen Devotee smiths from the broken shards of the sword Suku. Suku was a magical weapon which destroyed Osa monsters, carried by Tanman Kasin in Fourth History.''

Keth Adcrag snapped in his raspy voice, ''When they forged Devour, little man, they made it more useful than Suku ever was. Devour can put out four different poisons at once.''

And you'd like to rule it, Keth, I thought suddenly. It was in his voice. At that moment Devour turned and nicked the skin on my right shoulder blade. I held still, looking steadily at Caladrunan's boots. Something utterly idiot came to mind, so of course I said it: ''If you mean to poison me, Liege, you must know a dozen less elaborate ways.''

For a moment, the blade was motionless. Then it tickled over my skin again, sliding sometimes in my sweat. From that one cut, from the easy slitting of my robes, I knew that blade could cut my flesh as if I were melted fat. With his great strength he could easily cut me in two before I knew he had moved—and I was afraid of such ease. I was more afraid of showing it.

Caladrunan murmured softly, ''Do you know how many men have taken this test, Naga? And how many passed it?''

Even my brain felt cold. I said, ''Tell me, Liege. I do not know.''

Keth's rasping voice interrupted. ''Four men tried to assassinate Tanman, and came under this sword for it. None of them lived.''

The chill gripped and twisted in my gut. Because I was so scared—of those Flames, of the sword, of Tanman—I could get no more frightened, I felt a silly rictus of a grin come over my face, pressing crooked against the stone. I said, ''That sword likes to kill, doesn't it?''

I heard a thin bonelike high whistle from Keth's direction—and then a ripping sound. Cold sliced down my back. In reflex, I lifted my body and threw out my arm to block Keth's blade and push him away from Tanman, both hands clawing, all tangled in the cut robes—and my eyes hunted for a hidden assassin-blade. Both swords glittered in my face, from opposite sides. Both were bright red at the tip. Keth jabbed the ornate sword, saying roughly, ''So, you'd come at us, eh, little man?''

I felt my lips snarl back.

''Hold,'' Tanman barked. Keth shut his mouth. I knelt

there rigidly still. Tanman studied me. He said at last, "Well, it seems we do have a Sati here, and deeply ingrained at that. His reflexes knew that it was your blade struck him, Keth. Well, Sati, Harper—no one calls you a coward." He made a sharp hand gesture at Keth.

Keth Adcrag glared at me and stalked away through an Altar door. Different from the other door, it too was scratched with those meandering lines. I looked at Tanman. "At ease," he said, and I lowered my claw-flexed hands.

I shook my wrists free of the cut robes and knelt there, taking in deep shuddering breaths. I was afraid, I was not warm in any part of my body—but I was still alive, and able to fight. The crowd was roaring. A roar to get on with the spectacle: they wanted more than the minor nicks I'd got so far. I was impatient too. While I felt my life slipping loosely in my fingers, I was also tense, bored, and nervous—a trainee fault, that enraging combination that used to sap my strength before raids. I made a careful effort to remember my training, to regain my calm, to breath properly.

When I was steady again, Tanman said in a level and terrible voice, "Do you know what happens to a ruler who fails?"

I glanced up in surprise.

He spoke in soft, cold, incisive tones. "You wish to serve me. I may give you liegemen honor, titles, even wealth—and my enemies may give you a horrible death." He looked in my eyes. "A death as slow and as awful as you could possibly devise, Naga Teot. If I am pulled down . . . consider your worst nightmare."

For a moment I stared at him, feeling my hangover pounding. He knew; he knew what I feared most.

I answered him in a whisper, saying, "I know the history of your line—and of my own, Liege. I know what happens when rabble drag down a ruler." Then, in a slow, careful choice of words, I said, "Because you do not give *your* enemies such bad deaths . . . I came to you. You have honor in yourself."

Tanman's face trembled briefly, as if he had not expected me to say that. He said roughly, "You might have the right to say that if you knew me. You don't."

I glanced up, perplexed. "Was I being rude to you, Liege?"

He tapped one fingernail on Devour. "By desert standards, not at all. By Tannese protocol, you're frightful."

"I shall try to learn, Liege," I said, ducking my head.

"I will see to it that you do—if you survive this ceremony."

I swallowed. "Yes, Liege."

Keth Adcrag came out of the door. Keth smiled coolly and spread out a dark blue cloth before me, and stepped back. I looked at the things on the cloth: a torn scrap of red leather, a partially deformed pewter belt buckle, and a dull gray pewter urn full of black dust. Remains. For a moment red blurred over my sight, rage shook my guts, then chill. A sick hollow ache crept outward from my stomach, bile came up in my mouth. The death scent came pungent and harsh from the cloth. The stink hung choking close around me. It was the stench of Osa fire, burnt flesh, and funerary herbs. The herbs of a Upai death.

Tanman stepped forward, taking a leather bottle from a robe pocket. He poured a dark wine into the pewter urn. In his other hand, he held Devour bare and shining. Backlit, only the curly tip edges of his hair shone in the sunlight. He said in that same level voice, "Do you know what these are?"

I got up quickly to my feet. The urn rocked on its feet and liquid sloshed out, staining the cloth black with ash. I saw little chips of bone on the cloth. I rubbed sweating hands at my head, my hangover roared. All around me hung the strong stench of the most horrible of Upai funerals, the oily stench that herbs never masked. Even the pattern of leaves stamped into the red leather was Upai craftsmanship. My brother once wore a belt of leaves like that. . . . I drew in a ragged gasp. A thought bloomed in the center of my terror. Slowly, dreadfully, I looked at the back of the Altar.

The Flames shoudl have answered this sacrilege. It was profanity of every degree to bring the relics of such desecration into Tan's most holy Altar. Once these Flames blasted holy fire to the farthest wall when a scornful usurper-Tanman tossed a defiled object from some Wasteland into the golden Bowl. He took a hundred Tannese nobles with him in his impiety, thus opening Tannese rulership for the dynasty that produced Caladrunan. These Flames, for that reason, were called Judgment Flames.

But nothing happened now. The Flames towered up, serene, unwavering. I blinked. Red bands, rays and suns danced crazily inside my head when I closed my eyes. Perhaps I moaned. How many times had the Goddess turned Her face from the stench that hung about me now . . .

Tanman moved, holding Devour toward me, and he said coldly, "Pick up the urn."

I looked into his eyes. There was no mercy in that cold amber stare—only some deep and abiding rage. About me the stink of death oils seemed to get stronger. And his eyes said forcefully, *Obedience*.

Upai do not touch the dead after the burial rituals. Even the Nandos had not been able to break me of that taboo. He must know that, when he ordered me to pick up the remains of a dead man. I felt sweat run down my cheek. Keth Adcrag was smiling. I thought, Caladrunan must have a reason for this. He must. The man could not change so . . . could he? I looked at the urn. I bent over, breathing shallowly.

The instant my fingers touched the blue cloth, a shock of ice ran through my body. The funerary oils came through the cloth and clung on my fingertips. I murmured a prayer and clenched my jaws and straightened to my full height, holding out the urn. Hot salty sweat ran into my mouth. I glanced down: black dust floated uneasily across the surface of the wine among pale floating bone chips. My hangover roared in my head. I closed my eyes against it, and prayed hard.

At a rustle of cloth I opened my eyes. Caladrunan reached down and put his whole left hand into the black muck in the urn. I felt the blood drop out of my head, making my skull all hollow feeling. Tanman lifted up his mired hand, holding a pointed bone chip. He held it before my face. Wine dripped down his wrist, leaving sooty trails.

"Be still," he said, and traced a mark with the bone chip onto my forehead. It scratched my skin. If a man could be violated, it was happening to me. I let him do it—I could have reached out and broken his neck with one blow if I truly chose to, he was so close. I could have stopped him. But I did not. There was nothing inside me but shock, wreckage, disbelief. Even nightmares did not hold me like this. Inside me, some voice cried out: *what kind of monster has he become*?

"Look at me," Tanman said, and wrapped his sooty hand round my chin. He pressed lightly down, Devour lingering near my side, until I knelt at his feet and my head was fixed against a wet clenched hand as firm as iron.

His eyes were terrible and intense, focused hard on me: all pale-rimmed black pupil. I knelt there staring back at him like a beast pinioned under a witch stare. I still held his accursed pewter urn—he had told me to put it down. I let him use the dead. Perhaps dreams take too long a time to shatter. I felt like weeping.

Whatever Tanman read in my face, his expression changed—he looked as if he felt some grinding, internal pain. He must certainly have read in my face the truth, the Osa threat, and the bloody revenge owed for the deaths. So many deaths. Tanman let go of my jaw and looked away, swallowing. Devour hung down limp from his hand. I saw the muscles bunch and leap in his jaw above his beard. He said flatly, "Sati. Recite your Oath."

I heard murmuring from the spectators, even among the Devotee choir. Keth Adcrag said things a lot louder than whispers. Tanman ignored all of them. Later they would all whisper that Tanman wrestled for and captured my soul through my eyes, which was the most potent and dangerous sorcery of all. That, any timid witch-lore from the backhills villages would affirm: and perhaps the whisperers were right, though none knew how he did it. They did not know Upai funerals and Upai tragedy, but they saw me recite my Oath like a gana dragged sweating and stumbling to the harness post. How could my brother's friend bring the remains of Osa death into the holiest place in Tan—and he marked me with the ash of the dead! I spoke the bonding words of the Oath for the second time in my life—though something inside my throbbing head shrieked and wailed and flung about in wild grief. *How could he change so?* The crazy voice in my head rasped in hoarse whispers. I said, "I have the right, as an envoy of my people, to ask: Liege Lord of Tan, how could you bring Upai funeral relics of such—such depravity—into this holy place. Are you yourself allied to the Osa, and their acts of abomination—is that how you obtained the ash of dead men?"

Devour's tip rose sharply. It pointed, red with my own blood, at my gut. I said recklessly, "You dared to bring this before the Flames; you must answer for it."

Keth Adcrag drew in a sharp loud breath behind me; perhaps at last I had fallen into his plans to get rid of me. But Caladrunan held out one hand and restrained the Cragman. He said quietly, "Sheath that sword, Keth. We have confusion here—deliberately. It was my test. Despite what you thought, Naga Teot, you obeyed. You are more mine than you know. You are marked with my hearth-ash, with the honest bones and ash of my hunting, and with my personal wine. I claim you as I claim my personal servants and bodyguards.''

I heard Keth Adcrag break out furiously into Crag dialect. Caladrunan gave a very slight smile. But the tip of Devour did not relent. I tasted bitter copper on my tongue. I said, ''That was not just hearth-ash, Liege. There was a smell in that ash. Funeral herbs.''

Keth Adcrag spoke in Tannese so thickly accented that I could not understand him. Tanman turned his head, glaring, and the man subsided. To me, Caladrunan said, ''You smelled the offering oil I anointed my skin with, before I cut three drops of blood from my own hand by Devour's blade as a ruler claims his most confidential servants. As for the other things—the buckle I melted, and the leather I destroyed myself, to add to the test. They were made for me when I was a boy among your people—and they were precious to me. I hope you appreciate that sacrifice.''

Keth Adcrag stamped about swearing in Crag dialect. The red Cragman, too, had been tricked over what these things were, over what to expect; an unwitting tool, thinking to get me destroyed. Instead, he had helped test my Oath, helped prove it genuine. And he was not pleased. I glanced at Tanman.

· Caladrunan's mouth smiled then, but not his hard eyes. He said, ''The appearance I gave this, the herbs, were all part of the test of you. I am satisfied.'' Gently he wiped my blood from Devour's tip and sheathed the sword at his belt. Then he drew out a wooden disk on a leather thong from his robes. He held it up for the people to see. To me, he said, ''Take this as your envoy seal, Naga. You will not need another.''

It was pale haddoka wood, carven on one side with Sitha's dove and flame and grain symbols. The reverse showed a symbol of my own teacher—Reti's dune-line insignia, intertwined with Tanman's own sword-mark. Caladrunan put this into my cold hand and closed my fingers over it. He said, ''Reti left this with me to be given any of his Nandos who came here. Reti was already sick then, he expected to die soon. He wanted all of his men to know that, in joining my

service, his men would have his full permission and good
wishes.''

Keth Adcrag, at one side, sounded like he was swearing
seriously and at risk of his soul, under his breath. I put the
thong around my neck and touched Reti's seal. I felt I was
hearing the master's voice out of the past, for Tanman's voice
took on those antique cadences Reti had always used. I ran
my fingertips over the carvings, tracing Reti's sign. Of all of
us, of all his men, I was the one who stood here with
Tanman.

I glanced up once at Tanman. I think he knew I could not
speak at that moment, he had shaken me up too well. I
struggled with confusion and emotion, raw to the entire world.
Now he had the gana saddled and bitted, beyond fighting at
the harness post, Tanman could afford to be gentle with me.
He put his hand lightly on my shoulder, high praise to give a
man under so much general suspicion. Tanman spoke to me
then. The words fell into a quivering void in my mind and
sank there, never to be recovered. All I could focus my gaze
on were his eyes, deepset eyes lit with complicated depths
and emotions. I was certain he spoke the reassuring words he
always said to nervous soldiers; but it was the Great Oath I
gave to him, and he wove the threads down there in the root
of me, where I might never find them.

At last Tanman turned me to face the Bowl of Flames.
Devotee chants rose up on all sides. Ornately masked black-
robed celebrants carried burning bowls of incense past us.
The full ceremony of holy-day worship passed into me, and
through me, as through an empty vessel—what was there left
for me to feel? My memory of it was of the heavy-scented
air, the blue-white Flames binding me, and the choir voices.

Softly, a vibration in the rock, came the vast rhythmic
chants from the multitude at our backs, filling the domed
roof. They took their chants from the voice of the sea. To me,
it was the rhythmic breath of the living rock.

The Altar Flames shrank abruptly to a guttering blue tongue
at the end of blackened pipes in the holy Bowl. A Devotee
threw an offering of incense into the gold Bowl, and I started
and blinked as the Flames flared high into white brilliance.
An eddy of smoke swirled past in the intense glare. Caladrunan
ground his fingers into my shoulder, pressing pain and life
back into my body, grinding at an ulcer on my arm. I shook

myself a little. Tanman accepted an ewer of water from a masked celebrant. The scented smoke that the Devotees used lay heavy in my nose, a drowsy smell like burnt cupflower. I said, out of no particular thought, "These Flames are controlled, aren't they?"

Tanman shot a glance down at me. "You're learning fast."

Keth Adcrag said, "Liege, there is still time to reject—"

But Tanman took the ewer of water and splashed the water at my cheek, and as I blinked water from my eyes, he said, "You are accepted, Sati." He glanced once at Keth. Then he snapped at me, "Don't stand there, Naga, let's get you into some clothes before you freeze."

I swiped the water off hastily with my hands. He turned abruptly and pulled me along with him through a doorway. Devotees bent masked heads to him as he passed. Keth Adcrag trod close on my heels, as stiff and angry as a hostile dog. In the tunnelways soldiers formed ranks around the three of us; one of them held out to me a bundle of blue robes. I glanced down at myself.

Dark patches of fear-sweat stained my corad, I could smell the odors on me. I pulled on the fresh clothes over my leg bandages. The robes were cut to my size, as thick and soft as winter robes. Soldiers silently offered my weapons, a new weaponbelt, and leather armor much like my old armor— even my harpcase had been repaired. I put it all on, proudly, no matter how it hurt to strap armor over my sores.

While I dressed, Tanman spoke in a calm, genial tone to Keth Adcrag. "Could Vishna get away from his boats? I'm going to hold a strategy meeting at midday, all heads present. Strengam Dar already knows."

Keth said angrily, "With this Nando maggot listening, we—"

Tanman said in a deceptively mild tone, "Don't insult the Sati, my friend. He's trained and he's full of useful advice. We are not"—he gave Keth a long stare—"discussing his loyalty at this time."

Keth said sharply, "Should I return to the leather men then, Liege?" He spoke in the most formal Tannese court mode, which I barely understood for all its complex articulations of rank. The rest I could not follow at all.

Tanman said casually, "Yes, Keth. Thanks for your assistance with the ceremony. Good day." And Tanman strode off, calling me to come along. Keth stood staring after us, muttering.

We climbed up out of the bowels of Fortress by rising rock corridors. I had trouble keeping to Tanman's brisk pace. It was shaming, but they slowed down for me. The guard commander, Pitar, dropped back to walk beside me. He walked stiffly, very upright. He said, "This is the side way for you. You wouldn't care to meet that crush departing the main corridors—your kind is not popular here, Sati."

I gave Pitar a look. Tanman stepped briskly through a red-tiled gateway into a courtyard open to the sky. I said, "What is the likelihood of ambush?"

Something in Pitar's face changed. "Not very," he said, but he hurried forward to Tanman's side again. Beyond was a door, darkness. Three men vanished inside, and fire bloomed there: torches. For a blank instant I stared at it, and half turned away, right hand going to my scaddas. At my side Rafai's voice said softly, "We go up the stairs, Sati."

My hand dropped. I took a deep breath; I stepped into the darkness among the torches. The climbing was difficult with my gana-kicked leg, but I told myself it was as important as any raid or escape, and I finally stepped out of the stair gloom onto a broad flat roof.

The light sifted over me, a brilliant cool sun in a humid Tannese summer dawn. Light shafts darted overhead among the clouds in pale gradations of blue. Around me the roof was green as spring, full of trees and flowers in bloom, rows of plants in tilled order. I reached down and touched grass and my fingers came away wet with dew. A stone railing at the far end showed empty space beyond. I stood in a garden six stories above the streets.

Tanman turned about and looked at me. He said gravely, "We part here. Be courteous. You'll be safe until I call for you later." He strode back to the stairwell door with his men hurrying around him. The door slammed. I looked up then. Across the sky, a string of wild birds flew past. They were fish hawks, who hunted the sea in cooperation in all the old harp songs. It seemed a good omen. I looked down and stepped across the damp grass.

Three people sat together at the far end of the roof, lounging on cushions under a drooping pine tree. Lado Kiselli leaned against the tree, scribbling madly on a slate with his

brows puckered. His companions were two women: one was
short and round, her unveiled face looked like a dry fruit
seamed with shrewd squint lines. Her round belly pressed
over her legs as she laughed at some joke. A common woman,
without the veil—yet one of power, it would seem.

The other woman sat slender and perfectly upright. A cone
wound about with wheaten hair topped her head; her robes
and her full white veil were dressed with pearls. This woman
I had seen at Tanman's side, the night that Lado and I harped.

"Ai, Lado Kiselli," I said in a low voice, and they all
jumped and looked round.

"Goddess, you startled me!" Lado said.

I smiled, but I felt nothing really. I felt light and empty, a
little weak—like an empty refugee house, swept clean by the
wind, broken doors hanging scentless in the air. I knew, after
that Oathswearing ceremony, that nothing could have moved
me or alarmed me, only provoked my reflexes. The smell of
ash and funeral herbs seemed to fill my nostrils. I sat down
on a cushion Lado pushed toward me.

Lado turned about. "Lady of Fortress, this is the Sati—
also a Harper—whom we've discussed."

The wheaten-haired mystery spoke in a clear, regal voice.
"I never saw one of your kind trained in the noble arts
before." Her hand pointed at the haddoka disk on my chest.

I inclined my head courteously, and heard a noise. I spun
around almost on my knees, and crouched. A door opened
within a trellised grapevine. Keth Adcrag stepped out and
looked arrogantly about, feet widespread. "You," he said,
pointing at me. Then to the blond woman, he said, "A
moment with the creature, if you would, Lady."

The Lady of Fortress made a dismissing gesture with her
hand. Keth beckoned curtly at me and walked away straight
across the careful furrows of the herb garden, scowling. He
stopped next to a strange tree, picking at the furrowed bark.

I said, "Come to visit this garden?" And I held a crushed
mint leaf before my nose, to keep from showing my dislike of
him.

"No. I've never seen Upai nobility before, Naga Teot."
The name on his staccato lips disturbed me, as he meant it
should. He said in his raspy tones, "You look rather like a
frog."

"How flattering," I murmured into the mint leaf, lifting

my eyes to his. He looked aside. Cragmen always do. I said,
"Why are you wasting valuable time on me, when you are so
busy refitting your section of the army?" The chain of
conclusions—a high-ranking officer speaking to leather merchants, Tanman's obvious patience with this man's insolence—
all locked shut with a satisfying snap.

Keth looked angry. I thought he looked more than ever like
a weasel, with his sharp nose and colorless, deepset eyes. He
said, "Who has been gossiping to you?"

I smiled and dropped the mint leaf. "When the wind
blows, no one remarks that sand shifts."

He said, "Tanman ought to have had you gutted and
pegged out on the murderer's wall. It's outrageous that he
should endanger his own interests—and mine—over a petty
thing like you." He jerked at his robes. "I have a rival
Cragman on the Council, named Oldfield. He'll use you to
swing the Council voting against Tanman. Against me, too. If
Tanman got rid of you, we'd be able to muzzle Oldfield on
the subject of rebels."

I said, "The old lie that natives are rebels, is that Oldfield's
line of talk?"

Keth snorted. "Of course. Who else would the rebels be,
anyway? I ought to have you poisoned."

I murmured, "But you dare not defy Tanman," and I saw
the flare of anger in his eyes. I said, "And you are not ready
to challenge me directly, are you?"

In a heavier tone, he said, "I came here to discuss something with you. You ought to run, fool. Since obviously you
won't—this is your precise value." He plucked a caterpillar
from the strange tree beside us, and crushed it green between
his fingers and dropped it to the ground. "Remember that
when Tanman realizes he's hurt his own interests keeping
you." And he strode off past a trellised flower vine and
through a door hidden behind it.

I heard the door slam. I stood looking down at the caterpillar. With my boot toe, I nudged crumbling sandy soil over
it, and buried it.

CHAPTER

= 8 =

THE LADY OF FORTRESS stood on a cobbled path, beckoning me with one hand. I came to her across the furrows. I could not read her face through the white cloth veil. She said, ''You didn't learn your manners in Manoloki's camps. It takes a clever tongue to put Keth Adcrag in *that* kind of rage.''

I looked closer at her, but the veil hid everything. Even Nando face cloths revealed more: their eyes showed.

She said calmly, ''My husband told me about you, if you wonder. Keth has been bothering everyone to find out how my husband forced information out of you—as if anyone could force a Sati.''

I inclined my head a degree at the compliment. I said, ''Keth seems a dangerous man.''

The Lady's head moved forward like a predatory bird. In a taut voice, she said, ''He is Head of Cavalry—and he is more dangerous than you know, Sati. He did speak truth about our common enemy Oldfield, I heard that. Oldfield is shrieking in Council about rebels, while it is rather against my husband's interests to shelter you at this time. You also brought unexpected news about drug trade. It is plain you have no idea of the uproar you have created. So Tanman gives you the safety and comforts of the women's quarters until he calls for you.''

She bent down in a graceful crouch and plucked a handful of mottled leaves. She said, ''Sitha's mercy, you're not as clod-footed as Keth. I see he's crushed the ferns. My children are destructive enough here.''

I glanced at Keth's footprints across the pale green fronds.

I thought, typically Cragman. Of a rocky land, Cragmen did not believe the art of trailsign existed. Then I looked at the unfamiliar leaves in her hand. "Caladrunan's children?"

She inclined her head.

"And the nature of your . . . hospitality?"

She straightened rigidly. "Not many men would decline to enter the women's quarters, soldier. Even if, like you, they've never seen better than a street woman's den."

I found myself speechless. These Tannese, I thought. While I struggled with my embarrassment, we paced slowly around the garden perimeter. We passed Lado Kiselli without a word. Once out of Lado's earshot, she spoke again as if without pause.

She said, "I ask you for news, Sati. I order the women's quarters. Many women of exile cry here for news about their kin. Most were married, there are children, and few messengers arrive from rebel regions. Tell me what the last two moons have been like out there, in the raids, on the border, so I can speak with them. No military secrets—I want only a broad reckoning so I can perform my duties to these women."

I studied the blank white gauze falling sheer from her headdress. There would be factions within the women's quarters as in Tan itself; but how were they changed or distorted from the factions of the outer world?

She said softly, "Let me assure you, Sati—I learn much from the Cragmen, for the sake of my lord husband. Oldfield's business is known to me. Tell me what gentlemanly troop commanders will not, about the rebel area."

I said in a low voice, "Reckoning—as if there's a clear battlefield where bodies can be counted. Not so. I cannot make good of bad, Lady. The Nandos use caves and cellars of the ruins out there, dig for water. There is hunger. There are no holds—no whole wall stands—until you reach Black Pebble Ford in Tan. Deeper into Tan than you knew? That is the rebel front. In the eastern desert, where Manoloki's Nandos do not go, there a man can live. Not so in the raided zones. There is nothing."

After a long pause, she continued; her voice was perfectly controlled. "And the loyalists from those holds?"

I lifted my eyes. "They take no prisoners out there."

She walked steadily along the end wall of her garden, resting a slender gloved hand on the fine-grained stone. Faintly, at such distance from the cobbles and noise of the streets, I heard the ringing of a smith's anvil. "I thank you, Harper," she said in the same level, polite voice. "You speak excellently for a man who was not born Tannese."

"I am sorry to bring that news," I said, attempting to dignify it with a more formal Tannese mode.

In a firm tone she said, "The defeats will stop, that I promise you, Sati. Let us go in. I hear from the Head Armorer and my friend Lado Kiselli that you had a hard ride and that you are always hungry."

I smiled wryly. "Lado seemed well fed."

She said, "Not by our standards. The court has gotten lean lately—but I expect you wouldn't see that." She led the way into a vine-encrusted lath structure. The shade within was deep after the daylight outside. I heard a soft noise, I darted around the lath divider with one scadda poised in my hand.

There was only an old woman crouched among a clutter of muddy slippers in the shadows. She dunked a slipper in a tarred bucket, cleaning it with veined and knotted hands. She stared up at me with a grunt of surprise, blinking wide wrinkled eyes. Her thin face was many shades darker than my own. "Kuni?" she mumbled toothlessly, peering at me.

I felt a little thrill crawl over my back: her voice was pure Upai! I sheathed my scadda and greeted her. She sounded so old and senile, what harm could it do? Fortress seemed full of old people. I heard the Lady of Fortress stop at a door nearby, listening to us.

The old woman hissed in the darkness at me, "Ohh. Ohh. Sai—Sai—"

"Sai yom Teot," I said. Silence. The old woman blinked at me. I touched her bony shoulder and felt something surge up in my throat. There *was* some emotion left in me. I whispered, "Sai Teot."

The huge rheumy eyes blinked at me. A wet finger reached up and pushed my hood back, traced the tattoo on my forehead. She murmured, "Sai Teot. Sai Teot? There is yet another old woman to meet such as you. She knows. Orena é Teot." And she hummed it, smiling without teeth. A faded glint of shrewdness flickered in her eyes.

I gripped the old woman's wrist carefully. "Orena—that is my grandmother. Where?"

She drew back, pushing me away. "Not here! No! Out at the pig camps."

The Lady of Fortress said crisply, "I fear my Upai serving woman grows senile. I suspect you should ignore whatever she said. In the old days, we used to throw away muddy slippers. Now we clean them and give them to an orphan house." She opened the door into a stone corridor, beckoning me to follow. I patted the thin Upai shoulder and left her there among the slippers, humming tunelessly my name. The Lady of Fortress whisked swiftly away down the corridor. I said, "Where are the pig camps?"

She turned. "Oh, I expect she meant the Upai refugee camps. Didn't anyone tell you? Out by the slaughterhouses along the river. But in any case Tanman will not wish you to waste time on it."

I just stared at her. Whole camps of Upai here, at Fortress! She whisked onward, unmoved.

The stone walls were thickly scrolled with carvings and figures, many places on the walls were hung with gold-thread tapestries. The Lady swept up to a door flanked by two armored women guards, both taller than I was. They opened the door silently into a cool empty chamber.

It was a large rectangular place, walls covered with tapestries in a wild confusion of colors and scenes. Silver embroidered cushions lay scattered on the floor, nearly obscuring pale straw mats. The room around me carried the scent of dried herbs, a vague sweet draft of air.

The Lady swept over to a low brown lacquered table and seated herself. The dark doors closed silently. The Lady tapped the table, carven with beasts and birds and leaves in delicate pierce-work. "Sit, please, Sati. We can talk here."

Like a squirrel popping out of a tree, the pink-faced serving woman from the garden tossed aside a tapestry. She carried in a tray of food dishes, saying impudently, "Well, Sati, what fine swords—and curved, besides. I hear you're a well-armed male—in or out of harness!"

At my shocked look she let out a loud giggle. She set down the tray on the table, bobbed once to the Lady, laughed again, and vanished in a flurry of robes. A curl of stirred air touched my cheek.

The Lady held out one hand. "Harper, please. Sit."

Slowly I knelt down on a cushion across the table from the

Lady of Fortress, folding my legs under me as Reti once taught me. My sores complained. I thought a rude word to myself about the serving woman, embarrassed again. I scratched my cheekbone. The remains of Tanman's ash-signs were flaking off.

The Lady of Fortress said, "You should be flattered. Cherto is particular—and for her to tease a Upai! You must know the old Tannese fears of a native man's face up in the women's quarters. Shrieks, terror, throwing cushions. My women said the most awful things. Ugly native lizard, I'm afraid, was the most flattering. Of course, none of them saw you closely as I did last night in the Great Hall. You look quite different than most natives." In a softer voice, she added, "Strangely unprofessional emotion, Harper, when you sang Fourth History. I thought you might be crying—a man as calloused as yourself."

I looked silently away from her and flicked glances around the chamber.

"If you are uneasy about my motives, Harper: it is simple. Lado Kiselli spoke in your favor. And my husband asked me to accept you as a guest despite your Upai blood and your Nando past. There is no safer place for you at this time. Also, I wish to tell you a thing without mistake or distraction."

She paused, as if thinking out exactly what to say. "You saw my Upai serving woman, outside. She is very old now. She was with me since I was a child—or in all the rebel problems, they would certainly have taken her from me. She has served me longer and better than many Tannese, she has the virtue of complete loyalty. That is why I permit a Upai like yourself to serve my husband. It would be easy to destroy you here—for reasons beyond question—whether or not my lord Caladrunan desired it. And if he did wish you dead, you would never leave this room. Therefore . . . because you live yet, understand that my hand and my husband's hand shield you in friendship. Do not abuse our friendship. Do you understand?"

I lowered my head, thinking about air drafts and tapestries, observing eyes, and hidden places. My neck hair lifted. I was growing tired of that *watched* sensation. I said, "Yes. You are a brave woman, Lady."

Her voice came out metallic and controlled. "Where my husband and children go, I am as the tigress of the Wastes."

"I understand." The tent-mother had spoken. This was very likely why Keth Adcrag had not dared to kill me—with both Lady of Fortress and Tanman defending me, I was secure. Until I offended one of my new patrons.

The Lady said, "Good. Then we need never mention it again." She lifted dishes off the tray and set them before me. I stared at it. All Upai-spiced and heavily scented, the food steamed in white porcelain bowls. I looked up. Cherto glided in with another tray, smiled at me, and sat down at the end of the table. I looked away at the Lady, waiting politely for the Lady to eat of her food. It was desert manners to allow a host to eat first . . . to prevent embarrassments.

She took up a slice of some imported orange fruit on a spoon, dusted it in a dish of dried ground honey, and lifted it easily under her long veil. There were Tannese tools beside the dishes, but I was forced to use my fingers. Cherto sat watching me struggle. Amusement and interest crossed her face in broad cheerful sweeps hinting at what was rude and what Tannese might accept; I was grateful. The Lady of Fortress said, "Cherto had to fix the meal with her own hands, which she has not had to do for a while."

I glanced up.

Cherto said, "The old Upai nurse taught me last time how to cook your food."

I said, "I thank you."

She laughed. "Don't look so sour about it. I thought your people let women say whatever they liked."

I looked down at the food. It had been so long since I was around any women . . . or any Upai.

Cherto ignored my pause and said abruptly, "Lady, the women are going to scream about him every time he comes up to be entertained. They're shrieking already." To me, she said, "They think you natives are the ones killing their men out on that horrid border. They say you eat babies. Do you?"

The Lady manipulated another slice of orange fruit. She said quietly, "Harper, we may only be able to get a Kehran boy for you, during your service to Tanman. And that at large expense, I fear."

I choked on my food. After a moment, I set my hands on the table and stared at the two women.

The Lady's hands grew still. "Is the idea offensive? Forgive me. Customs differ."

I said in thick accented bursts, "Lady, bought whore-love is no vice of mine—and I don't eat babies!"

Cherto burst into laughter. I must have sounded quaint and outraged and provincial. But the Lady of Fortress relaxed and laughed softly, as if she'd half-believed the lies. I glared at her. I pushed aside empty food bowls in disgust. The Lady gestured. Cherto lifted a small silver pot and poured pale green fluid into tiny translucent bowls. The Lady took one and waved me to take the other. I glared at her again.

The Lady remarked, "Perhaps such astute judgment in a man deserves better than casual entertainment now and then."

A subtle sarcasm marred the even surface of her voice, perhaps a vocal habit. I said coldly, "My service to Tanman does not depend on how women treat me."

The Lady lifted her bowl under her veil. I heard her sipping. "Indeed? I was told you had a bad mouth on you, and it seems they were right. I will consider your case. Perhaps some of the desert hold widows might set aside their prejudices—"

Cherto interrupted freely. "Not that lot! They sit hashing over the same old news, half of it wrong, snapping at the servants—if there were some place to send them—"

The Lady set down her mua bowl half full. "They drain our resources."

I lifted my bowl of green fluid and sipped. It tasted of imported mua leaves; it hit my stomach with a hard authoritative glow stronger than any I had tasted in the desert. I blinked, took a deep breath. I set down the bowl carefully. "I heard that refugees were sent off to the Devotee Retreats, when a hold—even Fortress—could no longer care for them."

The Lady said in a dry tone, "It may come to that."

I said, with a tired flare of anger, "Your idle noblewomen could help refugees in the camps. Grant them lands to work, organizing kitchens, making clothes, finding medicines—"

The Lady tapped her forefinger on the table lightly. "As it has been done in wartime? No, Harper, don't protest. I know your views that it already *is* wartime. I am aware of the suffering out there, though you don't believe that. I have to find compelling reason to order women to work in the camps. It requires thought—but it's an idea that would make the women's quarters a good deal quieter. The Council will scream about appearances, of course." She lifted her mua

bowl under the cover of her veil, set the empty bowl down
with a precise clink. "One last thing, Harper. Don't go down
to the lower town, however much you fret about refugees;
and don't lose your escort soldiers. It is not Tanman who
governs there. You would disappear into some smokehole and
it would be unpleasant—and hopefully short—after that. Your
escort men are some of the best that Tanman could get."

I scratched my cheek. "They seemed noisy and clumsy. I
trust they are not—really."

She nodded her tall headdress once.

I said, "So involved an intrigue."

She said curtly, "You knew it would be when you came.
Cherto, please open the window."

Cherto pulled aside long tapestries, opened shutters on an
open arch. Outside was a balcony over a red-paved courtyard.
I stood up to see better. In the courtyard a line of children
came out of a lacquer door and walked around a white tile
fountain spouting water into the wind. They walked into a
stone arcade and around a corner out of sight. They were all
boys, pale and tall and silent, some with idiots' eyes. Others
looked gravely adult, with expressions too old for their faces.
A Devotee in a dusty black robe followed them.

"Nobles' sons," the Lady of Fortress said, rising to stand
near me. She was close enough I could smell the scent of
cloves and violets on her. Presently she said, "The third in
line is my son, Therin, Tanman's Heir."

"Ahhh," I said. A tall boy with pale hair and quick, alert,
even rebellious gestures of the head: looking about with none
of the dullness of the others. The Lady turned away. I said,
"May I see the boy at another time?"

I sounded more eager than she expected. She looked at me,
veil rustling.

I said, "I teach, Lady. That is part of Sati duties. It would
give me pleasure to teach the forms I learned from Reti. I did
not train anyone in Manoloki's camps. I would like to teach
your son. Perhaps I should ask Tanman?"

The Lady said, "No, until Therin is nine, you must ask
me. Tanman must permit you the time, but I must give the
permission . . . to teach my son." Her veil hung motionless
as if she did not even breath during some preoccupied
calculation.

I looked at her, wondering how she would decide. I would

like to teach again. I was good at it, once; and it offered a
future I understood. I discerned, by what I saw in the courtyard, that I didn't know the kind of boy lived in Tan. I had
taught combat to the eager, hungry desert boys who learned
to scuffle before they reached two years, not indolent Tannese
nobles. Remembering the look of those Tannese boys, I knew
there would be problems. But I was suddenly eager to begin
working. Perhaps it was the mua catching up my tired body.

The Lady of Fortress said, "I will consider that too. Cherto
will show you a room to rest for the afternoon. After that
ride, you'll enjoy the chance to rest and heal."

Oh well, I thought, and I followed Cherto out under a
tapestry. The servant women pattered down the corridor with
a ring of keys in her hand, gossiping. "Of course we have a
separated Household here, the Lady prefers a more regular
and structured schedule—for the children's sake—than is
possible for a Tanman." I listened carefully and said nothing.
When Cherto opened a door, I was certain it was the servant
woman's own room. The table beside the fur-heaped bed was
piled with necklaces and bottles and pomade jars. Over-
whelmingly the place smelled of Cherto's perfume, a heady,
musky hyacinth concoction. I covered my nose with part of
my hood and sneezed heartily.

Cherto laughed, lit a lamp with a flint spark-striker. She
reached up past me, opening an air vent with a wooden lever.
Before I could react to her close and heavily scented presence, she retreated, picked up a cushion, sat down on a
wooden box near the bed; I sneezed again. It made her laugh.
She pointed. "I have your harp if you'd like to play it. Pitar
sent it up while you were talking to the Lady."

I looked. My harpcase was thrown under a dark blue cloth
next to a pile of jewelry boxes. Are all Tannese cluttered? I
thought. I knelt down and pulled out the case, slid the harp
out to check on it.

She moved her foot. Her knee was not far from my shoulder. She reached out toward me. I sat back on my haunches
and eyed her. She murmured, "May I?" She fingered my
hair. Her hands were light, moth-delicate, on my braids. She
touched the tattoo on my forehead. She touched my cheek.
Her hand went down softly to my ear. When her hand went to
the robe loops at my shoulder, I drew back and got to my
feet. She lifted her head. I looked down into very shrewd

blue eyes. "Well," she said. "Do you keep all the old Sati laws—celibacy, the whole ruck?"

I turned away irritably, sat on her bed. I put the harp on my good thigh. "No. What song would you like to hear?"

She sighed. "Anything. It's a great honor up here, you know, to be serenaded by a Harper. Even if you do look like you're going to fall asleep."

I sighed. "Sleep!" But I lifted my hands and played a minor ballad. Her face grew dreamy. Perhaps that was as great a pleasure as any I could have offered her. As soon as I set the harp back in its case, she rushed over and pulled back the furs on the bed, spreading wafts of hyacinth musk everywhere. I blinked, and tamely lie down. I could hardly keep my eyes open. Perhaps the mua had been drugged. . . . I didn't think so, but I was so tired.

She fussed. "You can't lie down properly in full harness, can you? Well, all right. I'll open the vent for more air before I leave. I'll let you nap. . . ." And she went out, talking all the way. Her final murmurs faded, punctuated by the closing door.

I woke up at a noise much later, rolled groggy to my feet, scaddas in hand. I was alone. The door whispered barely open. A head hooded in black poked inside—a tall man in black Devotee robes.

"Identify yourself," I hissed from behind the door, holding scaddas hilt forward, ready. Two huge dogs shouldered their way inward, saw me, stiffened and growled. They would be tall as me if they rose on hind legs, an odd gray-coated breed like the Tannese war dogs.

"Have I fooled even you?" a familiar voice murmured, and the hood dropped back from his features. A nimbus of gold seemed to outline him, he was so bright in the oil lamp light. He closed the door quietly and set down his lamp, shifting the bulk of a folded black Devotee robe in his hand. He spoke a word to the dogs. They ceased growling and nosed at me with deep interest.

I sheathed my weapons with a grunt. I said, "Why the secrecy, Liege—"

He laid a finger on my mouth. "Drin," he corrected me, pressing my lower lip.

"Drin," I murmured. It was his boyhood nickname, from my people.

"I'm sneaking about because the women talk so much," Tanman said, looking like a boy on a wild escapade, not at all the dominating ruler. He sat down on a box, ruffling the dogs' ears, and grinned at me, looking me over. "For that matter, the men talk, too. You look better. The rest did you good." He smiled wickedly. "I've been checking rattraps."

I met his gaze. "So have you caught any—with me as bait?"

He laughed softly, a rich low laugh. "Yes." His smile didn't fit the Devotee religious robes at all. "We set up dummy chambers with your old clothes. A fine big catch we hauled in: some of Oldfield's higher-level bullies, some Cragmen drug-smuggling muscle, and a few curious fellows in veils and striped outrobes—perhaps you'd know them?"

I said, "If you mean those fools in the Hall the night I harped—no, I don't know those Nandos. I will get to know your rats . . . question them . . . if you wish."

Tanman lifted one brow, but it didn't darken his boyish good humor at all. He wrestled with one of the dogs. He said, "You're that fond of them? Indeed. Did you enjoy your stay with Cherti?"

"She tried to seduce me," I said in a bland tone.

"Tried?" Tanman said. "Unwise of her, the poor woman." He glanced around. "Well, the scent is a little overwhelming. Do you know when I started to believe your report on the Osa, Naga?"

"At Oathswearing this morning?" I said dryly.

"No, that was just to confirm—you know I had to test you in public. The story that you gave me, that cupflower drug trade information, leaked out by the first night you were here, and a certain Cragman named Oldfield was . . . ahh . . . livid."

I said, "Keth Adcrag seemed unhappy about me, too." I repeated his threats, using Keth's odd Cragman intonations; I repeated the Lady of Fortress's remarks in the same way. Tanman looked at me steadily, smiling.

"Well, then my lady wife keeps a close account, within her towers," he said. "So you've seen my son? You'll be meeting him. His flamed tutor just sent him up for insolence, poor child—hardly seems likely. Tutors! Therin will be going

out with us later; I haven't given any of the children enough
time of late. Bring your harp.'' He put up his hood, tossed
me the extra Devotee robe he had carried, and gestured for
me to wear it. I dared to put my hand on his arm when he
would have opened the door.

''Permit me,'' I murmured, and poked my head out. No
one. The dogs brushed past me, noses high. I gripped
Caladrunan's arm once and let go, and we both marched
smartly out into the corridor. There seemed to be no one
around.

As we walked, he murmured, ''I want to test some ideas
about messages leaking. We'll be at a strategy meeting, in an
area where eavesdropping is nearly impossible. If I bring you
along, and we discuss—dissect, really—important news, someone will almost certainly risk passing it along.''

I said, ''Military traitors?'' And I knew who I suspected.

''That's what I always did like about your brother,'' Tanman
said. ''He cut straight in. So do you.'' We passed through a
Devotee scroll room empty of people. He said, ''Do you
think the Head Armorer could put together a flamethrower to
study? You met him.''

I glanced up at him with hot dizziness crawling over my
flesh. Study—he'd innocently build *more* monsters, adding
more tragedy to the world. I took a deep breath. I knew as
well as he did that in Tan's military history those men trying
to stop the use of a new weapon often lost in the end, usually
to the very ones who adapted it for their own use. I said,
''With parts stolen from the Osa—yes, that's possible.'' The
face of the Head Armorer, affable and preoccupied with his
hordes of children, floated in my mind. Hardly the man one
expected to build such horrors.

''Is stealing such parts hard?''

I nodded. ''But not impossible. You want pressure gauges,
fuel needle-valves, air compression canisters and gears, I am
told. And the base of the gun tube with the mixing chamber
along with the flint-lock mechanism of ignition at the muzzle.''

''If you ever obtain the chance—'' Tanman gave me a
sudden shrewd look.

I said, ''I would steal such things in any case. Then the
Osa do not have them to flame people with.''

He looked at me steadily.

I squirmed a little in my leathers and admitted that there

was a cache of stolen parts in the desert; parts that Reti's men had taken over many years. Reti had cautioned us all that someday we might need to fight one tool with its own kind. He had also said that Tanman Caladrunan was trustworthy.

Tanman looked satisfied. He said, "It's sure to be a dangerous errand to fetch those here. Where's the closest loyal hold?"

"Lake Hold," I said blandly.

He gave me another look. "Down that way, near the Plains border, eh? Then we should take them to Lake Hold for study. Perhaps I'll have you select and organize the men to do that, and to clear it with Reti's other men. You'll be staying here, though. I've other jobs for you. My Lady wife was right, I've no time now to spare you for grandmothers who vanish, unless it's vital to your soul that you look." He frowned. Then he said casually, "You know your Histories. Not easy, learning those by sheer memory. Can you read and write? Many of Reti's men could, I know."

I squirmed some more at that. At last, with difficulty, I said, "Yes."

He gave me a look. "That bad, eh? I was afraid Manoloki was punishing native bloods for literacy. Some of our landholders have been. I've stopped it where I could."

I felt shamed blood flow up in my face. I don't know why it was so hard to yield such small personal secrets up. It wasn't as if I really thought him prejudiced, or a scourger of native scribes and scholars.

He said, "Why did you offer to train my son?"

I glanced up at the hooded face. "I'd like to see him practice. He was alert. He moved well, though he's so big. He could make a good trainee."

"Perhaps you should practice on some older ones before you train my son. You'll find some adjustments to us easier that way."

"Is your son a spoiled sort?"

Tanman laughed. "I like that courage of yours, Naga. I do like it. But let the boy grow up to the stage where your skill can do him some good. He's only eight."

I lifted my brows. I said flatly, "I was twelve when my clan died. You were fourteen and a Tanman."

Tanman put his hand to a door. "A different world, Naga. I don't know how you fared— I was a miserable little boy having to play king. Just tell my Heads of Military exactly what you told me at the first questioning, no more."

I inclined my head.

Tanman muttered, "Did Reti teach you to do that so negligently? So—elegantly?"

I smiled. "Reti would have hit me if I saluted him."

CHAPTER

= *9* =

TANMAN CLICKED HIS fingers and the dogs pressed around his legs. He gestured for me to listen with him at an elaborate stone carving on the end wall. Someone in the next chamber paced across gritty stones; I heard the leaders of Tan's Army talking. A deep and unfamiliar voice said, fisher-accented, "Tanman usually has good reasons for this kind of thing, Keth, you know that. You're restless as a child."

Keth's voice rasped, "Refitting is first priority. So he summoned us all and lets us sit waiting. He must have good reason, yes, certainly, Vishna— I merely pray we're not facing some new disaster!"

Strengam Dar's voice, like a whisper of dry reeds, murmured, "The city's been full of rumors since the execution of that door guard, Lumi. He was well-known—your insistence on execution may not have been wise, Keth. I also heard a fish-seller singing verses about Devotee stewards . . . something about nineteen barrels of royal wine disappearing."

"Stewards!" the deep fisher voice growled. "Taxmen, that's what they are. If my steward interrupts a conference of mine again, I'll break his pious Devotee back for him. I'm sure he listened to us at the last meeting we had. Spied on in my own flagship! I wonder if that's how our ambush on Seki's pirates was ruined. Someone passed news there."

Strengam's voice murmured, "How many did you lose, Vishna?"

"A hundred wounded. Sixty dead. On an island raid, of all things." The deep voice went flat and brooding.

I heard the gritty pacing again. Keth demanded, ''Do you have any proof that the steward—?''

''Of course not, or I'd have him in irons in my lowest bilge this moment,'' the fisher-tinged voice snapped.

Strengam Dar said, ''If half I hear is true, the present Elders are a menace to us all.''

At that point Tanman tapped a carved stone beast's nose, pushed an entire huge panel of carving aside on a gimbal, and walked noisily through the passage. The dogs surged ahead of him, parting the next chamber's tapestries; I stayed at Tanman's elbow. Tanman held away an elaborate silvered hanging, smiled into the chamber beyond. He said, ''Come, old friends, we'll talk elsewhere.''

The tapestry swung roughly aside, revealing the brightly lit room. Keth Adcrag came into the passage first, red hair ruffled by the tapestries; he stared up at Tanman. The dogs followed closely, eyeing the Cragman. ''You came out of nowhere, Liege— Vishna nearly threw his knife at your dogs.''

''Exactly.''

Keth swung around, and stepped back on seeing me. ''You! What are you doing here?''

Caladrunan said, ''Talk might be instructive. I hear that a Nando Leader-of-six-hundred is arriving soon—following directly on Naga's trail.'' The dogs nudged at Caladrunan's hands; he stroked their ears.

The other Heads of Military came through the passage, staring at me. The deep voice belonged to a tubby, muscular man who peered at me under a fringe of scruffy hair; Vishna turned and gave a hard nod to Tanman, and trotted away toward the chamber's outer door. Tanman said to me, ''Care for a fishing trip?''

We went down through the living cliff, chiseled landing after landing fading behind us in our torchlight, with the dogs scrambling eagerly ahead of us. Keth muttered about not having any of his escort soldiers, not even any of Tanman's men; no one answered Keth's grumbles, which lasted through more landings than I wished to count. We stepped blinking out of an iron-sheathed door.

I felt my head swing around in astonishment; Tanman smiled. Half the horizon was flat—utterly and mathematically flat: a span of color, blurred between slate and the gray of

Tannese fog, met the brilliant sky with such a *clang*! of
precision that I jumped. Then I realized men made that
clamor, and I pulled my eyes to nearer focus. Nevertheless, I
kept glancing at that absurd and unnatural line.

We stood on a harbor pier that jutted out of the shadowed
rock base of Fortress's cliff into sunlit water. The pier was of
fitted sandstone blocks; a large vessel moored at its end.
Green water slapped and sucked gently at the masonry; the
cool wind was numbingly wet on my cheek and reeked of wet
oak, pine tar, and an odd distinct tang like salted crayfish. It
made me hungry. The dogs nudged and pawed something
crawling across the pier toward the water.

Tanman stood pointing, naming and explaining what I
saw, while the others waited. The harbor lay within stone
embankments—arching jetties. Smaller floating walkways,
piers, divided the harbor, separating Tanman's stone pier
from busy traffic in other areas. The water constantly threw
up a glitter like a man in shiny scale armor, but flat. So flat! I
stared around fascinated. My questions made barrel-thick
Vishna laugh—while Keth narrowed his eyes at me. Bright
little chips of white, squares of dull dun and gray, Tanman
said were sailing ships slowly departing the mouth of the
harbor. Vishna added that most of them went out for deep
ocean fishing and he turned from me to the others, saying,
"Tide's passing. Time to go out, if you're going."

"Tide?" I asked Tanman.

"You're pitiful," he said, and smiled. We strode down the
pier to Tanman's vessel. The boat at the pierhead was ten
times a man's length, twice in width, painted black and
white, with one tall mast bearing a sword-marked banderole
and a raked boom. It was crewed by twenty men sitting at
oars amidships—they all shouted and waved when they saw
Tanman coming. The dogs ran up the gangway first, running
about checking on things, nosing at gear and men. When
Tanman himself boarded, he greeted the captain with a great
loud roar.

"Liege," the captain said, saluting Tanman in the mock-
ing, smiling way that Sek-bloods have. The captain was a
dapper narrow-faced man with the battered look of an ex-
pirate; I had seen such before, among the Nandos. He bore a
long sword scar on his skull, down his cheekbone, trailing off
near his mouth. His eyes assessed me coolly as I stepped in;

he could see how my bull-cut leg hampered me. To Vishna he said casually, "Good shrimp yield on the shoals. Three nets a ship last night, I heard."

The dogs returned to Tanman and sat at his feet, watching Keth and me. They openly disliked Keth; I, apparently, was still too much a stranger to trust, though they were perfectly at ease with the Sek-blood captain and the sailors. That level canine gaze was not lost on Keth, either. Keth Adcrag said abruptly, "Aren't you going to greet your brethren, Captain?"

Both the Sek-blood and I stiffened. No native blood liked to be so slurred together by an outsider. The Sek bowed a little to Keth, deeper by a faint degree to me. The Sek said easily to me, "Brethren? Hardly. Pardon, noble-born, but my mother would put to death a babe with features such as yours." One finger flicked out to gesture at my face.

I said politely, "Then how did she dare put teat in mouth beneath that witch's plow you call your nose?"

I saw Tanman smile, and Strengam Dar.

The Sek-blood captain grinned widely. "Few try me in the game of insult."

I smiled a little myself. "It is well-regarded in the desert, as a sport of children."

"As host, I accept polite defeat. You will taste it at next meeting."

"I always honor the challenges of weak opponents."

"A low blow, Sati. Since such a lubber as yourself will soon get sick, I will have to teach you manners at another time." And he sauntered off, smiling, toward what Tanman called a cabin amidships. We trooped after him down the narrow plank between the rowers, with the dogs threading in and out around us. Vishna threw rude greetings to the crew. All the metal fittings shone brassy bright, but there were oddments, steps, and ropes to thump the unwary.

The cabin was built of thick timbers and shining oak paneling nearly black in color. The captain said, "The riggers finished three days ago, an easy local tour should break her in nicely. We will have the cabin repaneled after your next raid, Liege."

Tanman chuckled. He fingered a particularly deep scar on the black oak. "That red-haired one, he fought pretty hard."

Vishna grunted. "Fool boy's stunt. They could've taken the ship, and you."

The dogs flopped down, panting, at Tanman's feet. The Sek
captain set a stack of slates on the cabin table, then five gold
goblets, and closed the door as he left us. A drum beat began
outside, and the splash and creaking of oars. The deck surged
under my feet; I leaned. Keth Adcrag fell on one of the
benches in a clatter of jade ornaments, rather faster than he'd
meant to. He pointed at me, growling, "He could betray us
all. He betrayed Manoloki. Just a flamed refugee like all the
rest."

Vishna snorted. None of the other military men bothered. I
said, "I swore no brotherhood oath to him. They assumed I
had." Strengam Dar merely picked up a slate and began to
write. Over his arm I saw glyphs of holds there—border holds
which had fallen. Strengam passed it to Vishna, and then to
Keth. Both men frowned. Vishna said to me, "Tell us how
that was done. Those holds didn't fall to any usual methods. They're all too different."

Tanman gave a small nod. I told them: Osa flamethrowers.
I described exactly what I was talking about, down to how
much time I estimated Tan had to arm and build before
irreversible Osa advances forced them into desperate measures.

Keth said flatly, "Fantasy."

Vishna stirred, glancing at Keth, but said nothing.

Tanman made an Upai fingersign my brother had taught
him, which pleased me. I reported what I knew about the
manufacture of the weapons.

Strengam murmured, "How strange a combination, bitter
desert earths and southern oil, to make fire that does not
extinguish with water— I wonder how difficult building flamethrowers might be."

I stifled the thought before it reached my lips: given the
crucial parts, any man skilled in wood and metal—certainly
such master craftsmen as the Head Armorer—could build
such a thing. All they needed was to learn the trick of its fire.

Vishna frowned. He said slowly, "The pirate Seki has
been trafficking heavily in southern oil trade lately. We've
found barrels jettisoned after hard chases. Seki brings the oil
into the Crag coast somewhere, Crag smugglers take it east
across Tan, sometimes by sea, to the ports off Marsh, where
we get a few more reports of sea jettisons. Then we never see
the stuff again. I'm certain it goes north in empty furships
into the Marsh swamps, perhaps as far as the highlands. Up north

with oil, south with furs in winter, dried fish in summer. It'd have to go back west across the highlands to reach these Osa you tell about."

Keth snapped, "Crag oil smugglers—not in my mountains. That would be Oldfield, he's the only one stupid enough."

Ah, would it be? I wondered. Keth seemed a little too angry, to me. I glanced at Tanman, who gave that odd placid smile.

Vishna cleared his throat, saying, "We've thrashed up and down Oldfield for years, never got anywhere with him. I want to know more about those Nandos you were talking about—highlands of Marsh are crawling with them, so I hear."

At a gesture from Tanman, I reported on Manoloki's dual involvement in drug trade and in supplying troops to the Osa, many of them half-trained Marshmen. On impulse, I asked, "Does Oldfield hire any mercenaries?"

Vishna growled, "Certainly. Oldfield keeps his own troops close to home. All his official levees, at least in my forces, are Nandos paid to take the place of clan men—nobody knows much about which sort of Nandos, though. Now we've learned there's different versions we might pay more attention." He glared at Keth.

Strengam murmured, "There are questions as to how Oldfield can afford it."

I glanced at the other men. "Are these Nando troops good?"

Keth laughed, a sharp noise like one of the dogs. A dog lifted its head and looked at Keth. "*I* expect Nandos to run away from a skirmish at the first chance. Who cares what sort—they all run."

Strengam sighed. "One of the certainties of my command."

Tanman murmured, "I am told that a Nando commander will ask for formal audience soon—a Leader-of-six-hundred, at minimum. It may be Manoloki himself."

Silence. I felt my heart beating in my throat, faster than the oar beat thrumming through the deck. Then Strengam Dar said grimly, "That one will bring assassin-Nandos. They won't be anything like the disgusting levees we get."

I agreed. "Manoloki has a crack guard."

Keth said sourly, "Oh? Good in whose terms? Yours?"

Tanman said quietly, "I put him under Devour. He has passed that test."

Keth glared.

Vishna looked surprised. "I thought commoners weren't allowed that kind of test—"

Keth rasped, "Not this one! He styles himself House Teot."

I gave Keth Adcrag a long, level look.

Vishna rumbled on. "A house? You?" He lifted sun-bleached brows. "I suppose anything's possible. A Upai noble House—I'd never thought of that."

I glanced at Tanman, and got a faint nod. I said, "Clan Teot was the Imperial line of the Upai before our empire was destroyed by the Osa, and we were driven into exile. My House is yet the ruler of Upai. I have the authority, on my name, to whistle up every Upai from the Po desert's farthest ranges to the refugee camps here in Tan. I can command desert Upai who know the old traveling wells protected for years from Manoloki's knowledge."

There was a long moment of silence. Then Keth Adcrag said abruptly, "Half the beggars in the streets make claims as high-flown as that. Why haven't you used this signal of yours before? You didn't tell us why you became Nando, either."

I felt my hands stir, my thighs aware of my scaddas: he had no right to ask why I became Nando. Tanman shook his head at me once. I set my hands tightly on my knees. "To waste my people would be stupid. When the time comes, I call in my Upai. I became a Nando when the Osa killed the rest of my clan."

Strengam fingered his mustache. "Might there be any other survivors of your House?"

I lowered my head slightly in respect to him. "There might. I still have rank and a certain authority . . . on my own name . . . in that case."

Tanman said, "I believe Manoloki is pursuing my Sati as a 'renegade Nando.' His officers, according to my reports, let Naga slip through; they never knew he was Upai, as well as Reti's pupil, until it was too late. He's on Nando records as a bastard of a dead Tannese noble, off a Marsh woman. The reports noted an impenetrable Marsh accent, no education, and a bad fourpeg habit."

Strengam Dar smiled, his eyes glancing toward the Sati

scars on my wrists. "I see. The Osa battles now. Is Manoloki closely involved in all—"

Tanman gestured with a flicker of thumb over fingers that I was to explain all.

I said, "Manoloki got the Osa to fight in *his* battles, not just their own. He trained his own men, secretly, to operate stolen flamethrowers. He was the first to think of using the Osa weapons against the Osa themselves. He finds the Osa yoke irritating. In anyone's hearing he calls them stupid, and a lot of Nando officers agree. The Osa tend toward settling into fixed positions with catapults, flamethrowers, entrenchments, that kind of thing. They're stretched on a long supply line over the worst mountains and the most difficult wasteland and alkali zones of the Po desert. They have few foot troops without Manoloki's raw recruits, and really disciplined Osa officers are rare— the Osa send their worst men to frontiers, to get rid of them. Their top officers seem to be busy somewhere else, perhaps politicking at home. Their best young officers use that incredible flamethrower mobility, but because of supply problems, they are constantly reprimanded for moving too fast. So the Osa command on your border counts on the machines to equalize troop differences in a creeping war of attrition against Tan. A war on civilians and grainfields."

Strengam Dar said, "Obviously, Manoloki has bigger ideas. He wants a short, big war, decisive in every way, does he not?"

I nodded.

Keth snorted. "His impatience is famous."

Tanman said then, softly, "What do you think of the Osa, Naga?"

I fingered the harpcase on my harness, not looking at the Heads of Military. After a moment I said, "Manoloki belittles the Osa too much. If *I* were the Osa commander, I'd use Manoloki's ambitions against him. I'd let him do all the fighting, then I'd invite him to destroy my other allies as I no longer needed them. Then, only, I'd smash him. The Osa always destroy or conquer allies; they believe in one ruler and one nation only. Were I Osa, I'd only fight Manoloki himself once he was depleted and hungry. And it seems to me that is exactly what the Osa have been doing." I paused, thinking. "Manoloki may think he can turn on the Osa and win. He always showed contempt for his opponent, even in his tactical treatises.''

Keth barked, ''So you're fit to judge Manoloki on tactics?''

I met Keth's eyes. We all knew that Manoloki wrote two of the master treatises on tactics used in all the siege and offense classes of traditional Tannese training—before he became a Nando for his crimes. I said, ''Who better? I've survived Osa fire. Manoloki hasn't. He's been held far in front of Osa lines, acting as their point guard—which partly explains the slowness of their advances. They don't intend him to learn any more about their weapons than they can prevent.''

Keth said, ''You boast. You imply that this Leader— Manoloki perhaps—is coming to Tan to kill you or take you back.''

I stared at the change of subject.

Vishna said dryly, ''Look at that slate, Keth, it wouldn't be so unreasonable. The Sati has already hurt Manoloki sharply with this report. And he'll feel it more when the Sati understands Tannese methods and knows how to work better with us. Personally, I don't expect any Nando is coming to pay off his damned debts.''

Tanman said flatly, ''They already tried once to assassinate Naga. Right in my own Hall.''

''No. To get you, Liege, while you were short of guards,'' I snapped. I was irritated. ''They were inept and slow. Roji assassins—the Marsh secret society. Not too well practiced of late, either. One of them was slow with a classic Roji fighting spur ankle-sweep.''

Strengam Dar said, ''Roji is rather an obscure style.''

I said, ''The way they present their knife wrist is characteristic. One of my training Hand had been a junior Roji.''

Strengam Dar lifted one brow. ''How do you compare to a Roji?''

I shrugged. ''I was better than the junior Roji was, if that's what you ask. I am consistently faster than their average recruits, that's all. If I had the size of your Tannese, I would be a truly formidable fighter.''

I saw eyes meeting around the circle. Strengam Dar said, ''How formidable are you, Sati?''

I said dryly, ''I won Manoloki's competition for the posting here. At higher levels of combat it becomes strategy—

tactics on the field particularly. And theoretical measurement there is impossible."

Keth said, "It's possible to try!"

I watched Keth's face. I said, "As a measure of personal skill, I could offer scadda challenge to Manoloki's sword. On the basis of his entanglement in Osa blood-debt for my people, it is justified any time I choose to issue challenge."

Keth snorted. "He was the finest swordsman of his day."

I laughed softly, shaking my head. "A gamble, yes. But he's also twenty years older than I, and he has a potbelly on him as big as I am. I'd do it just to see the look on his face!"

Tanman glanced obliquely at Keth and said, "I have more valuable things for you to do, Sati. Manoloki would have an arrow set in your back at a formal challenge. He has allies at court."

Strengam Dar leaned back and said quietly, "The simplest way to keep Manoloki away is to set a tax hearing on Nando land permits. Since the Pass of Bones debt is so far overdue, penalties would—"

Tanman smiled, and I understood that their sparring with me had been idle practice while they turned over ideas about how to treat Manoloki. Tanman said, "With a hard twist on the Council's tail, I could revoke his Tannese land permits. When he hears of penalties and debtor's prison, he'll stay away and send some minor officer in his place to rot for him."

Vishna growled, "Keep him out of Fortress and away from all our improvements, anyway. Don't care how many spies he's got, I don't want him looking at it himself."

Strengam Dar smiled, and Keth gave a fierce reddish scowl, and then they all burst into roars of laughter. Vishna said, "He'll gnash his teeth at that! Nobody has gotten to touch those land permits for years."

Tanman said calmly, "He did it to himself." Then he turned to me and began asking questions directly. I told them details: this pass taken, that outpost, the number of merchant caravans on particular roads, what they carried; the most successful attack methods against the Osa. I told them about pits, stake-trenches, rock-ambushes, tread-ripper wrenches, and the heavy oversized bows and metal-shod arrows that the desert men tried to use to pierce flamethrower armor, when they could get them. There was so much to say that we all had to drink hoarseness away before the talking was done. Tanman gave no orders; he hinted to me what information he wanted the generals to consider, that was all. All the men looked thoughtful by the end of it.

Keth said at last, "This rolling about on your ship is most uncomfortable, Liege. May I use a dory to get back to shore—much to get done—"

Vishna vented a roar of a laugh. "Seasick already, eh, Keth?"

Caladrunan gave the Head of Navy a stern look, and gave all except me leave to depart. "Seasick?" I asked puzzled. Tanman grinned.

Tanman and I stood at the cabin door, dogs standing between us and talking quietly, while two small boats were lowered from davits amidships. All the time we talked, we had been going around the arc of the harbor, not into the flat horizon beyond. Caladrunan carefully told me the names of gear as they used each piece. Six burly crewmen manned each dory; archers dropped into the dory sculling behind Keth's transport, to guard Keth. Tanman took no chances with losing his cavalry general.

Strengam Dar and Vishna waited at the rail together for the return of the two boats; I wondered if Strengam disliked traveling in Keth's company, for he could have gone. He and Vishna paced up and down the foredeck talking. From my place by the cabin door, I heard clearly snatches of their conversation over the creak of the ship and the voices of the sailors working.

Strengam said, ". . . I've dealt with desert men before."

Vishna told Strengam, "Ai, and some pirates are pretty good captains, too, if they'd only cease robbing honest men. It's like having a First Captain running wild, letting that runt live."

"Yes, well, he doesn't fit into anyone's organization. Possibly he'd do among my scouts. Possibly." Tall and thin, Strengam squinted off at the horizon.

Vishna spat, a boy wiped the railing. "I could use a cook with talent, not a bone-bottom refugee with no manners and the temper—so I hear—of a child murderer. I've no use for him. Maybe you do, you're a landgrubber."

Strengam Dar clicked his tongue reproachfully. "You know he isn't the one leaking information now."

Vishna said stubbornly, "No, but he could start doing it. Liege played him like a fishing smack on a lee shore during the whole briefing today. Tack and go about and never a blink from either of them to show that damned Cragman what was going on. I tell you, that Sati is a bucket of eels. And I don't like the way he looks at the back of my head for a sucker-hit when I walk past him. That isn't Tannese, that isn't. We're supposed to be fighting the same war—desert bastard. He doesn't fit and he's dangerous. I don't care if he did swear something or other on his granny's milk. His kind have no fear. And no discipline."

Strengam Dar's voice grew very dry. "In my experience discipline is something we have to impose on most men from above. Liege may work him differently than other officers. Detached duty, an aide, advisor . . ."

"Indeed," Vishna said. "You've seen him looking."

Strengam paced for a time. Over the sanding and pumping crews, I heard nothing. He said at last, "There could be advantages to that."

Vishna snorted. "I'd send him out on lots of raids."

"I doubt that will happen—Tanman spoke of easing Pitar's extra duties onto someone else. Pitar's wife . . . poor man, he just sits holding her hand."

I turned and said quietly to Tanman, "I'll have to show the Armorer how to build heliographs. A net of those would warn us sooner of enemy movement. Have you thought of buying up the desert ganas in the market here?"

"No, too bad-tempered. Nasty herd-mind—if they stampede they take all the stock in the area with them. We've bred it out of our lines. Bad, if they carry a whole cavalry division with them. Keth loathes the ugly monsters." Caladrunan studied me briefly and called Strengam and Vishnu. "Tell them why we should buy desert ganas."

I folded my arms, looking into the sea beyond Tanman's shoulder. But peripherally I noticed sparks of interest lit in their eyes. Vishna said, "Do you know something we don't?"

I rocked back and forth on the balls of my feet, balancing on the heaving deck. Then I ticked off points on my fingers. "They're stronger for their size than your Tannese beasts. More drought resistant, used to rougher forage and a lot more insects. Reti had a use for that nasty herd-mind." I rocked a little more, smiling at the sea. "During my competition for that fake position, I overheard a report about Manoloki's main encampment. He keeps his gana lines with a very few handlers, completely separated from both his riders and his infantry. Less chance of theft and desertions, until right before battle. Do you know what a gana stampede of size is like, running over a poorly organized camp? Thousands of horns clicking, and sparks flying, and dust . . ." I rocked a little more, eyes half-shut.

"You're suggesting we drive a wedge of desert beasts into Manoloki's lines and take all his mounts away with us," Tanman said.

"And you don't need many riders for it."

Vishna was silent, shoulders hunched. Slowly he began pacing back and forth beside our group. Strengam stroked his chin, eyes bright. "Amusing thought, isn't it?" Strengam said, with delight in his tone. Vishna pursed his lips, eyes blank as he thought.

I said, "Reti learned to direct a herd-mind out of necessity, all of our beasts were desert bred. Manoloki's men never did understand why their beasts turned on them and ran with us. Of course, we never left anything behind to explain it to their officers. Vanished into the desert, lost to a man, poor souls." I was smiling still.

Strengam murmured, "And so inexpensive . . ."

"Keep them penned awhile, feed them up, train them with some of your Upai refugees who can ride," Vishna suggested brusquely.

Tanman began to grin. "How few riders would we need?"

"Only a squad or two each, on the point and leading flanks. The beasts there direct the flow of the herd, have the largest effect on its speed. Of course terrain is important, too; they won't charge a hill. If your riders fall . . . It's dangerous work, riding point in a stampede."

Strengam said, "You know some fellows who'd like that kind of work, Vishna? After all, Keth won't want to send out his Crag cavalry for this."

Vishna snorted.

I smiled. "Why should we tell Keth about it? Let me send off word to the border— Reti's men would come, to the right message from you, Liege."

Vishna slapped his thigh.

Strengam said, "There're more like you?"

I blinked. "Of course. I was one of the younger ones. Some of them thought I was too civilized—learning harp— but they forgave me when I came up with ideas from my History training. One of the old men was an expert on ambushing flamethrowers. He was in hiding like the others, if he's still alive . . . I forgot to mention contacting Reti's men while Keth was here."

They exchanged glances. They all, slowly, began to grin. Tanman said, "Suppose I have you send off word for Reti's old officers to come here. Tan might make a good place for a company of Reti's expatriated officers."

I frowned. "Send them to your gana training site along with Upai scouts I'll send word to. Reti's men wouldn't like it up in Fortress—too many assassin-crannies, bad memories about rockpiles like these—too many people they wouldn't tolerate. Reti's men kill when they're nervous."

Vishna grunted. "Strengam and I can start working on the site. Better they work under my nose, away from Keth and Oldfield and that lot."

Strengam said, "My clan owns a stretch of land by the Tejed River fords that might do perfectly—that place where you drill your marines for island work, Vishna. Keeping a reliable force there might be an excellent defense idea anyway, with Crag rebellion tensions risen so high. We could also recruit refugee men and boys, breeding wouldn't matter."

Vishna said, "I've some old marine friends up here in port, too old to fight, but they might be willing to come back, train some youngsters. Reti's men work the beasts. You've got some good trainers, too, don't you, Strengam?"

Tanman said, "Nothing official or noticeable yet. All very casual, very innocent. Strengam generously gives land to a refugee camp, where Vishna's marines drill, while any trained refugee men are allowed to eat, practice their old skills and keep fit. . . . I'll send down squads of officers I trust, to learn about disabling flamethrowers and climbing desert cliffs and scouting—I understand it's very different from our wheatfield maneuvers." He smiled at me then. "And if the time for official attention comes, then a certain Sati will be commanding those irregular troops in the manner he sees fit, whether it's traditional or not, under my personal name. With the help of your advice, both of you, Strengam and Vishna, but casually. That way both of you can swear you knew nothing about it, if clan politics get messy. I'll have to take care of funding.''

Strengam lifted his brows. ''Will they be listed as your personal guards?''

Tanman smiled. ''Let's say, my personal task force.''

All our heads jerked up at the grate of wood rasping on wood; the dories had returned. A seaman was swearing about paintwork.

''Here's our boat,'' Vishna said. Tanman waved dismissal, smiling, and all three men chuckled. Strengam and Vishna moved off, talking. As the two dories rowed away, Tanman turned from watching our main oar banks at work. He waved and said to the Sek-blood captain, ''Take us on out, Leo, we won't need the dories today. Work's over for now.''

CHAPTER

= *10* =

THE OARS CREAKED faster to the drum. We drew out of the headlands of the sprawling harbor, past the scrawny pines and oak that marked land's end. The deck rose and fell sharply under the open swells. I braced my feet. The dogs at Tanman's side swayed in place. Sailors pattered back and forth past us, ropes swung from hand to hand. A sail billowed up the mast, a huge expanse of blue in the sun, with a sword of white upon its center; the ship creaked as the sail swelled taut. The fresh cold air flowed over my skin wet as oil. I peered overside at the water, fascinated. We were racing along now, oars inboard, at a speed surpassing any land methods. Tanman turned about, looking up. Then he looked at me. "I had this boat built when I was twenty. Isn't she beautiful?"

I glanced about. Beauty in boats I couldn't judge. At last I ventured, "It's orderly, Liege."

He smiled. Men pattered in and out of the cabin, changing everything around, taking chairs belowdecks and bringing up a folded bed, hanging tapestries, straw mats, and gauze curtains that smelled salty. Tanman gestured absently for me to sit down on the bed as he turned to the Sek-blood captain. "Leo, I'll see my son now."

"I'll go now before your son comes up—" I stood up.

He gripped my shoulder and thumped me back down on the bed. "You're staying here! I don't want you running about anymore on that cut leg, you're looking gray. Besides, you're to observe my son, you're a prospective tutor. You can tell me what you think once you've seen him. Get up there, pull

119

the curtains shut. I don't want to frighten him by calling you
in later, rank titles and all. He's nervy enough, sent up for
insolence and all that nonsense, he'd be scared silly of a Sati.
I'll tell you when I want you to show yourself."

I said doubtfully, "It will startle him, finding me here.
Should I let him hear me, before he sees me?"

Tanman beamed. "I knew you'd understand. Now remember—even if I'm busy and I don't catch you at it, no
running and straining this leg my bull cut up—and no tearing
blisters. I don't think I could stand to see you nursed through
more nights like the last few."

I nodded. He could stand it, we both knew that; whether I
could withstand another bout of cupflower drugging was another matter. I made a face and drew back into the cabin
shadows cloaking the bed.

Tanman's Heir was announced both by Leo and a shuffling
scuff of boots scraping the decking outside: eloquent reluc-
tance dragged at every step. It seemed the delight of a journey
was not enough to dilute the specter of punishment from the
boy's mind. "Liege—Father?" A thin voice, reedy with nerves.

Therin at eight summers was nothing like his expansive
father. I lay watching from within the bed curtains, wondering why the Devotee tutor had sent the boy to his father for
insolence. Insolence! The boy's bright yellow hair was the
only unruly part of him. He didn't look sly, or a rebel—not as
I had been at the same age. He looked like an active, burly-
boned boy anxious to please; I saw touches of clumsiness that
proper training would have smoothed away by now. "What is
this about yelling at tutors?" Tanman rumbled.

As Tanman interviewed his son waves of whitish green
washed through the boy's cheeks; freckles stood out appall-
ingly plain, blots like dust on his skin. "Yes, Liege, then
he—then Karidi told me he'd beat me, but he wrote on that
slate across what I wrote, and he—he sent me up to your
guards—" The boy clenched his hands into his robes over his
stomach.

I moved a little on the rumpled bed furs, watching intently.
Someone, I thought with growing concern, has tried to ruin
this child for any useful life. Made him into material for a
cowering puppet-ruler, punished him for very slight rebel-
lions. I hunched my shoulders. At the same age I would have
bit that stupid tutor's leg for the trespasses the boy innocently

reported. Certainly he had not been handled respectfully as Heir, with greater needs and duties than most boys. Pious Devotee ruination—and his lady mother's obviously preoccupied, sometime-affection. It was getting late in the child's history for Caladrunan's gruff, sympathetic rumbles to repair the damage and overcome the fear. "You don't look so well," Caladrunan said, frowning. "A touch of sea wobbles?"

I watched silently as the boy clutched his mouth, fled for the slushpot next to the bed, and vomited. I could see his hands shake as he tugged frantically to straighten his robes afterward. "You'll feel better soon," Tanman murmured.

Therin coughed and mumbled. While the boy's back was turned, I parted the bed curtain and looked steadily at Tanman. He cocked one brow questioning. I pointed at the boy, then myself. It was fear made Therin sick. His present tutor would be his death by sheer incompetence—when the boy was a man grown, when the damage could not be undone. Tanman considered my gesture, brows lifting. I let the curtain fall silently in place as the boy began to recover. Therin didn't even glance toward me. While I watched the boy's wretched face—trying hard to look normal and failing utterly—I felt another flare of rage at the Devotee tutor. Karidi, I thought. I will remember this man's name too.

Caladrunan sighed, gazing at his pale son. "Well, it's sure to be chaos for the rest of the day if Karidi lost his temper with you boys so early. When did he leave you to copying out slates this morning, the lot of you? Any assistants—no? What, no one?"

"First bell," Tanman's Heir whispered, "they all left." His chin was somewhere down in the folds on his belly.

Caladrunan cocked one brow. "Early indeed—and his assistants too. Time old Karidi was retired and given something harmless to do." He turned his attention toward me. "Naga, would you give him some decent tutoring today, some Histories?"

I said, in my mildest, laziest voice, "Yes." And I yawned.

The boy whirled about and stumbled as the deck heaved under him. I said softly, "Liege, I think he's too upset, or too ill, to think about Histories."

Slowly, cautiously as a redbuck testing unsure ground, Therin approached his father's curtained bed, and me. I parted the gauze and looked back at him, and we measured one another. "Are you sick?" I asked mildly.

He shook his head violently, which was a mistake. His fingers briefly clutched his middle; then he got it controlled. Huge agate-green eyes rose in some mute appeal to mine. The spark of courage in the boy's eyes struggled with the shriek of *Alien! Alien!* Too many times lately I'd seen it in Tannese eyes—I didn't like the fear either, which fought so strongly with his courage. Tanman's Heir should not cringe.

Perhaps the boy read the anger fueling inside me, and mistook its direction. I was not angry with him; he was just a child. But he read anger, and he stepped hastily back into a surge of the deck, flailing, and bumped the bedside table where my scaddas lay. The blades slid out part-way.

I gripped his wrist before he accidentally cut himself on the bare scadda blades there. I held him safely isolated through his reflexive jerk. Finally he stood still, breathing hard, aware I was not moving. Slowly, gently, I drew him forward to sit on the bed near me, and I released his arm.

The boy darted a nervous glance at his father. Caladrunan murmured an order. I reached across the table, lifted a wine decanter slung in a net at the table's edge, poured a goblet full. I sipped the wine just as I would for the boy's father. While I rolled the wine in my mouth for off tastes, I looked at the deck mats rumpled by Therin's struggles and considered training schedules. I also allowed Therin to take a longer look at me. Among the Nandos I learned that Tannese required a long stare their first look at a Upai, and it was no use going on until they'd got it. When I was satisfied with the safety of the wine, I put the goblet in the boy's hand.

He gulped at it like water. I watched in resignation as he choked. Not, I thought, very experienced. Just as well; at least they hadn't tried to ruin him that way.

Caladrunan shifted where he sat at his worktable, and looked up from slatework. "What did you say Gerin's strength was at Keddorin?" He frowned in concentration. Therin had already been consigned to capable hands and forgotten.

I consulted with myself. "Fifty archers," I said, and yawned. I felt sleepy. Therin stared into my mouth. I explained my teeth were gold-drilled where faulted, in the Sharinen manner Reti had insisted maintained their health. "Perhaps First History might suit you, Heir."

The boy's eyes brightened as I began reciting. Therin began to relax when he saw I would not be like Karidi; which

only deepened my fury against the Devotee's poor handling.
He asked questions, timidly at first. The curiosity was a
reassuring character trait to plumb in an otherwise anonymous
little boy. If I freed all the banked fire and vigor of a
Caladrunan in his son, he would make a Tanman indeed. All
the startling and strict sense of fairness those questions revealed, this was not a quality one expected of a mishandled
eight-year-old. I wondered, had Capilla, Lady of Fortress,
never noticed the damage done her son—or had she shown
me her son, precisely to extract him from Karidi's grip. She
would shrug off a change of tutors as Tanman's inexplicable
whim, I was certain of that. Then I wondered mordantly
which noble she had placated by giving her son to Karidi.
Tanman had apparently trusted her with the choice; perhaps
he'd had little choice, too. I thought of the town-choked
undefended Fortress walls, and something in me tightened
again.

I soon had to use the slushpot at one cabin wall, revealing
my sores and crippling stiffness. I tried to move unobtrusively,
using the bedposts to help me. I thought unhappily, if you can
stand to swear an Oath before the entire nobility of Tan, you
can stand this, my fine Sati.

I felt thoroughly ridiculous when Tanman strode in from a
meeting with Leo and scolded me about bandages. He bent
down and examined my thigh with his hands, poking at the
wrappings; he told his son how I'd hurt myself—while I
squirmed mentally in embarrassment. He clucked over the
riding sores when they bled. The boy stared at me, with those
large green eyes; they seemed rather steadier than I might
have liked at that moment. I changed the subject hastily to
Therin's progress in training.

As I'd hoped, Caladrunan sat down on the bed and relaxed,
stretching out his legs. I could venture to make a few jokes
while I gave my judgment of Therin's progress—sometimes in
Tannese, but breaking for privacy into the Upai that Caladrunan
had learned from my brother at Redspring Hold. He seemed
to remember some of it, enough to gratify me.

Therin listened alertly, eyes shifting between us. He understood my Tannese quips. I thought, I'll have to be quick to
stay ahead of this one.

Near midday the Sek-blood captain brought food. We moved
out to the shade side of the cabin, what there was, and sat

down on the deck like the rest of the sailors. The dogs panted, begging food discreetly of Tanman. I tasted his food first, steaming fish and spiced mua and fresh chopped fruit, while Tanman joked with his son about getting the bottom of the bowls all his life. Therin frankly gorged; I wasn't much better. I ate all my food and on his insistence, half of Tanman's—I didn't object very much when he thrust one bowl after another at me. Tanman would point and name a piece of ship's gear, or a sailor's task, quizzing both Therin and myself while we grunted understanding with our mouths full. He also greeted passing sailors by name, asking about their kin and talking about past raids. It was amazing how it made their faces light up. He was nothing if not a politician of the people.

Caladrunan yawned at last and retired to the bed in the cabin, dogs at his feet, sending his son off to a small bunk below. I sat at Tanman's open cabin door, one scadda scabbard across my knee, watchful; the words I heard had new and alien meanings, so I learned most about the ship by watching how things were done. That odd flat line was three-quarters of the horizon now, rocking up and down past the slender brass rail that rimmed the deck. "Rouse, you luffing bastards, rouse!" the first mate roared.

In the middle of the afternoon, Tanman sighed and rolled over. He rubbed his eyes. "Let's go swimming."

I grunted and stood up. "Where?"

"In the water, Dance of Knives," he said, smiling, and stretched. He came out on deck."

I stared at him. "But it's got no land under it, Liege."

He grinned, whacking me lightly on the arm. "Can't you swim?"

I blinked. "In rivers, yes."

"Goddess! You fool, rivers are dangerous. Look at those rollers—those are nothing." The deck sank under my feet and rose gently. He laughed. "Come, I'll show you." He ripped his robes off carelessly, threw them into the cabin, strode to the rail. And jumped over. The dogs barked wildly after him.

I hurried to the rail and looked over, mouth open. A bright golden head bobbed in the green water. He flung hair out of his eyes in a spray of water, beckoning, and laughed. The Sek-blood captain said, "You shed your robes first, Sati."

I glared at him. The dogs barked. I threw my weaponbelt

across the deck into the cabin, and my harpcase. I kicked off boots, wrenched off robes, and did a somersault over the rail. But I couldn't figure out how I was supposed to hit the water: I waded or rode into river fords, never jumped. I landed on my bottom, feet kicked up over my head—and got quite a shock. In the depth of hot season, the ocean hit me with a wall of chill. It didn't taste like water. My mouth filled up and salt clawed at my sores and eyes. The disturbed surface far above me shimmered like a desert mercury pool. I thrashed and clawed upward until the water went foamy around me; I choked on all the salt. I popped out on the lee side of a roller, in the midst of seaweed. Weed flapped about my head like a net. I sputtered and spit out water and started swearing. My legs milled as if I was running. The next roller lifted me up and dropped me.

Tanman swam over in two lazy strokes of his arms and grasped the seaweed, parting it. I kicked out of it; a spillet of foam smacked my face. I coughed helplessly. His hand grasped my arm, held me up. For a moment our eyes met. Here, he had me untrained as a babe; there was no one between us, no one to stop him drowning me. No one could protect him from me, either; just the two of us, under the glaring sun. "Do you want to learn to swim?" he asked calmly, sculling his free hand through the water.

I coughed, lashed some seaweed impatiently aside, and he grinned. "You're learning." The bandages for my sores began to unwind in long tangles. Raw flesh shrieked and congealed in the chill. "Lie back," he commanded, putting a firm hand under my back, and taught me how to float in the swells. At last we floated together, bobbing in the water and grinning like idiots at the hazy blue sky. Foamy water slapped and washed my face; I floated heavily, and mostly I had to strain my head up to get a breath. "Not enough fat," he said authoritatively, tapping my chest.

I trusted him to help me before I really needed it, as he was an excellent swimmer. By the time I had learned enough, adapted enough from river fording, to get about, my body was growing clumsy in the thick cold water. Caladrunan swam to the side of the ship and shouted. They dropped a line. He timed the roll of the ship, leaped up clear of the crusts of weed and barnacles, and went up the rope hand over hand up the side of the ship, long thin legs stilting along like a wooden child's toy. I understood now that Caladrunan greatly trusted the Sek-blood captain—a trust that must be earned many times more than my own portion was. The dogs went into frenzies of greeting on the deck. When Tanman was safely up, the rope floated out airborne to me, and slapped the water by my arm. Tanman's face peered over, watching, while his son's face shouted in excitement beside him. Therin waved. I climbed after, shivering.

The moment I stepped over the rail, a bucket of fresh water doused me. My hair plastered down over my face. I parted it, blinking, and saw Therin's grinning face slowly stop grinning. Caladrunan clicked his fingers at the barking dogs. He said, "You're bleeding."

I glanced down. I hadn't many bandages now; my sores were running. I looked up at a ring of sailors' faces. One of them held out a cloth. I mopped my hair with it and stepped slowly through them toward the cabin. The dogs nudged my legs, licked my hand. Tanman took my arm, saying, "Dry off over here in the sun." So much solicitude for my comfort! I crouched down beside him, leaning against the sun-warmed cabin wall. "Back to your slates, Therin," he said, and Therin grinned and hurried away. Then Caladrunan said quietly, "Well, that woke us. The swimming was to clean out those sores; the herbalists suggested it."

I glanced at him, surprised. I smiled then, thinking how he'd found yet another—and more polite—way to get me to bathe. He was looking at my ribs. He pushed aside my hands, looking at the harness marks. At first I flinched when he touched me. He kept examining me as if he didn't notice the reflex. Gradually, I got over it and my skin eased to smoothness and I let him look. He said, "Cat jumpy, aren't you—I promise I won't pull your tail. Are the sores all open and fresh?" He peered about. "Looks like that did the work. You had dirt worn into the flesh so they wouldn't heal. There's bandages and clean grease in the cabin. I'll put herb extracts on the worst spots. I need you in top form." A dog nosed his knee anxiously.

He told the dogs to sit down. His voice lowered suddenly. He told me in that lower tone, "You're never seen a whale, have you? Great gray things, bigger than this ship, alive. You can see their eyes sometimes. I saw a white whale once. It was sleeping at the surface, and then it dove down into the water, all green and dim . . . I think sometimes my soul has done that, gone away into the murk, into the rubbish of ruling. And you . . . you reminded me. Just flashes of white, down in the gloom, in the water. It—you know, it used to be right there on the surface, when your brother and I were friends. Boys. You remind me of that time. You are so much like him. Did you know that?''

I looked past him at the sea. Something hurt in my throat. I shook my head.

After long silence in the sun, he muttered, "I thought you knew. That was why I gave you a chance to prove yourself.''

I stared. I almost saw the glimmering vast green depths and the whale he spoke of, there behind his eyes, in the silence; he'd mourned my brother. My very face made that grief fresh. He'd known all my dead clan, probably better than I did. I could see, too, that few men saw him in such pain. He did not permit it.

I was not made of that stern stuff that could leave him to suffer, to labor up through the depths all alone. "Ai, Drin,'' I said softly, "Breathe deep. As you taught me to breathe. Don't drown in that water—''

A sailor trod by, shattering the moment. The dogs stood up briefly. More loudly, I said, "I should dress these.'' I lifted one raw shoulder.

The stillness went out of his face. "I'll do that. You look exhausted. Go in the cabin and lie down. I'll get some other things.''

The cabin was dark, warm; fragrant with the odors of wood and tar and cordage and damp salty tapestries. Slowly, stiffly, I lay on the straw deck mat. Caladrunan carried in a bundle of clean rags, ordered the dogs out, closed the door, and opened the two portholes. I asked, "Why are you doing this, I can—''

He knelt, grinned, and ruffled my wet forelock. "Why not? You won't trust anyone else but me to handle you.''

"I can reach around myself—''

"Stop squirming.'' He washed away salt with herbal water from a crock, dipped his fingers into a jar of goose grease, and spread it on my leg. Then he bandaged it with brisk hands. "So *don't* moan or whine, then,'' he said, as if amused. I said a few nasty words; he laughed.

He did the worst ones carefully. Examining and cleaning,

he went from my scabbed shoulders to my ribs to the back of my knees. I did not think about it, did not move, did not insist again that he let me do it myself. For a Sati, few more intimate acts of trust could be permitted: for another to dress his weaknesses. It was as heady a liberty as getting drunk.

He leaned back finally, lit a lamp and held it close. I let out pent breath. I relaxed my clenched hands, let myself sprawl out defenseless. He glanced into my eyes.

"You have your tests, too, don't you?" he said, examining my neck again, holding the lamp, its scent close all around.

I was going to answer, when something—the smell of burning oil, the way the lamp lit his face—set off a daylight reliving. It was a bad one. Dimly, I saw his face past the bloom of flame, and I cried out warning to him past the exploding torch of fire. Past the screaming. Arms crushed up around me. For a moment I struggled. Then, "Drin," I cried out for help, desperately squinting past the flames, straining to see through the nightmare-fire, and then I felt something inside me slowly give way, terrible and slow and inevitable like a bridge cracking over a crevass. I hung on like a child even tighter to his arms. And clutching and clinging until the end, I fell screaming into that darkness.

I knew I was kicking and flailing. I'd been told about it after other relivings. Sometimes they thought I was Goddess-marked: epileptic. And tears—there were always tears. Sometimes it lasted only a little while, sometimes the horror went on for two bell passes or more. But I never knew how long the caves of fire had claimed me until it was over. I felt my ribs arch up, and my body surge against some hold. I had to flee, my body lunged against the grip frantically. Quite clearly, Caladrunan's voice spoke Upai in my ear; sane, calm voice. I heard him—the voice of kin, of childhood, of safety. Then I could hear myself rasping and hacking in the dark for breath to scream again. Caladrunan said, "Kigadi, don't—don't. No one can harm them now."

I fumbled, gripping this rock of sanity. I begged him not to go, not to vanish into the gloom, though all I could get out was his name. "Drin," I gasped. He didn't pull away. When the fire bloomed stronger, his voice still reached me through the roar of flames. My mother's burning hair trailed sparks, and the black nozzle of the flamethrower rotated toward me. And away.

When I screamed, he cupped one hand firmly over my mouth, quieting the shriek, and I was dimly grateful. I thrashed, beating myself on the matting, and screamed, and screamed. Screaming that went on . . . something in me, strained to breaking, finally snapped. I blacked out.

With the darkness, some final knot of resistance unraveled in me. Coming to, I emerged into my new life. The nightmare relaxed its grip once I was defeated; nothing was left of an opposing will for the horror to feed on. It was resistance that made it strong. I knew that with all the wan clarity of great weariness. Strength of mind was spent as strength of body had worn away: the last bit of determination built over the years, the force and drive, gone. There was just me, and I was a shaking mess. I came up out of it shivering. I lay there limp and exhausted, sweat greasing every limb. The Goddess had wrung the last measure of water from me. When I opened my eyes, Caladrunan was looking down at me, his face intense and worried—yet he stayed still. I blinked.

He looked at a tear trail on my face. "Do you remember what you said?"

I lifted my eyes wearily to his. "No."

"Well, it doesn't matter." Unsmiling, he added, "I swear I will cure you of this affliction. You have a strong mind. You'll heal."

I closed my eyes. "No. Not strong now. Later. After revenge. Maybe." I swallowed and opened my eyes. Thought and anxiety returned. I whispered, "The Nando reports about me . . . partly right. I always ran away to hide when I felt the reliving coming on. I am afraid of fire, always. Afraid. I will run, or kill, or go into fits when they try to use fire on me . . . I am a flawed Sati. These relivings . . ."

He bumped the uneven stubble of my beard roughly with his knuckles. "Attacking from hiding, and running away if you're seen, seems the only sensible way to wreck a flame-thrower, my friend—*I* fear them! I understand."

I looked at him steadily. "You wanted a message sent, to call in Reti's men. It goes through someone called Fat Nella."

He blinked, scrambled up, and tossed me a slate. "Write."

I slept that night curled up in extra furs on the foot of his bed, while he sat working on his slates. No dreams of mine broke the regular slaps and creaks of the ship, the scratching of Caladrunan's chalk on order slates. There were no night-mares, no sweaty awakenings to nothing. There was peace, instead. I hardly opened one eye when he lay down.

When I woke it was dawn outside. Caladrunan stirred and opened his eyes. For a moment he looked into my face— and then he smiled an irresistible, wicked, little-boy smile. He punched me on the arm. "I wrote down, afterward, what you told me when you were yelling—do you remember yelling about putting white magnesium into brick facades on fortifi-cations to resist Osa fire? During the reliving? No? Oh, well. Strengam's buying up ganas and I have work crews clearing ground for your stampede camp."

"Very good," I said, rather blankly. "White magnesium? Why would I be yelling about that?"

"You insisted I should know about its fire resistance, about building ravelins, casemates, scarps and redoubts of such bricks. Maybe you were thinking of outworks for Fortress."

"Reveting—casing the outside—is the best we can do in a short time." I snorted and stretched with crackling noises. At his look, I said, "I always wake stiff if I sleep too long."

"What you need is a good hard working-out," he said. "You can't pin me, I'm so much heavier—"

"I can pin any man!" And I grabbed him. He broke it with a head spin.

We ended up wrestling on the deck. He was pretty good, and he got indignant when I tried to throw the bout. "Don't patronize me!" I admired him for daring to wrestle and tumble with me beyond his trained level; once I disabused him of the idea that size meant a win against me, he enjoyed the feel of his strength against mine; and he was controlled, unlike most amateurs. He called and stopped in mid-bout once, to straighten my bandages and scold me. "You're fit now—I'm losing and you're enjoying it!" He scolded me until I laughed and grabbed him and took us both over in a rolling tangle. I suppose that was the start of our real friend-ship, laughing and scuffling among the deck mats like com-mon soldiers and making his guard dogs whine unhappily outside the cabin door.

His boat, Tanman told me when I asked why we were here, was standing station as a brief substitution in an anti-smuggling blockade. Boring work, he added, and expensive to his trea-sury, but vital. He pointed out the signal flags run up to communicate with a blocky-looking ex-merchantman to the southwest. "Can't maneuver, but I put some Sharinen cannon on her, and you'd never guess she had teeth by the look of her," he said with obvious satisfaction.

Despite the festive mood of both Caladrunan and his son as they climbed up and down companionways that morning—Therin was reciting to his father names and crewmen's duties, ship's anatomy, and Tannese fleet requirements for cordage, cloth, water and provisions, repairs and dry-dock services—a great deal of work got done that day. While Caladrunan read message slates, I wrote up slates of questions and arithmetic for Therin, and set the boy to work. Caladrunan rose and stretched and tossed me a courier bag. I read slates of names and statistics: review of duty rosters of Tanman's guards; ranks and powers of his nobles. While I sat memorizing, leaning with the deck and glancing at the horizon tilting oddly past the portholes, Tanman scowled over inventory figures, payrolls, and disputed quartermaster's bills.

"Can I aid you?" I asked quietly. After a startled look and a brief test of my morning's roster labors, he pushed over a stack of household slates.

"Tally those, it depresses me too much," he said. "My lady wife makes economies, but . . ."

While I calculated, he stretched and walked out on deck. He and Leo paced past the door. ". . . you'll find out how charming Upai are when you make him angry the first time," Leo said. "You'll need a trysail bent on and reef all tops."

I lifted my head. Tanman's voice rumbled. "What do you think I am, a lumbering freighter?"

"I didn't think you'd heard the rumors, Liege. The great majority I listen to believe in the justice and virtue of your rule, but—" Leo's voice shrugged.

Tanman sighed. "—but we have always the vocal minority, the Cragmen, the younger sons of small holds, the hedge-lords, the smuggling lords, the—" He flung up his hands and let them fall in a clap of silk.

"That, and the Devotees lending them too much legitimacy. But I am thinking of a Sati, so very visible at court. A *native* blooded Sati. The conservatives will flay you unless you can think of good reasons to keep him—and they'll destroy him if you don't keep him close. Too well I recall how it was with me!"

"I may have to take him away from court awhile, train him to Tannese rig."

"A certain no-name friend will arrive shortly," Leo said then. "I see the tender coming now—ah, and it seems they brought our dories back, excellent. About a half bell-pass, Liege."

I was stacking slates when Caladrunan trod inside and closed the door. He stared at me. I said, "What's wrong?"

He shrugged like a gana twitching off an insect. "Nothing, yet."

Abruptly, without conscious decision, I said, "You heard about your spy-trap already. About who leaked the briefing."

He stared. Slowly he said, "It has been leaked. By some officer who was there. Exempting you and me, that's as much as we can tell."

I said impatiently, "Why do you need Keth Adcrag so much?"

"Numbers. My legislating abilities hang on Keth counter-vailing Oldfield's bloc." He went on about Council nominations and voting blocs, hereditary taxing licenses granted by his father, exchanges of futures in grain, silk, and wool crops for Crag metals, and the influx of smuggling monies, which diluted Tanman's taxing powers and the value of official coinage.

I felt stupid. I wasn't understanding what he was trying to explain, and it must be important. Finally I looked down at my hands, stretching my finger tendons out backward. "I hear someone calling, about water level. Why does Keth resist better Tannese defenses?"

Caladrunan snapped, "You have a maddening ability to blow all my thinking to bits." He went to the cabin door, bellowed out a name. There was a brief-muttered conference. The figure that appeared outside was no sailor; the man advanced in long strides, swept out an elegant salute to Tanman, and turned his gaze to me. After a moment he entered the cabin, took up a clear disc of glass from a robe pocket, and set it across one eye. Wings of gray marked his dark hair.

"May I approach?" he asked me directly.

I slid a sidelong glance at Tanman—never taking the periphery of my sight off the stranger. At Tanman's word, I gave a stiff nod. The man's high-bridged nose drew uncomfortably close, the nostrils flared.

I didn't need to make such effort. "Mua," I said distastefully, unable to avoid the distinct odor of it in his direction. The man must use as strong a brew as the Lady of Fortress.

"Red spice," he replied amiably, and nodded once. The clear eye glass was tilted to take in all of my person. "Delightful. An unusual combination of talents and for you, my Liege, an unusually useful set." Then the man gazed mildly into my eyes. "Try to contain that terrible temper, I advise you, young man. You may get what you want without excessive violence." Then he turned and marched out again, Tanman beside him—while Tanman waved me to stay where I was. They murmured together; though not so low I couldn't overhear.

He told Tanman, "I agree, his report is probably true. Obvious in the lines of the mouth, the heavy jaw muscles. That look of childhood pain or illness is indelible as any beggar-child's. What a hostile eye! And those hands—I'd like to see him move."

Tanman beckoned me to walk forward like a prize beast.

"See?" the man murmured. "He heard me, the hostility is grown. Look at the stride, the springy pouncing movement as the boot comes down. But no sound at all. That is ingrained training. And the hands, they hardly move at all—when they do, it's all in short strong arcs near his weapons. He's done manual labor lately, but his hands were used mainly on weapons and the harp. He moves better than I would expect of a rider with such severe recent wear from stirrups, on the instep-straps of his fighting spurs. Were I you, Liege, I should teach him to put on gloves when writing parchments or slates, if he means to hide his literacy."

I rested my hands on my weaponbelt as I stopped beside Tanman. The stranger tilted his lens at me. I said dryly, "Of what so-called native tribe am I?"

Tanman nodded for the man to answer my question.

"Of a Upai noble House, with such elaborate forehead sigil—that tattoo at the hairline," the man replied easily. "And not much traveled with fellow Upai of late, either, judging from a large variety of clues, ranging from your general health compared to that of your fellow refugees—and of course your entirely new Tannese pig-leather harness—to your posture and accent. A most remarkable accent: perhaps more like the ancient Empire accent than any ordinary Upai will ever speak. Your blurring of border accent and the cadence taken from the old harp Histories enforces the antique rhythms on your words. Unique. I feel quite privileged to hear it. I studied Sharinan records of Upai Empire-period poetry."

"A scholar?" I said in Upai, glancing at Tanman.

Both men grinned.

"A spymaster," Tanman said, "who prefers to work quietly under more noticeable Heads of Military, or heads of accounting records."

"Either might be useful at this time," the man agreed. "Both fronts must be covered, as the drug smugglers are likely to be caught only by careful record-checking of revenues and inspection of loads at the gates. Of course, due to this young man, we already know what to expect will happen on Fortress guard patrols." His eyes shifted once to Tanman, and back to me. "Assassins."

"Why expose your existence to me?" I asked.

The man smiled. "Because then you might remember what sort of skills bring you the information I will be rendering you, to better perform your duties. Some of the Tannese officers, though estimable guards indeed, tend toward short memories of both myself and our enemies' patience."

"You think I remember longer?"

"I would say that was obvious." The man smiled and gestured toward my harpcase. "If you will excuse me, Liege, I'd best get to work again."

Tanman nodded once; and the man went over the side along the chains into a waiting dory, speaking to the gray battered-looking fishers at the oars. In a moment the man turned, swung a slicker over himself amidst a jumble of shifting fishers, and was indistinguishable among them.

"He's good," I said.

Tanman chuckled. "Reti left one man with me, when he came."

I slanted a glance at Tanman. "I never knew that."

"Few did, thank Goddess. He has been invaluable—which helped you earn the right to prove yourself likewise." Tanman waved me to go back into the cabin, and shut the door after himself. Then he snapped through a series of inexplicable orders.

I went through them as patiently as I could manage. He taught me a series of postures, dance steps, salutations, respectful comments, and put Tannese eating tools in my hands. He worked with my grip on the tools until I used them on our midday meal as he wanted. "Oh Flames, we have to get a fitting off before the Armorer leaves for Lake Hold—" He wrote down measurements of my arms and legs and thickness of body, holding up a marked leather thong to me. "I don't know how the Armorer can do this all day. Hold still, haven't you ever been measured for riding plate before?"

"No," I said, some of the mystery lightening for me. "I never had much metal. I cut my old leathers myself. Why not use the size of these?"

He glanced up from deck level. "I'd say not! No wonder you arrived with riding sores. Look at this!" He gestured up at my corad.

"Um," I said. "Blame that on Manoloki and the Osa. I had to tie it funny, the sores . . . is that too dangerous now? I'll wear armor over everything—"

He sighed. "Not in that way, no. Dangerous to the modesty of ladies, to the dignity of the court and myself, to— Goddess knows what else. You can't wander around court like that. Will I have to teach you how to put on court robes, too?"

I looked at his robes, with all the elaborate layering and cross-ties. I said frankly, "You may have to."

He groaned.

"I'm sorry," I said, contrite. "But Liege, aside from being careful my hidden weapons stay in place around your enemies, I don't understand what clothes have to do with protecting you and your family and your country."

He groaned again, putting both hands over his face and slumped onto his bed. "Goddess Above and Below, what have I done to myself?"

"Acquired a source of more well-digging songs than you will ever want to hear."

He made several odd choking noises, and finally spluttered into chuckles.

"What's so amusing?"

He sprawled on the bed and laughed until tears ran down his face into his beard. "Oh, Naga," he gasped at last. "Oh, Goddess, if I'd known what I got myself involved in on that hunt . . . I'd have done exactly the same thing, I fear."

CHAPTER

= *11* =

THE DROVER PASSED up a wad of leaves to me. I sniffed; my new gana ambled beside the man's wagon. I chewed one leaf and nodded, passing down a jade chip. I chewed three leaves, stuffing them in my mouth in a wad. The drover grinned and spat black juice with great accuracy. Dust puffed up from his team's hooves, coating another powdery layer on his legs. His hands adjusted the ring-lines of his team of heavy ganas, and touched his switch to the lazy one to make it keep pace.

I spat, creditably knocking down a leaf on a bush. I grinned at the drover. He pursed his lips and knocked over a dry blade of grass passing beside his wagon.

"What is this, a spitting contest?" Caladrunan said, riding up beside me. His son jogged unsteadily on a short, fat beast next to him. I passed over two dry leaves. Tanman looked at them dubiously a moment, and stuffed them in his mouth. "Gaaak," he exclaimed, making a face at the taste.

"Black leaf," I explained. "Desert delicacy. Cuts thirst. You never spit in the desert, you see. Only in Tan. Spit in the desert and you're marked ignorant by every thief and robber who sees you." I chuckled, remembering one fine outlaw trap I had baited by deliberately spitting black leaf as I went about my business in a border town. Then I glanced at Therin. "It's also like mua if you swallow too much juice—but stronger."

The drover grinned, making an idiot-face imitation of a man juiced on black leaf, eyes rolling. Tanman laughed, and spat messily, and grinned as we jeered at his amateurish effort. Therin looked shocked, and then had to attend to his fat beast as it wandered toward roadside forage. The drover knocked down a locust disturbed by one of his beasts; Tanman rode onward, chuckling. I turned my head, squinting for any movements in the dense dusty green blots of oak scrub we passed. Nothing.

I paced my mare to Tanman's bull, a half-spear before Therin's fat little beast; the boy could speak to either of us easily. The rustling of dry grass marked the passage of Tanman's hunting cat, a great tawny creature with insolent eyes, and an independent spirit which propelled it frequently off its lazy wagon-perch to scout the land. Tanman's guard dogs rode, disconsolate and leashed, in a wagon well back in the column to keep them from getting footsore; I could hear them whine.

The gana teams lifted their ears, snuffling and whistling as they began pulling down the long steady slope toward water. The River Tejed glittered among the trees. I pointed. "Someone there, Liege."

A small blue-robed figure stepped out of the trees and waved at us. Tanman told two men to run ahead to check, and grinned at me. "Sitha, dusty going here. When Rafai gives the word, Naga, between your mare and my bull the first one in the water wins. Somebody's got to persuade the teams to get in and cross it, you know."

"Don't want to wet my blades. I've got to shed my belts and my—"

"That armory of yours? Lado—Lado Kiselli, take this fellow's belts. I think if we take away *all* your things and get you wet, Dance of Knives, you'd lose half your bouting weight."

"Look like a starved dog," I agreed.

Rafai, in the trees, waved. I whooped. My mare was already in a full charge before Tanman's startled yelp of reaction could chase me. The mare pounded down the road, ears laid flat, but Tanman's bull came pulling close on her flank. Both of them were fast animals; I was pleased. While I shifted my weight and leaned close, I grinned. Terrain rushed past at my eye corners. I hung on with my knees as my beast veered through the curves. She spun about in a throw of dirt, flinging up her head, before the glitter of sun on water. I left

her back in a long flat dive. Water sprayed up over my face
and arms, splashed down on my back.

The river came up to my knees as I stood up. I yelped as
Tanman dove off his bull straight at me, knocking us both
down into a wash of muddy water. I twisted, scrambled free,
and ducked another rush. I gasped, laughing. I smacked water
at Tanman, scooping up wild handfuls and spraying it everywhere. Tannese wealth! When he smacked water at me, I
lifted my arms wide and stood squarely taking it, laughing.
"Sitha, Goddess of great surprises and lots and lots of
rain!" I crowed. Water ran down my face and chest and wet
down my leathers. I shook my head vigorously, tossing water
from my braids. Therin charged in then, spraying water at
each step, and the three of us had a rousing water-fight. We
looked at one another at last, panting, and we all grinned.
Fording was hard on armor sometimes. I splashed more water
about my legs, and watched slow muddy swirls spin about my
knees. I could drink it if I wanted, it was not at all like sea
water. A little gritty perhaps, that was all. Such a peculiar
feeling, this constant luxury of fresh water. Dizzying, almost.
I clenched my fists, catching at the water. "And you shall
never have it, no *Osa'aa'ei*, not ever," I chanted at the
running water.

"Come, let's lead the beasts in," Tanman said, wading
closer. He clapped my wet shoulder in an explosion of water
droplets, slapping leather on leather. "We've got a long ride
yet."

I tensed and looked around at movement. A marshal was
trying to hold Tanman's beast, and failed. "Your flamed
bull!" I yelled. I ran in great smacking sprays of water. "Get
off my new saddle, you stupid—"

Tanman stood in midford and roared with laughter, while
his son grinned. Ignoring the marshal who tried to grab for
nose-lines, the bull crowded my reluctant mare toward the
water, clattering and thumping his armored forelegs at my
saddle and tangling his own girths with my saddlebags. Stupid animal, I thought. She isn't even in season. I ran right at
the beast, yelling ineffectually. Bulls stopped for no man.

The mare, however, put her ears back and delivered a
terrific kick backward. The bull let out a startled whistle, fell
away from her, and stumbled hastily away when she threat-

ened to kick him indelicately again. The bull gave me a long
reproachful glare.

Tanman shouted, "Flamed bitch! Naga, you wouldn't laugh
if you got it there, and he's very sensitive to being laughed
at—'' Water fanned from his big Tannese boots as he splashed
toward me, ''—have a bad time catching him again if you
keep laughing—''

I pointed at his bull, giggling. The beast's eyes were pale-
ringed with astonishment and dumb dented pride. "Serves
him right!" I said, amused at the affronted dignity on Tanman's
face so like his bull. Insult my beast, insult me—until he
looked again at his beast, and himself started laughing at the
animal's absurd expression. Five days of swimming and fishing, watching Therin skylark among the sailors, reading stacks
and stacks of Tanman's courier slates, working through the
impossible backlog of duty and accounting slates, stretching,
and sleeping on Tanman's ship, had nearly healed my travel
sores and my knotted muscles; so, one gusty morning on the
foredeck, I asked quietly about seeking my grandmother—she
might have knowledge we needed. Caladrunan did not answer
me directly. I assumed he had a reason: he looked thoughtfully at an inoffensive line and up into the yard it secured.
Work on preliminary legal arguments in a Council presenta-
tion on the case for army mobilization had left him a bit
owl-eyed and preoccupied. "You sent off that message on the
escort ready at dockside? Therin's beast to meet us there? I
don't know why I always forget my scribes when I leave
Fortress, Goddess knows I always end up needing them."
Finally, he told me that I would go with them to Lake Hold to
see their clan.

In Fortress port, he pointed out a whole stable of beasts for
me to pick among, and Pitar offered a rack of tough campaign
saddles likely older than I was myself. He said, "Spares. And
don't tell Keth I've got these, either."

I nodded. Lado Kiselli, who met us at the pier, merely
laughed, and shook his head. Tanman's guard escort all
thought it modesty when I chose a scruffy barred-legged mare
instead of the doe-eyed beauties of breeding that they debated
among. The mare's markings were proof of desert-bred stamina and drought-resistance and the same irascible bad temper
that saved my first mare from so many thieves. The new beast
had since proved her dominance over prettier ganas with

some wicked bites and kicks. Therin's beast obeyed my mare without arguing, which was good for the boy's safety in emergency.

I'd asked Tanman's reasons for the trip, as I rode my ugly mare beside Tanman's bull through the summer heat, toward the ancestral family land of Tan's rulers. He chuckled. Caladrunan thought it best that I learn to act Tannese in gradual stages; his clan at Lake Hold, he told me, was less formal and less rigid than Fortress court. Safer besides from my new-made drug-trade enemies, he told me cheerfully. I looked at him askance. And the rest, I thought, he wouldn't tell me. Yet.

Despite my drive to find my grandmother, I hadn't liked breaking the idyll on the sea. I didn't want to meet any clan at Lake Hold. I didn't want to bear the Tannese noble prejudices and sly malice I'd seen in Tannese exiles among the Nandos. I didn't want to fight anyone, I hardly even wanted to harp for Tanman and his son. It was as if I had retreated deep into myself to rest; I had been reluctant to come back to life outside slates of numbers and crisp Tannese reports.

He saw it, of course. So did Lado Kiselli—he told me I must sing him songs he'd never heard before, or I could ride strapped across a pack beast with my tail in the air like a redbuck carcass. Tanman agreed. I had grinned at the idea of either man trying to tie me down, which was the start of my return to active life.

So far, it wasn't bad. Therin was a delight to teach. In night camps I gossiped with the guard commanders and scouts, as they watched my arms practices; while I repeated difficult scadda throws over and over because I was dropping or fumbling or missing—but no one jeered my efforts. They seemed to like my long harp practices well enough. The men asked me for some music every stop. No one remarked on my native blood or offered to bully me. I never asked for more favor than that.

I tossed back my wet braids, grinned at Tanman and waved my wet leather helmet with a whoop. His bull snorted, wild-eyed, and wheeled toward Tanman. The beast dodged aside a step when Tanman tried to grab the nose-lines. I whooped again, and the bull dodged both of us. I clicked my fingers; my mare came to me, nosing my robes for the dates which I used to train her. Datefruit was one thing I had not hesitated to ask for.

Tanman glared at me. "Call him," he snapped.

"The bull won't come to me," I said. "But perhaps a few of these will bring him to you, Liege." I tossed the parchment wrapped sweets to Tanman.

"Desert tricks," Tanman muttered, but his bull came to him eventually. We could have chased him for a bell pass without laying hand to reins using the old Tannese cavalry methods so rigidly taught. Pitar, sitting on his beast nearby, looked both interested and disapproving. Of course, they all found my riding habits a bit odd; I had got the mare used to my mount and dismount being wherever I chose it to be, even rolling off her hindquarters. I was fond of her already, with pangs at my disloyalty to the dead mare who first let me scramble up. Never, I thought, will there be another beast like that. But Tanman's gift came a close second, and I was grateful. "Swine," I murmured, unwrapping a date, and felt velvety soft hair nuzzle my palm.

The gana teams were plodding toward us and toward the water, ears flicking forward and back. Tanman shook his bull's forelock, patted the brawny shoulder, and rummaged in a saddlebag. The beast moved restively, whistling. "Time for your physic," he said to me, and cut up a hard-rinded fruit I had seen more than enough of in past days. I groaned as I accepted it from his hand. Sour juice ran stinging over my cracked lips and fingers; I wiped my hands on my thighs and mounted, gently swinging my tender legs over the saddle. Tanman watched me. Pitar watched Tanman in an anxious way. Lado's gaze looked sardonic. And Therin, catching cross-currents, glanced among the four of us.

Lado Kiselli rode up then, hot and red-faced and pulling aside his robes from his saddle sores. "Pack of cow-clod rustics," he muttered, and rode his placid beast straight into the water. He climbed stiffly down, splashed muddy water over his fine clothes and his face, and looked at us woebegone. His beast stood patiently beside him, head drooping. Tanman laughed at the sight and apologized together, urging Lado to come out and take some wine from Tanman's own bag.

I had already noticed that most of the soldiers carried wine in their travel bags rather than the regulation water-vinegar

mixture. Tanman seemed to be bowing to common custom in
ignoring the rule Pitar had carefully explained to me. Tanman
was generous about sharing his wine with thirsty Harpers;
Lado had already drunk up his own wine, disdaining vinegar-
juice. My bag held vinegar-water cut with black leaf juice, a
vile combination useful for curbing desert thirst, exhaustion
or infected wounds, and little else. Therin carried boiled
water in his bag, and wondered at all the fuss.

Lado wiped his lips of Tanman's wine and thanked his
benefactor in ripe, ungentlemanly, heartfelt terms; he groaned
loudly as we all led our beasts across the shallow ford ahead
of the first team. My mare jerked and jibbed at the reins and
the water, but I soothed her across and gave her dates and
made much of her. Lado made an acutely sour face when he
saw this, and whacked his patient beast a bit harder than
necessary to make it climb the far slope of the ford. I glanced
at Lado's face and began to understand why that skilled
performer refused to tramp the roads like other Harpers.

Late that afternoon in camp, Lado mumbled about new
songs for Midwinter Feast. "Begging pardon, Liege, but your
lady wife was quite unpleasant. She liked nothing I could
offer."

Tanman thumped my shoulder. "Tell me then, what are we
going to do for Midwinter Feast? Lado?"

Lado and I lifted our heads, eyes blinking, from our goblets. We'd broached a barrel from Tanman's travel-hoard, and
we were both a bit drunk. Tanman had decided that he'd had
enough of morose Harpers—and Lado's silent sour expressions of pain—and he'd ordered us both to drink up. I looked
at my goblet and blinked. I'd been quite cheerful about
complying on the wine, I remembered. This Tannese drinking, I thought. I can't think.

"What are we going to do?" Tanman demanded, bright-
eyed, aggressive, happy.

"Get women," I said solemnly, "and prong the—" I
stopped when Lado stared at me. He burst into high giggles,
spluttering behind his hands. I lifted my puzzled gaze to
Tanman, and felt a silly friendly smile wander across my face.
I hadn't told anybody I was a huge liar, either. He did not
look amused. I blinked. His face blurred out of focus, and
bits of sunlight sparkled painfully bright on his face.

Entirely too bright.

Suddenly I felt icily and utterly sober. *No*, I thought, not here! Not where men could see, and fear, and gather tales to repeat. *No!* My hands and feet went numb. A tiny pinpoint of light glowed suddenly on his bright hair, light seared the center of my brain. It was a seed-point of brilliance which grew larger with frightening speed, whirling outward and opening as it blazed, an aureole spinning in my inner sight. Corruscating fire flared wider, blasting actinic lightning everywhere, brilliance unbearable. I stumbled up to my feet, shoving aside goblets in a clatter of fear and pain. I lifted cold stumplike hands clumsily to my face, trying to press away the burning nimbus that seared my head. "No," I said, but it was impossible to fight. This, I knew—this was a raw force that lay denied and twisted behind the ugly visions of my relivings. "No!"

Dimly past the glare, I could see faces, familiar faces, horrified, staring at me for the peculiar quality of my voice. My voice echoed in my head, coming in a long, slow rumbling like drums within a cavern. Some hidden source gave life to these rings of sound, echoing and expanding and spreading full-blown into the glare of the Goddess's fire with a great *bong!* as of a bell tolling the pass of the Goddess's day and of the night. Words tolled past. "Get ink!" I cried out, frantically clutching my head together against the acid light. I had to hold the plates of my skull together over it, radiance streamed through all the cracks and seams in my bones. "Ink! Black leaf to treat the body of what they did—"

Breathless, Tanman's voice gasped, "Here, here. Naga, here."

Lado gasped, "Keth said Naga was a witch, but I didn't believe it."

"He isn't," Tanman said grimly. "He's something else, and Keth won't like that either."

The light flattened, became a broad shimmering plain. The lines of battle glittered painfully bright across the map of light; it hurt my weak brain to look at it. Lines—the great scratched Bowl of the Altar of Tan flattened into this blinding field, with the scratches of gold and iron upon it sprouting horribly into menacing cliffs of armor and thickets of pikes. "Parchment!" I cried out, and the voices of wolf packs and of gore-crows belled through the tent of Tanman. "Ink parchment write down map map—"

My hand was grasped, a stick forced clumsily between my
rigid fingers, the end dipped in a bowl of fresh-made soot
ink. Perhaps I had been bellowing words at them while they
made the ink, but I could not remember. Briefly through the
glare I saw Lado's sweating face, red with drink, as he
steadied the ink bowl. Therin was at his elbow, shouting
something about Oldfield and witches. Tanman's hand forced
mine down, down to the feel of parchment. Rapidly, with my
head and neck arched unnaturally in the grip of the vision, I
wrote until the stick was dry. My hand was forced aside to
the ink bowl. The glittering map extended pitilessly in length
as my hand struggled to follow. "So fast, so fast," I gasped,
whimpering in pain as my hand dashed onward helplessly in
the grip of the light.

The blaze of it grew steadily more unbearable until I didn't
see map lines at all. My legs began to twitch. I flung both
arms futilely over my eyes, gasping. Sweat creased down my
face. I stumbled blindly forward, but hands pinned my body,
pushed me back from the tent brazier, herded me away from
the fire. Again and again they pressed me back, away from
the relief real flame could bring. My body twisted and jerked
in Tanman's grip and then the tent floor spun up toward me.
My body jerked and danced like a fish on grass. My eyes
were wide open. I was entirely aware of my uncoordinated
writhing, but I could not stop it. It horrified me. My teeth
clicked together over shreds of incandescence, spangles were
dimming in my bones. Dimly, through the fading glory of the
light, I saw Tanman and Therin and Lado spin past my eyes;
then my head jerked backward.

"Goddess Above and Below," Tanman gritted, low and
frightened, close by me. Lado flinched; blood trickled from
the knuckles he lifted to wipe his lip.

Therin stooped close, a spinning frightened face above my
own, with narrowed eyes. "Look at the tremors in his face,
Father. And the rigid fingers. It's the drug the Devotees use
for visions, isn't it? And look at his legs, they're arched back
like that—I remember I saw it last Midwinter at a ceremony,
Father!—Liege."

Tanman's eyes became yellow rings of fear. "If Naga uses
the vision-drink of the Devotees!—"

"No," Lado said, close now and angry. Lado's mouth was
grim. "He didn't do it. I think someone drugged him without

any of us knowing. One of our trusted escort perhaps. Sitha knows how we'll keep this quiet, 'witch' will be the least of it. We'd better tie him up while we can still handle him. The Devotees go into seizures sometimes."

Words spilled out of my mouth. I was unable to understand them. I managed to make a small groan of pain and of questioning for myself, when they tied me with cords. Tanman patted my straining, twitching cheek. He spoke soothingly; the twitching eased a little under his voice. Lado was writing something on slates, bending close by me, and sometimes he nodded at the spilling words streaming over my lips like water. Then Lado's face writhed away into something horrible, and drugged illusions swallowed me. Solid things melted through my body, things of air and wind and delusion shattered and cut at me: it felt too real. Flavors combined in my mouth in nauseating complexity. And the relivings, twisted and distorted into fantasmagorical sights, went on and on and on. Bodies rended and tore apart, burned, smoked, and cried out in children's voices at me. I screamed. I tried to control what was happening, tried to turn aside from what I saw, but this only twisted it into new forms.

The main virtue of the Devotee drink was that its effect was brief in outside measurement. Best not to expose a brittle Devotee mind for too long to the Goddess's unshielded might—or to expose a man's own mind to him too honestly, for too long. He might go mad. Tanman tried, knowing this, to make his voice an anchor for me. I heard him clearly over my own noises—a roar of Tannese earth and rock, crying out stability to me. They told me, as I struggled, that the Devotees normally added a euphoric distilled from mua to bring a seer out of his vision relaxed and smiling.

But my enemy had not done me that small favor.

I was fortunate in having them all, quick-witted, to help me. They forced me to drink strong mua, one goblet after another, while the visions consumed me and I gibbered. "Only thing that will keep him from drowning in himself," Tanman muttered grimly, lifting another full goblet and forcing my teeth open. His face smeared into a green death's head with Cragman hair, and his voice howled. But I managed not to bite him again. They made the mua as vilely strong as they could, then they used my own drinking bag full of vinegar and black leaf.

So I came out of it gasping, weeping and giggling help-lessly at the sight of my mother decapitated by the tread of an Osa flamethrower. One moment I could see the blood splat-tering exuberantly up the side of the metal rollers, and the next moment it was all gone; I lay there blinking up. My mouth felt stretched into a rictus as I looked at them. I could feel the mua and the wine and the black leaf, all still active, collide in me. I giggled and spoke. Tannese words would not, stubbornly, come to me at all. It came in Upai.

Tanman sighed. "Best go now, Therin, go rest while you can and my thanks for your help tonight."

Odd, I thought, I can understand what they're saying, but I can't find the words for myself. Tanman handled me with ruthless speed, which was as well because my body tried to eject all the conflicting drugs in as many ways as possible. When I could, I apologized in Upai. I was cheerful, after the mua and black leaf, and I knew my voice was slurred from the wine; but I was puzzled. Why would Tanman bother soiling his hands personally? Lado murmured. Tanman snapped, "Because he'll hurt anyone else but me, same as he bit you! Any other silly questions?" I blinked sleepily at him. He looked quite cross. I couldn't remember who made him cross, I wanted only to go to sleep. I wrapped my forefinger in a twist of my hair and closed my eyes. It seemed sensible that Tanman should hold my head and shoulders in his lap, with his big hands spread over my back, while he called in soldiers and demanded answers. I went easily to sleep.

I was horrified to wake up slung over his shoulder, bobbing up and down as he walked. He carried me, wrapped in a blanket, before a sea of faces lit by torchlight. Perhaps he felt me tense in his grip. He muttered, "You're still asleep," and shifted my weight a little closer. He spoke loudly in Tannese, but I was too drunk or sick to translate it in my head. When he let go of my shoulders, I let my head and my arms flop; I felt too awful to open my eyes very wide to all those blurs. A long moan of fear, anger, or awe—it was quite impossible to tell which—rose around us. I listened blankly to angry talk in Tannese; then he wheeled about and men cried after him in fear. He marched along so rapidly and angrily that I kept still—I was afraid he might throw me to the ground. But he put me down and quietly dismissed Pitar and Rafai. "Naga," he said. "Are you quite all right?"

I dared to open my eyes cautiously. I blinked at him. The words, the tone, were deceptively gentle. His face was flinty.

The Tannese words came then, slowly, when I needed them. "I try," I said, slurred, wanting to apologize, and began to sit up.

"You're still too drunk. Lie back, there's a fur folded for your head. Good. Where are we? What's the first line of Fourth History? All right, that's enough of the History. I do like having an instant and expert source. What is it?"

"Cold," I said, shuddering. "Poison? Did he poison you—I have to find out what he did—"

"No, Pitar is questioning the man you identified. I understood you. Lie back."

"He—what man? What man, when?" I said, feeling I'd missed something. I felt as muddled as after any reliving. "The Osa—did they get through at Black Pebble Ford—"

Tanman shook his head. "Their machines haven't even reached Manoloki's rear positions." He threw a fold of his huge outrobe over my body. It was warm, from being next to his inner robes. I sighed.

"Better?" he murmured.

"Mmm," I agreed, eyelids drooping. "Is Therin—" I stirred. "I bit someone, I don't know who—did you send for extra guards for Lake Hold?"

"Go back to sleep," he said, "Therin is fine. You can apologize to Lado tomorrow, and yes, I did."

I yawned. I opened my eyes then. His robe felt marvelously warm. My muscles soaked in it, revelled in the heat. He sat down next to me. I said, "Can't guard if I'm drunk. Never get drunk again, promise. Only if you say to."

"I *did* tell you to, this time."

"Oh. You did? Only time," I said solemnly. "Stinking Osa take advantage—watch Tejed Lakes up at your hold. Keth has a Cragman camp out there."

"You're menace enough sober," he said. "You worry too much. Go to sleep. Goddess, you're so thin, Naga—I hardly realized you'd be twice as drunk as we were. I couldn't tell, you never *sounded* funny."

"Harper!" I muttered, half asleep, "Drink you silly any time, bet on it. . . ." He was laughing softly as I fell asleep.

When I woke up in the morning, Tanman sat writing on slates by the tent flap. Reports to his lady wife perhaps: his expression was grim. I felt grim, too—and not very proud of myself. I hadn't been much guard last night. But if I was left sleeping near Tanman, I was still expected to be his guard. I wrinkled my nose at the close, unpleasant smell in the tent, stinking with every breeze from outside. I could guess what he'd done: an execution. Perhaps, Fortress-inured, the stink didn't bother him. Crackling stiff muscles, I asked, "Which one was it drugged me? And how?"

He looked up. "Do you remember I made you eat some sour fruit, as a medicine? One of my more religious officers was maneuvered by persons unknown into needling Devotee drug-fluid into the rind of the fruit before you ate it. With wine, I am told, the drug becomes much more active."

I slid a glance toward the tent flap. The religious man was undoubtedly hanging dead on a tree out there as an example. I said abruptly, "The marshal who was having trouble with your bull at the fording, when we were having the water-fight. You carried the fruit in your saddlebags. Your bull was fighting the man, he hated anyone fiddling with the bags too long. So he didn't have time to needle all the fruit, only a few."

Tanman sat back studying me. At last he said, "Yes. He couldn't tell me who got him to do it, just that it was a Devotee. The man admitted it when he was arrested. We figured out what he used—Therin recognized it first. You told us who he was last night, and how he'd done it to you, when I asked, it's interesting you remember that part now."

"What?" I got up. "I don't remember figuring out anything like that—"

Tanman gave me a long, keen look, and turned his head away. "You remember nothing of what you said last night during the—fit?"

"Something about a huge map of lights, Liege," I said uncertainly. "And relivings. I must have made a howling fuss, embarrassed you and your son, I left you vulnerable to assassins—"

"Your fresh clothes are on that rack with your armor. Rafai cleaned your leathers and robes for you, I hope satisfactorily for your tastes," he said calmly, writing. "Do not discuss this with anyone but me."

I swallowed. "As you wish, Liege." I dressed hastily.

He turned back to me with his eyes a hard glitter of yellow

in the light of his lamps, no warmer than the gray predawn light throughout the tent. "How does it feel to be the next prophet of Tan, Sati?"

I looked up from latching my weaponbelt. "What? I don't understand what you mean—"

He crossed the tent in three strides. I met his eyes. The hard glitter softened faintly. "You really don't know what you did," he whispered, eyes briefly ringing white all around as if amazed. He took a step back, all the while staring at me. His eyes narrowed. "Well, if you don't remember, you don't, and we have a day's ride ahead—are you fit?"

"I think so. Your wine was better than the last drunk I had, my head doesn't hurt as much."

He turned abruptly away and stood looking down at the stack of slates. On the top he spread out a parchment marked in scrawling, untidy symbols. "Very well," he murmured, staring at the parchment. "Very well, I'll accept whatever help I get, however it comes." He rolled the parchment and put it in a leather case, calling for Pitar. He gave Pitar the case. "Guard this as my life—and do not make that guarding obvious," Tanman said somberly. "Is Therin ready to ride?"

"He is, Liege." Pitar glanced briefly at me; his eyes slid away from mine. But he saluted Tanman and went out with a brisk step, carrying the scroll case under one arm.

Tanman said, "Manoloki had no idea what he threw away in you, Naga. Nor do the Devotee conspirators know what wolf they have unleashed."

I said, "Manoloki never did know the value of things. Or of men, either."

"But I do?" Tanman said sardonically.

I hooked my scadda sheaths on my weaponbelt. Deliberately I lightened my tone. "Of course you do. After all, *I* chose to give you Great Oath, not some other lord, and *I* have excellent taste in employers."

He blinked, smiled slowly. "Oh? Is your judgment infallible then?"

I shrugged. "You kept me and my Oath. Obviously you know the value of fine things." And I made a haughty face.

He laughed then. It seemed a good omen for the day. I went out of the tent flap with him. Guards began moving in behind us to strike his tent.

"Permit me," I said dryly. I went over his bull and his

riding gear with a careful hand, while the other guards eyed me, as if unsure whether to be insulted or to fear me. I checked Therin's and my own beast likewise. When I had mounted, I watched the tent-striking. I pointed out several things he could order done to secure his tent and his camp better; he merely nodded, listening to my diffident suggestions.

He said little during the day's riding, and that little to his son; he hardly reacted to Lado Kiselli's brave efforts to amuse him. Lado finally gave it up. My fellow Harper was even more uncomfortable on beast-back than the day before. I could only bring Lado out of his miseries by a long talk on his own harping inventions: pitch-changing levers and adaptations of melodies from native songs discovered in port taverns. Then, of course, I made him sing some of *his* songs for us all as we rode. When we started the long last grade up to the walls of Lake Hold, Lado looked almost happy. "A real bed, by the Goddess," he sighed.

Early in the afternoon of our arrival, I went to the balcony of Caladrunan's chambers on the fourth floor of Lake Hold and looked down. Village houses crowded out to the edge of the forest. The laundry lines were full of flapping colors. The wooden palisade built between forest and village was not at all what I considered defensible, not against flamethrowers. Rubble of fallen walls or low masonry barriers would have been better. And the western pass into the desert zones that Manoloki ruled was only ten days' ride from here.

I heard Caladrunan move up behind me. Devour sang softly in scabbard at each step. He told me he'd never figured out what metal part struck his scabbard to make that noise; after years of it, he no longer worried about it wearing or damaging his extraordinary sword. He thought instead about having to use Devour. Caladrunan said, "Don't worry about secret passages or spy holes here at Lake Hold. There aren't any. My relations are too frantically fearful, they keep each other honest." He snorted. "I know this place. I spent a lot of time trying to find some, right after my coronation. They all thought they could safely keep a boy locked up here, with my kin frightened into serving as jailers—while my regents ruled at Fortress."

I turned to him. "Getting out of here, getting rid of your regents—you didn't tell me about all that. It sounds quite a story."

"It was. One of my regents helped me: the only honest one. Ropes down the wall, the whole tale. You'll meet him in the next few days. I want my son to meet him, too." Caladrunan's face was closed, bitter, as if the place had ugly memories for him.

I said, "I wish I had been here."

He roused, lifting his head to the breeze. "I'm glad you're here now. I think I'll take some rest. We can endure the rest of my relatives later."

The ride through the village into the hold—more of an unplanned parade, everyone waving and shouting—and the official greetings had been wearing. Lado had had more sense—he had evaded all official ceremony and somehow got himself buried in the women's quarters, telling eloquently how he'd languished all the ride long for lack of such necessities. Therin had been sent off to bed looking transparent. To me, it was all a blur of dust and faces and too many people peering entirely too closely at me, and I was glad to be out of it. Everyone was certain I was the Goddess's prophet.

Tanman turned away and went into his private chamber to a table. I closed the balcony door and barred it. "Sit down," he said casually, pouring wine. "I have a surprise for you. There are beggartowns—refugee camps—up here at Lake Hold, and I'm told there are Upai among them. As you asked me on board ship, I had a call put out for your grandmother in the camps near Fortress. Some days ago, Fat Nella sent a note that Orena traveled up here to check on your people. Nella also said that there was a rumor among the gangs: some important noble up here is said to be trading in smuggled goods. He's also exporting slaves raided from the camps—which can only be smuggled to pirate press gangs. You should check this rumor, Naga—see if any refugees have disappeared thus—with your grandmother. That is one reason we came to Lake Hold."

"If I cannot find her, I can still check with people in the camp." I clenched my hands on my knees, about to rise.

He smiled. "Drink your wine. It doesn't have to be done today." He turned away, pulled a stool opposite me, and sat down. "That's better. I don't like to tower over the conversation quite so much. Today I'd like you to go around with Pitar to check the local guard watch. Check their readiness, learn their routine, look for penetration possibilities—weak coverage, overlooked ambush sites, faulty scheduling, slovenly personnel management. It shouldn't be too bad, here, but you'll want to know what local faults my guards must move in and compensate for."

"You relieved the old Lake Hold watch commander for a bribery scandal, didn't you? Wouldn't the watch—"

"I promoted the fellow who kept the watch intact during the senior's nonsense. Yes. Now, once you're able to do some of Pitar's Fortress work, I'll give him extra time off-duty. I overwork him, and he needs to be with his wife, who is ill. Strengam got up here yesterday. At the ceremony he said he had forty young officers interested in new training. We can screen them for loyalty and send the top ones on to work at the fords with Vishna's marines and Reti's old Nandos. Edan Dar's son commands at Black Pebble Ford now, he writes that he'd be willing to field the experiment there. Oh—what's that?"

I leaned forward; our heads were very close together. "Servant with piles of silk in the outer room—probably clean robes for you, Liege. Among the account slates that mask the project expenses, Vishna's liaison man sent a report. Not good news. Their first trial runs failed, the herd failed to cohere for any practical distance. Perhaps they had too many inexperienced riders—hard to break that habit of preventing a panic when you herd. But eight more of Reti's men drifted in since those runs and they've been testing and working on reliability and scare methods. Smoke pots work the best, but we don't want the beasts trained to something that will let the Osa control the stampede. We haven't reached the stage of absorbing another herd, yet."

"Speaking of difficulties," Tanman smiled, "the Head Armorer is up here sputtering about parts. Can you advise him about what goes where in that cache of junk my men retrieved?"

I gulped at my wine. Finally, in a low voice, I said, "Well, I've done flamethrower raids. I can destroy them. But I don't think I'd do well at building more of them. Relivings." I shivered slightly. "The Armorer's problem likely is the different sizes, ages and types of throwers, and damage done in removing parts. Spiking the air vent will make the mixing chamber useless except as models to work from. I hope he remembered that the gun is the simplest part, the biggest messes are the steam engines that drive the treads."

"He wants to see how all of it works," Tanman said.

I groaned. "When he can't even work their alloy?"

"Very broad-minded of you."

"The Nandos knocked most of the nonsense out of me."

"And most of the humor?" he said tartly.

I looked down at the goblet in my hands. "No, the Osa did that part."

When I looked up, his face looked pale. Then grimly he said, "I deserved that." His hand fisted, punched my shoulder lightly. "Any luck getting mining surveys out of that Devotee scholar at the ceremony?"

I shook my head. "Old charts. I looked at his strategic scans of the border near Bitterspring. Either the surface halo markings were wildly inaccurate, I knew there was an exhausted mine on the site, or it was in an active zone of a Waste where you couldn't send anyone for more than a half day. Even then they'd get sick." I shrugged. "At this rate we'll end up fighting the Osa with your navy. If we last so long."

"Such impatience. I hear the heliograph tests went well, so I sent a signal corps to Black Pebble Ford. Strengam said he'd got together a lot of nobles up here, to hear me talk about the war. It just might make the difference in Council, with my fat, complacent lords. He's friendly with some wool clan lords—"

I shrugged irritably, glancing around the chamber. The servant had gone away. "Maybe that will help. The Osa can move so fast, when they choose." I looked down at my hands. Tanman said, "Look at me. You're Upai, be proud—best and toughest friends in the Three Countries. Don't look down, I'm not afraid for you to meet my eyes! I'm not Manoloki."

I looked up quickly, startled. For a moment we stared into one another's eyes. "It may be slow, but I will swear to you, Naga, that I will do my best for your people. I will try to fight your war. Will that suffice?"

"It has to," I said simply. Then, "You were going to rest for awhile."

He closed his eyes, nodding, and slumped back against the

wall, tilting his head. It was the only rest he meant to take until late at night; on our first arrival he had scheduled altogether too many meetings and receptions and inspections. Aware of his driving appetite for work, I sat motionless in the heat of the afternoon, to avoid rousing him to his labors again. I was glad for the quiet of the chamber. My whole body relaxed slowly and my nervous skin began to smooth out as I sat in the wood-scented gloom. Shafts of dusty gold light spread from the high narrow windows across the thick straw mats, sparkled on silver in his robe. Sunset light glowed on his face, on the wiry red and gold beard. Eyes closed, he said, ''Rub my neck, will you?''

I got up, pleased at the trust, and shifted my stool around behind him. My hands massaged his neck and the back of his head and the jaw muscle that twitched and jerked under tension. I stroked his hair as if we were both children together. We were there a long time in the declining gold light.

CHAPTER

= *12* =

"SECURITY STINKS," I growled, glaring about.

"Your problem is, you prowl too much. You have a terribly snooping attitude, you lack all respect, and you prowl." Pitar's voice was dry. So was his humor.

"I don't like it."

Pitar raked one hand at his hair, and turned about looking distracted. "Will you stop that, and sit down?"

"Too much stuff all over the walls—troll-shit. And little iron railings and statues and—" I poked a finger at a thing, appalled when it whizzed and answered with a clang of tin, a whirring of gears, and the expulsion of a fake bird on a long metal tongue. I hit it and knocked the whole thing over in a jangle of parts. I sprang back, scaddas poised, and gingerly poked the dead thing. Nothing.

Except that Pitar burst into howls of laughter. "That *was* a music box!"

"If you're a troll," I said crossly, poking it. "That wasn't music!"

"What do you want, a bare room? These Lake Clan snobs will never be impressed by that."

"Yes, I'd like a bare room," I said fiercely, sheathing my scaddas, whip-whip of iron on leather. "With a target painted on one wall. Anyone who gets nasty, Tanman can point for them to go stand there while you and I take a long stare at him. That might impress the Lake Clan snobs."

Pitar chuckled. "I rather like that. I might second the idea

155

when you suggest it to Tanman—but you know he'll never agree to it. No dignity. All that nasty raw force, no subtlety.''

"You Tannese," I said, disgusted, and Pitar laughed again.

I said, gathering what patience I could, "In Third History, the Tanman—''

"—was undoubtedly killed by some nonsense invention like that box you murdered,'' Pitar said. He sighed. "You Harpers—Histories, all the time Histories. No, don't tell me, I can already hear the lecture!'' He marched toward the door, where he turned. With sudden passion he yelled back, "History makes a damned cold lover when you need some comfort on a long night!'' And he left, slamming the door.

I looked at the door, remembering that Pitar's wife was slowly dying, and found myself stilled and silent. His phrase rang through my insides. Slowly I kicked at the tuneless jumble of the music box, and watched the parts skitter over the stone floor. I closed the door quietly after myself when I left.

I got no more comfort out of forcing my way on Tanman's name past the guarded gates of the Upai refugee camp, outside the hold paling, late the same day. I was dismayed at how my Tannese escort caused everyone to fall back in fear. Skinny faces snarled and arms thrashed in gestures of hatred at the blue-robed men. "Animals," one soldier said, eyeing the mob swirling around us.

I had shed my own blue outrobe before coming, but the beggars knew my leathers were Tannese as well. I held out my hands, clapped them sharply, and spoke with more staccato words than most Upai conversation ever used: the flow of tones became rough, imperative. "Has our pride come to this, throwing rocks at fools?'' I snapped. "Does no one know the tent of Orena's family, here?''

The starving faces became sullen. I listened to muttering. Yes, Orena é Teot had come, and gone again, and if she wished me to talk with her, she would indeed find me. They looked skeptically at me, as if I might dare print ink on my temple and impersonate the Teot heritage.

"You little know the urgency that brings me?'' I asked, with heavy sarcastic tones, "you little know our joint enemy? Shall I name them for you, and blast this place with the

ill-luck of that name, and of my rage against the enemy?''
My arm jabbed out rigidly.

It got very quiet. Apparently even here they had heard
something of me, and of what I'd done in Tan so far. More
quietly, I made my escort move aside, and standing in turn
before each woman of the camp's ruling council, I asked my
questions. I didn't like the answers. Fat Nella's rumor was
ghastly true: this camp had been raided once a moon, and the
able men taken off; the rest were left to starve. The local
guards stood aside when masked archers swept through at
night. The people had little strength for anger; and even now,
the crowd soon dispersed.

There was no hiding from *me* the problems of the beggartown, as the gate bailiff had done with Tannese camp
inspectors—even now he peered resentfully after me, and
fretted at his men. If I stayed long, he would find forces to
overwhelm my escort: so the women warned me. He seemed
powerful to them; his crimes ran on in pitiless Upai precision
from the women's answers.

Aside from prostituting the young women, he bartered camp
food for his stake in drug trade, and did his best to enrich
himself from supplies for vanished Upai. There was not
enough food when an honest man held the gate, the Upai told
me. Thus, had been a man murdered to open the post for this
bailiff; and now hideous children were dying everywhere.

Hideous stinking invalids lay in every tent I opened. Constantly, little hands cupped before me, plucked at my robes,
gently gave way as I moved.

I said nothing to my escort, I simply carried them along
through the camp with me; they had eyes. I merely stood
looking at the young Tannese soldiers who buckled in place
and vomited. The older ones merely looked weary and
disillusioned.

"Drug trade," Ben said at last.

"No doubt Nella tipped us to a rival's operation," I said
bitterly.

"Tell the bastards at the gate what these people said, the
bailiff's men will jump at you and we can chop them for
attacking, stop it all now," Ben said.

I looked at him. "And hurry it up before the other thugs
get here, is that it?"

"I'll send off Ibiculé for reinforcements."

"Send two."

"You've got a high opinion of our ability to defend you."

"I've got an opinion on this camp," I said. "Leave that big ugly enforcer beside the bailiff for me."

"With pleasure, noble-born."

The talking part didn't last long.

I asked, with great impartial care, to see the camp supplies reserved for this moon, and the record slates. My timing, as I'd known when I arrived, was fortuitous: there had just been a delivery to all the camps, from the very draft train we accompanied. And already, the women told me, the medicines and grain were taken, gone, the sailcloth for tents, half-gone. "Oh, and I'd like to speak with the herbalist who works here," I said.

The bailiff said, "You cannot. You lack authority."

I smiled. "Fine. I'll go up to Tanman without your explanation, and present the testimony of the people inside your camp."

The man flicked his hand; the hulk beside him lunged forward.

I stepped aside and let the big man rake his belly along the length of my left scadda. They never expected the body-shift to the right and weapon attack to the left. Tannese swordsmen reflexively shifted body-left to free the sword and arm as the arm hinged out to draw the blade. With a little surprise, I noted the man's cuirass was not even metal-studded under his robes. His leathers parted like the skin under it. Had they grown so arrogant they didn't armor up even at surprise inspections? Steam swirled out, and blood spurted with each heartbeat. I poked him again and wrinkled my nose. Dust flew as the man fell.

Ben, at my eye-corner, was using a neat filleting gesture on a red-haired camp guard with a thief-fast hand. Ben swore at a rip in his outrobe and leathers, and stepped around the staggering man to the next one.

The bailiff pulled something from a waist sash, leveling it at Ben. Without waiting to see what it was, I bashed it from his hand with the back of my scadda's forte. Then I punched the pommel up in his face to occupy him, and turned to help a youngster overwhelmed by a bigger veteran tough. I parried a heavy dagger and the youngster got a ragged decapitation

going—sufficient, but messy. I flicked my blades to drain
them, glancing around.

The other camp guards were running away, pursued by
three of my escort. Apparently, Ben and I had targeted accu-
rately the leadership and excised it. I turned back to the
bailiff, who was sitting on the ground holding his nose. When
I went toward him, he shrieked, scrabbling backward on his
bottom, grabbing for the tool I'd knocked out of his hand.

Ben picked it up instead. "Sharinen," he said laconically.
"Smuggled or stolen, probably." Casually he swung the
metal barrel. The bailiff cried out and tumbled over and over,
and lay still.

I looked after the man. "Breathing," I said.

"Good," Ben said, with such force in his tone I looked at
him. "Liege doesn't like anybody treated the way these
people were. Look at those little babies! Didn't anybody
notice what was going on out here?"

"I think they saw a lot of hungry animals they couldn't talk
to," I said. I saw Rafai riding up the hill toward us, waving
his sword. His party split, one group pursuing running men,
the other riding on toward us.

"Saw what they were bribed to see," Ben said darkly.
"Anybody could tell what was going on. Have to arrange a
new guard out here and some new supplies, flame this bastard's hide."

"We'd better check all the camp inspectors, and the bai-
liffs." I wiped my blades even as Ben sheathed his sword. He
pulled thongs from his robe pockets and stepped over the
bailiff, efficiently searching the man's robes and binding him.

"Thought we might need these strings. Liege will carve
this glutton up," Ben grunted.

"Physically?" I glanced around, putting loose weapons in
a pile.

Ben looked up and grinned. "You haven't heard the rough
side of the Liege Lord's temper yet? Ai, this sack of slime
will *wish* it was physical."

Later that night in Tanman's chamber at the hold, I stirred
uncomfortably, lifted my head, rubbed at my eyes. My arm
felt stiff. I'd fallen asleep in Tanman's spare chair sometime
after dusk, while he paced about and worked on slates by the
light of a rack of brass lamps. "You're awake?" he asked
cheerfully. "Rafai, this stack of estimates goes back to

my private archives. Where's that stack of bills of lading? Naga, I'm going to prove my case so thoroughly Lake Clan's smugglers will leave for better shelter. Troops need at least one secure site to fall back to if Black Pebble Ford is breeched.''

I moved my legs, flexing muscles. I was in my leathers yet. For a moment, drowsy, partly in my stupor, I blinked at him.

"And you the fellow with so many mine-tax reports to read," Rafai said lightly to me.

My own fault, I'd asked for them when I got back. "Unfortunately I just—'' I waved one hand to indicate how I'd drifted off. I yawned, and scratched the old scar hollow on my shoulder where I hid little knives.

"Rafai had a nice long nap waiting for the camp bailiff to answer questions, that's how he comes to look so fine," Tanman said dryly. "Why don't you go to bed, too? I forgot you were there."

I stretched, crackling joints carefully and luxuriously. I settled back in the chair and rested my head against the chair back. "Fine here. If you need anything . . .''

"We've lost him again. Go get someone to warm up a blanket, Rafai.''

I stirred when I felt the bulk of a fire-warmed blanket draped around me. My head fell to rest among the cedar-scented folds. "Fine," I muttered contentedly.

"Go back to sleep," Tanman murmured, and pushed a layer closer around my shoulder.

I was disoriented briefly when I opened my eyes; the place was dark. Then I turned my head and realized Tanman had moved his lamp away behind me so the light would not shine in my face. He sat alone working, intent, absorbed in his slates, oblivious of me. I got up silently. So as not to surprise him, I hummed softly, and then more loudly, and walked up. He jumped.

He looked at me, mouth flattened. Then he smiled. "That was polite of you. It also startled me.''

"I was trying not to.''

"Sit down here. Hungry? There's a tray of fruit here. I'll show you how to eat it politely.'' He took the little silver fruit knife, placed it in my hand, and adjusted my fingers.

"This knife is dull for that," I said doubtfully, tossing up the apple and sticking it.

He laughed. "No, hold it in your hand while you cut it."

"Thus?"

"Thus," he agreed, smiling. "So you throw things about when you eat apples?"

"I trained on dried apples," I said. "They have the same resistance as leather, in the desert."

"And you still train that way?"

"No. On feathers, and clay pellets." I crunched the slices. Then, belatedly, I said, "Is it incorrect to just talk to you, without the salute and saying Liege?"

"Quite," he said, smiling, and leaned back in his chair and stretched. "But you may talk as you please when I use the informal mode, in private like this, and I don't think anyone will object."

I nodded. "I should tally those mine-tax reports, there were some fraudalent-looking figures, and I can't seem to find any good new iron surveys—"

"New, in such terms, would be done in my father's reign—and he was not investing in exploratory shafts or equipment. He liked silver plate. So, of course, we pay the Cragmen shortage rates and a rickety plant bought from Sharin, here at the Lakes, is generating all our silver thread. I wish it was the other way around now. I married Capilla to get alliance with the silk clans who control metal imports." He inspected me critically. "You still have that bruised look about the face, the eyes—not enough sleep. I don't want you making a practice of it, Naga."

I looked up, surprised. "I thought you worked men hard. Pitar and Rafai have too much just maintaining watch strength for daily coverage, let alone travel and screening audience visitors. I didn't want you to fail for lack of information or analysis, and there's so much work—"

"I watch men when I work them. You're working too hard. Why do you twitch like an animal in your sleep?"

I grimaced. "Dreams," I said, and tossed the apple core into the slushpot with a clang.

"Bad?"

"Not this evening, no. Not for how tired I was. I've been sleeping well. Before—" I felt suddenly embarrassed. My nightmares were impairing my performance, obviously. I straightened. "It's nothing important."

"Don't lie to me, Naga," he said sharply. "How bad is it? I don't want to hear what you'd tell some hill-bandit employer."

I rested my hands on my thighs, taking a deep breath.

"Stop looking like a little boy I'm yelling at," he said, "and just talk to me. They're like relivings?"

I jerked at a strap on my left knee-guard.

He said quietly, "Is there any place—any time or routine— you don't have the dreams?"

I jerked at the strap. "Yes."

"Where?"

Head down, I said, "Where you are. The complete and imperfect bodyguard!" Then, savagely, I added, "I'd sleep on the floor, or across the doorway, or anywhere here, just fine. But off on my own, ever since the Oath swearing, it all comes back in a—" I made a disgusted gesture. And I didn't look at him. Too well I remembered him calming me from a half-drugged nightmare my first night. "I sound insane, don't I? A witch, like the Cragmen say I am."

"I think there's a pretty obvious cure for it."

"It is obvious, isn't it?" I grimaced. "I can't help it. I just—I feel like a fool, but these dreams, they have a bad habit of repeating. Gets—tiresome after awhile, same old thing all the time." I felt my shoulders hunching, and forced them down again.

He slowly and deliberately took up an apple, cored it, sliced it. He held out half the slices. "Take some."

I took some, ate them.

He sat back in his chair, frowning a little, eating apple slices. "Perhaps not a witch . . . You have given us some interesting ideas in your—ah—seizures. Like the map, the magnesium bricks, and some exact fortification demands at specific garrisons. I've no doubt the Goddess will call on Her prophet if She wishes, wherever he is. I knew *I* needed you about as my guard, I was not aware you would benefit also. I'm trying to consider if there are any problems."

"It's stupid, that's what," I said bitterly. I picked up his apple core and threw it—clang!—in the slushpot. "I'm not a prophet!"

He looked at the pot. "Do you ever miss?"

"All the time, in practices," I said crossly.

"I haven't seen you miss anything around me."

"That's exhibition," I said.

He looked at me.

"I know, it's been a long time since anybody used that tone with you. I'm sorry. You can have my head bashed in for it. I'm sure I'd be sorrier then."

"A long time, yes," he agreed, and opened up a foreign fruit with a hard green rind. "Given the circumstances here in Tan, my having your head bashed in would not be smart. If my men endured what makes a Sati sweat and lose sleep, they'd go mad. You don't have to be embarrassed, Naga, I just want you to get your rest."

I laced my fingers tightly together. In a thicker drawl than normally, I said, "You do have a way with you of cutting right in along the bone, don't you."

He glanced up. "What, about embarrassment? I didn't stay Tanman by being blind, you know. If I *asked* you if you wanted to sleep nearby, you'd say, 'no, of course not,' like an utter fool. I know that pride. So I'm telling you. You will report if the problem changes, and don't try to cover it and lie to me again."

"Yes, Liege," I muttered.

"Louder."

I repeated it.

"Yes, Caladrunan," he said firmly. He tossed segments— wet, fluid-filled sacs—at me. I caught them, tasted them, waited; nodded. He said, "You saw how I did that?"

"Peeling?" I said, picking up another of the fruits, and repeating how he'd peeled it.

"You're faster than I am," he said, sounding disgusted. "Peel the others then, Lord Hungry."

I tossed him sacs, grinning.

Then he said, licking his lips of juice, "You know what I miss in most of my friends, my nobles?"

I looked up, surprised, with half a foreign fruit in my hand.

He pointed. "The simple ability to accept food from their hands. I just can't take the risk, these days."

I looked down at the fruit. Then at him. I said, "I tasted it first, it seemed all right—but I don't know this fruit either. Are you—"

He smiled. "I know, I saw you do it. Don't look so appalled, it's fine. You see, because in Tan you were never anyone else's man—maybe Reti's—we can all think you trustworthy to me."

I blinked. Then I set down the fruit and frowned. "I'm not hungry anymore. In the desert I swore Oath, at the Altar I swore an Oath, and I meant it."

"This is Tan. You must understand how people will view it, as being a convenient Oath."

I stood up, resting my hand on the back of the chair. "Convenient," I said, in a rather deep register.

He looked steadily at me, waiting.

"Convenient," I said. "I'm sure the Osa found a great deal here convenient."

"Not in my Hall," he said crisply.

I looked at him bitterly. "And in Keth Adcrag's hall? Oldfield's hall? Some nobles seem to have a poor understanding of fealty."

He agreed, popping a sac in his mouth. Ruefully, he said, "I failed to teach them, too."

I surveyed him rather grimly. "I think they chose not to learn. You know all about teaching someone loyalty." My voice scaled up to a parody: "Isn't that risky, a Sati armed, right near you?"

"Mmm," he said, with his mouth full. "Indeed. Particularly if somebody wakes up that Sati without warning. Like a bear in a bad mood: sudden death. Have some more of this, it's very good. Do Satis have trouble learning trust?"

"No," I said, jabbing three fingernails through the skin of an apple, and lifting it. "This Sati will have no trouble distinguishing between his friend and his friend's—" I smashed the apple on the edge of the table. It fractured in three pieces across the core, and fell neatly apart. None of the pieces shifted more than a handspan from the strike-site "—enemies."

That night Pitar woke me at the change of watch, speaking quietly outside the chamber door. I glanced at Tanman as I pulled on my leathers and belt, and I slipped out holding the heavy door with my wrist. The two duty guards outside could not stiffen any further, or they would have.

"I went over your suggestions," Pitar said, "and implemented some immediately. From your wake-up orders, I thought you'd want to see the sort of lighting and visibility we have here at night."

I nodded. "Do the men know we're inspecting?"

Pitar smiled. "The ones who saw me pass; but no, the rest do not." He spoke quietly to the sentry at the outer meeting room. Though we avoided creaking the wooden floors, we went through the guest chambers with no other effort to be quiet. Neither of us wished to startle armed men.

Each chamber opened directly to the next, without back passages for servants' work, as Lake Hold was an old place. Though built of timbers, it had only twice burned in its long history. The rooms were lit now by big oil lamps near each door; Tanman's entourage slept on straw pallets on the floor. In their furs, the sleepers looked like a pillaged storeroom stock, flung in swags and humps across the floor. No one stirred as we passed. Pitar said, "You can always tell night commanders—when they walk, they creep like cats, and talk constantly." He sounded proud of it.

"I suppose the steward screamed about the extra oil and torches."

Pitar's teeth flashed in the gloom within the large wooden main hall. "That he did, noble-born." Humps and blankets and burlap sacks lay everywhere on the hall floor; the local soldiers and servants bedded down in common warmth. The place was lit by a single long stone hearth that lacked any hood, shedding a shadowy haze throughout the air. It vented somewhere in the black rafter space. The coals winked like glaring eyes, sparked, and vanished again in the long bank of ash.

I looked up from the firebed to the blackness overhead, and felt a slow creeping cold across my back, as if we were being watched.

"I thought you said nobody could climb up there," I murmured.

Pitar had the sense not to throw his gaze up. He waited, poised. Then the odd feeling eased. I shrugged, puzzled. He said, "Well, Tanman's sister was seen up there once, but no one else knows how she did it. They had to make a ladder just to get her down. Rafai can check for markings in the dust up there, come morning."

"I have not met Girdeth yet."

Pitar laughed soundlessly, shoulders moving against the light of coals. "You won't forget her soon. Come, I've secured the women's quarters, too, against any threat to Liege's kin."

We passed down an outside balcony past closed chamber doors. Guards stood at some of the doors, apparently surprised as we approached. Over the wind, Pitar said, "This balcony is due to be closed in before the weather goes bad— some sort of removable panels. Not terribly secure, any of this— They move into the guest rooms when it's snowing. We didn't light the storerooms underneath here, I couldn't talk the steward into that. I had the main pantry lit, you can see a bit of light out of the eyeloops in the floor along this sitting area here. I've set each watch's underofficers to looking in the loops as they patrol along here."

"Much grumbling about extra work?" I asked, and looked approvingly at the torches streaming in the topmost bailey. At least a guard could see any movement or change of shadow-forms, if he stayed alert.

Pitar chuckled. "Reminded them you may have saved Liege's life, first night in Fortress hall—stopped all that. So, how do you like turning into an accountant?"

I said wryly, "It wasn't quite what I expected. But I find it soothing, which is odd."

"Fellow like you with his letters and his numbers, now that seems odd. Ai, Liege has surprised a lot of people on this. Now, here's that stair to kitchen and cellar, under the hall baffle between doors. Wish we had some Sharinen lenses, expand the light of that cresset there—no room for more lamps."

"I've been thinking the Armorer could direct it with some flat white surface like the roofing slates, perhaps make a harness of brass to hold the slates in place without taking too much room."

"He hates that kind of work," Pitar said.

"He'll hate worse his meals falling downstairs. Or somebody climbing up from in a storeroom, leaping from this stairwell into the hall without so much as shadow to give warning. We should at least put tables across the direct aisle to the dais. The Armorer may also have some brighter-burning stuff than oil which we could burn here, so long as we're visiting."

Pitar chuckled. "I'll leave you to convince him of all this."

"I'll present it as an engineering dilemma. They usually bite on that." I waved at the kitchen around us, making wit on our surroundings.

"Our good Armorer has had more practice at evading fix-it requests than most," Pitar said. More humped forms were huddled in the kitchen, clumped about a draft oven built in the brick pier that, on the floor above, became the firepit. The chimney seemed to vent into copper pipes. Pitar pointed. "Those two pipes go out to the bathing shed. Water picks up heat in here and goes back out. Tidy arrangement, all fed from the rain cistern on the roof. There's even a hand pump for this at the well, when rain is gone."

"Any holes a small person could climb through, above these pipes?"

"I checked that today—no sign of any, no fresh cuts or disturbed dust."

I looked about. "I'd guess the cook is due down here soon, and he'll throw us out. Any burrows into the food lockers?"

"Found one, boy-sized, in the buttery. Got a carpenter to that right away. I tell you, the steward thought I was impugning his management!"

"Only one hole, I congratulate him," I said dryly. "The hold lockers I've seen were riddled." We climbed the stairs past the cresset and made a quick traverse to check on Tanman in his sleep. Then we went along the outer sentry walk, which ran in isolation along the outside of the hall, and down steps to bathing shed and guarderobes above the river. The isolation reduced the stink inside.

"Can't keep this well lit, the wind hits that corner hard," Pitar said. "The young men like to come out here with the pleasure women—from the village, strictly."

"I know, there aren't any of that sort *living* up here," I said. "The steward's scribe was quite careful to explain that to me."

Pitar laughed.

I said, "This walk is terribly exposed. I'd put some outworks around here, to keep people around it more—maybe extra gana pens beneath the walk, we'll need more stables than these baileys have now, if Black Pebble Ford forces fall back to here. And why not make this area productive—"

"Some sort of stinky work like tanning pits," Pitar added. "which uses saved-up guarderobe mess, Sitha help us all. I'm surprised they didn't already think of that practical combination. I think the local tanners use bat guano built up in the Lake caves. I know the silver plant up there has something like tanner's ponds. I'm told the Cragmen use seabird guano off those miserable cliffs of theirs, for all sorts of mining industries.''

"Maybe that explains Keth Adcrag's temper.'' We went back to the hall door, and out: down the outside ramp into the yard of the upper bailey. Beside the bailey palings, inside a blockhouse lit by cressets I'd insisted on, we climbed more stairs—and came out on a parapet at the lip of the hold's main palisade. Pacing briskly along the wide and well-built parapet past sentries, Pitar and I discussed outworks, rubble barriers, fire-resistant facades, and funds for feeding levied laborers to do the work. We paused on the side overlooking the hold village. The wind came at our backs and whipped Pitar's outrobe in long dark furls, embroideries aglitter by the streaming torchlight.

"I think a heavy gate would not balance out,'' Pitar said, pointing. "We have to weigh the needs of trade coming in and defense, or your business begins to drop. Hold Nebvahrar—''

"—wonderful defensive crag,'' I agreed glumly, ''—abandoned for lack of surrounding trade or crops. This is well built,'' I said, gesturing at the palisade. "It's just the wrong material.''

"Well, these kinds of timbers take a good long while to ignite. Did I show you the furnace and hypocausts that warm this pile? They learned it from piping the hot springs in Fortress; like the bathing shed, they pipe the steam around. Well, the timbers they burn down there take a year to need replacing. And—'' Pitar turned into the light, so I could see him grin, ''—the Armorer is down somewhere there, fiddling with a pile of junk. He keeps odd watches, he just might be up working.''

I grunted and went downstairs. Across the bailey a man was replacing torches that burned low. Pitar led the way to a shed; he spoke to the guards taking turnabout, within and without the heavy door, in the cold.

Inside—lit by more such lamps I'd insisted upon—was a cut stone stairway to the piers beneath the hall and kitchen floors. A spider web billowed in a draft. Sitting, arms dangling between his knees, a skinny figure loomed over a glaring firebox door.

"This light is not that good,'' Pitar said.

The Armorer shifted, coughed. "It's always bad in here."

I looked around at the tidy piles of metal, glimmering reflected light. Within the firebox, timbers glowed—thicker than the piers around me. There was very little odor; only stone and sifted dust from the floors above.

"So," the Armorer said, propping his thin face in two long sooty fingers. He stared mournfully at me. "*You* sort these parts and explain them."

I looked coolly at the Armorer, and at the parts, and shrugged. Instead, I explained our requirement for a light-deflector to brighten the kitchen stairwell.

He stood up so quickly he bumped his head on a floor joist and yelled. "Out! What am I, some flaming tinsmith's apprentice? I built your flamed heliographs, and let me say those plated glass mirrors were near impossible. Out!" He rubbed his head. "If that's all you can tell me, out! You're ruining my concentration."

I looked levelly at Pitar. "I see," I said. "And when will we see new flamethrowers built?"

The Armorer scowled. He did not seem the same personality I'd seen before, among his children. Perhaps Tannese did not travel well. "I'll cobble up something in the morning. Which cresset is it? Oh, that. Flamed fools, you'd think the cook's runners would have got that done years ago. Antique, all of it. Can't even use the lathe-built designs they've got in their own silver plant." He glared. "Well, do any of these heaps make sense to you?"

I said, "They take these out to make a thrower fail so I'd think they were the most important bits. That's a fuel-and-air mixing chamber that's had the vent spiked—"

"I knew that. No, these bits over here. How do they transfer steam chamber pressure to the axles?"

I glanced at Pitar. "I think it's time I got back."

"You're no help at all," the Armorer said.

Pitar said, behind me, "I think that's the idea. He doesn't like the damned things, you know. Good night."

At the stairs I turned and said, "Armorer, how is the Fortress of Tan vulnerable, within your region of mastery?"

He heard me perfectly. "Underpinnings," he said crisply. "Look downstairs sometime. That whole rock's alive."

"But Fortress never quakes—" Pitar said, "—never sapped or taken—"

"So who says it can't?" Rafai's father shrugged when I thanked him. The Armorer muttered as we left, and glared at a pile of gears.

The next morning Tanman did not order food up to his room as expected. He read a message slate, lifted his brows, and just after first light broke over the palisade, Caladrunan and I marched down with escort to the hall for the first meal of the day. Rafai was peering at the rafters. Though up and yawning, few of the hold people were really awake as Tanman greeted them. Then he spoke to a girl striding through the main door. A girl who, though she had the pale hair of Lake Clan's nobles, did not even wear a veil over an alert face. She turned, holding something hidden in the flare of her robes. She lifted it upward from the fullness of her clothing.

As Caladrunan began to speak, I was charging her. My harpcase swung under my arm as a shield, my scaddas were out in my hands—and Tanman's hand flew up in the imperative stop signal.

I found myself, scaddas extended at arm's length, looking at the end of the girl's cocked crossbow. She glared at me.

Tanman began to laugh. "Girdeth! Put that thing down. He's one of my friends!" He looked heartily amused. At his sharp gesture, I sheathed my scaddas. But the girl didn't move, training the tip of the bolt on me when I moved. She examined me unblinkingly from head to foot for ten long heartbeats. The others in the Hall were staring, motionless as startled cattle. Meanwhile, Tanman smiled, chuckled, and poured himself a goblet of wine from the common barrel by the door. I stared at the crossbow and the girl's pale green eyes. My hand itched to smack the bow from her grip, for safety's sake.

She said, "You must be that Sati, my brother's pet. Mother sent word, dear brother, to make sure of him. She said he was prowling all over the hold last night."

Tanman said, "So, I'm told, was Pitar. Mother is senile, as you very well know. Naga, meet my sister, Girdeth—she with the temper of a grass-fire!"

I inclined my head a degree, watching her.

"I don't like his looks," the girl said. The bolt point held steadily on me. I didn't much like hers, either.

Tanman said easily, "Put it up, Girdeth. You're being rude to a hero, and inconsiderate besides. The poor man's not had his food yet."

"Where did you find him, in a kennel? Since when is this—this!—a hero?"

"Since there were assassins in the Great Hall some days back. Ask Lado Kiselli, I'm sure he'd be eloquent."

She finally took his word for it, and lowered the crossbow. The instant the point started down, I reached out and snapped the wood shaft of the bolt. The bow-cord sprang free of its cocking and snapped her thumb in recoil. She let out a cry and almost dropped the thing. Uncocked, with no more bolts in hand, it was not much of a weapon. I relaxed slightly. She stared at her reddening thumb, and then at me. And stamped her foot. "How did you *do* that?"

Tanman chose to sit at a common trestle table; he put down three pewter goblets. Tanman drawled languidly, "He is faster than your trigger hand, Girdeth. Now please do have some food, and drink the wine I've poured before it gets warm, both of you."

She made a very rude stable-boy gesture at me. I jerked the crossbow out of her hand and set the center of the cross-stock on the table edge. An inferior weapon, it smashed in pieces. "Cheap," I said, regarding the damage.

Girdeth sank onto a bench opposite her brother, and leaned her elbows on the table, gazing at the wreckage. There was a dent in the table. She lifted her eyes to me. I looked at her more carefully than before; she wore the expensive silks of a noble at court, and a lot of jewelry—which I could see no reason for, in a place so familiar and safe that she did not even wear the ubiquitous womanly veil.

I rested my hands on the table amidst the debris. "Do you treat all your guests this way?"

She said crisply, "Only those who look like they'd slit someone's throat for a good price, creeping about the hold all night. I suppose it was your fault, all those new security orders. It quite ruined my day's plans!"

Caladrunan said hastily, glancing at me, "Oh, be fair, Girdeth. That's his job. And the scars add a certain—character, don't you think?" He held out a goblet of wine to her.

"I agree. I've seen better-looking hangmen."

He laughed. They looked very alike now, these two, with their light eyes and wheaten hair. They were both tall and big-boned, and looked close kin. She stared at me, saying judicially, "I expected better of you, brother."

Caladrunan chuckled, "One of your soft housebred nobles, eh? Tall and handsome and languid and so-o-o slow. Well, meet a real soldier."

"I've met others," she said coolly, and sniffed. It was then, unexpectedly, I saw the glint of wild mirth in her eye—the suppressed giggles of laughter exactly like her brother's. I could not take the put-on noble arrogance seriously anymore. I revised my first guess about her age; she was in the throes of Tannese adolescence, which I felt sure made her capable of a great deal worse than this. One long ringed finger snapped out to point at me. "You laugh at Tanman's sister?" she growled.

I said, "Why not? I laugh at Tanman, sometimes."

She snatched up a piece of her crossbow, threatening to hit me, and I snatched it away from her. She yelled in frustration and grabbed her wine goblet. Wine sloshed over the table. Caladrunan grabbed her wrist. "What is this, brawling with the men?"

She glared at her brother. "How did he do that? I can beat *everyone*—"

Tanman released her wrist. He said, "Naga comes of a clan whose men snatch the necks of desert vipers. His training included tests of speed."

She drawled, "Has nonsense like that been necessary?"

Caladrunan nodded silently.

Girdeth abruptly crossed one knee over the other inside her robes, sipped at her wine, played with a pearl necklace. She adjusted a filmy wrap at her bosom, checking to be certain of my expression with sly upward glances through her lashes. To her finely tuned feminine perceptions it must have been blindingly obvious that her charade had none of the usual effects. Trouble, I thought stonily, if she does this to poor silly young guards. My first impulse was to upend her and apply a piece of crossbow to her behind. Then she smiled at me with Caladrunan's innate disarming candor. "Oh—you *are* annoyed. You're a real charmer, aren't you, Pet?"

"Pet," Tanman said, amused.

"Pet?" I said hostilely, feeling my hackles rise.

"It's perfectly obvious you're going to be my brother's favorite little scruffy. I like to keep people's names straight in my mind."

"My name is Naga Teot!"

Caladrunan said gently, "You're offending him, Girdeth. Try to remember your court manners, please."

She glanced over at him and said casually, "Oh, by the way, Pupo, Aunt Spit wants you to trot over and see her this morning."

I lifted my brows, looking at him. I was not alone in obtaining an offensive name from Girdeth. "Pupo? Aunt Spit?"

"You keep out of that," Caladrunan said hastily.

"Pupo is a kind of fishing worm," Girdeth said. "Haven't you any nicknames like that? Grub? Plith-plath? Like Lado said—Black Man? Or some such?"

Tanman abruptly reached out and twisted his sister's ear until she howled; she beat at his wrist with her rings, while he grinned. She growled as he let go. He had never told me that his family was crazy like this; I watched them in astonishment as they settled back in their chairs, both apparently well-pleased by the exchange.

She snapped, "Wait until you meet Aunt! She will really pop your ears."

I found myself joining Caladrunan in his coughing fit. Some lady! Girdeth had the mouth of a teamster.

He said, "It ought to be interesting, Aunt and Naga together. Naga could win the foulmouth title in Fortress, without knowing there was one to win."

Girdeth lifted feathery pale brows. "Oh, Aunt will have a time with him."

Tanman explained to me, "My mother used to fine anyone who uttered a foul word. Great-aunt Agtunki is exempted for her age, which I never thought was fair."

Girdeth laughed. "You got it, remember, when you were seventeen? It was terribly embarrassing, the Liege Lord of Tan asking his mother to excuse him from wearing a fool's mask. Two moons married, too."

I smiled. "Liege, did you have to wear the mask?"

Girdeth chuckled. "No, he had to read History translations to Aunt Agtunki—Aunt Spit, to you, Pupo. I don't know which was the worst punishment." They both laughed merrily.

Then Girdeth said, "Aside from new orders they didn't like, Mother and the steward were muttering about somebody lighting all the lamps and torches last night."

I glanced at Caladrunan. "Me," I told her.

Caladrunan said, "For my guard shifts, at night."

Girdeth said, regarding me critically, "You do look the sort who'd slink around at night, except you're too dark. Too much sun."

I said indignantly, "I am this color!"

"All over?"

"Aren't you white all over, like fishbelly?" I retorted. "Or do you save special colors for special places—"

Caladrunan's hand came down on my shoulder, hard. He said, "Let's not forget that Girdeth is a lady, even if she does."

I shut up.

Girdeth said, "I see what you mean about his mouth." Then she gave me a sunny smile. She looked half her real age. Conspiratorially she said, "I'm the family radical. The rest are terribly stuffy. Aside from Aunt—she's just odd. I suspect you'll throw the lot pop-a-nocky. What would happen if a man walked in here yelling with a butcher knife?"

I blinked. After a moment, Caladrunan said, "Don't taunt him, Girdeth. That's going to be his duty. And so is staying awake all night with the lamps lit, sometimes."

Her eyes turned grave. "He'd better be good. I heard that there were a few times you almost got hit, Pupo."

He smiled, tapping one of her braids with a mock-fist. "All here, in one piece."

Girdeth tossed her head and said, "Up *here* we only have assassins up for midday drinks, noon precisely, on the fourth day of each moon—or the second Feast day, whichever comes first."

I didn't say anything, but I didn't think that was funny.

Girdeth reached out, trailing one finger on the table. "Oh, I've annoyed you again, you're rattling your robes. How much of an armory do you have stashed away in there, anyway?"

I twitched aside before she could touch me. Caladrunan told me dryly, "She's been learning from Aunt how to insult people. Pay no mind."

"She's rather hard to ignore," I said.

"Make the attempt," he said.

"Yes, Liege."

Girdeth said, "Pupo, do you enjoy bossing the pet around?"

"Yes," Caladrunan said, in a sharper tone than before. "I

prefer to use men who are good at things. And quality tools.''
With his hand he swept the crossbow shards off the table.

I said, ''Girdeth, how did you come to have this bow
design?'' I knew my voice was low, and a little too soft to
pass as angry—unless someone knew me. Unfortunately,
Caladrunan knew me that well; it hadn't taken long.

Caladrunan sighed. ''I told her about it. She tries having
things built sometimes. She wanted to see how much strength
it took to cock it—apparently not near what the archery
masters insist.''

Girdeth glared. ''Talking military—I suppose this means I
wasn't supposed to build it.''

''Now behave yourself. Don't stick your lip out. Naga
would have flattened anyone else ages ago, the things you've
been saying.''

''He broke my crossbow! And he's been insulting me right
back—''

''He's earned the right. Now leave him alone.''

''He's rather hard to ignore,'' she said, mimicking my
tone, even attempting my accent.

I smiled. Not altogether pleasantly.

Caladrunan said, ''Where's the food? And Aunt? Never-
mind. We're supposed to go out on a hunt sometime this
morning, we'll have to skip Agtunki.''

''You'll be sorry if you leave Aunt till later. She's in one
of her mischievous moods.'' Girdeth stood up and destroyed
all impression of coy femininity by shouting for food at the top
of her lungs.

''Hunt?'' I said to Caladrunan. ''It's past dawn.''

He beamed. ''You'll enjoy it. The dogs aren't as good as
my Fortress packs, but there's lots of game, and you'll get to
show my cousins what you can do in the woods.''

''I'm not here to entertain your sister or your cousins. I'm
here to keep you from breaking your neck.''

He just gave me a sunny look, exactly like Girdeth's, and
smiled at the servants. Girdeth flounced off after a brief hug
from her brother. We ate in silence together under the eyes of
the serving men. They kept staring at me, and whispering
away from the table. As we finished, Caladrunan called for
his hunting bow to be carried down, and his gana to be
brought around. He smiled at me. I glared back. I had no
intention of going on any public hunt, but it seemed I had no

choice. I did go over all his gear with extra care, mistrusting the Lake Clan guards.

As it turned out, I was right not to trust such guards. None of them bothered to keep our beasts secure, or us; without his own escort, Tanman would have been alone. The dog pack barked and wandered about the mounting courtyard and some ill-trained mongrels nipped at the ganas. Nobles came up whenever they pleased to us. We were mounting, out in the courtyard, when a blond youth stalked up toward us on foot.

Both our ganas reared, bared their teeth, whistled. My mare gana snapped out her head, reaching to gore the idiot with one horn. The youth leaped back rather too late—if I hadn't jerked the mare's head back with a kick, she would have ripped his soft underparts away up through his head. As it was, she knocked him hard with the curve of her horn, throwing him down.

"What kind of a fool trick—" Tanman roared.

I snapped a command and my mare snorted and came back down on all four hooves. I looked at the youth, then at Tanman. Caladrunan had been in the midst of settling in his saddle when his bull reared. I was glad to see it had not ruffled Tanman's balance at all, he was nicely set in his saddle. I backed my mare away from the fool on the ground, though she hissed and hooked.

"Well, cousin—Liege," the youth drawled, rising, dusting himself off. "Glad to see you're ready for the hunt, and still as good a rider as you ever were."

Caladrunan said, in elaborately polite court dialect, "I wish I could say it of you. You saw the ear-marks on these beasts, Eran. You know better than to spook anything trained in my fighting stables. These are not parade ganas. Surely you must remember what little you did learn."

In court dialect, it was impeccably scathing; the youth flushed red. Looking closer, I could see that the youthfulness was only an impression. There were not enough deep lines to mark his face at a distance; he looked disgruntled, and somehow, irresponsible. Eran was slighter built than Caladrunan, and younger by perhaps six years—but no youth. And there was resentment in there, under the misleadingly childish face. Eran grinned, making the best of it. "Murderous lot, those beasts of yours." He walked up toward me, holding out his hand toward my mare. The mare bared her teeth and lowered her horns. She had proper instincts. Eran edged back ten paces. "So, tell me, my cousin Liege—is he as friendly as his ugly mare?"

"Less so," Caladrunan said coldly.

Eran looked up at me. "Until you tell him so, eh? And maybe not even then."

Around us in the courtyard, other members of the hunt were mounting their ganas, coming from various doors, stretching and yawning. They cursed at the dogs. Like most of the gear, the beasts were for show. Ours were by far the fittest— and ugliest—mounts. Eran said, "So is he as good as the stories say?"

I looked down at Eran. Something about the court dialect he used, not quite fully formal, still slid away from my complete understanding. I had the feeling I was being subtly mocked. Eran was fifth in the line of succession, and his arrogance was as traditional as Caladrunan's plain common sense was not.

Caladrunan said, "What do you think, Eran?" And he made a Upai warning sign at me, to restrain myself but wait ready.

Eran's face sobered. "Some of the cousins expect to find out. They've started a boar. It's in a cave off Duck Lake." He paused. "A big boar."

Caladrunan stirred, glancing at me. I could see Eran expected me to be impressed. I was not, after working with Reti's huntmaster. I said finally, "Pig meat," and I dragged the breath into my nose in such a way it made a ruckling, snuffling noise.

Eran looked startled.

I said, "Don't you have anything more interesting?"

A slow smile started on Caladrunan's face. I, too, could play snob. Of course, I had not added that, besides being boring with so many dogs as this to waste, boar could be ugly on close work, sometimes not worth the meat it gave. Tanman settled back in his saddle as if satisfied to see me hook Eran like a fish. I thought, Eran, who is your master, who sent you to bait me? Who set Lake Clan's disgruntled top bully on me?

Eran said slowly, "Interesting?"

I said, "Reti's men hunted boar and red deer for food in the mountains of the desert. It's dull work. Yedda and screamers were more challenging."

Tanman said mildly, "I remember Reti sent me a bedfur patched up of yedda pelts. Cattle-killers and sheep-stealers— the man-cunning ones. He told me he didn't hunt the wild yedda who run the deer herds, they weren't clever enough." Oh, he was enjoying himself, and the look on Eran's face.

Eran said, "I didn't realize you were both such—discriminating huntsmen."

"Oh, Reti said his men each took down a yedda alone, to make rank." Caladrunan's face was suspiciously bland.

"Not always," I corrected. "Sometimes yeddas were just in the line of work. I remember I took one pelt out of a Upai camp, two scouts helped me. The beast was messing up our surveillance of raiders, kept panicking livestock and waking people up at night. Not at all what we wanted, so we killed it."

Eran said, "I see."

I said to Tanman, "Are you wanting me to come? You'll have no problem with boar, you've got enough of a dog pack here."

Caladrunan's eye glinted; now I was prodding him. He said smoothly, "We can both use the exercise."

Eran said, "Please excuse me, Liege, my beast has just come."

Caladrunan waved his hand. Eran made a big circle well clear of my mare, saluted Tanman, and went off. I saw him talking in low tones to several men before he actually mounted his beast; those men looked at us slyly.

I said fiercely, "Who was that, the local Lord Haughty?"

Caladrunan smiled. "You didn't do too badly yourself."

"I'm getting tired of proving I have a right to be here while stifling all my reflexes for family."

At that point the mounted huntsmen began to edge toward us, riding up one at a time to greet Tanman. My mare was nervous around so many strange riders and beasts, but at least they were mounted. After Eran's provocation, she would have trampled footmen. The male members of Lake Clan all rode up to politely examine Caladrunan's health, check his memory of their names, and stare at me—though none of it was quite put that way. One of the loud elder members began entertaining everyone with Sek-blood jokes. I found it in poor taste. Somebody eventually diverted him into jokes about young girls, which were just as bad.

Caladrunan seemed to find the whole thing amusing. One of the huntsmen passed around a wineskin; Eran took a monstrous slug from it, swaggering in his saddle. I would have tanned the huntmaster's skin to hold my wine if he allowed a hunt to go out like this; but it wasn't my hunt, nor Tanman's, and we both kept quiet. What made it into an incident was that Caladrunan offered the skin to me. I didn't want it; but it was plain no one turned down a drink from the hand of Tanman. No one else'd drink after me.

So I picked up the skin and smiled grimly at Caladrunan and tilted it up. I drank all of it. About five goblets' worth, it was quite enough to make me drunk. No one said a word. I crumpled up the skin and tossed it aside where the servants could get it later. I licked my lips. No one seemed to be looking exactly at me, when I glanced around. Caladrunan smiled. I said in a low voice, "I hope I don't actually fall off when all that hits."

"We'll still be riding on the way there," Caladrunan said, in a lipless murmur. "You can ride asleep. Most of them will be asleep—they'll never know the difference."

"They won't forget that little stunt."

"That was the whole point. I meant them to be impressed. That's the language they understand."

I said a rude Upai word. I was smiling all the while, which made my jaw ache. He smiled back at me. I said, louder, "How long does it take to get a troop on the road? I'd have Rafai howling if he took this long to get a party mounted."

One of the huntsmen near us turned in his saddle. He was a third or fourth cousin, who looked fifteen years older than Caladrunan; he was also cut across the nose with an old white sword mark. He said, "Patience, Sati. Some of this lot find it difficult to rise at dawn, and would be upset if we left without them. Not many of them are army quality." His voice was impeccably polite and his gaze steady when he looked at me. He hadn't been drinking.

"You were in the army," I said bluntly. "You didn't retain your rank in your name, for me to be aware of your title."

He smiled. His posture in the saddle gave it away, of course. "It seemed unnecessary after retiring. I can hardly expect my wife to salute me at bedside."

Tanman chuckled along with the man.

He said, "Eran has been very proud of himself since he won his latest challenge. Perhaps you've heard that he's been growing friendly with one of Keth Adcrag's friends, an officer who was sent over to Bada's Well to get disciplined. They drink each other's brains out."

Tanman said, "I know the one. Perhaps you could speak a few words with Eran. I shouldn't like to see Naga kill him."

Aider nodded, inclining his head. "Eran's pushing it, drinking away his speed. He's very good for this area, of course."

Caladrunan said, "Naga is better."

"Oh, yes. I'll speak to Eran carefully, you may be sure. But it would be stupid if your Sati took some wound just for the follies of that young bull. Especially since you tried so hard to find his people out at Redspring Hold—"

Caladrunan grimaced. "Aider—"

Aider lifted one hand. "I think he ought to know. By your leave, Liege. Years, we thought most of the Upai were dead, all the inquiries we made, all the searching, we found no one— Liege did try, for your brother's sake who was his friend. I knew Reti once: loyal as a burr. It made me feel good to see a man who's loyal, who speaks his mind and stands up for the real virtues." He smiled, looking modest and embarrassed. "Get carried away, don't I? But if you need anything on the hunt, or after, call on me."

I looked at Tanman, astonished, and then at Aider. "Thank you. I will."

He nodded and turned his beast and rode sedately away to take his position in line.

Caladrunan said, "My fourth cousin, Aider. He was one of my regents, the one I told you about who helped me escape. He advised me until I was twenty. Best one of the lot. He retired from the army to straighten his properties—he was a fierce fighter in the border raids, he got captured on the Crag border just a year before you got here. He was released on a private ransom given to some of Manoloki's Nandos, after nearly dying of starvation."

I looked at Caladrunan. "You didn't tell me that before, either."

He gave a wry smile. "Aider doesn't get noticed much these days—and he prefers it that way. His wife was driven mad during his imprisonment. She has good days when she talks, but for long periods she doesn't speak or move. She doesn't even eat unless you put the food in her mouth. He does everything for her himself. He only left her to servants now because I asked him to come on this hunt with me. He needed a bit of hunting, I thought. And I'd like you to put together a complete sand map of the desert, for Strengam, Aider and me to study.''

I folded my gloved hands together. ''I feel an idiot, drinking that way in front of a man like that.''

''He knows Eran as well as I do. I just thought that you'd like to know that not all Lake Clan are Eran's sort.''

''Yes,'' I said. ''Thank you.'' The line of riders finally began, in a straggling formation, to leave the courtyard.

''Where's Lado?'' Tanman asked.

''Sleeping late. He was up late last night dancing with the ladies and playing fourpeg. I think he was planning on going to a party tonight. Your son is at slate lessons I wrote out for him.''

''Party? I don't recall any party for today. The only one I know who runs parties up here is Aunt. My dear Aunt. Goddess help us all. Well, Girdeth did try to warn me.''

I added, ''Guard slates reported a lot of guests arriving and departing the hold, they're lodging in the village. Several wool clan boys came here.''

''They wouldn't dare—'' Caladrunan began.

''They would, for a prize like your sister.''

''You're right. That lot would. And my dear Aunt didn't send me a security report on her party ahead of time. That old reprobate!'' Caladrunan looked more annoyed than angry.

I dozed much of the ride into the lake hills. The wine sloshed uncomfortably about my brain. I had guilty thoughts about failing my duties whenever I snapped out of a nap. The hunt itself was not like my old hunts.

The jeweled and robed Lake Clan men rode along while the dogs quartered the brush with villagers on foot. It was not a meat hunt to the nobles, but a vermin-killing hunt; the greater numbers meant no shortage in shares of glory after. There were many good places to stop the boar, but no one tried to make the squalling boar stand to for archers, quickly, as I was accustomed to; I had never had time or numbers to track a boar so long. The dogs snapped and barked, driving the fleeing boar toward a net strung between several trees, across the path to its lair. Among the gashed and baying thickets of dogs, the boar didn't turn on any rider, just plunged headlong into the thick cordage and rolled up in it satisfactorily, and lay squirming and shrieking pigly obscenities, slashing cordage with its tusks. That net, I thought, would have held a bull gana easily. Three simultaneous spear jabs, one by Tanman, one by Aider, one by Eran, finished the job.

I stood by the tusks, ready to slash at the snout and distract it if it should lunge for Tanman, but I wasn't needed. All in all, a safe and productive extermination disguised as a dangerous noble outing. I could see everyone was red in the face and dusty and satisfied. Like cats at a kill.

The villagers moved in silently to retrieve what they might of the tough scarred old carcass, blooding it on the ground, setting water buckets over a fire to scald and scrape off the bristles. They didn't try to string it up on a gamble stick to hang it; it weighed too much for the tree branches.

Eran said then, passing me, "You didn't even try to spear it, Sati. What was that prattle about difficult game?"

Aider heard, and said curtly, "He took the head. Shut up before your own mouth slits your neck, you fool." It seemed his earlier attempts with Eran had not gone well. He climbed the scuffled leaf-strewn slope past Eran toward the ganas, looking disgusted.

Others heard the remarks. Some of the younger men muttered at Eran under their breath. More clearly, one languid dandy said, "You're going to insult a Sati, Eran? You're crazy."

Eran said, sticking out his chin, "Who knows whether he really is a Sati or not? Out in the desert anybody could say—"

I reached out, hooked Eran's neck with one hand, and shoved his face down into the steaming boar entrails. When he began to kick and struggle hard enough for air, I let him go. He slithered and struggled to his feet, wiping his face, and yelled, "Now I'm going to—" His hand pawed at his sword sheath.

I shoved his face into the entrails a second time. Let him up. When I glanced up, Caladrunan was standing nearby with a water skin in one hand. He grinned and handed it to me. I opened it wide and tossed it over Eran, drenching him. He sat in a puddle of gruesome mess. He gasped and spit and wiped his eyes. I flicked away some grains of blood from my robes, and waited. Eran sputtered, sitting there. Finally I held out my hand as if to greet him, and I said with Tannese hateur, "Naga Teot. Sati of scaddas. And you?"

Caladrunan burst into laughter along with everyone else.

Eran shrieked, "Goddess Above! How can you stand there and laugh, damn you, Pupo?"

I heard Caladrunan's little chuckle tickle over a second time into a full-grown roar of joy.

I folded my arms, watching Eran. I said, "In the desert, you are not properly a Nando until you've had your face shoved in a carcass by your trainer. It is considered an affectionate initiation."

Eran sputtered rude words, lurching to his feet. "Spare me your affection!"

Some of the others glanced uneasily at one another. Eran shouted onward, "All right. You caught me by surprise, anybody could be. How did you do it, like this?" And he made a grab at me.

I twitched aside. He grabbed again, and this time I blocked it, slamming him to the ground—mainly because I used the slick mud and the force of his own wild off-balance swing against him. He made a soggy splash. For a moment he lay there defeated.

Behind me, Tanman said gently, "Naga has his ways of proving what he says. Best go wash in the stream down there."

Eran muttered sullenly, climbed to his feet, and went off holding his grimed hands away from his sides. Since his clothes were ruined, it was a futile effort. Caladrunan turned, went to his cousin, Aider, and slapped him on the arm; they were both laughing. I glanced around at the younger men, who were tittering at Eran behind their hands. As expected, I sighed to myself. It was invariably necessary to fight or outbluff the resident bully whenever I poked my muzzle into a new Nando outpost. I was disappointed that Caladrunan's kin were no better.

When Eran came back, carrying his grimed outrobe, he passed me wriggling his shoulders like some street woman, with an extra flounce as he passed Tanman. They all laughed at that small wittiness. All the way back to the hold, Eran regaled the party with jokes. He must know it stung Tanman every time he told a joke about natives; he seemed content with that kind of revenge. I kept my own face masked in polite disinterest. At the main hold gate, he rode off looking about as cheerful as any of the other saddle-sore riders. But I wondered as I watched him go, and wondered if I had made a grave mistake to offend him.

CHAPTER

= *13* =

I BENT OVER the sandmap, moving models. Tanman slapped another model into my palm. I placed it carefully, triangulating from two other positions on the map. I frowned. "Not sure of the exact height of that hill," I said, smoothing the slope with my littlest fingernail. "Only heard about it."

Tanman's Heir shuffled forward. I glanced at his boots and he picked up his feet. "Aren't there any more of our holds out there?" he asked curiously.

I glanced at the boy, then at his father. "No."

"But didn't we used to have a hold called—called—" he frowned. "I think it was there." He pointed at the narrow slot I'd dug to show Pass of Bones.

"Tan used to," I agreed softly.

The boy's eyes met mine. "What happened to it?"

I glanced up at his father. Tanman nodded once. I said, "It was burned. It is an Osa death camp now."

"A war camp?"

I felt my mouth tighten. Carefully I placed another model. "A death camp is where the Osa kill people they have no more use for."

"Why?"

"They can't feed them," I said grimly.

"Would you do that?"

"I," I said, "would let them go. At least they might travel, find food and ways to live. But the Osa do not want Tan to find out anything about *them*, or the war, until it is too late."

185

The Heir looked soberly at the map. "They've been winning, haven't they?" he said.

I smiled grimly, siting a model of an enemy munitions dump, as last reported. "Not any more. Here are our latest advances, as you see."

The boy looked at his father. "Why do they want a war anyway? They aren't fighting for honor or rank, so why—"

Tanman looped a long arm around his son's shoulders. "In all our Histories we've never been able to figure that out, Therin. Which troubles me: you should always know the motivation."

Bending over the map, extended by another table to show the desert I knew, I said, "The Osa are afraid of anyone not like themselves. Their priests tell them to crush, control the world, or it will devour them."

The boy's clear eyes examined me. "Did your people try to prove that we wouldn't bother the Osa if they do not make war on us?"

"No. We exist, we bother them, either Upai or Tannese. They want a deepwater port so they don't have to trade with their hated enemies, the Sharinen, for so much they need. They see no trust in treaties or agreements, so the Osa conquer. We are lucky the Sharinen keep so much of their energies occupied." My eyes checked cross-relations and measurements among the various symbols set in the sand. Then I said dryly, "In any case the Osa would never let my people live, they hate us so much. There is bitter blood between us."

"So you didn't come here because you wanted to," the boy said, still studying me. "You had to, for your people."

I lifted one brow.

The boy's jaw jutted out. "You made friends with my father because of your people."

Tanman opened his mouth, outraged, but I held up one hand. I said, "You must understand this, Heir. Yes, in a way." I rested my hands on the high sides of the sandmap. "I had a duty to them. As you have to your people, to learn as much as you can, so later you can lead them."

"*Had* a duty to them?" Tanman said.

I lifted my eyes. "I swore an Oath. Now I have a duty to you, first. Only after that, to my people." I stretched my fingers backward against one another, paling the palms of my hands. I muttered, "Might as well be here working for some good, I'd never make a decent camp Upai. Too long in the desert."

Both of them looked at me. Finally Therin said, "I sneaked out once to a beggartown outside the walls at Fortress."

"The refugee camp?" I said evenly. "Who were your guards that day?"

The boy smiled. "I can't tell you, you'd be nasty to them."

I gave him a sidelong look. "It better not happen again. I would take you myself where you wished, if it was asked, if Liege allowed—guard commanders do not impose stupid restrictions for arbitrary reasons."

"Yes, noble-born," the boy said, returning briefly to the subdued creature I'd found under Karidi's tyranny.

"So that was what made Karidi angry enough to send you up to me. And what did you think of refugees?" Tanman asked.

"They smelled bad. There were sick people. Nobody was helping them!" Therin's voice went fierce. "Shouldn't somebody—"

"Your mother is organizing the women to help," Tanman said gently. "Perhaps you should talk to her about what needs doing."

"The other women just laughed at me about how horrid it was. Mother would believe me! She does what I want her to, if I ask the right way." The boy swung around and glared at me. "You don't get moods, do you? I've a hard enough time with Mother as it is."

I smiled. "I never vent a mood on trainees, Therin. My trainer Reti never did, and he beat that into us."

"He beat you?"

I sighed. "Indeed he did."

"If you're made my tutor, are you going to beat me?"

"If you do things like run off to town, or to camps without proper escort, after getting warned—yes, I will beat you." I spoke evenly. I looked at both father and at son. Tanman merely smiled.

"I heard you beat Eran," Therin said.

"No. I knocked him down."

"Really? How?" The boy's eyes shone. "If I could do Sati things to some of the boys who want to bully—"

I glanced up at the boy's father. Tanman smiled. "Off you

both go to the training courtyards," he said, making shooing gestures. "Go on. I have to talk with Strengam about planning Council strategy to fund building a river diversion channel to protect Fortress. It was, so to speak, ordained." He laughed when I stared at him in surprise.

There was no time to ponder. Only two bell passes after our return from the hunt, I must adjust my thoughts to complete impassivity: Tanman warned me of that. With my hair still trickling beads of bathwater down my neck, I followed Caladrunan up a long flight of shallow steps. We went into a pavilion built of lacy pierced-wood panels and tiled floors, standing at the crown of a low garden hill. The place was entirely open to the weather. All around us the breeze smelled of flowers. Irises, symbolic of Tanman's clan because they were found throughout Lake Hold territory, stood in groups of formal figure, the stiff green fans rising among scented and varicolored other plants. The other flowers were imported plants and strange to me, blooming in that dry season at the tail of summer.

In the single chair, among the shifting dappled shadows of the pavilion, sat Tanman's aged aunt. For a moment—a glimpse—I saw whence came the sense of watching, the ancient quality and frightening aliveness of joro statues, which I had seen in Caladrunan; the woman might have been a leaf-drifted statue for many seasons. Agtunki sat in a dappled shaft of sun within the pavilion, brooding behind her white translucent veil. Her crossed hands glittered with rings and large gems. Her thin right hand rose from her lap in a crackle of thickly embroidered robes. "You!" She gestured past Tanman to me, beckoning.

I had heard about Agtunki as I stalked Lake Hold's halls. I didn't want to get any closer to those pitiless eyes than I must; but Tanman waved me toward her. When I stood near enough to spit, her hand relaxed into her lap again. She said severely, "Kneel. You're giving me a neck-ache."

Tanman nodded slightly at me, and I settled on my knees before her on the chilly blue floor tiles. Her gold slippers rested on a cushion a hand span from my knee-guards. Behind me, Tanman said, "We were bathing, Aunt. We just got back."

A wrinkled translucent finger rose and touched my jaw. Her finger was cold. She touched a tendril of damp hair. "I

can see that." Her hand dusted lightly up the side of my face.
"What lovely skin. Such a nice, even color—pity about those
scars. Hard mouth. Nephew, you have quite an exotic taste in
servants."

"He isn't a servant. He swore Oath to me."

The finger tapped my cheek twice, deliberately. "So they've
been giving you a hard time on this, Nephew—what did you
expect? I heard about his drinking at the hunt, of course, Eran
couldn't wait to tell me so. You have to watch natives, they
don't drink well." She tilted her head critically, veil rustling.
"At least you select the best when you choose such things."

Tanman said dryly, "Good taste runs in our line, Aunt."

She snorted. "You've only to look at Eran to figure otherwise. But I must say no one else would have the genius to
train such unusual material up to—you didn't? How interesting. He is naturally like this? Fascinating."

I tried not to think of anything in particular. But I didn't
like her tone.

She said at last, "Girdeth saw it instantly, you know,
Nephew. You can just stop being so stuffy about it." Her
hand turned my chin. "Interesting. I heard that the Upai
didn't wash and ran about in raw goathides, stealing things."

Tanman said in a low, quiet, and dangerous tone, "Aunt,
that's enough. If I cared to have Naga insulted, I'd throw him
to the dogs at your party, instead of coming privately."

Agtunki reached forward, fingered one of my wet braids;
she seemed to look closely into my face. Behind the thin veil,
she had bright blue eyes, hooded and shielded in heavy fallen
old lids. She said, "Nephew, is this child capable of speaking
more than four words together?"

Caladrunan laughed uproariously at that. He waved one
hand. "Shall I ask him to recite Histories for you? How long
would you like? I'm sure he could go on as long as you cared
to listen."

Her hand waved impatiently. "Nephew, don't be silly. Can
he converse? Can he keep a decent wit about him? I've a
terrible shortage of any decent food or wine, those damned
refugees soak up all our reserves, so we need brilliant conversation to cover any lapses. I can hardly count on Eran's dim
lot to supply it!"

Caladrunan shot an amused glance at me and paced about
smiling to himself. "I told him to be quiet here. Naga has a

mouth like a leaded whip. I didn't care to watch him use it on you, you old scandal-mongering witch.''

Ruffled, Agtunki snapped. ''Oh, really? And you tolerate this kind of insolence?''

Caladrunan smiled at me. ''Naga only applies it to fools.'' He grandly waved permission for me to speak.

I snapped, ''Whoever the fool happens to be—we still have a garrison inspection before dark.'' I glared at Agtunki. Out of the corner of my eye, I noticed Caladrunan wince.

Both of them looked at me.

Agtunki tapped her forefingers together. ''You're right, Nephew, he has a tongue like an ox-whip. By all means bring him.''

I growled, ''If you complain of my voice, reverend one, let me explain. The Osa made me rasp like this when they tried to kill me. It's called smoke damage in a Harper's voice, O reverend one. Perhaps you've heard of the Osa from those smelly refugees.''

There was the tiniest flicker of movement in the draping of her veil. Abruptly there was something cold and very unfrivolous in the tones of her voice; something quiet and patient—and deadly. ''I have heard, child. That I have. And those witnesses will be kept safe until the right time. You would be wise to speak little of the Osa in public.''

Tanman leaned against a pavilion post. ''I'll tell Naga not to speak at your party. It should make things easier.''

Agtunki tapped her nails together. ''But less enjoyable. Some of your out-cousins have got very stuffy lately. It's time you shook them up a bit.''

Caladrunan laughed suddenly. ''Get me to do your dirty work—shame, Aunt.''

She folded her hands together. ''Keth Adcrag's lot has been snubbing me lately, and spreading the most astounding rumors about you, Nephew. I think it might be good for you to bring this nasty child to my party. Nobody outside our boring little clique has come since you brought along that woman, I forget her name—the one you had the abominable good sense to marry. I rather liked her. Possessive, though, like all the silk clans. What was her name? Capilla.'' Then Agtunki reached forward and patted my cheek.

I sat completely still on my heels, looking at her. After a moment she stopped. I said, enunciating each word distinctly,

"If you do not remember such details why do you feel qualified to concern yourself in Tanman's private life?"

Her hand returned to her knee. I thought she smiled behind her veil. She said, "What a charming little monster you are." She turned to Caladrunan. "He might even be good enough for you, Nephew."

Tanman said, "I think you like causing scandals, Aunt."

She smiled within her veil. "Now I'm too old to fuel them myself, I instigate them. Go away, both of you. You're interrupting my nap."

I inclined my head just a little to her, while Caladrunan chuckled. The old woman settled back into her chair more comfortably and smoothed her robes, resting her thin hands in the sun. Caladrunan strolled away. When I turned after him, Agtunki murmured, "And such a nice body, even if *I* prefer them big. But those scars— Pity." I looked back at her, startled, but the veil revealed nothing at a distance.

The formal garrison inspection consumed the rest of the afternoon. We took tours of the barracks, the garrison kitchens, the holding area where new-arrived refugees awaited transport to the more distant permanent camps, and we spoke with the tired herbalists who ran an overcrowded hospital below the hold walls. Tanman finally withdrew to his private chambers and sent away chattering officers and demi-nobles. He wanted some rest before the lengthy entertainment Agtunki planned. Because he knew I was off duty, he made me lie down to rest on the end of his bed. "Mine is better strung, you won't get so stiff."

"Promises come back like ghosts to haunt—"

He made a sour face at me. He had put on his sleeping robe, at my urging, but he didn't look at all ready to rest. He couldn't settle, or nap, or even sit still in one position. He squirmed. He fiddled with slates to no purpose. He broke chalk and swore at himself. Finally he sat down on the side of his bed, hands on knees, staring into space. I lay on my back watching him, waiting for him to say what was bothering him; I was drowsy. I also had a headache from the hunt wine and the pressure of thinking about things—particularly about hungry refugees tugging at my robes for food.

He said, "Do you know, I was thinking today how tired I was of company. Chatter, politics, favors, squabbling, all the time. The hold steward thinks *I* can conjure up food for the camps out of nothing, so *they* won't have to pay for it. Got to fight it, all the time . . . There's no room for just . . . me. Reeling like a flaming drunk from crisis to disaster.'' He mimed rolling eyes and shaking hands.

I smiled. I couldn't help it.

He glanced around and went on, ''That clan gathering at the hunt this morning, the garrison—what a lot of clacking mouths! And my outrageous aunt.'' He shifted on the bed, looking at me. ''Our spymaster, through Agtunki, sent me a slate. They expect Manoloki to show up at her party.''

The smile left my face, my teeth showed in a rather different expression for a long still moment. I lifted my eyes. I said levelly, ''At the party. I could kill Manoloki.''

He stared. At last, softly, ''Getting rid of Manoloki would only shift leadership to another Nando exactly like him, you told us he's got six or seven of them jostling in line—and we checked on that! And it'd unsettle the known factions in his camps, I might lose all my spies to some purge. Oh, I've assessed the cold practical realities on Manoloki. I've sent my son off out of harm's way, before you ask. Men Aider trusts are escorting Therin.''

''But—''

Caladrunan's lips quirked. ''I won't destroy the very laws I've worked on so hard for so many years, for so little reward. Especially not so publicly! Besides, I don't believe murders will do your mind any good. So I will not let you murder Manoloki. I promised Sitha Goddess I'd keep you sane.''

I stared at him in amazement. ''Sane—? But I never asked you to promise anything about me myself—''

He gave a grim smile. ''You didn't have to ask. I swore a small thing to the Goddess about the laws I've already broken for you, about the fits I seem to ease for you, about the great responsibility of directing a Sati of scaddas.''

I muttered, ''A mad Sati at that.''

He shook his head. ''No. Not madness. Rage.'' He fidgeted for some time with the hem of his robe. ''I suppose you want to spend time with your people around the refugee camps, but I don't want you to. You're sure to find more like that bailiff you brought in, and I don't know yet how well you contain that fury of yours. I hate worse the idea of you raiding with

Upai warriors. Even though I know your raids as Tokori Efresa did help us here in Tan.''

I started violently, grabbing at the furs under me.

He smiled sadly. "How could you hide that from me, Naga? Didn't you know Pitar reported events on his watch last night? The two of you have the hold commander, the head carpenter, the steward and my poor old Armorer in frenzies—how could you hide such a tactician's mind from me? Who else could possibly be Tokori Efresa of the Upai?''

I drew in a shallow breath, and unclenched my hands. Tokori had a large bounty on his head in some places.

"You did promise that I need never fear Tokori Efresa.''

I lifted my head higher. Then I said, "That was a foolish thing to tell you.''

Caladrunan smiled briefly, and sobered. "I had to figure out where you were in Efresa's hierarchy to make promises like that. And I didn't remember that Upai groups had much hierarchy.''

I sighed. Well, he hadn't survived as Tanman by being a fool. He said, "I wish we'd heard more from Strengam on the wool clan nobles who will be coming. I'd know better what would move them to support a Council resolution for war. Goddess knows, we're fighting it already in three places on the border, it'd be common sense to acknowledge that. Blame the Red Tyrant for all these stupid restrictions. Back-lash laws.'' I watched him fall into his own thoughts again, and frown; he didn't seem to like his thoughts. Then he gazed at me, and away. He fidgeted with his bed robe, looking deeply unhappy.

A sudden alert bloomed in my mind. I climbed over furs and knelt beside him on the bed. "What makes you look like that? That I didn't tell you I was Tokori?''

He shook his head. But he didn't meet my eye.

I bumped his shoulder with my fist, lightly. "Your jaw is jumping. You'll make your muscles stiffen up. Shall I go get someone to answer questions?'' I was anxious to understand the sudden turnings of this Tannese mind that governed the fate of my people. The mysteries hidden in such a different life could be sudden, frightening, and absolute.

He turned and gripped the rising shoulder muscle at the root of my neck. His thumb hooked beneath my collarbone. He felt the reflexive jerk, and his eyes glinted cold lights. I wouldn't fight him; but he shouldn't push my reflex training any farther, I might hurt us both. I looked down at that hand and up again; I had shown him how to break this grip, to escape a broken collar and dislocated shoulder. A hard fast punch with his other hand and I would have a broken shoulder—he wrapped his free hand around my windpipe.

"What is it?" I asked, alarmed now. He was quite able to rip out my throat with that hand. Few other men, perhaps, but his hand could.

With his hand on my throat, he said, "There were rumors being spread as we came through the port a few days ago. My spymaster reports more every day. I heard them here this afternoon. Very convincing ones."

I studied him. His fingers bruised the muscles beside my voice box. I said, "Rumors. About me?"

"Yes."

"Assassination plots? Witnesses who would say all, but for fear of—"

"Yes." His eyes were very close. Huge, amber irises—pupils widening and narrowing with each flicker of sun and clouds in the outside light.

"I haven't heard it myself yet. Of course, I'm not settled with an information net, so I can't help you set counter-rumors," I said, raking back through my memory for possibilities and sources of rumor. I recalled uneasily that great blooming fire in the Altar Bowl of the Fortress, the lines marked on the Bowl, and wondered about Devotee plots.

He looked startled, and dropped his hands. "Oh, Naga," he chuckled suddenly, curling up, and laughing as if he were suddenly relieved, and happy. He said, "Only you would say a thing like that. Not even your brother ever had that audacity."

"Can you tell me what the rumors actually say? Or is it secret—"

"No, later," he said, lifting his head and blinking at me. "Never mind. I am capable of limping along with my own spies until you're properly settled."

I frowned. "I didn't mean it to sound insulting—"

"You've the desert honor, Dance of Knives. Promise you'll keep that much of the desert for me."

I blinked. "I'll try."

"Good. I'd best reread Agtunki's message and give her some kind of answer."

"You were supposed to rest." I frowned at him.

"You've met my aunt. Do you think she'll give me any peace until I do answer her?"

"In the desert she would not insult anyone! She would be grateful she has her family left alive."

"Agtunki survived the Red Tyrant, she'd know that better than anyone. Maybe fretting over kin is how she shows it, Naga." He turned abruptly away, leaned over to the bedside table, poured water in a goblet, and brought it to me. "Drink," he said gently. I took the goblet from his hand; I breathed across the water's surface, murmured a prayer word, and sipped, then I thanked him and offered it back. Accepting it, he said, "I forget too easily that you cross huge gaps to meet me. In the desert, I am certain, I would find many unpleasant faults in my conduct. I expected there would be rumors about you—after those attempts on you, I should have realized there'd be more elaborate plots. There are rumors about Eran, too. I shouldn't have grown angry over Manoloki."

I said, "Here in Tan, I try. I get—angry. Court, Council— Tannese are so slow. Osa are not. Their war is not."

"Yes."

Fighting along the edges of anger and the need to talk and the desperate wish not to hurt, I said, "All the Upai—it's like a sickness we have, this anger at all the lost people. As raiders we strike at things, we can't wait. We wait— I waited!—for so long, we've got no patience left. Manoloki is coming here—"

Caladrunan rested his hand on my arm, lifted the goblet before me. "Now. Not so tense, please."

"I lose all my flamed training when I hear his name!" My hands flexed, clenched, flexed open, made claws.

"And that only makes you angrier at him, yes?" He said it in Upai.

"Yes." I closed my hand over his, and gulped more water from the goblet. "It does. It does. Is it wrong, even in Tan, to want to destroy this creature—the damage goes on so long after he leaves—the one day he led the Osa to us, one day! he destroyed us as a people. We are—we are all like broken things, we are beggars, the women kill their babies when they have no milk. Upai! Upai women, killing babies." I shuddered. "I heard of Cragmen slavers hitting camps hardest just

outside Lake Hold's borders—a day's ride from Keth Adcrag's
camps at Bada's Well.''

Caladrunan's hand gripped hard on my shoulder, making
an old sore cringe into life. I whispered, ''The stories they
tell, over and over—and they look at me with eyes like
stones. Like dead people. Nothing will heal it. I saw these
women, in the camp—their legs like sticks of wood—they
begged food from me—''

''Yes,'' he murmured, and his eyes were full of pain, full
of the same rage and anguish I felt. ''Did you hear the bailiff
was convicted in local common court? You spoke with those
Upai among the herbalists' patients in town—did you tell the
herbalists where to find translators? You did? Good. Goddess, I'd love to have a whole troop of Upai to parade in
Manoloki's face tonight.''

I clutched at the hand on my shoulder. ''Is it wrong to kill
this monster? Why don't you let me—''

With his other hand he set down the goblet, hard. ''I don't
think you're a cold murderer, Naga. It would change you.''
He got up suddenly. ''I've made my decision.''

I stared while he changed into official robes for Agtunki's
party. I braided and bound my hair into a tight spiraled pad. I
said in a dead tone, ''Nice of you to explain it to me.''

He said, distantly, ''Yes, it was. I did not need to explain
any decision to my Sati, did I?''

I met his eyes. ''And to your spymaster, and to Agtunki,
need you explain why I still live?''

He heard the tone of my voice. He turned and looked at
me. ''We will see what Aunt's intrigues are all about—then
we will decide what to do about it. Not before.''

I said, ''Yes, Liege.''

He turned away, shrugging his shoulders into his outrobe.
''Odd, when you're better secured meeting with enemy am-
bassadors than you're allowed to be in the heart of your own
kin and blood.''

I stood up and straightened the hang of his outrobe for him.
I said softly, ''I will do my best whatever happens.''

''I know that.''

I looked up sharply at him. He smiled and said, ''Wear it
loose, will you? Old Upai Imperial House style. Remind them
who you are, and how they might fare at Manoloki's hand,

who are not so high-bred nor so strong as you are, Dance of Knives.''

I put up my head proudly, ''Remind them how they would fare at Manoloki's hand instead of *yours*, Liege.''

''Caladrunan,'' he said mildly.

''*Kigadi*,'' I said instead.

CHAPTER
= *14* =

I TURNED IN the darkness among the square pale marble pillars, looking back through the inner colonnade of the pavilion. Light spilled across the blue mosaics, slipped over the steps like water. Inside, the robes of the women of the court glittered with gems, billowing in the breeze—like crinkling petals of red and blue and white and darkest green cupflower drug blooms. The men escorted them with stately gestures; the men were golden-haired, tawny, russet as deer. Modulated crisp voices and graceful gestures seemed to be bred into this court with its wealth.

At the sides of the pavilion, the fat men discussed business, eyeing the women and eating from celadon green bowls. Agtunki held court in one corner. Tanman moved among his kin with his guards of honor; even Tanman's youngest relations had come, greeting him with enthusiastic voices and visible awe—but his son was halfway back to Fortress now, out of Manoloki's immediate reach. Tanman smiled regally, murmuring gracious words from his great height. I'd helped Pitar select his guards; he was well protected. It would not be an evening of pleasure for me.

Certainly it was not pleasant. There were no beggars allowed in these gardens, never had been; a Upai soldier had no place at such a traditional Tannese gala. I had come expecting trouble, but not the sort I was given: for the first time I saw myself full-length in the plate metal mirrors of Lake Clan's new Pavilion of the Wind. The extravagance of the pavilion shocked me, but the sight in the mirrors was worse.

198

I had never considered myself small.

I did not think small in challenges or combat, which was part of my strength— I felt larger than most men in some intangible way, a truth usually verified by experience. But among all the mirrored golden Tannese shifting gracefully in courtly patterns, I was a thin shadowy glitter with a spray of honeysuckle in my hanging hair, and alien. *Alien!* I saw that cry in my own eyes this time. Worthies of other nations, other races, had not been invited to this Tannese affair, just myself. I didn't have an excuse, success as a battle officer perhaps, to bring me there. At best I was Tanman's commander of guards, foreign nobility—Tanman's half-mad assassin, at worst. No matter what my other accomplishments, I would not have been there if I were not a killer and Tanman's favorite: thus all their pork-pie eyes said, their controlled easy voices, when Tanman took me around greeting his noble kin. As I harped for them, nervous reservations held strong in their pale eyes. I found fear an unflattering honor, and fled the mirrors.

Where I stood outside, the mirrors reflected only works of copper sculpture cast by prominent artists, the central work a writhing Sek-blood impaled by a copper spear—symbol of Tan's conquering might. The sculptor had done too excellent a job; I saw nothing heroic in that vivid battlefield agony. It did not do Tan honor, either, I thought that copper could find better use in Tan's defense.

So I stood in the outer wind, stars high and sharp behind me, and I watched. I turned my head. My hair rustled at my shoulder, slipping loose down my back when I looked at the sky; hair dressed in the old Imperial manner.

But there were darker reasons to avoid mirrors. Agtunki's spies warned us that Manoloki was certainly coming, invited or not. The Lake Clan guards would be too polite to turn away such a powerful man. I must guard Tanman with my bare hands before those mirrors, if necessary; and it might be. I might have to reveal my talents before the entire assembled Lake Clan nobility, including Eran and his uneasy loyalties. Pitar and I organized security as well as we could; I prayed it would be enough. It was the fifth bell before dawn, by the angle of the thin new moon above me.

Manoloki was sure to arrive at the last possible instant, for a full audience, with the guards all dulled and tired—if not already drunk. That was Manoloki's way. I drew my chest harness knife and felt the smooth oily iron with the tip of my thumb, brushing it against my calluses. The metal caught the cold light and glinted. I drew a weapon rag from a robe pocket and cleaned the knife and resheathed it. A giggling couple fled down the pavilion steps past me, never noticing me in the dark as they hurried away. They were not the first ones. The pines rustled throughout the garden while I listened to shadows. Torches streamed in the breeze. The vine woven in my hair plucked at the wind; a blossom fell loose on my shoulder.

I drew in a deep breath and let it out slowly, dropped into a light meditative trance. My hearing was more acute that way than in any other state. On guard duty in the desert, or during long martial ceremonies, I spent long passes of time wide awake and perfectly alert, but relaxed. Near me pine needles rustled. I smiled: to become part of a tree, rooted in the earth, still and enduring—a paradise, an entire existence of meditative quiet. I thought it an honorable transformation. I didn't think I would mind dying, to go to that.

Words whispered past me into the bushes—another couple slipped away giggling into the garden, arms entwined: Lado Kiselli and a woman. They didn't see me.

The next one was alone. I drew in my breath. In the waning garden moonlight, she glowed like a blue pearl. Caladrunan's sister lifted her pale head and strands of hair floated on the breeze, fine as spider webs. She folded back her white veil. "Good evening," she said calmly. "I hope I didn't disturb you." Her dress glimmered against the dark pines.

"No," I said.

"I came out to get a breath of fresh air."

"So did I. You are very beautiful."

Girdeth gave a rude snort. "And you are very direct. Most men take a bell pass or more to get to saying that."

"The moonlight," I said vaguely. "Reminds me of the desert."

"Ah, yes—riding and hunting at night. My brother mentioned you see like a bat. You enjoy the night?" She padded closer, her gold slippers glinting.

"Sometimes."

"Is it the company, or the setting?"

"I'm not interested in witticisms, Girdeth."

"It livens dull evenings."

"I prefer doing something productive."

"Lovemaking, perhaps?"

I turned aside silently, clearing the way for her to return to the pavilion.

Then she said, "I'm sorry. Truly, I didn't mean to offend you. Living with Agtunki, you learn to sharpen your claws wherever you can. I didn't mean anything by it." She laid a perfumed hand lightly on my arm. "Please, forgive me."

"Apology accepted."

"Oh, that's right—you have to be militarily correct." Her hand, still on my arm, tightened a little. "I never meant to actually insult you, you know. I've got into the habit of breaking through the protocol, the nonsense—I was only six when Pupo was made Tanman."

"I understand."

"We have a long-spaced family, but I expect you already know that. Pupo says you're an absolute tyrant about taking care of him, making sure he gets some rest, eating the right things . . ."

I said seriously, "I try."

She gave a little laugh. "Well, he is my brother, and I do worry about him. I've been hearing some alarming rumors of a plot to kill him— You will try to be good for him during this war that might be fought, help him, good influence on him?"

"To the best of my talents," I said. "The relatives seem happier to argue with him and cause trouble."

She sighed. "I know, not the usual ruling clan. More like a big rowdy bickering family, instead of conspirators whispering in the halls. We're—we're so naive up here, you know. I know that. It's frightening sometimes."

I smiled. "All Tan seems that way to me."

"Naive? I suppose we are."

"I hope it doesn't change."

"You mean, doesn't *have* to change," she said tartly.

I bowed to her a little.

"You know, it's so refreshing to talk to a man who doesn't patronize me."

"Upai," I said briefly.

"Oh, is that what it is?" Girdeth moved along a garden

walk, her hand resting on my arm. "So your women can just go where they like and speak with whoever?"

I said, "Of course—a lot of our women could make liver pudding of a stranger who offended them. Many of our women are knife-dancers. That's one of the things we had to learn."

"I'm sorry to hear that's why they're so free," Girdeth said earnestly.

"History." I shrugged. "And your chaperone?"

"I sent her off to eat. She won't come up out of the trough for another bell pass at least. I picked her for it, you see. She's a darling otherwise, so it's quite pleasant. I'll have to think of some other plan at Fortress when I go to court."

"Devious woman," I said lightly.

"Harper, why did you say I was beautiful?"

"Because you are."

"You like my brother, so you flatter me."

"No," I said, as gently as I could. "I love your brother."

For a moment, all misty hair and white silk, she looked down at me. Then she touched my cheek lightly. "You permit the most outrageous liberties with your person. Most men would be foaming at the mouth by now."

"I know my limits."

She chuckled. "Oh, Agtunki would be shocked if she heard about this—no one else in sight . . ."

I said dryly, "She touched me. Everyone seems to do it. They don't think I'm quite real until they've gotten a good pinch."

Her hand drew back. "Oh, I didn't mean it like that. . . ."

"I know you didn't." I put her hand back on my arm.

"Well, you should hear the stories people tell about you, that's half of it. Why, the stable lads can run home and tell their dear old clan that they polished your saddle buckles. And the refugees tell fantastic stories. I visit them, you know."

"Do you? I polish my own buckles. Security."

"You know what I mean. Servants do it to me—to all of us, all the time. You've always got to be careful when you open your mouth . . . tiresome."

"Technically I, too, am a servant."

"Nonsense. Pupo thinks the world of you."

"Well, I think he's scorched marvelous, too."

"You can put on a very nice court dialect, when you want to."

"Don't tell anybody. I don't dare use it anywhere, they'd laugh."

"See what I mean, always being careful?" She patted my arm.

"Gets to be a habit."

"You do interesting things with your voice, Naga. Do you get tired of habits?"

"Everyone gets tired."

"Tired of pretenses?"

I looked at her a moment. "Yes."

"Don't look surprised. No one ever said that Caladrunan's mind didn't pass to me, too. Only that I couldn't use it." She snorted. "Maybe in peacetime, I could do more."

"Maybe. You may have to do altogether too much, before this war is done. Somebody has to organize those refugees." I touched her hand. "I like talking to you."

"I like it, too. You're nothing like what Lado told me."

"Oh?"

"Curiosity plucked the goose," she teased, veil ruffling.

"I suppose he said I was foul-mouthed and unkind."

"To put it lightly! He told me you make that maniac Keth Adcrag look the very soul of sanity."

I looked down.

"Is it true?"

I felt a large struggle going on inside me. What came out was ridiculously quiet compared to the uproar in my head. I hardly knew Girdeth, but by her manner tonight. "Yes," I said, just above a whisper.

She said, "You admit you are . . . a little prone to fits."

"Fits," I muttered. "That's putting it nicely. I fall on the ground and scream and kick anything in reach. Sometimes I bite."

"I imagine, being a Sati, that makes you dangerous to be around."

"Yes. Caladrunan can stop them. He has."

She lifted her hand to my chin, turning my head to her, looking into my face. Her brows lifted. "That's amazing."

"That's what I think, too."

Her hand tapped my nose. "Well, I hope you get better. I have to go back inside. Good night, Naga." And she brushed her lips against my brow, and padded away with golden-shod steps.

I felt, more than saw, the stir among the sentries then. The alert became a subtle shifting of guests beyond the colonnades. Rafai stood briefly on the steps, gazing out into the garden: the sign I'd waited for. The unwelcome Nandos had been sighted. I checked the harpcase slung on my harness under my arm, test-drew all of my weapons. I went up the steps silently, briefly startling a sloppy Lake Clan sentry. I slipped into the lamplight, amid the celadon and crystal dishes and perfumes.

At the foot of the northern dais, Rafai flanked me to left and Pitar to my sword-side—had I used swords. Tanman sat in his chair behind our shield. His face did not change when he saw us unite, he was more disciplined than that; but I felt as if, when we united into one powerful group, he was as glad of it as I was. A bell pass dragged by, time in which to quietly recheck final arrangements. I had suggested some nasty surprises to Pitar, should Manoloki try any of his known tricks. "The gall of the man!" Pitar fumed repeatedly, "walking in and expecting to be treated like a guest!"

I glanced at Pitar wryly, knowing the Tannese would do just that, in fear of Manoloki's might against individual nobles. In fear of traitors among their own kind, too; no one wanted to rock a fragile balance. Then I saw the Nandos enter at the far door, speak to the announcer, and a cold feeling spread all down my back into my legs. My lips peeled back from my teeth. "Naga," Pitar hissed, "don't do that! You'll scare everyone."

I snapped, "Let them! Do them good to see truth!"

Manoloki crossed the pavilion with smiles and greetings for everyone, purposefully reminding them that he had fought for and with many of the nobles here, in the past. Manoloki was a tall man, as one might expect of a one-time Tannese sword expert. He was swathed in expanses of red silk; but these days he didn't bother to wrap a Nando cloth across his coarsened face. He was flanked by two large, masked and muscular officers, who were in turn trailed by a familiar slender man with reddish eyebrows—a Cragman under that veil. The trailing one leaned forward, looking at me, and spoke hastily to the men before him. One nodded; all three looked at me. "They didn't know my face," I grated.

Pitar whispered, "Do you know them?"

"The thin one led my escort into Tan to betray me," I said levelly. The cold prickled at my scalp. "The other two, no. He has found men I've never observed in a fight."

I knew why Manoloki brought the big Nandos. So did Pitar. Manoloki, once a Sati of sword, had a potbelly worthy of the fat merchants at the sides of the pavilion; he would not be fighting his own fights tonight. That was a Nando commander's gesture of contempt and success. His hair was oiled, he wore rings across every knuckle. Beside me, Rafai snarled in a rare burst of wit, "Meet the new Red Tyrant!" I saw Pitar give a slow, toothy grin.

Manoloki pushed his bulk before us. He glanced insolently up at Tanman and gave a brief wave of his hand, meant to pass for a salute. I saw Pitar's mouth drop open at this insolence. In the utter silence, Tanman let Manoloki stand there. The Nando sighed and saluted properly. Then, ever genial as a host, Tanman graciously gestured permission for Manoloki to sit down. Manoloki promptly turned and waved his escort to sit down. Pitar frowned at that; Tanman's permission was sufficient, no one else commanded here.

I stood, hands loose, watching Manoloki. I had already planned how to dodge, attack, and destroy all four Nandos, to varying opening attacks—which insured it would not happen. Manoloki would know we were prepared for him. He and Tanman conversed in civilized voices. The force of hatred pressing in on the Nandos, from every blue-robed guard around them, was palpable. I had some trouble to keep from showing my teeth.

Manoloki spoke politely of the sculptures and the pavilion . . . lingering thoughtfully on the spear-impaled Sek-blood who looked so native, so like me, he thought, as he gestured languidly in my direction. Servants brought delicacies on long trays. Manoloki didn't bother to have his officers taste the food for him, he felt completely safe; he ignored his men. In contrast, Tanman waved his guards graciously to eat with him off his trays. I did not dare so much as glance at a food tray. We all knew I was the lone effective guard for Tanman's person in the first moment of a Nando attack; I was the one with the fast reflexes. The others could back me only when it was half over. Of course Manoloki remarked on it.

Setting down his goblet, Manoloki said, "No music,

Harper?'' And he laughed, his jowls shaking. He laughed that careless, superior laugh of his—contemptuous because he could see how he was feared. No one thought lightly of moving, alone, against Manoloki. I stood quietly, saying nothing to the jab. Pitar looked white with rage; Rafai was muttering.

Tanman remarked coolly, ''A Harper of Naga's status chooses when and what he cares to play, in any hall—and chooses when he will *not* play.'' A gibe at Manoloki, for having lost me. Harpers had refused to play for tyrants, no matter what it cost them; a ruler without Harpers was a man repudiated by his people. And Manoloki had no trained Harpers now, however pitiful. Tanman had counted it a major victory when such vote was announced by the elder tutoring musicians.

Manoloki replied, ''Then do you rule him, or does he rule you, Liege Lord of Tan?''

Our part of the pavilion grew very still.

Tanman said coldly, ''Why, do you need him back as trainer, to teach you how it is done?''

Manoloki remarked, ''Concern motivates me, Liege. There are rumors that your dark Harper is . . . easily enraged. Does he obey, or does he rule here?''

Lake Clan nobles around him in the chairs of audience rose angrily to their feet, but no one approached Manoloki.

Tanman said quietly, ''You never ruled him.''

The nobles were silent now. Everyone stood quite still. If Manoloki did not back down, he would be a dead man. The cost might be terribly high, it would start a civil war, but he would die. I heard Strengam Dar's voice to one side, muttering to one of his sons, gray brows lowered. Briefly, I wondered when he'd arrived, and then merely thanked Goddess that he had. With his sons, he had the strength to hold this unstable group of nobles quiet. The pavilion mirrors reflected us over and over, side to side; by a trick of reflections, the writhing Sek-blood statue loomed in the mirrors above Manoloki's head.

Manoloki said at last, ''I never ruled him, I admit it. But I am not a landholder, nor a ruler like yourself, Lord of Tan. I am merely,'' he inclined his head an insolently small degree, ''a humble Nando.''

Tanman snorted. ''You question a man who outranks you,

Nando! Naga is a second-degree Sati. You only rose to the first degree of sword in Tan. Your humility does not seem in much evidence here.''

Manoloki remarked, ''Forgive me, Lord of Tan—but it is natural to question these things. One must wonder who rules here, as some say your Sati is a witch. Still others, that he is subject to fits and gives orders from his visions.''

Tanman smiled faintly. ''Certainly it is the rightful portion of a prophet to pursue visions. Or even an ordinary man. Having become Sati and Harper, Naga now pursues more . . . spiritual goals.''

''Oh, a prophet! Religion has become an endemic disease among the beggartowns, you know. Fanatics babbling nonsense. Perhaps your prophet's followers should call themselves Women of the Harp,'' he sniffed. His voice was as crisply disdainful as a noble who had never left the circle of the court. ''As anyone can see, that black servant is not worthy of gracing such a noble court''—he glanced around at the Lake Clan worthies with a gracious wave of the hand—''as this assembly. I never meant him for such high service, when I gifted him to you. Had I known your—desires, I would have sent a better man.''

I felt a white hot rush of rage go through me, piercing the cold. I started forward, blood roaring in my ears. Someone clicked their fingers twice, sharply.

Tanman's hand. I jerked, turning one ear slightly toward him. Tanman said calmly, ''Oathswearer, you will answer any insult to my person . . . when I desire it.''

I gritted my teeth together. I inclined my head to him in silence. He was correct, of course; Manoloki was not insulting me directly, but Tanman's wisdom in keeping me.

Manoloki laughed. ''Oh, so this little native might challenge me? Or will the Women of the Harp make me tremble with fear?''

I clamped my lips shut. He meant to goad me into rage, to begin a brawl he could later blame on me; he'd nearly succeeded. Those officers of his must be Satis themselves, or he wouldn't tempt fate.

Girdeth's voice rang out from one side of the pavilion. The sound of the clear, calm voice shut off Manoloki's grating laughter. ''Oh, certainly, Great-aunt! He would have ordered a man to go out and challenge Naga—if he had a better man who could fight fairly, by himself. Clearly, he does not.''

A little flick of warmth softened the coldness settled like snow melt in my middle; I saw Tanman smile again faintly.

Tanman said calmly, ''Next time I click these fingers, Manoloki, you will see to what degree I rule here. Now we will discuss Nando debt payments.''

Manoloki glanced up at him, briefly astonished. Perhaps he was not prepared for that kind of debate; perhaps he'd forgotten Tanman's long and unforgiving memory. Manoloki countered, ''You pass Judgments at parties?''

Tanman smiled again. The Nandos didn't seem to like the look of that smile. ''I pass Judgments as I find it necessary, not at set times.'' His hands, I saw from my eye corners, gripped the arms of his chair. ''Your payment of last moon, as I sent word, was defaulted. Your Nandos did not serve out their contract acceptably to repay debt for Pass of Bones. They were untrained and they fled repeatedly from the field. We had to use dogs on them.'' A murmur from the nobles at that classic proof of dishonor.

Manoloki's voice was incredulous. ''You worry about debt payments when our whole realm is threatened by the rise of rebellion, by the invasions of raiders like that Upai there, by—''

Tanman leaned forward. ''Those foreign invaders being the Osa. And you have contracted with these Osa, Manoloki. We have sealed copies of your documents. You work with the Osa to the scale of two thousand jades' pay per day. Exclusive of looting and pillaging rights for your troops. You expect to get paid bonus upon the Osa invasion of Tan and the overthrow of Tan's Fortress.''

I felt a flare of excitement: Tanman's spymaster had been busy! Tanman's voice remained calm, deliberate, but he noticed the effect on listening Tannese nobles. More and more of them were crowding up to hear. I heard whispers of outrage at the Osa pay. Tanman said, ''Your troops were used to attack the outer holds of Tan. You have a thousand men at Black Pebble Ford. Don't speak of traitors and rebels to me! The Osa ambassador admitted using your aid.''

So, I thought grimly, Tanman too has been active, forcing an Osa ambassador to such concessions of the truth—and at a distance too.

Manoloki flared, "That is the function of Nandos. We supply troops to those who can afford us. Naturally if one country is too weak to hold its territory it must forfeit land to another—which has resources and needs that ignorant beer-headed farmers do not begin to understand—"

He saw his mistake in their faces. His words did not please any noble of Tan. With Manoloki's main bulk thrown into the enemy effort, any of his smaller contracts would be turned to the Osa side; unlike Reti's Nandos, Manoloki's Nandos did not have a scrupulously clean record of impartiality on their mercenary contracts. Nobles might ignore a skirmish in some-body else's far-off borderlands: direct threat to their homes was another matter. These stubborn blue-robed sons of pig farmers, circumscribed by the habits of custom and tradition, who'd ignored the threat before, seemed to see it now. That famous Tannese complacency had just been swept away by Manoloki's own words.

Tanman had made his point. The Nandos were traitors; and when it came to forfeiting land, Tannese nobles—indeed all Tannese—were the most conservative loyalists to be found.

Manoloki began again. "We cannot control the ambitions of countries, Lord of Tan. We supply a reasonable service, we can't help those who do not avail themselves of our trained skills."

I heard more angry remarks at that. Men here had seen something of Nando skills, and lack thereof; and Strengam's burly sons were spread throughout the group of nobles, loudly telling what Manoloki did not wish heard about a recent score of Nando battles.

Tanman waited until the noise quieted. Then he said lev-elly, "I doubt that the landholders of this country will any longer hire the cowards you have offered us. For your insults and for the display of your disrespect for Tan, your debt has been raised to ten thousand jades. If you do not make accept-able payment at the next court, Nando, your land permits in Tan will be permanently revoked, your properties confis-cated. I have quite a few refugees eager to work that land in my name; it will not lie undefended.

"Fines and imprisonment will be leveed on your officers as we find them in our territory, at subsequent defaulted pay-ments. As a further step, we would no longer honor the face veil of your Nandos; branded outlaws will be destroyed. At

such time, I'd send letters recommending the same to my
fellow rulers in Marsh and Plains, who already generally
agree with me. If you think this threat of punishment trivial,
please recall what happened when all my fellow rulers revoked land permits in the outer provinces, to your great
discomfort during the drug harvesting this fall. . . . I did not
exert one hundredth of my available force. Think well,
Manoloki, before speaking again.''

Manoloki shifted in his chair. It was almost comic how
clearly we could read his expression: he'd thought to show
the Tannese nobles how weak and divided they were, to cow
them with his single dominating presence. It might have
worked, at a different gathering—perhaps in the past. But
now I could see it wasn't going at all the way his advisors had
told him it would. The slender red-haired Nando, of evil
memory, looked unhappy; undoubtedly, the one responsible.
Manoloki glared at him once. Then Manoloki said, ''You
speak of Nandos as cowards, Liege, yet you keep my free gift
to you—that flawed Sati—as if you had no skilled soldiers. I
could offer you better in debt payment, if you like.''

Tanman said blandly, ''Better? I think you would find that
difficult. An officer from Reti is valued wherever he goes.''

Manoloki smirked, a heavy movement of the lips. ''Oh, so
the rumors were true? I had no guess that this . . . this sort
was so much to your . . . well-known tastes.'' He lifted one
languid finger to point at me.

''No doubt your own well-known fondness for killing little
girls in private, Manoloki,'' Agtunki's voice replied crisply
from one side, ''gives you the impulse to say such remarkable
things. You thought we'd forget your bizarre desires that
brought you down from high power here in Tan. Ah,'' she
cackled, ''but I'm an old woman, and I remember what made
you Nando, where these youngsters may not. Not getting any
younger, are we, Manoloki?''

Manoloki's face congested. ''Untruths—misunderstandings
among my friends. The Nando veil protects—''

''But you're so proud you don't wear the veil anymore!''
Agtunki's voice snapped like a parchment flattened in a giant
hand. ''You fled before the sentence could be branded above
your eyes. Your troops win battles now by fleeing on the
contracts of honest lords. Face your sorry past when you dare
come here, man of outlaws. I suspect I know where arise

these rumors you recite, Manoloki. It comes from your twisted vision!'' She shook her veiled head once. "It is too bad. You were brilliant once.''

"Be careful, old woman, who you insult,'' Manoloki growled.

Tanman said then, very patiently, "Is that a threat against one of my kin?''

The place was again still. The blood pounded evenly and rapidly in my ears as I waited for the click of long fair fingers, and for Manoloki's slightest movement.

Manoloki visibly swallowed. His eyes darted around, noting Tanman's extra guards posted quietly all around him. Then he said, "I came to—ah—offer alliance with Tan.''

Tanman sighed. "I've heard that too many times before. What think you, my kin, my noble friends?''

The reply came at large among so many people, and united: a peculiar sound that made my neck hair creep. To describe it as a rumble would leave out the snarling quality of it. Two hundred Tannese gathered close, with Manoloki and Tanman and me at the center of their mass, gave a collective growl. Twice.

Tanman lifted his hand lightly. "Friends, please. Do not let this spoil Agtunki's fine gathering. Manoloki, I believe it safest for you if I bid you leave.'' Then he glanced at me and smiled. "Perhaps Naga Teot should escort you to your camp, to insure your safety from any . . . ruffians. I would hate to think that I left my guests, invited or not, to manage their own security. Your three officers might not be adequate.''

Manoloki glared. He said, "I go, strewing praises for the hospitality of the Lord of Tan, and of his many kin. I would not deprive you of the least of your multitudes of liegeman, Lord.'' Somehow he managed to make it sound vaguely as if Tanman cowered behind ranks of guards—but only vaguely. Not directly enough to set off the crowd. He rose, giving me a long insulting look, up and down, as if I were a Kehran boy.

At one side, Agtunki drawled, "Look long on your own mistake, Manoloki. Now we know how very badly you want to be rid of our dark Harper, we'll appreciate him more fully.''

Manoloki gave the old woman a cold glare, which moved Agtunki not a bit. Manoloki inclined his head a brief jerk to

Tanman, and sauntered out of the pavilion with his officers slowly, so as not to set off the animals; the Tannese were still, in places, growling. The Lake Clan senior men muttered, knotting into fierce little groups with rumpled brows, jabbing fingers punctuating their talk. Hostile glances followed Manoloki's path.

I sat down on a harp stool when he was gone.

I thought, Manoloki's remark about weaker countries was a grave mistake with Tannese of any political leaning. Even the most radical wouldn't like it—admitting that once the Osa came, no Tannese would rule here again. I glanced up at Tanman. He was sitting very still. Then, slowly and deliberately, he uttered the Upai word for swine, the most obscene of several synonyms. And he let out a great long breath.

Caladrunan looked from Pitar to Rafai to me. "You did well," he said quietly. We inclined our heads in deep respect to him. I felt a burst of dazzling pride in Tanman's mastery of Manoloki; Caladrunan had just proved to the heart of Tannese nobility that he was the new way.

Lado Kiselli strolled up then, with Strengam Dar smiling behind. Lado nudged my harpcase and murmured, "You should celebrate. The lot of you made Manoloki look an idiot."

Strengam said then, "I commend you for that powerful display of just who *does* rule here, Sati. That was well done."

I blinked and looked at him. Then at Lado. Then I flung back a tail of hair and began to feel annoyed under their gazes.

Lado grinned. "If you keep balling your fists and lashing your hair about, you'll break some hearts tonight, Black Man."

I turned abruptly away from Lado's smiling face. They didn't seem to realize that the rage Manoloki provoked had been real, and was still there in me, waiting. The mirrors created endless fading corridors of Tannese, myself a black blot among them; I was out of place among the light faces and the crisp embroidered and silvered robes of nobility. I gritted out, "Whose heart?"

Lado's light trained voice replied, "Oh, at least four different connoisseurs are hiding behind veils, wishing they could buy you off Tanman."

Strengam made a warning gesture at Lado and said hastily, "Come have some wine, noble-born. You're missing the best food we've seen in some time."

Tanman gave a little smile. "Thank you, Strengam. You two, take him off, put him in a better mood before he starts a fight. Go on, Naga." He gave me a look that meant I was supposed to be polite if it made me burst to hold it in. With Manoloki's lot gone, he was safe enough. I walked away growling under my breath.

CHAPTER

= *15* =

AT DAWN, TANMAN and I stood in the garden, watching the sun rise. He had finally packed off the last of the persistent guests; his guards of honor looked rumpled, grouchy, and wine-sodden. I felt a little sleepy myself. But Tanman stood watching the sun, red and gold and white across the fall leaves. As his guards, we stood with him, and kept silent.

He knelt down slowly, on the headland above dormant furrows, squeezing soft clouds of black earth between his fingers. He squinted as he looked out over the tilled garden to the fields beyond. I watched him, between glances outward for his safety, and said nothing. He murmured, "Best earth between the desert and the sea, and everyone wants it." He let the earth crumble moistly from his hands, dropping in soft flaky piles, perfect for plowing and sowing, rich black earth as light as the honey pastries that had been served last night. Tannese soil—Lake Hold soil—would grow anything. It was no surprise to any of us that the Nandos wanted its wealth, nor that the Cragmen in their hungry numbers among the bald stones of their hills wanted it; while the Osa wanted the rich fishing port below Fortress. Even my people wanted some of it. Melon-growing soil, my people said in praise of it, and rubbed forefinger on thumb to describe its texture. I felt a sudden pang for the simplicity of the old life, for the feel of earth on my hands. My mother had grown melons in soil like this along the Redspring; I remembered playing in the mud with my brothers at six years old. No pampered noble life— like Tanman. This body was born of the earth.

214

I sat down on my haunches beside him and we watched the sun rise. I heard the guards grumbling about in the background and ignored it. Everyone had been on extra duty to foil assassins that a disgruntled Manoloki might send. Tanman's fingers stirred the dark soil. "Everyone wants it," Caladrunan said again, and I heard deep weariness in his voice.

I turned my head to him. We shared a long look. I lifted my hand; he clenched it in his big bear paw and clasped it. Then he sighed. "You give me the heart to go on, Naga. I don't know what I'd do without you."

While I stared at him, he rose, stretched, and yawned.

"What is that smell?" I said sharply.

"Nice, isn't it? I asked for Upai recipes to be sent ahead to the cook. I wanted a Upai meal to be made for us here. I've missed it." Caladrunan smiled, the light flickering gold through his ruffled hair as he walked. "Ah, Pitar, there you are. On to the hall, I'm hungry as a winter pig."

I lifted my head. "Excuse me, Liege, I must check on something." I gave Pitar a brief look. In a low, calm voice, I said, "Guard well, Pitar." I turned aside from their alerted faces and up the ramp, past sentries, down the stairs past jostling servants, into the kitchen. Potboys, assistant cooks and table stewards scattered in a shattering din.

One of the killers got away. The other didn't. When I emerged into the hall, there was blood on my hands. I knocked aside a yelling sentry pawing for his sword. Servant men and women screamed around me, making such an uproar my shouts did not penetrate. I raced up the hall past grasping hands and obstructive bodies toward the dais table, where Tanman had just reached for a piece of hotly spiced Upai meat—his second. He had obviously been laughing at one of Lado Kiselli's quips, with his mouth quite full—until he heard the chaos at the other end of the hall, and saw the cause. Me, rushing up the single clear pathway.

The aisle had been blocked and interrupted by tables on my own security orders, to slow any straight-line charges. Now it might hinder me too long. I leaped, hurdling tables and startled faces, spattering drops of blood on the way. All I saw was Tanman, with that one bite already in his mouth.

I wasn't going to reach him in time. Already guards were lunging after me thinking: a Sati charging Tanman! with hands already red! A hand brushed my boot, fell away as I

leaped. In midair both my scaddas left my fingers. Then I
came down in the heaving barrier of Tanman's off-duty guards,
all struggling to get up from table and turn toward me.
"Poison!" I screamed as hard as I could and felt something
thump my shoulder numbingly. Missed killing me by a head
blow, I thought dazedly, while my arm gave way and I
sprawled across the table and goblets and the food. I strained
upward, trying to see past the tangle of arms and swords and
shouting mouths. A rookie's sword thudded into the table an
instant after I rolled past him—Esgarin, picked up from the
Devotee stable. Ironic if he killed me. I rolled right into
Rafai's sword tip. I gasped as the blade cut the skin near my
mouth. It wasn't a heavy blow, just enough to part the outer
skin. But the tip, with Rafai's characteristic alertness, leaped
down and caressed my throat where I was stretched open
above my armor.

"Halt!" Rafai roared like hold war-bells, and veterans
came back to themselves, ablink at such authoritative command. Men drew back a little, swords ready; the dull rookie
blade was still wedged in the wood beside me. And Esgarin
still smelled of ganas as he ran messages. Odd how distinctly
I noticed it.

"Poison," I muttered, holding quite still. Then I heard
Tanman coughing and rising, his robes rustling, in the silence
near the high table.

He said, "Pitar, if you would cut my sleeve free. Thank
you." I heard his step approaching. "Put those swords away.
Rafai, perhaps you should send some of these fellows to calm
the rabble. Did you catch all the poisoners, Naga?"

Rafai's blade lifted from my neck. I sat up gingerly, touching my mouth. Amazed, I looked at myself. I was missing
one boot and my outrobe had been torn away, my leathers
wrenched half-off, and my inner robes slashed in three places.
I dripped the food and blood and wine splashed on me. I said
bitterly, "One got away, the Nando who commanded my
escort"—I said some unpleasant words—"when I first came
to Tan. I don't think we'll catch him now. The other was
Eran. Liege, I think they poisoned the dishes for your table
alone, though how they knew which ones . . ." I shook my
head.

Tanman looked at my robes. He rubbed the center of his
chest, where the great force of the scadda pommel had thumped

him. It also knocked the bite out of his mouth while hurling him backward, as I'd hoped: phenomenal luck, which I had no right to expect. The very thought of it made me sweat. The other scadda had pinned his sleeve to the table, preventing him from taking another bite. He said mildly, ''And did Eran fight as excellently as his reputation?''

''No, Liege,'' I said curtly, moving my numbed arm. Somebody had cudgeled it with a sword pommel. It felt most peculiar. ''He drank away his speed. He was just good enough to prevent me from getting the Nando and getting him, and to you in time. I chose your life over the Nando's death.''

''Rafai,'' Tanman said, and Rafai sheathed his sword, turning to the other men of his watch and barking orders. Hysterical hall guests were herded out and soothed; another section began sorting out equally hysterical servants. Tanman turned as Pitar stepped up. ''What kind of poison was it?''

Pitar looked at him with miserable eyes. ''Cyanide. The bitter almond smell is more noticeable in the dishes not yet brought you, Liege.''

Tanman said thoughtfully, ''Bitter almond. I think only a Upai could distinguish the proper smell of these dishes.''

I sighed. ''I just wondered about the odor, at first. Until I watched Eran talking casually to the head cook. The Nando poking about the sauce pots was just extra proof. I doubt the cook saw them do it.''

''You should have warned me of your thoughts before you went to check. Did you think I'd ridicule your suspicions?''

I lowered my head, ashamed. Girdeth had laughed at me. Pitar had lifted his brows at my suggestions about kitchen precautions, though he humored me. And Tanman simply trusted me to guard him. I clenched my hands together, head bent.

Tanman's hand rested lightly on my shoulder. ''Pitar. Naga. Look at me.''

We both looked up. He gripped my arm and Pitar's. ''It was Pitar who heard the warning first, and knocked the wine goblet out of my hand—also poisoned, no doubt—when I was coughing and might have drunk it. And it was Naga who saved me from an extremely unpleasant death when no one else suspected the odor. Not even, apparently, the cook. Most ingenious and classic—it nearly worked. Is there any proof, do you suppose, Pitar, of Eran's crime on his person? In his rooms? Among his confederates? A pouch of that poison?"

"I'll search, Liege," Pitar said, light springing into his eyes. He strode off.

I looked after Pitar's hurrying figure. Slowly, carefully, I rubbed one hand in the other, and brushed off the wet bits of gristle still clinging to my nails. I looked up at Tanman, who was staring at my hands. I said quietly, "I'm afraid Pitar won't enjoy it. I left a bit of a mess. I didn't want to get my blades stuck in Eran. I knew I might need them later, and I had no time to play about."

The listening white-faced rookie had ceased to pull at his stuck sword. He turned away and vomited against a table leg. I looked at my hands and smeared them across my clothes.

Tanman said levelly, "You fought Eran bare-handed?"

"He only had a cook-knife to hand, not a sword. Skilled, I'll admit he was that. He nearly had me in the hearth-fire twice." I touched my cut face, thinking. "I didn't like that. When he tried it the third time—" I shrugged and brushed my hands together. "You know what that means? Someone saw a fit, or sorted through all the rumors correctly, or someone guessed by knowing what Osa flamethrowers are like. Someone informed him about my dislike for it. Even our escort soldiers didn't know it was like that, they thought I *wanted* fire."

The hold commander came running up then. "Two of our men went to Eran's chambers. They found a man there packing jades and papers. A cavalry officer from one of the Bada's Well commands, they recognized him. He's in a cell now, but he's in poor shape, they fought—"

"Dead, Liege, nobles-born," another soldier added laconically as he saluted. "We couldn't stop the bleeding."

I clenched my hands, looking at my bruised knuckles. "That's too bad," I said softly. My arm tingled now, numbness fading. I stood up, I flexed my fingers, and pressed my elbows tight against my ribs. Control, I thought fiercely. "The Cragmen are good miners. They do know about the cyanide process that is used in that old silver plant on the Lakes. Do you even know it? Gold and silver, low-grade ores—and the Cragmen mine both, and sell silver to the pirates because Lake Hold grips the legal silver market tight-shut." I lifted my gaze to the frowning men and felt my lips peel back from my teeth and a great shuddering of rage shook my body.

They all, Tanman among them, stepped back in alarm. My fingers strained in the air and clenched tightly. My elbows clenched hard in on my ribs, pressing inward to hold in the rage. Sati rage. I arched my neck trying to control it. Softly, carefully, I said, "Liege, are you well? Have you taken poison from the food?"

"I am well," he said. He looked both alarmed and puzzled. He lifted one hand toward me, but did not touch me. Not quite.

I felt the deep shudder rattle my armor again. Red haze clouded the corners of my vision. The roaring of a large fire filled my ears. Close, too close, a reliving was coming on me while I was angry. "They make the poison from heating, heating a season's filled tanning urinary, heating the dung of caves and of cliffs upon the sea, and running water makes power in the copper Goddess-Combs of the ancients, to draft from the poison slurry plated glory for a heating in the crucible!" Neck still arched, I opened my eyes widely and stared at Caladrunan. It was doubtless an unnatural-looking posture; but it helped. Grating, word by word, I said, "I do not want to be angry."

"No," Caladrunan murmured, still not quite touching me. "No, you don't need to get angry now. It is over."

"For a while," I grated between bared teeth.

"For a while," he agreed, and his fingers moved slightly in the air above my arm.

Slowly, shuddering with effort, I lifted my clenched hand and opened the fingers. They quivered, tendons standing. Then he gripped my hand in his. He took a step closer to me. For a tense moment my grip and his contested in strength, shaking force against force. I shuddered, forcing up my other hand and opening it. He gripped both my hands, meeting my strength as firmly as I needed him to. Cords jumped out in the back of his wrists. I forced my head to come up, straightening my neck, and I closed my eyes; I shuddered until my scabbards banged my knees. It was only then I realized I was growling like a beast.

He said, his breath jolting when my grip shook him, too, "There is surely some way to stop this."

Pitar said in a low tone, "For Goddess's sake, Liege, you're putting yourself at enormous risk—"

"Not from Naga," he said softly. Almost crooning the words. "Not from my Oathswearer, my Sati. I'm safe, Naga."

I opened my eyes. I wasn't growling anymore.

"You must be worn out after that. You're not angry now."

My hands grew still on his; gripping hard, but not with such punishing force. His grip likewise eased, meeting my strength steadily, but not any greater. I swallowed, tasting such a strong metallic tang on my lips and tongue that I was nauseated: the taste of rage and recent fear.

Tanman said aside softly, "Get him a drink of water, Ben. I'm dry, Goddess knows he must be." He met my eyes steadily as he spoke.

Slowly, I nodded. He let go of my hands. There were smears of red on his fingers, outlining where my bloody hands had stained his. Where there was no blood, there were bright pink imprints, sign of bruises to come, where I'd gripped his wrists. When he put a bowl of water in my hands, I drank it mechanically.

Tanman said over the rim of his own water bowl, "Well, it looks like the bathing room for you, Naga. Those robes are ruined. It would be interesting to learn who told Eran about highly spiced Upai food, and when I would have it prepared. Did the cook know about the poison?"

Pitar shook his head. "But he doubtless told Eran aforetime exactly when your food was being planned for, Liege. I've already imprisoned the cook. It seems Eran struck up a friendship only a moon ago, when your plans to come here were first discussed."

"The combination of food and poison was someone else's plan, not Eran's own. Eran," I said harshly, "had limitations to his inventiveness." I touched the table, leaning briefly while I shook myself into order, and stretched out the knots formed by rage into my muscles. Popping bone noises made them look at me.

Pitar said in an odd flat tone, "The local men are going to turn over the entire hold and the town for the Nando who got away, Liege. The hold commander and I plan for more than usual thoroughness."

"Look for him in Manoloki's escort, out in the hills. Or in

Keth's cavalry command," I said evenly, with no particular emphasis.

Pitar eyed me. "You hold long grudges, don't you?"

I looked over at the dais, where one scadda had fallen and the other still pinned a scrap of Tanman's sleeve to the table. Both were probably nicked and utterly ruined. "I have a long memory." I looked down at my feet, one booted, one bare. There was a lick of old burn scarring over the brown top of my bare foot. "Grudge seems such an inadequate word for it."

Pitar snorted and turned away, shaking his head. "Can't carry the whole world," he muttered as he strode away toward guards who were questioning servants.

"He's right," Tanman said.

I kept looking at my feet. I thought, with sputters of red licking at my sight, *yes!* That's the problem with all you Tannese, you don't remember, you don't care, you don't ever think— But I didn't say any of it. Finally, I said, "I'm sorry I frightened you."

He put his arm around my shoulders and began walking. "Come. You look exhausted."

"I need new blades. I'm not going to that bathing shed and leave you vulnerable now. The investigation into—"

"Pitar will half kill himself over that, trying to make up for missing the poison. Do let him redeem himself."

"Did no one taste the food?"

"That's done by the kitchen here—apparently not, this time."

"Damn fools."

He smiled down at me. "Not now that you're here to show us the error of our slovenly ways."

"Pig farmers," I said, choking out the words over a tight throat. "Silly hornheaded pigherds."

"Let us hope," he said, opening the door to his private quarters between very alert guards, "that we can continue to be silly pigherders for a lot of years to come."

While I stripped and washed in his private chamber, dipping water from a basin, I silently called myself a lot of bad names. I washed the fear-sweat off, shivering though using water that was, in truth, not all that cold. Caladrunan kindly pretended he wasn't looking at me through the worst parts; he busied himself with slates and made a lot of clattering noises.

Dry at last, I huddled in one of his oversized bed-robes—they were like blankets on me—and I looked at him. He lifted his head and looked back. I said, "No one asked if you were angry, too."

He gave a dry little smile, fingering his chalk. "You did, you remember? You asked if I was well. I never thought you meant merely bodily health when you asked a thing like that."

I shivered, though it was not cold in the hearth-lit room.

He tapped the chalk. In even tones, he said, "In fact, I *am* angry. I will be angry until this war is fought. I think I've lived my whole reign being angry at someone or something or other. I'm tired, just now, of being angry." He smiled that small smile; the wisp of humor barely lightened the gravity of his face. "You can certainly move flamed fast when you choose."

I shivered again.

He shook his head sharply once. "Why don't you take that robe with you and go over to that lounge. I'll warm some blankets for you by the fire. Go." He smiled. "Stubborn man. I'll feel better if you let *me* make sure you're cared for."

I stared at him, settling down as he wanted. He began working with blankets; the hearth light flickered over the grim planes of his face. He was angry. He was deeply, dangerously angry. When he carried over the first blanket and draped it around me, muscles jumped in his jaw. His hands were very gentle; which only made me oddly certain of his anger. I said, "Should we be with the men, in sight, to prevent rumors of your death?"

He said quietly, "They'll come to me. I'll have to hold some sort of Judgment tomorrow, to quell panic when later rumors begin flying." The grim look eased. "I did my duty. I'd rather be up here with a friend."

I smiled, feeling warmth burn my ears in a sudden teary pleasure. Surely he knew the effect of such remarks, surely it was deliberate praise; but it warmed me, steadied me. I murmured, "Thank you, Liege, for that."

"Why not? It's true. You're much better company than that pack of sentimental drunks down there in the hall. You, at least, know when to be quiet and let me think my own thoughts. Do you get anything from it?"

I blinked. "What do you mean—of course—the Liege Lord of Tan—"

"No," he said impatiently. "No, not that at all."

"Just as a private person, as your friend?"

His face cleared of its scowl. "That's it."

I pulled my legs unde   ne, knelt before him. I clenched my hands together on my knees. He reached forward impulsively, touching my shoulder. He said, "No speeches. Just tell me."

Quietly, deep in my throat, I spoke then a far more serious binding than any Great Oath. I said, "I would do anything for you, Drin."

His hands drew back a degree, clenched together, as if what he saw in my eyes frightened him: so much more than he had expected, more than he'd known, enough to frighten him terribly. *Anything*, I said, and meant it. Other men, I knew with an untaught cold clarity, would have faltered there before me and my promises, before the cold mad gaze of a Sati. I thought grimly, let us see if the Liege Lord of Tan commands a Sati now.

He slowly drew himself together, reached out his two hands, and cupped the flat planes of my cheeks. Leaning forward, he said, "Let us hope I will never have to ask it of you, Naga. Let us hope that much." His eyes were utterly sober.

"Yes," I said, meeting his eyes.

Softly, brokenly, he said, "Let us have that much hope."

The delegation of Eran's relatives came to apologize for the faults and errors of their prize swordsman, their spoiled and frustrated son of nobility. The hold commander's men had found them at the main family home, at an early meal. I dressed myself and listened to them from the shadows.

They were not very humble; yet, bewildered by the things Eran had done, and deeply shocked. That much was clear even to me, where I stood hugging a shadow of Tanman's bed.

"But why did that man kill our boy?" Eran's distraught father asked. "Surely if he was able to—"

Tanman said, with touches of iron grating in his voice, "Perhaps because Eran was trying to kill him. The commander explained some of the facts of the case to you?"

"He did, but I don't understand why— Liege, we had such hopes, Eran had just made so many new friends."

"Did you know these friends? The Harper Tatéfannin stays with you? I see. If you'd tell me about them? I need their names." Chalk scratched as Tanman recorded the answers. No borrowed scribe, now, for such sensitive material.

"They wouldn't let us see—see our boy's body."

Tanman looked up. "That was by my order. It was for your best interests, as it is not a pretty sight. If one or two of you feel able to stand it—and be very sure you are able—then one of Pitar's men will take you there."

"But why—"

Tanman's jaw muscle rippled. "What Pitar's officer did not explain to you was that Eran dropped cyanide into my food with every apparent intention of assassinating me."

I watched their faces closely. The florid head of clan, the angry brothers who were drinkers, the vague and distraught father, and the single grimly upright woman who was head of the clan women—all looked equally stunned. No small thing, considering how easily someone could have warned them before they came; but no one had dared tell them. The head of clan went ash white. They all knew the punishment for Eran's crime.

Tanman said politely, "If any others of you share Eran's political convictions, I give you leave to say so openly now, and suffer no penalty for it but banishment from Tan. If I find proof of similar attempts among you later, your entire clan to the last child will be forfeit to my rage." His eyes moved, like mine, over the blanched faces of Eran's younger brothers. "Think well on it. Inform the hold commander by sealed parchment tomorrow on whether my rule is tolerable to you, or not. If any clan member decides he should quit the region of my rule, my hand will not punish other, honest citizens of Tan. Beyond that time limit, beware."

The head of the clan lifted his head, his skin gray-looking and his face somehow sunken, but still dimly proud. His mustache bristled. "For those of us who are honest men, Liege, are we to be watched, to be mistrusted, maligned? Already everyone probably thinks us murderers, although Eran put himself as much above our laws as above yours!"

I thought coldly, in the desert border holds this man would

be too disgraced by Eran's crime, to argue about being watched. But I said nothing.

Tanman said, "To be watched may help preserve your clan's safety as well as mine. I have no wish to see innocent clan members falsely framed by outside enemies, to point to a family already once accused. It would hide the real assassins, you see. And I have no wish to let riots affect you either. Do any of you find life under my rule so intolerable you want to end it?"

The head of the clan grew more normally ruddy. "Well, we may find things that need changes—my wool taxes—wine tax—" He cleared his throat. "—but none of us want to be banished just for such nuisances."

Tanman smiled then. "And the voting at court, which you must attend to elect Council members?"

The man cleared his throat. "That, of course, and—"

"Just enough of your complaints!" Eran's father said raggedly at his clan's head. "Enough! You filled Eran's head with your complaints when he was little—"

The woman said acidly, "And you drank yourself into stupor when Eran was a youth. I hardly think this will bring him back to us. Shall we go now, Liege? I believe we've learned all we can, and little else productive will get said from here."

The two men were already arguing. Tanman waved his hand in dismissal. The brothers still looked puzzled as they left.

I looked at Tanman, who threw down his chalk with a gusty sigh. "Not the brightest of my relatives, I'm afraid," he muttered.

I said, "I'm unsure how Eran became fifth in succession out of that lot."

"The woman who was so delightfully calm is Agtunki's youngest and only living sister. Agtunki abdicated her own right to the royal prerogatives which then passed to—oh, never mind!"

"I saw the clan blood relationship. I meant Eran's tested competence, in succession judgments by you and the Council."

Tanman's voice became dry. "Even I, my dear Sati, can be as blind to the obvious as these people were. 'A bit childish,' my notes on Eran ran. 'Drinks too much. Sometimes offensive to inferiors but charming to most. Skilled swordsman. Gets along with Cragmen'—an important point.''

''Accurate enough.''

''As far as it went,'' he said, the iron grating in his voice again.

I said softly, ''I can hear Pitar coming down the guard room. Probably with those papers confiscated from Eran's rooms.''

He sighed. ''Goddess, that hearing of yours!'' Pitar was announced. Pitar told us both, ''Liege, several long strings of colored knots were found in Eran's quarters. I brought them—''

I stared at the clump of strings he held up for Tanman. ''Osa,'' I snapped, reading the knots. ''Orders to proceed, repeated in two different ways, with strong emphasis, sent at different times. Apparently Eran was shielding a local Osa nest, or someone wanted you to think so. Whoever got these strings, he was reluctant to do what he was told.''

Tanman gazed at me thoughtfully. ''Pitar, bring out your collection of strings. I would like him to read them. Naga, we have so far been baffled by most of the knots. The older ones were confiscated from some of Oldfield's thugs—they tried to swallow the evidence.''

Pitar returned with an innocuous-looking quiver full of arrows: innocent camouflage. A side pocket opened under his fingers. One by one, sorting them in consecutive order of capture, he handed me the strings. I read them aloud as they came to me, while Tanman recorded my translations. ''Not all these are Osa,'' I said at last, ''but most of them are.'' I glanced over the collection and began to grow angry. Very angry. I tapped one laid upon Tanman's table. ''*Terminate proceed*, here. Who died then? It was just before I came to Tan.''

Tanman folded his hands, glancing at Pitar. ''Some days before you enlivened my hunting in the woods, Sati, a cousin of my lady wife was attacked and her hands given scadda-style butterfly cuts. She was in her private rooms in Fortress. She lived long enough to describe a short man, dark-handed, of foreign accent.''

My scalp prickled. I looked up into Tanman's face. Slowly, I said, ''And it was thought that I—''

''Undoubtedly just as Manoloki desired to be thought. Or

Oldfield. You recall the rumors and witnesses which caused me doubt about you.''

"But then why send me to you at all?" I frowned. "There were so many easier ways for Manoloki to dispose of me. Why? To discredit you if you kept me, to create factions at your court? But they weren't certain that you *would* keep me.''

Pitar said diffidently, "Perhaps it was merely a contingency plan in case you did get to Tanman with your information. Perhaps they simply wanted to disrupt the women's quarters and create problems with the Council vote on accepting refugee natives into Tan—''

Tanman smiled. "Stopping Tokori Efresa's ride into Tan must have been difficult for them. I understand that your escort kept trying to dawdle at the border with you, but you wouldn't let them do as they pleased.''

Pitar turned slowly, staring at me.

I lifted my eyes to his, staring back levelly. Then I said, "They'll find it no easier to stop Tokori Efresa when he takes blood for blood for this threat to your life, Liege.''

Pitar met my eyes for a very long time. Then, by dawning slow degrees, Pitar smiled. "By Goddess, we've got that one working for us? I'd hate to cross that one.''

I lowered my eyes to the strings. "Wise man.''

CHAPTER

= *16* =

PITAR RESTED ONE foot on the iron grill before the hearth, and turned his boot toe this way and that. His face was weary, after screening all the nobles who must see Tanman to be reassured he was alive. He also had no idea that I was not asleep in my roll of furs and blankets. "Ai, Naga was right, we aren't likely to catch the Nando bastard now. I've another thing bothering my mind."

Tanman tilted his head, sipping wine, and set the goblet on the mantel. "Tell me."

Pitar leaned against the mantelstone, murmuring, "Naga. He's got no one else. That's not good. He's too much putting it all onto you, Liege, what ought to be for his own kind. I don't like it. He's—not Tannese. It's too much. Too intense."

Caladrunan stood, arms folded, beside Pitar. Both men studied the hearthfire. "Has Naga been rude or hostile—to you? To the men?"

Pitar moved uncomfortably. "No. Just that—difference. Pulling like a trysail bent on for a gale, even when it's quiet around you. Flat dead calm, unhuman even, away from you. He's learning to hide it, I can tell that. Never real plain until you know him, but it's a thorough deep change. I've never seen a soldier change like that before. Gives the boys creeps. They saw it clear enough today!"

"They know he'd kill any one of them if they crossed him against my safety," Caladrunan said. "It might simply be that."

"But that's the difference!" Pitar said. "That's just it,

228

your safety—not even his own. What do you suppose I've
ordered if you died and he didn't, suddenly?''

Tanman looked at the bluff mustached soldier and simply
blinked.

Pitar smiled without humor. ''Protect your Heir first. And
chain Naga hand and foot, second.''

Caladrunan gave a deep sigh. ''The boys'd be lucky to get
close enough for that. Better to barricade him wherever you
found him for a few days, until he regained his sense.''

''If he ever did,'' Pitar said, looking at the fire.

''That's possible, too,'' Tanman said evenly.

''He's put too much over onto you,'' Pitar repeated.

Caladrunan sighed. ''I know. I know it, Pitar, and I'm not
sure what to do about it. He won't—trust anyone else far
enough. I don't know entirely why he picked me for all this.''

''*He* picked—*you're* Tanman—''

Caladrunan smiled. ''I was picked by him to rescue his
Upai, and I'm well aware it wasn't any orders or yelling of
mine that got me the honor. There's a lot of the cat in our
friend.''

Pitar narrowed his eyes. ''And you like it that way.''

''I guess I'm as weak for that kind of flattery as anyone. I
always thought free will was a better soldier than fear or
bribery. Manoloki has been proving me wrong on that, a lot.''

''Idealist,'' Pitar growled. ''What will you do if you stumble, working among these puzzle-pieces and the Sati turns on
you?''

Tanman frowned. ''There's that chance with any man.
More risk if he does turn on me than with most other men.
But I think the breaking and saddling period is settled, and it
won't ever be so hard in the future as it was. Or so I think.
The rest of the raw edges can be taken at leisure.''

''How long are you planning on keeping him?'' Pitar waved
one hand in protest. ''I assumed this was temporary—''

Caladrunan lifted his head. ''I am not sure. Perhaps as long
as he chooses to serve me, Pitar. Oldfield is in open Council
war with half the members. We might all die tomorrow.''

Pitar made a sign against magic, denying the evil thought,
and shook his head. He muttered about woolly-headed ideal-
ists as he left. After a decent interval I rolled over, stretched,
and got up silently. Tanman shot me a keen look, poured me
a goblet of wine, and sank back into his own thoughts.

That evening, while the last of the reports were trickling in, we sat in chairs before the hearth—just close enough to see by, not so close it plucked the strings of my irrational fears. I sat half-turned to watch his face, to watch beyond him the rest of the dark chamber. Tanman set aside slates with a gusty sigh. "How would you react if we were in opposite places?" he asked, flopping one hand lazily on his chair arm.

"You mean, if this were the Upai Empire, and you an inferior and despised carrier of disease?" I said lightly.

His lips puckered. Then he smiled. "You have a wicked tongue, O Upai."

I tilted my head a little as I answered. "Undoubtedly it would be more unpleasant for you there, than it has been for me here. The rulers of the Upai were notoriously arrogant—worse than your Red Tyrant. They drove the Osa, who were once a starving Upai hill clan, to insane hatred of them. That's how the Empire was overthrown. The Osa atrocities when they took power made them hated in turn." I rested my chin in my hand. "Not that there was much to excuse all this. We ruled widely and absolutely, we feared nothing, and our nobles were weaker than yours are. And, of course, so much power . . ." I smiled wryly. "Reti taught me all this history, because I knew no Upai to give me the history of my clan. Reti considered it important." I looked up sadly.

His hand tapped the arm of his chair lightly. His eyes were low-lidded, half-closed. "And if I had come ragged and desperate to you, Upai ruler?"

I rested my chin in my fingers, thinking. At last I admitted, "I don't know if I'd be as careful of your dignity, your honor, as you are of mine. I would like to think so. But—" I flapped one hand inadequately, aware that my feelings had always been obvious to him despite my attempts to curb them. I went on, "—I don't know if I could be as patient as you've been with me."

He opened his eyes and smiled. "It hasn't been easy."

I sighed. When I spoke, the words came struggling out slowly. "I believe it gives you the greater ethical right to command me. It proves you have the self-restraint of the Goddess, which I too often lack. Reti told me that often enough!"

His arm stretched out, his hand touched mine. "But your

discipline is greater than mine, Naga. You're a Harper. A Sati."

"Small things, not large," I said sadly. I cupped my fingers around his. I drew in a deep breath, let it out, and let go of his hand. "As a ruler, I fear I would still be greatly . . ." I drew in a deep breath, my pulse grew loud and hard in my ears. I twisted my hands together, looking away from him at the fire. At last, bitterly, I said, "Who knows whether that's just the distortion of what's happened to me in this world. Maybe, if things were different—" I whispered, "—if I was different . . . I wouldn't be so starved for the kindness you've given me." I rested my head on my fisted knuckles. I chewed a callous. "If I'd lost you there in the hall, with the poison . . ."

Hearth light flickered orange shapes over his beard, the planes of his cheeks, the heavy brows. I clenched my teeth because everything inside me rocked perilously over abysses; I could keep control if I did not move. In one of those inner crevasses, relivings lurked, rumbling to get out. In another, flared the baffling and painful white glare of that map of lights. I gritted my teeth against all of it. "You should rest," I said.

"Of course, and so should you. But—" he sighed, "there are more reports coming. Let's hear that harp of yours." He smiled. "Please."

I thought of a song and grinned, lifting my brows. "Have you heard the song about the farmer, the pig, and the traveling pleasure woman?" I scrambled to get my harp, while he swatted his massive hand after me.

"I've heard Lado do parts of it, when he was drunk! You should blush to speak of it!"

"Upai don't blush," I said airily, and strummed my harp. "Past time you heard what your pitiful court bawlers cannot begin to approach, a truly—truly—obscene song."

He began to laugh as I finished the first verse, he roared freely at the second, and by the fifth one he was rocking in his chair helplessly with tears streaming down his cheeks. I grinned with satisfaction. "Stop, stop," he gasped at last, "stop, I can't stand any more. How long does this go on?"

I said blandly, "Twenty-three verses are traditional with Harpers. I've added another eight original ones, and I've adopted ten of Lado's—"

"Oh, I can't stand any more tonight," he gasped, wiping his eyes. "Save it for a day when I need it. Goddess, that was better than a goblet of wine, I'm worn out! I'll have to save reports for the morning."

"That was my secret intent," I said, putting the harp aside. I put the outer door guards on night notice and returned to help Caladrunan out of his inner robes, holding thin silk bedrobes for him. On the ship he had let me help him like a dressing servant, if I happened to find it convenient—and if I could figure out how the robes were supposed to be worn. Sometimes he had to redo everything himself.

I sat beside the head of the curtained bed then, moving a fan at the air. He settled himself among the piled furs. I knew suddenly that I would not risk sleeping tonight, not even close to him where I could sleep easily; I didn't want to. I would sit up and guard his sleep, until all risk from Eran's conspiracy was over, and Manoloki's escort were well off in the distance. Caladrunan seemed to sense the decision in the same moment I made it. His face relaxed. He smiled, rolled over in bed, and drowsily flung his arm across the furs. I looked at him, fanning him until he slept.

While he snored, I drew maps and made measurements in the nap of the bedfurs, and I scowled in worried dissatisfaction. No amount of clever thought would change the equations of logistics and supplies and troop strength necessary to attack the Osa in the nest of their invasions, at Pass of Bones. They had so easily destroyed the Upai; and Tan seemed so fragile. For all their difficulties and mistakes, the Osa knew it as well as I. I hated them for their smug assumptions that their equations could, in the end, blot out all that was once Tan.

So far, I thought dismally, as I looked at my exhausted Liege Lord, they were doing an excellent job of it. I bent my head tiredly into my arm and fanned my sole hope for the future.

Sometime in the middle bells of the night, he stirred, blinked, looked at the marks in the rumpled furs, and then at me. He placed his hand lightly on the back of my bowed head. In my ear he said gently, "A general shouldn't have a conscience. It hurts too much."

"Go to sleep, you stubborn pig farmer," I muttered.

He chuckled, patted my shoulders and drew back, pretending to obey my common sense. I waved the fan and pretended I could say more, if I chose. I fanned the hot, still air over him, shifting furs for him when he moved in his sleep; I watched the shadows and angles of the wooden bedchamber. Once I renewed the oil bowl of the night lamp. One-handed, while fanning him, I practiced harp fingerings, scadda thrusts and parries; it seemed a good time to practice one-handed maneuvers to maintain the muscles and reflexes.

But altogether too many times I found myself sliding onto the floor on my knees with the fan clenched in both hands, praying. Perhaps it was all unreasonably too much to expect of the Goddess. I felt the sweat run off me as freely as at a fight.

Perhaps prayer had some effect I didn't anticipate. Four bells before dawn, the chamber doors resounded to frantic banging, voices and dispute. I stood tensely a sword-span from the foot of Tanman's bed, listening, with two table knives in my hand. I wanted my ruined scaddas badly.

Aider's voice rose above the roar. "Let me in! This is confidential and our business is none of yours! Need you more authority? Here's Girdeth—she can explain to her brother why you did not admit us!"

I turned swiftly and tapped Caladrunan's foot. He jerked about, grasping blindly for Devour's hilt near his head. "What?"

"It is I, Naga," I said in the dimness. "Aider and Girdeth are outside disputing with guards. Shall they be admitted?"

He sat up. Then he roared, "Pitar, let them come in!"

I unbarred the inner door cautiously.

Aider, outside, was standing muddy and disheveled between two of Pitar's men. Rafai stood grimly supporting Girdeth, who looked ragged, all her torn finery spattered with clots of grass and dirt. A bead dropped from a ripped necklace. "Let them enter," Caladrunan said softly, from behind me. "Rafai, see to their escort, undoubtedly they're in rough shape—"

"Escort!" Girdeth cried, running in. "They're dead!"

"Hush, dear," Aider said firmly. "Let us report properly. Naga, would you close the door, please."

I glanced at Caladrunan and obeyed his gesture.

Aider drew himself up very tall, once again a soldier. "Cousin, Liege, we were beset while we were returning to

the hold in my wagon, from my lodgings in the town. Girdeth
went with me this evening to visit my wife. Tonight she was
distrait. Girdeth soothed her, and—'' He started trembling,
and drew in a deep breath and straightened again. ''—my
wife gave us grave news.''

Tanman nodded once for him to go on.

Aider said, ''I brought Mimuri and her servants to the
Pavilion of the Wind during Agtunki's party, because I was
afraid to leave her alone. I didn't know he would come—
that fat spider. She—she told me that she was molested
once by Nandos while I was held captive for ransom. I would
never have brought her to the Pavilion if I had known, but
she was afraid of the Nandos and grew upset when she heard
them. During Manoloki's talk, when everyone was preoccupied, she escaped all her servants and hid in the garden.
There she saw a man she feared during the time that—that
the Nandos drove her mad. He spoke to a Nando about a
document. She hid until they moved far enough for her to
flee. When I took her home she was so disturbed I understood
nothing by what she told me, but she spoke to Girdeth later
more coherently. Girdeth impressed on me how vital it was
you should know of this, that we should bring Mimuri to
speak with you. As we were trying to return here with her,
we were beset by archers. Girdeth was nearly dragged off the
wagon, my servants killed, my escort—and my wife—'' His
voice faded. ''—she—''

''Shot dead,'' Girdeth said quietly. ''We think she lost her
embroidered outrobe in the garden, which would tell the
overheard men who she was. They likely recognized me and
tried to take me for ransom. Townsfolk saved us.''

Caladrunan went to the table and sat down on a stool,
pulling slates before him. He began writing. As he held them
up I ran them to Rafai at the door, who dispatched them with
vollies of supporting orders. Caladrunan said, ''Aider, I will
have your wife's body cared for. Girdeth, what exactly did
Mimuri say? What did she overhear? The other man's identity?''

They glanced at one another. Girdeth said, ''She overheard
the Harper Tatéfannin in the garden.''

I felt my breath go out of me in a soft hiss.

Girdeth's eyes turned to me. ''Indeed, Sati. She described
the man beyond doubt—and I think Aider can tell you that
Mimuri went incoherently wild the one time Tatéfannin came

into her sight at court. We were days bringing her back to venturing from her chambers. The Harper was talking to a man with a red Nando cloth on his face, and that man's description sounds so terribly familiar—''

Aider gave a slow grim gaze at the floor. "Could have been twin to the Devotee tutor Karidi, slightly older."

I touched my tongue to dry lips. "Does Karidi have a brother? Some more distant relation who looks like him?"

"Had," Tanman whispered. "Outlawed. Go on, Girdeth."

Girdeth took a deep breath. "Tatéfannin told the Nando, 'Force Keth to sign it immediately, our offer only lasts so long.' Mimuri said there was talk of which Tannese holds and Crag provinces they would each rule when Fortress fell, which holds Oldfield would give away. Mimuri was terribly lucid, and frightened. The other signatures are supposed to be on the document already—all but Keth's—as an official notice of who gets what, after Tan falls. All the major names are there, apparently, and it's been sealed. The thing is to be resealed, after Keth signs, with the old Crag Imperial Seal, the original, that was outlawed by the Red Tyrant.''

Caladrunan looked up. "They hope to contain the Osa with some piece of parchment?"

Aider said, "Apparently they think their collective oath-sworn alliance would stand against the Osa, if it came to that.''

Tanman shook his head. "I've unpleasant news for them."

Girdeth cried out then, "Manoloki's meeting in the Pavilion was a cover for this other—but we don't know where the document is. She told me their message phrase, and neither Aider nor I understand it!''

Aider said, in grim tones, " 'Sealed goat by wolf of light in home devoured.' Apparently they mistrust their messengers."

Tanman pulled at his beard. "Sealed goat is clear enough. The old Crag documents were put on goatskin parchment to make them official and final. Only temporary documents went onto their damned reedpaper." He pulled viciously at his beard. "Come to recall, they've been putting a lot of their proposals on paper lately, as if they don't want any of it to last after some future point. Which just makes this document all the more dangerous." He frowned. "Home devoured. Home of Devour, my sword? That could be anywhere in Tan."

"No," I said crisply. "Devour's first home was in Sharin.

It was given to Tanman just before the first Osa war, to fight
monsters—it was known as the sword Suku. The broken
shards were reforged into Devour—''

''Thank you, Naga,'' Tanman smiled. ''Harpers.'' He shook
his head, smiling. ''Well, then. We're looking for some sort
of ancient place, in Tan. Tell Pitar I want the map, Naga.''

''Which map?'' I asked briskly.

He lifted his head. ''He'll know which one,'' he said, in
such an odd tone that my neck hair crawled. He meant the
map of lights I'd drawn in my fit. I opened my mouth, and
closed it, and did as I was told.

Pitar indeed knew what was meant; he contrived to hide the
map case among all the other things Tanman had sent for.
Caladrunan spread out the map, glancing over the markings.
He murmured, ''There are two parts to this map. One is large
scale, visible by the meandering lines of terrain. I can't tell
where it is. The other seems to be of a smaller area, rectangular, perhaps inside a building.'' He pointed at a scrawled
character. ''Tell me, Naga, what that means.''

I squinted at it. ''On its side, it would be the old Upai
character warning of a burial chamber in the Wastelands. But
upright . . . Reti told me he saw that character written out on
ancient caves which held discoveries in the hills of Sharin.
Reti said the Sharinen gained much of their technology from
studying the tools and broken things. This character would be
put on a place where they find such things. So, in an ancient
context like this one''—I flinched a little, remembering the
context of this map—''it would mean—''

''A chamber of old things, like Devour.''

I nodded.

He tapped the table beside the map. ''What does 'wolf of
light' mean?''

Aider said quietly, ''Electrical storms cause flares on the
mast tips of ships. In many of the Crag dialects, they call that
'wolves of light'.''

I tilted my head. ''That's odd. My Nando escort into
Tan—they were once Cragmen—they used that phrase for the
Flames in an Altar building they sacked—''

Caladrunan glanced from me to Aider and back. ''Hmmm,''
he said. ''If I were a Cragman, I could certainly regard the
Great Altar as a large 'wolf of light'. Here's a Tannese

character. 'Mouth.' And this one reads 'pipe-bend,' a rather odd thing to put down in a trance, don't you think?"

"A fit," I muttered. "Not a trance, a fit."

" 'Control valves' here, it says. You wrote it with the Tannese prefixes peeled off and sometimes tacked on the ends of the characters, Naga. I finally figured it out with 'mouth.' Pig-Tannese, in a map? What an irreverent fit-spirit."

I opened my mouth, and closed it.

"And right in the middle, we have this Upai character of yours, which means an old chamber. What does that collection of words seem to indicate to you, Aider?"

"Down in the piping for the Great Altar, there's a place the Devotees have not been telling us about. Where possibly we might find that parchment awaiting Keth's signature—convenient to them all. Very likely the Devotees were in on it all along."

"Goddess grant we get there before Keth does. Maybe I can prevent him from joining that alliance. I have to keep *him*—nobody else can hold those Cragmen in check." Tanman straightened, closed his eyes briefly, and folded his arms. "Goddess Above and Below, it all fits, entirely too well. The hard part will be finding that chamber in time." He opened his eyes. "Aider, I ordered clean clothes and armor to fit you. Also things that might fit Girdeth—if you want to come, sister. It'll be a very hard ride, not one of your hawking jaunts."

Girdeth said, "All this is based on that map that the Sati wrote—"

"—in a fit, yes," Caladrunan finished. "Mimuri's testimony started this, and she's mad—but I believe her. You have an alternative answer to the riddle?"

She frowned. "No. But I've heard before from the court women visiting here that Tatéfannin is Oldfield's man—and Oldfield likes word-games. He could mean his riddle to be used in several different ways to get in, when we finally find the place. It would surely amuse him to befuddle or even scare Keth for a while, judging by what I've heard about him."

Tanman lifted his brows. "You're right. We'll puzzle over understanding the chamber door when we see it, though. Are you coming? You've earned the right."

Girdeth grinned above her torn veil. "I'll ride you all into the ground! Send for my leathers and an Army crossbow for me, will you? And I'll just borrow some of your robes to go over mine, Pupo. I hope you gentlemen don't mind. I've a feeling we may run into some of the same robbers as Aider and I met before.''

"I've already sent a decoy troop out the west gates," Tanman said briskly. "Naga, I sent for scadda blades. Here they are. The Armorer stayed up to cobble something together. It won't be as good as a more lengthy consideration, but—''

I picked up the scabbarded blades, slid them out. A slow creeping feeling went down my neck. "These are no improvised blades. These are written on and signed and—''

Unfolding heavy robes, Girdeth looked over my shoulder. "Well, what a surprise! Look at this, Aider.''

Aider examined the blades by the lamp flame. The three of us looked at one another. At last he said, "Entirely appropriate, I must say, for Ganek Tanedi's master blades to reappear to fight beside Devour.''

In a rather hollow voice, I said, "I didn't know Ganek Tanedi was a scaddaman.''

Aider gave a toothy smile. "He lost a hand during a skirmish before the Osa war, that's why he became a swordsman, and that's why he wasn't famous as a scaddaman in all the ballads. But he was for years a Master of Scaddas like Reti—perhaps he even invented the rank and the weapons. He fathered my mother's line, the old reprobate, that's how I happen to know this trifle of history. Apparently the Head Armorer has been digging about in interesting places for weapons.''

We were all wrestling into clothes and armor as we talked. I helped Aider buckle his cuirass and then I disentangled Girdeth from the shirts of a leather riding coat as she pulled it on. She thanked me and said, "Go on, strap the blades on! Ganek would be pleased, wouldn't he, that his old weapons were being used?''

"I'm amazed they're not rusted to bits," Caladrunan said.

I lifted my eyes to his. "They're of the same metal as Devour.''

He smiled and clapped me on the shoulder. "Let me be the first to blood them, then," he said, and nicked his finger on both. "There. Now pray we make it to Fortress in time.''

I swallowed. "I'm a bit afraid to do any more praying now."

He glanced at me. "You and me both, Kigadi."

I shrugged into the last of my armor. As I turned, Girdeth took a grip on my arm. "Hai, scaddaman," she said down in her throat. "Give me a kiss for luck, would you? I'm scared to death."

I looked into her eyes, startled. Beyond her, Tanman smiled. He took her arms and kissed the top of her head and beckoned me to do the same. I took her hand and bent my head low in salute over it, and kissed her cheek lightly. Aider gave her a hug. "All right," she declared, "let that lot beware of crossing us now!"

CHAPTER

= *17* =

"GUARDS," I MURMURED as I stood tight against the wall, with Devotee robes over my armor. I glanced back at the three behind me, all in black Devotee robes. "Three. One across in the doorway opposite the Devotee chamber, two beside the chamber door." I saw Tanman nod once.

Aider murmured, "Do you need a diversion?"

I glanced at Girdeth, and smiled. I beckoned her, making gestures, and she grinned in turn. Tanman frowned, looking worried. Girdeth strutted past me and around the corner. I couldn't see any of her armor under the stolen Devotee robes; the way she moved hid it well. "Well, my boys," she said, in such a classically easy tone I wondered if her brother was scandalized by it. "Let's not be hasty! A girl has a living to make, you know. The robes? Well, the housemother wouldn't let me out just like that, you know, I have to be devout in my . . . attentions."

I saw Aider grin in appreciation as I spun around the corner and ran toward the Devotee guards. I moved silently.

Girdeth had done her job, passing the guards and turning them away from me. My scadda pommels took the nearest two down without a sound. My hand continued in the same line of force to crack jarringly against the third guard's turning head. He went abruptly sidewise, and fell down like a pile of rags, and was motionless. I stared about for any running rescues. Nobody.

Girdeth looked down at the third man. "I think you killed him, Naga."

240

Aider and Caladrunan were already binding the other two guards' bodies and hauling them out of sight beyond the corner. I dragged the dead one there, and felt unhappy; Caladrunan had ordered no killing. I said, "I didn't think I hit him too hard."

Girdeth stared at me. "Don't look so upset. I'm sure Pupo will excuse you for it."

"My knuckles hurt."

"I should hope so. They're bleeding."

I looked at my knuckle-guards. She was right.

Caladrunan came up and grabbed my arm and hit my face in two tart little swats. "No more of that," he said. "Now let's get into this damned chamber, shall we?"

I grimaced at him and pushed open the door and went in. Inside a Devotee sitting on a stool peered around at me. "Dodenaca, is that you?" He pushed back his hood, showing ruffled thin white hair. He squinted, peering at me. Incredibly near-sighted, I thought in amazement, and relaxed. I glanced at the slates spread out all around the man.

Tanman came up beside me. "Isaon," he said warmly. "I'd forgot you still worked down here. How are you now? You used to tutor me."

"Oh, I did?" He smiled. "Well, I have such a faulty memory. I'm afraid I tutored so many that I've completely mislaid—"

"Caladrunan," Tanman said lightly.

"Oh yes, oh yes, such a sharp boy, I recall. We got so far as to enter into celestial mechanics, you recall? I wanted to—"

"Isaon, we have a problem."

"Yes? If I'm in the way I can move my slates, I'm sure—"

"Where is the pipe-bend?"

"Pipe-bend?" Isaon blinked. "Pardon, I wasn't aware any gas pipes deliberately bend, even down in the caves they bored direct lines— Perhaps you could show me, the Devotee brothers rather discouraged me from exploring some upper parts of the gas mine—you know it is a working gas mine, don't you, that our ancestors tapped and made? Oh, well, I see, you didn't." His finger stabbed out at one of the slates I was looking at. "The Altar burns fluids brought up from faults in the rock of the cliff. I believe ultimately the reservoir of gas may lie out to sea. Anyway, they developed a series of holding and automatic distilling tanks deep in the rock, with marvelous disposal methods for ridding the raw exudate of its less useful components. The Altar up there is just a later tacked-on use for what was originally—I say it quietly, you see—a source of fuel. It still heats our springwater for the bathing rooms, you know. The Devotees obtain their excellent Archive ink from the soot off the Altar burning. I believe originally the mine was of practical value.''

"That is heretical," Tanman said, obviously impressed by Isaon's words.

"Oh, but it's obvious in the physical evidence," Isaon said earnestly. "The problem is, the whole thing may be unstable. You know we lose bits of the cliff regularly, faults in the rock shifting and dropping into the sea. I wondered if that shifting might be taking place at deeper levels, and I checked on things installed long ago. Marks have indeed moved measurable distances since they were first put in. Parallel lines no longer are parallel, and so on. Perhaps you mean an accidentally bent pipe? I've tried to warn the Devotee high ranks, and they do let me make my observations and report to the highest councils, but I don't think they find it very serious. Whenever I get to talk to someone outside like you, I try to tell them—''

"You never leave here?"

"Well, over into the next chamber, to sleep. It's just an old storage area—"

"Take us in there," Caladrunan said abruptly.

Isaon rose, blinking. "Oh, certainly, if you wish. I've no idea what you do now, sir, but it's plain you're no Devotee. Is it proper?"

"Indisputably," Caladrunan said, straight-faced. "I am now Tanman Caladrunan."

"Oh, quite," Isaon said, in a rather uncertain tone. "I'd completely forgot the connection. Well, this way. Here's the door. You'll have to duck your head. It's quite uncomfortable in places, you have to squeeze through, but some of my most valuable observations of the rock movement were made here, and I wouldn't give it up for the world. See here, the thing goes in fits and starts, as I've marked with this tar line, here and here—''

Isaon carried along a lamp, jabbing it unsteadily at the lines and fissures of the raw cliff rock as he walked along the winding corridor. "There—I showed that insolent young Cragman, Dodenaca, my work, and he laughed and scarred up the rock with his spurs! I've no idea why all these Cragmen want to see it if they laugh at my work."

"Do they come often?" I asked softly.

"Oh, nearly every other day," Isaon said crossly, "in and out, and nodding like fools at whatever I tell them. It's enough to make a fellow feel like a doddering old man, I will tell you that, when I'm nothing of the kind! They've threatened me at times, too. That's who Dodenaca is, one of those damned Cragmen. You've an odd accent yourself, young fellow." He peered at me.

"Upai," Caladrunan said briefly.

Isaon peered at me. "Happen to know a lady named Orena é Teot, by any chance?"

I nearly choked on the dusty air. "How did you meet—"

"Lovely lady. She sold me some Sharinen-made rock climbing picks and tools. Indeed, I must have bought up most of her stock. All contraband, of course, with no Sharinen treaty signed yet, but she told me a great deal about her people and told me some of the history of this place. Apparently the Upai who first came to this harbor were the ones who built the Great Altar over the gas mine to begin with. Silly use for it, making an altar of a dangerous unstable site I must say, young fellow, and I told her so—she was rather amused at that. A very old lady Upai brought her here, I think one of the Lady of Fortress's servants. The old woman was lost down here when we first met, Goddess only knows how. Poor old thing—disgraceful. Here is my humble abode."

There were intricate carvings and relief writings over all the domed stone walls. In places I could see traces of old metal brackets and braces which had rusted or been torn out. Isaon waved at it. "All Upai, that. Orena read some of it to me. Lovely language, Upai. This used to be a Upai prayer chamber. Singularly appropriate for meditating on my findings and measurements, don't you think?"

"Where do the Cragmen go?" Tanman asked.

"Oh, they wander around and spit on the carvings and talk among themselves, I get too disgusted to keep track of them in here. I've nothing of value, or they'd take it."

"Faults," I said. "Rock-climbing tools. You have other places you go?"

He shrugged. "Just down into the rock. Here." He pressed the tongue of a carved stone animal and the stone tongue easily depressed. A narrow strip of carvings slid back into the wall's surface, exposing a dark side exit. I looked closer at the stone animal and its tongue. The carving was roughly of a wolflike or doglike form, within a Upai character which meant spring sunlight. The Tannese character for light was scratched crudely above it. Tanman glanced at it and nodded once, significantly: wolf of light.

"Are there other chambers like this one?" I asked. "Down in the rock, near the mine and the pipes?"

Isaon beamed. "Yes, very small ones. I'll show you, if you like. Tell me what the written carvings mean, if you would, where we come on them. It might help in my observations, you never know what earlier men have seen in the rock."

I licked dry lips. "Isaon, do you know anything about the pipes and the burning, and the regulations of the gas itself?"

"Not everything, but a good deal, yes," he said.

"Would it be possible to set it wrongly? To make it . . . devour its home?"

Tanman's face went pale in the unsteady lamplight.

Isaon's brow wrinkled. "Why, yes, if someone was silly enough to try. I could check the settings down there, if you like. The main controls are up top, I expect you know that, but all the mechanics of it are down here. When it goes odd up there, they all troop down here and half the time I have to show them the proper settings anyway. They send acolytes to me to learn the settings now, at least. Such silly, flighty little boys, I hardly think they remember a thing. Come, let's look at the settings."

He carried his lamp down into the blackness. As we followed, I felt my heart get louder and louder in the flickering, pressing dark. Isaon said, "Now the heavy feeling you get in the dark is quite normal. The smell people often remark on is leakage from the garbage pits up top, partly, but also leakage from the mine's automatic disposal of metal wastes. The Devotees retrieve sulfur and special oil deposits at the main pit, and there, let me tell you, the stench is immense. I'm not sure what they do with it, but I think they sell it to someone."

I stopped short in the narrow ragged rock corridor. Girdeth bumped into me. I said softly, "They are the ones selling to

the Osa supply lines for their hellish fire. We didn't know
where it was coming from."

Tanman turned, stooping, and touched me. "You're sweating. Are you all right?"

The smell of Isaon's lamp barely touched the draft of filth
from the depths. I clamped my teeth tight. "Go on," I said.
Then, gritting, I said, "The Osa smell . . . like this . . .
when they run their machines. And fire them off."

Isaon said, "How interesting. They must burn poorly distilled fuel gases. Here you can see the supply pipe, how it's
begun deforming under the rock movement." He stooped,
bending in the light of his lamp. "How odd! My tools were
moved, they're out here in plain sight. I keep them back in
the crevass there, so the Cragmen won't stumble over them so
easily and take them if they come down here."

"Look around here," Tanman said quietly to Girdeth, Aider,
and me. "Feel for a wrapped packet, in cracks within reach."

I felt over the rough banded sandstone beside me. Then my
fingers stumbled over an arm-thick hole lined in cold ancient
metal. I gingerly poked a scadda into it, expecting an ancient
trap or a snare, or some nasty Cragman trick. Nothing. Then I
reached in with my hand, and touched something slick lying
on the metal lining of the hole. I grasped it, drew it out.
"Here."

"Lamp please," Caladrunan called to Isaon. We huddled
over the leather packet as I carefully opened it.

"Cover your faces," I said, "in case they've put some
kind of ambush powder in it."

Girdeth said, "You have a nasty imagination, Sati."

"All in good cause," Aider said grimly.

I folded back the last hard leather wrapping. Inside gleamed
a dark reddish wax seal on a cream-colored rolled parchment.
I glanced up at Tanman. Carefully I lifted it, examined it for
any signs of tampering or damage, and breathed out a deep
sigh. Aider pulled open his robe and brought out a rigid small
case for scrolls, handing it to Tanman. Aider said, "I rather
anticipated we'd need that."

"My thanks, all of you. You too, Isaon," Tanman said.

Isaon squinted. "Oh, dear. It's important, is it? Well, it's
good you retrieved it then. We still have to check the readings
on the mine, you know."

"You're right," Tanman said, stowing the case in his own

robes. Girdeth carefully wrapped up the outer casing as it had been and stowed it, with a fierce grin, back in the hole. "We'll post some men to pick up whoever tries to retrieve that," Tanman agreed.

Isaon fussed as he led the way, lamp dipping to remark on ancient marks and calibrations in looped metal tubing, on ancient glass-faced disks. "Here again, you see, the pipe has actually begun deforming under the pressure of the rock shifting. That'll have to be replaced eventully, you know. I'm studying now how to shut down the mine safely with all the improvisations and bypassed safety mechanisms we deal with these days. We've lost so much."

"Pipe-bend," I said suddenly.

Tanman turned in the lamplight and stared at me. The flame guttered in Isaon's hand. The old man blinked at me with a rather preoccupied expression.

Aider said from behind Girdeth, "Isaon, we should check—or you should check—the readings close around this deformity."

"I have, they're quite good. I also checked the last one."

Girdeth murmured, "Is there another place where the mine's pipes are deformed?"

Isaon turned uncertainly about, sending shadows leaping over the walls and humps of the tunnel. I felt my lips draw back in the eddies of sulfuric odor. Tanman gripped my arm hard and released me, saying harshly, "I am trying to remember the map now. It seems we have been following the map's larger part, if the meandering lines I thought were terrain are actually the lines of tunnels down here."

"Perhaps we ought to look at that map," Girdeth said.

Isaon turned, saying, "I don't know what all this talk of a map means, but I've drawn quite a good one and placed copies on the walls at regular intervals for convenience. A great lot of bother, but someday worthwhile, possibly. Here's one, you see?"

"The Cragmen know that? They can see all the tunnels on this map?" Aider said sharply.

"Yes, if they've disturbed my tools, certainly they could find the maps. The problem is to know which of several control systems they've tampered with. There are so many possibilities." His finger tapped the sooty markings.

"Home devoured, pipe-bend and wolves of light," Girdeth murmured, gazing, beside her brother, at me.

Staring at Isaon's map, I said, "I first saw this map scratched on the underside of the Altar Bowl at my Oath-swearing." I turned to Tanman, eyes staring wide. "It is the same map."

Isaon became animated. "Your code-phrase reminds me of a set of carvings near one of the systems—now I recall, a steam-pipe bend is there. The line goes to warm the hypo-causts and bathwater up top in Fortress and if that was poorly valved, it would shatter the main gas line to the Altar—I know, you all think me a silly man, but the truth is, there are such a great number of different ways that—" Isaon moved abruptly around a rock buttress, and we were thrown into flat darkness.

Girdeth's gasp of alarm made me blink and forget my own terrors. "Here," I said to orient her, and felt her hands on my belt at the back, even as I grasped Tanman's belt in the same way, and felt safe between them both.

Beyond the twist in the corridor of rock, Isaon was darting impatiently and holding up the lamp. "Come now, it's aston-ishing we haven't all been blown up by now if they've tampered with the steam line. Come, come!"

Isaon, once moving, did not linger. We stumbled, more in darkness than light, with Aider getting the worst of the stum-bles at the end of the line. Girdeth gave a high nervous giggle at some rude words Aider muttered. Isaon pattered on be-tween toothlike columns that stretched from pitted floor al-most to ceiling level—and rock cones that hung from the chiseled hacked ceiling down almost to the floor. Water dripped between the teeth. Tanman's sword scabbard brushed one of the stone teeth; the thing gave off an eery ringing clear note. The hair crawled on the back of my neck as I slipped between the vibrating rock and its faintly humming neigh-bors. The noise of waterfalls became suddenly loud in the dark ahead.

Isaon climbed down a stone slope, using hand and foot-holds hollowed into the rocks for a much larger set of men than ourselves. Tanman was the only one who climbed easily from one hold to the next. The rest of us had to stretch, securing one another, while Isaon slid down the stone slope and occasionally checked himself casually by stuffing a hand or a foot into a passing hold, meanwhile holding the lamp above his head. I stared down after him. The light went farther away with every heartbeat. The source of rushing water, far down in the darkness, echoed loud, pervading our bones. Aider and Girdeth and I lifted one another from toe-holds to fingerholds when our hands would not support weight at an awkward angle; the Devotee robes were a nuisance. We were perhaps more cautious of Girdeth than she needed, but she didn't object to it. At the bottom Isaon said cheerfully up to us, "There's an easier way back up on the return. I think you'll find it quite interesting."

"What about the steam pipes?" Girdeth gasped.

"This is it," said Isaon, patting a carved stone facade on a column as thick as five men. "It's inside here. I've checked this already. The next set of gauges are just down this metal walkway. The walkway's quite sturdy. Someone ripped out all the other fittings, so this is the only catwalk intact, to my knowledge, anywhere outside Sharin. Have you been to Sharin?"

Aider said grimly, "No, we've only bought tools, weapons, from Sharinen traders."

I said, "I've fought a few times beside Sharinen soldiers." They all briefly looked at me. I finished dryly, "They're good."

Girdeth stepped down then on the metal walkway beside me. At Lake Hold, her gold slippers had been discarded in favor of heavy forester boots with iron grip-bars on the soles; they clattered as she walked. The walkway beneath us looked like a metal fishnet frozen in midair, edged with strips and crossbars of the rustless metal. Depthless darkness lay below, with the rushing grown to a jarring vibration, and drafts of heat and eddies of stench; I felt as if I were breathing in the muzzle of an Osa flamethrower. Girdeth, as she and I came up close to Isaon, gave me a hard look. I wiped sweat out of my eyes. I hadn't sweated so much in the desert before battle. When I glanced over at Aider, his face was oddly shadowed in the low lamp set on the walkway; I noticed heavy beads of sweat on his face. Aider knew that horrible smell, too.

Isaon's face looked old and white in the lamplight. He fidgeted, tapping glass-faced metal disks and turning levers to no effect. Isaon said quietly, "They did their dirty little games here, my friends. But how did they know . . ."

"Maps, the Devotee acolytes you trained," Tanman said softly.

"Can it be repaired?" Girdeth sounded weary and frightened.

"I am doing so. But this shut-off valve is locked open with age—" Caladrunan strained. Tanman's fingertips barely brushed the high round wheel overhead.

"Let me," I said. My voice sounded oddly harsh. I drew in deep breaths of the tainted air. When Isaon moved aside, Aider and Tanman both bent to make their backs a platform on which to stand. I noticed torn holes in the walkway where a platform—intended to reach this wheel—must have been removed. The ancients, I thought coldly, were not so giant as they seemed.

Isaon held up the lamp as high as he could. He said to Girdeth, "He's the smallest of them, which is good for getting up there, but surely he can't—" Then he said hastily, "Young man, it turns to the right hand at the top."

"Watch," Girdeth said, in a harsh echo of my own tones.

I stepped up on their backs and clamped my hands on the wheel and threw my considerable leverage into jerking the wheel to the right at the top of its arc. Aider made a muffled cry as my boot heels drove into his back. Nothing happened, while I held my leverage and balanced myself on the leather-armored platform of my friends' backs. Tanman shifted very minutely, and I said quietly, "Hold, Liege."

Girdeth cried, "I see flakes of gray shifting around the stem of the axle!"

Aider grunted, "I won't sleep on my back for a tenday."

Tanman said, "If he doesn't get that valve turned, we won't any of us be sleeping in a tenday. Oh, Goddess. You're right about our backs."

Isaon said, "I see gray flakes falling, too!"

Then suddenly, the great rushing noise I had associated with the hot depths below the walkway ceased. The air became still. The rushing sound had come from the great stone column rising out of the dark toward the rock overhead, rising toward Fortress chambers. For a moment the feel of all that stone weight came crushing down on me in the dark. I wrenched, I gave a last straining, mind-hazing heave, and the wheel spun forcefully under my hands, jerking me forward. It threw me off their backs.

I felt myself falling toward the walkway's edge, toward the

depths. Red haze still blurred my sight. But Girdeth was in the way, face white as cloth, white hands spreading like wings. She caught my arm. Somehow she spun around, using my own motion to wrench me sidewise, redirecting me with all the grace of a warrior; my boots swung over space and stumbled back onto metal mesh. For a moment we swayed together in the center of the catwalk, my limbs clutched on her in animal panic. Slowly I relaxed. Then Girdeth let go of me, patted my rumpled robes. Tanman gripped my shoulder and brushed some gray flakes out of my hair. I drew in three deep rapid breaths, feeling my armor heave under the disguising robes as I breathed. "Thank you," I said.

Girdeth smiled an odd slow smile. "Well, I couldn't let Pet go flying out there into Goddess-knows-what nastiness. I'm sure you would've figured out something without my help, though."

I said dryly, "You needn't flatter me to save my dented pride. I'm quite glad enough that you caught me when that flamed wheel turned, I hardly care about the rest."

"All right then. You owe me a handful of favors!"

"I'll do for you six things," I said.

"You've a deal," Girdeth said.

Tanman chuckled. "Remember not to play fourpeg with this shark, Girdeth. He can't make you any promises. It countervails Great Oath."

"Oh, you mean little man!" Girdeth cried out, and laughed, and I saw tears glitter in her eyes. I didn't duck aside when she smacked my face lightly. Girdeth, I thought, had had enough adventure for a while; she wanted to go home now. Her hand fumbled out, gripped my arm. Tanman dropped his arm around her shoulders, squeezed tightly.

Aider saw her face, too; he said, "Shall we go on?" Then he glanced at me. Under his breath he murmured, "I hope you don't have hysterics."

I looked squarely at Aider in the lamplight. I didn't pretend deafness. I said, "No. Just fits."

Isaon was looking inquisitively from one of us to the next. Aware of the look, I turned and began walking down the metal mesh into the dark. Isaon hastily followed me, holding up the lamp. The old man pointed out a spiral metal ladder, climbing up into a black man-sized tunnel in the rock. The light did not begin to penetrate its height. Isaon said, "What are you listening for?"

"Cragmen," I said. "How far up?"

"Up into Fortress itself, this goes," Isaon said. "And wait until you see where!"

"Tell me. I dislike surprises," I said evenly.

Isaon looked into my eyes, and hastily away. He said reluctantly, "It goes up into the women's quarters, near where the youngsters stay. The Heir, and those sort of young rascals." He gave me another quick look, and swallowed.

"So you know where the Heir sleeps, Isaon? Do the Cragmen also know this, from your tunnel maps?"

"I didn't think there was any risk. I never saw the Cragmen get out of the storage room, until today, where my tools were disturbed and you found that package—" Then slowly, he added, "Well, sometimes the numbers of who came and who left became rather confused, some were coming and going all the time when they were with me—"

I turned to Tanman and briefly outlined the risk to his son. I saw a yellow flicker in his eyes as the lamplight flared high. "It's good you told us of this, Isaon," Tanman said, in such a flat tone that I wondered about the life of any Cragman who wandered into our path on the way up. Tanman said, "Climb, all of you. Isaon, brief Naga on the pathway ahead as we go upward. If you and Girdeth cannot maintain our pace, you will follow more slowly with Aider as your soldier. But Naga and I must reach the boy. If the Cragmen have already passed this way, my son is at too much risk. He is up there by now, I sent him off from Lake Hold for his safety—into this new threat."

"How much likelihood?" Aider said briefly.

"High. Altogether too high for my liking."

So was the old spiral metal stair. It swayed slightly to our weight. Girdeth and Isaon were eventually forced to fall behind us, for fatigue; Aider's face was worn in grieving lines, and he did not seem to mind staying with them. They opened one of the wooden ports in the side of the steady dark bore of rock, and took the lamp with them into a side corridor, deep in the dungeon gut of Fortress. Aider promised that he could get them to safety from there. Using a chunk of stray wood from Isaon's tunnels as a torch, Tanman and I climbed onward in the dark until my breathing came as hot and loud as his; his worry drove him pitilessly. When the torchwood was gone, we climbed in blank blind darkness. I finally persuaded him to conserve his strength in regular fifty-step pauses. When I stumbled and fell once, he grabbed my weaponbelt and we stood quite still until the swaying in the metal eased. Whispering, I panted, "Step was gone there, my foot shot through."

"Did you sprain anything?" he panted in return.

"No. Just a scare. I'll feel ahead with my hands now. No matter what Isaon said, this thing is falling apart."

"That last crossbrace was torn away."

I gasped out a joke. "Corruption in the construction crew. Inferior metal."

He swatted at me and I began climbing again, brushing my fingertips round and round the rock tunnel as I climbed.

I went more slowly in the blind dark with the risk of fallen steps and fragile metal. It had been better preserved down in the sulfurous depths, which seemed odd until I noticed salty crystals grating under my hands. I felt back to him with my hands and made him aware of it. "We're in the cliff near the harbor waterline, I think," he whispered.

"Should we take one of the side portals into the corridors?"

"Not yet. This is probably the fastest way through Fortress."

The salt on the railings had become irritatingly abrasive. Each portal door, now, I felt over to find the chisel-mark that years ago told Isaon where the women's quarters' doors were. He had, Isaon admitted, found it convenient to visit a lover when he was much younger—but no less crazy, I thought to myself as I climbed. I wondered how he'd any strength left for his lady-love. We didn't speak for a long time. The portals began to come at regular intervals, marking each floor of Fortress. Eventually we left the region of salt behind.

"Here," I muttered at last, finding the mark, and very cautiously slid back the portal's bar. Even Tanman's breathing seemed frighteningly loud. I drew open the door. Blackness. My hand crept forward, slid onto straw mats. A floor of stone lay beneath the matting. I swung my head, patted Tanman's arm once. Drafts of cool herb-scented air spun past my nostrils and down into the hole behind me. Tanman lifted me and pushed. I slid out onto the floor silently and turned to help Tanman squeeze his greater armored bulk through and free. Then I closed the portal and felt the bar thud automatically into place on the far side.

A tapestry fell in place over the portal in a rustle of fibers, threads catching under my rough fingertips. My eyes adjusted to a dim light beyond an open archway. Tanman said harshly, "I know where we are now. Isaon's directions are a few years away from being useable. Grip my belt."

I did so, though I was apprehensive for his safety; I'd have felt better if I moved ahead of him, first into any ambush.

We passed into the next room, where a low-burning lamp illuminated someone's private scroll-room. Feminine scents filled the air, cushions were rumpled and casually tossed about. "Therin should be up here with his mother today." I saw Tanman's jaw ripple with anger. "They may be safe," he said.

"They may also be holding more than just your son to ransom," I said. That was the kinder idea of several possible events. I didn't add any further to his misery.

We trotted through a maze of rooms, some used, some not, and startled a women's quarters guard as she turned about on her regular beat. She barely had time to recognize Tanman before we plunged past her. I thought it strange, but he didn't call her to follow and aid him. Nor did he ask assistance of any of the other guards we passed. "Why go alone?" I asked.

He gritted his teeth when he answered. We were running down a blank corridor with pools of scummy water in the cracks of stone paving. We burst into an archway; he impatiently tossed open an iron grill gate. Outside lay a red-tiled courtyard, with a white stone fountain spouting water into the morning light. Both of us blinked, dazed by the sun. He said grimly, "If Keth Adcrag is involved, I want to be able to keep it all among ourselves and retrieve the situation without getting any of my guards murdered by Cragmen to protect the secret."

"Have you—" I stopped a moment, considering his mood, and went at it differently. I said, "Is it possible that Keth led the other Cragmen on as if he were going to sign the document, and changed his mind? Did Keth intend them to betray themselves to you?"

He gave a brief humorless laugh. "Keth is resourceful. He planned this to get rid of Oldfield, get rid of all his Crag rivals, yes. I think they wanted him to be signing that document down there, close by when Fortress's gas mine blew up—so he turned their plan on them. It's likely he actually set up Mimuri's flight into the garden. I've long wondered about some of the servants who care for Mimuri, but Aider won't hear anything against them. If the servants are Keth's spies, Keth would know about Mimuri's weak spots, Girdeth's friendship. If he told his servants to conveniently let Mimuri run away and overhear—even steer her subtly—he knew Girdeth would hear about Oldfield's plot eventually.''

I said, "If Keth *knew* the news would travel on to you, then who tried to kill Mimuri and kidnap Girdeth and Aider?''

"Nandos. They probably discovered one of their own men was not quite what he seemed. Mimuri was not difficult. The tricky part was setting up the meeting in the garden where Mimuri could overhear: Keth had to get Oldfield's man to talk to the messenger Nando at a certain time and place. While Tatéfannin thought he was talking to Manoloki's Nando—he even assumed Manoloki had a distant leverage on Keth—in fact that Nando, or the one who set up the meeting, was a double agent in Manoloki's organization, working for Keth. Thus the meeting was overheard. Later Mimuri's dropped outrobe must have been discovered, since the Nandos tried to stop the message with Aider and Girdeth's deaths.''

I scowled. "Keth's part in it sounds almost . . . loyal to you.''

"Keth plans for both sides of big events. He certainly plans to look innocent when Oldfield and the others are brought to trial for treason. And technically, he would indeed be loyal.''

"Why not act more directly—warn you in certain time to prevent the blowing up.''

Tanman smiled grimly. "I have to salute his deviousness. His advantage among the Crag nobles would balloon if Fortress blew up with the four of *us* there—and you know it was close. Lay out proof his plan murdered me, and his people back home would love him. It's almost a holy war, getting rid of the oppressor—Cragmen have been trying to overthrow Tan since the world began.'' He gestured for me to arm myself openly.

I had Ganek Tanedi's ancient scaddas in both hands as we plunged into a warren of narrow corridors and small stone rooms. The proportions of the furniture spoke of children's quarters. "They've moved," Tanman said savagely, face contorting. "This is the third place to look, he wasn't in any of the others, and how much lead time they have— I don't know where my son is!"

I said slowly, "Wolf of light. Do boys get taken to the Great Altar areas at times? There must be plotters who still expect an explosion, about now—it also puts your son close to the Devotees, in case the explosion only sputters."

He rolled a wild look at me, spun about, and ran.

We burst in on one of the balconies of the Great Altar. The entire place was deserted and echoing, but for a solemn line of boys in the benches near the Altar dais. A tall black-clad figure, pacing behind them and gesturing with a scrawny hand, had more to do with their solemnity than the impressive surroundings. I whipped my black Devotee robes aside and sheathed my blades and straightened myself even as Tanman did—before we could be seen as soldiers. Curious heads turned up toward us, jerking back into line at the crack of the Devotee's voice. Karidi snapped. Therin's tutorial reprieve had ended when he was sent back to Fortress for his safety— ironic on too many counts.

"My son," Tanman breathed. The hard lines of his shoulders went suddenly lax, and he leaned weakly on the balcony. "He's safe here—since you turned off the steam pipe, Naga."

"Unless Devotees or Cragmen attack directly," I said quietly.

"They won't—they don't dare anything *directly!*"

I slanted a look at Tanman. I could well believe the Cragmen feared to attack Caladrunan directly, as fierce as his face was at that moment. I wouldn't have wanted to fight him, the way he looked. He drew in a deep breath. "But we will go down to floor level, out of Karidi's sight, and we will stay close to prevent any trouble. Dance of Knives, you will kill any man who even touches a weapon near my son. Pick your spot carefully."

I said softly, evenly, "Yes, Liege. And if it is Keth Adcrag himself?"

He snorted. "Keth won't risk himself here, knowing about the gas-pipe plot." He slapped the wall in irritation as we moved down a broad flight of stone stairs. Flame motifs covered all the available surfaces. I kept noticing more of them at the corners of my eyes, reminders of death and stench. Some level in my brain seemed to open and a little spark of light glowed briefly there. I shook my head sharply and blinked. Not now! I thought. The light faded like a pale coal. Dormant. Waiting, not gone.

Within a cluster of pillars and buttresses, I listened to the Devotee tutor bully and lecture his charges. Tanman's son and Heir had a flat, stubborn look on his face, resisting what he was told. I wanted badly to reach out and grab Karidi by the neck; but I stayed still, watchful. Now and then my eyes darted to the low Flames guttering in the Altar Bowl, checking for any flare or surge.

Tanman, meanwhile, went to a nearby doorway and rummaged among empty Devotee slates stacked there on a table. Rapidly and quietly he began writing on a slate; he closed the rather scarred cover with a snap. He held it tucked under his arm. "Orders, for later," he murmured. I nodded once in hiding, not daring to ask; his face was remote and forbidding.

When the midday bell tolled through Fortress, the Devotee tutor gave up, barked orders and the line of boys filed out. I followed, flicking from one column and buttress to the next, watching shapes in that great shadowy place, listening intently. The boys marched down steps and went around a colonnade toward the red-tiled courtyard and the fountain. There was not a guard in sight to notice us as we followed. "Out into the open now," Tanman murmured, pulling his Devotee hood over his face. I mimicked his staid, even pace as we followed the boys. Karidi glared back at us once, perhaps because our robes came of a different elder's sect, then he forgot us in a noisy scuffle among the boys.

"See anyone?" Caladrunan murmured.

"No, Liege," I murmured back. The boys burst into their quarters and scattered free of their tutor, running for their sword-training clothes and scuffed leather padding. Wooden swords stood in baskets outside the practice courtyard door. A large scarred soldier stood bawling names and cuffing running boys as they skidded past him. "Walk!" he roared. He inclined his head a faint degree as we walked sedately past him; his hand accepted the covered slate as Tanman held it out to him in passing. The trainer barely glanced at it, slapping the cover shut and calling for a messenger to run it over to the guard quarters. Tanman stalked on as if nothing had happened. Out of the side of his hood-shadowed mouth, he said, "I have to have my own net of friends, you know."

I smiled in the depths of my own hood. Tanman's son was safe now, away from the Altar, supervised by a trusted trainer. "Do your friends include Karidi?"

Tanman snorted. "Of course not, pompous conspiring old bag. Wife's choice. Isaon could explode his preachments in a quarter-bell pass—complete with practical demonstrations to prove his points. Isaon's out of favor with my lady wife, however, since he spilled something nasty on one of her women during a court magic show."

"Magic show?" I blinked up at him. "But I thought—"

"Oh, it's pretend," Tanman said impatiently. "Come now, don't be so superstitious. We'll pick up Karidi . . . when I'm ready."

"Isaon would be a better tutor for your son," I said.

"You'd be a better tutor," Tanman said. "If you still want the job."

I blinked again. "Liege, I am no Tannese. I don't know now if I'd be adequate for everything the boy needs to know. Perhaps weapons training—"

Tanman reached briskly for a wooden door in the courtyard wall. I lifted my hand, stopping him; opened it and glanced through before he could risk himself.

Within was a dusty pile of torches on the stone floor, and a dim stairwell that led upward. I could see arrow-slits to open air in the spiraling well and pillars above us. Tanman stepped in and closed the wooden door after us, so we stood in a dim twilight. He murmured, "I don't think the Cragmen had any backup plots—"

"On the contrary," a calm trained voice rang down from above. Lado Kiselli stepped lightly down the last spiral above us and stood looking at us. "But Strengam and I just now managed to contain the most blatant threat, Liege, as your orders requested. There are rumors of more mischief to come, but nothing clear as yet. I've put your—ah—scholar of secrets onto it. Did I interrupt anything?"

Tanman slapped my shoulder lightly. "Not at all, Lado. What was the backup threat?"

Lado gestured a harp-calloused hand upward. "Twenty men in hiding on every probable route up to your quarters, and trailsigns set to make you think your entire family was taken—bait to make sure you took certain routes, I think. I hadn't believed them capable of so much subtlety. I'm certainly glad you had us rousted out of bed back at Lake Hold. That sandmap our Black Man here built, gave us a wonderful shortcut around some Cragmen riders—smugglers with Lake Hold friends, we think. We destroyed the map before we left, as you asked.''

Tanman nodded. ''Thank you, Lado. Is Strengam up there also?''

''Off picking traitors out of Fortress guard watches and throwing them in dungeon, doing a quiet bit of questioning.''

Tanman lifted a brow, and glanced at me. ''Nothing I'd hate to hear about later, was there, Lado?''

Lado also gazed at me. Soberly, levelly, he said, ''No, Liege. Much as I would have liked to extract some pain from those men, we didn't.'' His eyes seemed, in the dimness, to be testing me, asking if I thought him weak for obeying his Liege Lord's express wishes.

I smiled a little. ''That wasn't easy, I'm betting.''

''No, it wasn't,'' Lado said levelly.

I flourished a Harper salute of respect to him, which made both of them smile slowly.

''Come,'' Tanman said, throwing one arm around my shoulder and ascending until he could do the same to Lado. ''Come, my Harpers. Has Keth appeared anywhere?''

Lado gave a grim smile. ''No, Liege. Not him, not his friends, not his men, no one—Conspicuous by their absence. But Oldfield's men have been blundering about like cows. Appears the great lord of Crag fled and left them adrift in the middle of this whole operation.''

Tanman sighed. ''So he got away. Goddess, my leg muscles are in knots after the climb up from Isaon's hole.''

Lado exclaimed, ''Isaon, your old tutor? Thought he'd died.''

''Not quite,'' Tanman smiled. ''We'll have to sit through a long lecture on the mechanics of the Altar plumbing, if we've any sense at all, and give Isaon the men and metals he needs to repair it, and the whole affair will be a boring nuisance.''

''But for the knowledge that the thing could blow up if he wasn't fixing it,'' I said blandly. ''Have you ever seen an Osa flamethrower blow up?''

''No.'' They both looked at me.

I smiled Lado's own grim smile. ''That Altar plumbing

could leave a crater the size of this Fortress, carved into the cliff. And not much else but rubble.''

They climbed stone spirals silently for a while. At last, thoughtfully, Lado said, "Oh, that reminds me. Girdeth marched into the women's quarters in men's robes and armor, and—ahem—more or less told your Lady wife she could eat pig-pies when your Lady wife remarked on Girdeth's clothes—''

Tanman chuckled. "I can guess. I've a bunch of angry women to sort out, too. Do you know what else I've got to take care of, in the next few days, Lado? My Council, in full." Tanman reached into his robes and drew out the case holding the scroll retrieved from in the bowels of Fortress rock. He said quite pleasantly, "Do you know what's in here?''

Lado glanced curiously at me, and back at Tanman. "No, I've no idea. It's something nasty, by the look of you."

Tanman smiled. "This is a parchment sealed with the Crag Imperial Seal. Untampered. Untouched. In its original wrappings.''

Lado lifted one brow. "Indeed. Do I get to see the fun?''

"You do, my dear Harper. As does my other Harper, who found it. After all, you're on the Council, Lado, and he's my bodyguard, so both of you are legally privy to it. We do need *two* such Harpers to witness the event officially for our records.''

"You know, Liege," Lado said, grinning, "you're insufferable when you're like this.''

"Good," Tanman said, slapping both Lado's and my shoulders. "I've earned it after all the pig-pies I've endured from that flamed Council. It's past time I exposed those fellows who caused me so many problems.''

Lado lifted up a harp-calloused hand, which I met with my own long-nailed fingers. Tanman's sword calluses covered both. "To success," Lado said. His face in the dim light was fierce as a face in battle.

I grinned at them both. "To justice," I said, which made their brows quirk in surprise.

Then Tanman said quietly, "To my men, who made it possible.''

CHAPTER

= *18* =

TANMAN, ARRAYED IN five layers of ceremonial blue robes, armed with Devour in a silver-chased scabbard upon the baldric on his back, stood holding out the Crag parchment scroll with its traitorous Seal clearly displayed. From side to side he held it, so all the Councilors could see it. I stood, scaddas bared at my sides with the ancient writing on them glinting light; I held post two steps below Tanman's Great Hall dais, to his left. Pitar, holding a bare sword, stood to Tanman's right. Pitar's face was still as stone, and savage with warning. We were symbols of Tanman's bared justice. Silent in her dais chair sat Tanman's lady wife like silk-draped marble statuary. Beside her, Girdeth sat upright, yet somehow within elaborate veiling seemed to lean forward with eagerness.

Tanman Caladrunan said, "Is there anyone who disputes that this is the Seal of the Crag Imperial House, which was outlawed in the time of the Red Tyrant, and outlawed by every Tanman since? Does anyone have proof to dispute this Seal's authenticity?"

Silence. No one moved in the Great Hall. Light fell from the many narrow clerestory windows among the overhead beams, streamed over ceremonial robes hastily thrown on, limned the disgruntled uncomfortable faces. They grumbled when they found no Hall benches to sit on, no servants with wine, no tables—but there was no room, else, for the crowd. This was not the small Advisory Council; this was the full Court Council, with petty lords dragged by messengers from their business all over town and countryside. The disgruntlement was beginning to leave their faces; speculation, fear, apprehension replaced it. And in some faces, a suppressed glee: Vishna, among a pack of squinting sea-nobles, was fairly rubbing his hands in delight. Aider stood nearby, head bent, his long face somber. Lado stood near, watching Aider with concern. Pitar and I were too busy scanning the crowd to console him.

Tanman said, "You have all seen that this Seal is intact and untampered. We will now discover its contents."

The crackle of wax and parchment seemed painfully slow. There was a brief rapid murmur, then silence, as Tanman's hands spread out the scroll. He held it up, side to side, and began reading. I tensed. Someone at the back uttered a sharp scream, there was a scrabbling of Tannese boots on granite floor; a grunting, heaving tangle of guards departed. Another complement of guards replaced them, watchful. Girdeth muttered, "Thought they could brazen it out, thought it wasn't genuine! Any more?"

I noticed a few gray-white faces; they excused themselves and began filing toward the doors. Guards surrounded each noble as they went out. A few shouts echoed outside, but not many. The Lady of Fortress turned her head and moved as if to draw away her sweeping robes from that direction.

Tanman read, "We, the following names and nobles of these lands, do affix our symbols to a pact of covenance and alliance, as was done in old days, and do swear to support the following rightful lords in their rightful territories, listed below. Whereas, the usurper Caladrunan, and his son and Heir, shall not long hold the power in these lands, we shall aid the efforts of our liberators, Manoloki of the Nandos, and the foreigners, the Osa, and expect to pay thereto their rightful due as our legitimate laborers. Equally and severally we shall unite to withstand any attack upon—"

There were more pale looks, and bent-headed departures. There was some loud dispute outside between Tanman's guards and the escort of one noble. That was cut short by a full guard watch, all hand-picked by Pitar; the guards returned serenely after, straightening their blue robes. Quiet held the room. Tanman read off the names and elaborate titles chosen by the Crag lords and their sympathizers. Keth Adcrag's titles were not there.

"—and lastly, the Most High Exalted Prime Mast of the

Goddess, His Excellency, the Ruler of Fortress of Tan and its
surrounding lands and forests, Oldfield, of Crag's Royal Lin-
eage, Bearer of the Seal of Crag.'' Tanman waved the parchment. ''He unfortunately fled his would-be realm around
midday today, taking his Seal and his authority with him. It
seems there was a plot to hasten his exaltation here, and my
own demise. So! I see there really weren't all that many of
you interested in a change of order. I am pleased by your
loyalty, my lords of Tan. Are there any others who would
like, voluntarily, to announce an affinity with the Crag lords?
You need not fear reprisal. You would be granted retirement
to Crag lands. Perhaps those forfeited by Oldfield, such a
popular man in his home province.''

Pitar gave a grim smile. As everyone knew, retirement to
Crag lands meant being a lord over an impoverished stony
land and an unruly people; but by the look of Tanman's face,
better to choose that than to be discovered a traitor at a later
time—a choice like the one given Eran's kin, at Lake Hold.

''Very well,'' Tanman rumbled. ''There is one other matter to occupy us now, my lords of Tan. The war.''

There was a murmur at that.

Tanman lifted his arm. ''There is war among us. Think of
those lords no longer among us because they no longer rule at
the borders of Tan. Our country is smaller than it was. And
these—'' He snapped the parchment. ''—these are the cause
of it, not the likes of this.'' He pointed at me. ''This man
saved my life thrice in the past days. This man passed every
loyalty test we have, here in Tan. This man swore himself,
and his people, to my cause. They serve me now as army
scouts and map-makers. They are not the source of the attack
on Tan! This—'' He snapped the parchment again and tossed
it on the black table beside his ruling chair. ''—this unspeak-
able conspiracy of mercenaries, foreigners, and rebels is our
true enemy. And I will make war upon it, within and without,
as Tan's safety and security requires me to do. No more lost
lands! No more murdered people! No more!''

Aider was the first to lift his hand. In a quiet, faintly
uneven voice, he said, ''As our ancestors chose their captains, I swear fealty in time of war, and I say, no more lost
lands.''

Lado was the next, and then Strengam; Vishna and his
sea-nobles roared out as one giant blurred shout, and then

three nobles were repeating it steadily in unison, men I did not know. Then more, and more, of them.

Hands lifted, sometimes wavering as they spoke the words, but agreeing that Tan's patience was exhausted, and it was time for war. For an Osa war, a serious thing. When they were quiet again, Tanman looked at Pitar and me. Pitar smiled, and made a beautifully correct salute. "My fealty, Liege, has always been yours. No more lost lands."

Tanman looked at me.

I crossed the silver scaddas of Ganek Tanedi across my breast and bent my head. "I renew my Oath to you, Liege Lord of Tan. And I say, no more Osa atrocities. No more lost lands."

Tanman rumbled, "Let the parchment of war be drawn up among us now, lords of Tan, to answer that abominable list of foresworn names. Let our debate on a diversion channel to defend Fortress, end in positive commitment. Let our enemies be warned, we of Tan stand as one. As *one!*" His hand lifted highest of them all, rising above the forest of arms in salute toward the light above us at the windows, symbol of the Goddess. "I have more news! I will read you the latest report from the border forces: 'New herd technique a complete triumph. Seven enemy emplacements captured in night raid, three flamethrowers destroyed. Our casualties thirty-six dead, forty-two wounded. Known enemy casualties four hundred thirty. Their cavalry routed and infantry retreating in increasing disarray. Enemy requests for Osa intervention intercepted during our pursuit northward. I salute you, lords of Tan. From the hand this day of Edan, Dar's son, commander of the Liege Lord of Tan's first division.' "

Lado let out a howl, and Rafai joined him, and Pitar pounded on his back, grinning. Ben yelped out, "Parade the banners!" and Tanman's loyal nobles picked up the chant, stamping feet together. Uncertain faces vanished into the general excitement. Girdeth tugged on my braids until they fell down, and I bruised Lado with a careless smack of my hand. Tanman stood grinning at us all. After my first uncontrollable yelps of joy, I tried to sober up. I told myself sternly, this is only the first step towards the first battle of a long war, we have yet to drive the Osa back across the desert. Then I forgot all that and yelped some more. Men were hooking down the tapestries on the Great Hall walls, and marching them like trophies around the hall and out.

I glanced up then. The Lady of Fortress held out a slim, gloved hand and smoothed her husband's robes. Silently she folded back her blank veil and, marked by brilliant turquoise eyes, her aristocratic face smiled into mine. "The report came by the net of heliographs you gave us."

I blinked at the people parading past us. I said pleasantly, "They all die in this war, you know." Tanman looked at me appalled. "I saw it in a fit . . . black logs upon a burned field. Will you put on a feast for the poor bastards? Small enough gift for all that carnage. Or is that too expensive?" I smiled at him. "As expensive as making one Tannese flamethrower?"

The muscle in Tanman's jaw flexed a moment. Then he said, "You and I can try our consciences as friends concerned together, later—and I hope it will be so for many years. For now, you have what you prayed for, your war."

"Our war, Liege. I prayed for peace," I said absently, staring at the gold light glancing and flashing on the banners.

"Come," Tanman said, "we've a parade to lead." And he lifted Devour high, bare and shining, overhead.

I flourished him a salute, threw back my head and let out a Upai raid-howl, the likes of which few Tannese had ever heard. Lado, then Girdeth picked it up, seconding me like dogs, and then everybody was doing it, even Tanman's off-key boom.

Then he plunged down from the dais into the midst of his nobles, making requests for the use of toll roads, for supplies, for men. The humming night was destined to be punctuated with howls and impromptu marches and torchlit parties at the slightest excuse. My sensitive ears did not mind a bit. The first of my tasks had been accomplished. Teot's War had begun.